Praise for Lisa Brace's novels

'Compelling, heart-breaking and gutsy.
I couldn't stop turning the pages.'
D.E. White

'A powerful novel about skill, courage and determination.
I was completely invested.
Lisa Brace's writing moves seamlessly
between tension, poignancy and humour in a compelling story.'
Gill Thompson

'Lisa Brace writes vibrant, strong, fun and well-rounded characters. A great read and a wholly satisfying ending.'
Sue Fortin

'A beautifully written, wonderfully astute examination of modern society that teaches us what's most important in life.'
A.A Chaudhuri

'A brilliantly heart-warming and refreshing story.
I couldn't put it down.'
Anna Jefferson

The Fastest Girl on Earth

Lisa Brace

Blue Pier Books

First published by Blue Pier Books in 2025.

Copyright © Lisa Brace, 2025.

The moral right of Lisa Brace to be identified as author of this work has been asserted by her in accordance with Section 77 of the Copyright, Designs and Patents Act 1988.

Cover image © That Agnes.

Blue Pier Books values and supports copyright. You are supporting a small publishing house and its' authors by purchasing an authorised edition of this book and for respecting intellectual property laws by not reproducing, scanning or distributing any part of it by any means without permission, in accordance with the terms of licences issued by the Copyright Licensing Agency.

No part of this book may be used or reproduced in any manner for the purpose of training artificial intelligence technologies or systems.

In accordance with Article 4(3) of the DSM Directive 2019/790, Blue Pier Books and Lisa Brace expressly reserves this work from the text and data mining exception.

A CIP catalogue record for this book is available from the British Library.

All correspondence to hello@bluepierbooks.co.uk.

*For the daydreamers,
the truth-seekers,
and the adventurers.*

"Let us hurry, and do great things while there is yet time."
~ Louise de Bettignies

Prologue

Dying was nowhere near as exciting as living.

In fact, Evelyn contemplated as her soul began to exit her body, had she known how boring it was, she would have preferred to have disappeared off the face of the earth in a fiery ball of flames or submerged fifty feet underwater.

Instead, she had this.

A morphine-infused calm, which had coated the pain of her injury in a sheen of otherworldliness but which, she acknowledged, she'd had enough of to leave this world without ceremony.

And enough that the result would be irreversible.

Not that she wanted to change her mind.

Evelyn was well aware that she'd seen and done more in her forty years on this planet than most people would fit into three lifetimes.

But right then, taking a final glimpse around her Mayfair apartment before her last gasp took her, she wondered why, when the whole world had been at her feet, she had been left to die alone.

1902

Chapter One

London

'Mind out.' The cry came from a man quickly moving his horse out of the path of the young woman crossing the road, with no heed as to what was around her.

'Sorry,' Evelyn called after him, fighting to stay up in her too-high heels as she made the short walk from the Tube to the offices of Napier & Sons, wincing a little in the sunshine. She rearranged the fox fur which was threatening to fall off her shoulder, and cursed her friend Hena for the third cocktail they'd enjoyed the night before, hoping the headache clouding her thoughts would disappear.

At twenty years old she hoped this job would keep her parents at bay, especially their plans for her to marry some countrified gent and send her off to a draughty dark house in the middle of nowhere.

That was as long as she could get her nerves in check and she could formulate an entire sentence without stumbling over any of her words. Shyness was, she felt, one's way of reminding you of your place in the world.

If she could overcome her innate shyness, which sometimes paralysed her at some of the high society dances she attended in London, she could climb higher and find her true place. She was certain of it.

Brushing down the pale-grey coat she wore to cover her skirt and blouse from the dust that was kicked up from the City's roads as horses, carts and cars skittered past and tucking a stray strand of light blond hair behind her ear, Evelyn took a deep breath to calm herself.

She was Evelyn Bloom and today was the first day of the rest of her life. She could just feel it. As of last week, she had been plucked from the secretary pool at Napier & Sons by Sharp, the manager of the firm, and promoted to his personal assistant. Despite the nudges and winks from the other secretaries that Sharp was after more than her secretarial skills, Evelyn had shrugged off the rather lewd suggestions and saw this as the opportunity she'd been searching for.

As long as she could walk through the door.

'After me, then.' A short man who was the size of the jockeys she regularly bet on at the races, sidled past Evelyn and went to push the door. 'Or, are you coming in too?' He smiled and his face quickly became warm and welcoming.

'I'm coming in, it's my first time at this office and I'm not too sure where I need to go.' She spoke quietly so the man had to incline his head to hear her a little better.

'Well, where do you need to be?'

'Mr Sharp's office.' Evelyn replied to the man who, at not more than five foot three inches, was on her eye-line. He openly appraised her, looking quickly into her brown eyes, then down her body. When he'd finished, he shook his head and sucked air into his teeth in a way which irritated her greatly.

'Makes sense, follow me.'

He turned on his heels and pushed through the doors, behind which a gentle hum of hard work from the entirely male workforce was revealed. Evelyn was painfully aware of the sound her red heels were making as she click-clacked across the glossy marbled floor. She focused instead on the dark oak panelling and the severe-looking men all captured in portrait form that lined the stairs that she was being directed towards.

As she rearranged her matching red bag to the other hand, so that she could grip the handrail better, she caught sight of a man in dark-blue overalls below the stairs. Upon catching his eye she nodded her head slightly to acknowledge she'd seen him, then realised he was leering at her, hoping to catch a glimpse up her skirt. Flustered, and realising the helpful short man had disappeared when she was distracted, she stumbled a little on the stairs as her heel made contact with the carpet that lined the central sweep and she stuck out her gloved hand to grab the handrail.

'And where do you think you're going?' A steady hand gripped her elbow to stop Evelyn from slipping. A hand which, she quickly ascertained, belonged to her new boss. Victor Sharp. On seeing she was no longer in any sort of danger, Victor stood back and indicated they should continue up the stairs.

As they made their way up the staircase Evelyn took the opportunity to sneak a peek at the man who was in charge. With neat black hair that looked as though he'd come to the office straight from the barber shop, greying lightly at the temples, and with a little weathering around his eyes, Evelyn estimated him to be in his mid-thirties. He had an elegant moustache and a ramrod posture.

'Are you well, Miss Bloom?'

Reddening at the realisation that Sharp had caught her looking at him, Evelyn nodded and smiled tightly, looking ahead as they reached the top of the staircase.

'I'm quite well, thank you, Mr Sharp,' she replied. 'I'm keen to start work for you.' She smiled as he opened a door for her.

She could have sworn she saw a flash of something in his eyes as she spoke, but it was quickly replaced with quiet pride as he showed her to his enormous office. Evelyn considered the large oak desk sat in the window bay, the deep-green leather chair facing away from the view, the two oxblood-red leather armchairs flanking a fireplace and multiple paintings on the dark oak walls portraying scenes of motor cars, hunting and her own passion, horses. There was little other furniture she could spy, save for a drinks cabinet and a few low-slung tables.

'Yours is here.' Sharp opened another door Evelyn had mistaken as part of the panelled wall and revealed a cosy, light-filled room, painted in a soft green with a smaller version of the same desk as his and an armchair sat in the far corner decorated with numerous pink roses.

'Oh,' Evelyn exclaimed, charmed by the room.

'If you don't like it,' Sharp had mistaken her delighted surprise for disappointment, 'it doesn't matter because you won't be in here very often.' He looked at her and she expected him to clarify, but he just continued to stare, a slight smile tugging on the right corner of his mouth as she tried hard not to squirm under his gaze. He turned on his heels and left the room, shutting the door behind him, the action causing a light cloud of dust motes to dance into the air, glinting in the soft sunlight.

Evelyn exhaled, then removed her coat, unwound her fur from her neck and looked behind the door, relieved to see a coat stand. She had just hung her coat up and was making a move to see what the papers on her desk said, hoping they would give her a steer as to what her job was going to entail, when the door reopened.

'Tea?'

Sharp had appeared with a tray, replete with a dainty set of two cups and saucers, a teapot and flowery milk jug. The contrast of the well-dressed stiff-backed man, and the tea set caused Evelyn to bite her lip to refrain from smiling.

'I'll be mother,' he told her and began to arrange the teacups and saucers on her desk with precision. 'Take a seat. It's your room, after all.' He spoke with a quiver, Evelyn realised, a light tone which seemed to imply he was finding their interaction amusing.

Evelyn sat and watched as he poured out their tea, nodded when he offered milk and accepted the cup and saucer. Realising he was pouring out a tea for himself too, Evelyn began to look in the drawers of her desk.

'What are you doing?'

'I'm looking for a notepad, Mr Sharp.' She spoke with as much authority as she could, fully aware of how shy she could appear. 'I assumed you were in here to tell me what you needed doing. I am, after all, your personal assistant. In fact, I'm rather surprised you're serving me and not the other way round,' she admitted, then raised her hand to her mouth, concerned she'd spoken out of turn. Ten minutes into the job and she'd be out on her ear, proving her mother right that women shouldn't be in the workplace. Her successful jeweller father would be thrilled if she gave up trying to work and instead married one of the well-off men in their circle. She shook her head at the thought. *No thank you.* She couldn't understand how women filled their days when they didn't work. How they must feel like birds in gilded cages if all they ever did was be kept, bought nice things and dressed up.

Sharp had taken a seat across from her, his leg crossed loosely over the other, the dainty tea cup and saucer carefully balanced in his right hand, and Evelyn snapped back to attention, watching as his face became animated as he spoke. 'First, you won't need to take many notes, I need someone a little more useful than a personal assistant. Second, I prefer the tea I make to anything anyone has ever made for me.' He sipped his tea as though to make a point, dabbed his moustache with a handkerchief from his top pocket, and placed the cup and saucer on the desk, before fixing his attention on her, his hazel eyes glittering in the morning sunshine. 'And third, do you drive?'

Evelyn had become more and more confused as he spoke, and the last question surprised her completely.

'I, ah, well, that is, I've been driven,' she replied, unsure as to where this conversation was leading. 'But I don't drive – not many women do,' she reminded him, 'though I'd like to, especially as I work for a motor car company.'

Sharp nodded, seemingly pleased with her response.

'Lessons start Sunday.'

Chapter Two

London

'Ever been in a car?' Leslie, the young salesman who had been directed to spend his day off teaching Evelyn to drive, spoke to her with ill-disguised disgust as he helped her up into the driver's side of the Napier motor car. It was parked in the large warehouse at the back of Napier's offices which housed around ten cars, all of which were in the process of being sold.

'Yes, I've been in quite a few. It is 1902 you know,' Evelyn replied curtly. She waved her hand around as she spoke. 'My father's considering one of these,' she added, hoping her lie would soften up the instructor who clearly saw teaching her as beneath him.

'He'll join our many other customers then. Our *male* customers,' he emphasised, 'people who can be trusted behind the wheel of something as expensive and dangerous as this.'

'Oh, don't worry about my safety.' Evelyn smiled, hoping to win him around, but failing as Leslie smiled unpleasantly back, exposing yellowed teeth.

'Oh, I'm not. I just don't want this car to go up in smoke just because the boss has a soft spot for you.' He jumped up into the car, pressing his bulk into Evelyn's side. 'I don't want to die in a puff of smoke either, so if you can keep your attention on the road and not on your hat, I'd appreciate it.'

Evelyn grimaced, she'd only lightly rearranged her hat in preparation of leaving the garage. She decided not to antagonise the young man any further and smiled tightly.

'Of course,' she said as she took some buttery, deep-brown leather driving gloves from her navy handbag and pulled them on, ignoring the fluttering feeling in her stomach, and the hard stare from Leslie for wasting his Sunday.

'Now what's the first thing I have to learn?'

Leslie continued to stare at her. He had a glare which would, Evelyn decided, turn hot water to ice but Victor – Mr Sharp – she corrected herself, had explained she had to learn to drive and she was damned if some boy with a chip on his shoulder was going to stop her. So she stared back, willing her heartbeat to calm down before it gave her nerves away.

Evelyn gripped the steering wheel, the cool of the metal still perceptible under her gloves, and looked at the view from the top of the car. She was up comparatively high and would, she felt, have a good view of the road when they made their way out of the garage. The black leather seats were comfortably upholstered and all the chrome fittings shone in the relative darkness of the garage. The Napiers really were charming cars. Evelyn decided she'd have to encourage her father to buy one.

'Switch on the current,' Leslie told Evelyn abruptly, pointing to the dashboard which had the letters A and M on it. She moved the switch from A to M, then looked up expectantly at her teacher who sighed.

'I'll start it then, shall I?' he said as he leapt out of the car and headed towards the bonnet where Evelyn saw him moving about recalling similar actions from her a chauffeur pushing and pulling the handle at the front when she visited her parents at their home. At first, there was nothing, just Leslie huffing at the front of the car. Then, a split-second later, the vehicle burst into life as he jumped into the passenger seat next to her. 'This is why driving is man's work, I can't imagine you starting a car.' He shook his head, chuckling.

Evelyn kept her retort in check but vowed that next time she would be the one starting the car. After all, if she were to become a motor car owner she would need to know how to get the thing moving.

'Hold the wheel,' Leslie barked and Evelyn did as she was told.

'Move this forward,' Leslie showed her the ignition lever, 'and give more air by pulling back the lever, here.'

'They make the car sound different,' she noticed and spotted the tiniest flicker of interest from Leslie.

'Indeed.' Now, see that?' He pointed at a golden lever next to her right, one of many.

Evelyn nodded.

'Slowly release it, that's the side brake. Don't be rough with it,' he cautioned, and she did as she was told again wondering why Sharp wished her to go through such a palaver. Surely she could be sat in the passenger's seat and get as much benefit.

Evelyn would have squealed if it had been anyone else bar Leslie in the car with her as the Napier lurched slowly forward and they began chugging towards the wide exit of the garage.

'Turn left here.' Leslie pointed and Evelyn slowly moved the steering wheel, noting the car turning at her request. 'Quicker than that or we'll veer into the other side of the road,' Leslie barked and pushed the wheel to force the car sharply left. No sooner had they begun to pick up speed, Evelyn realised the car was making a noise again.

'Time to change to second speed,' Leslie announced. Evelyn did exactly as she was told and was relieved to feel the car moving much faster along the road. She grinned as they whizzed past roads, concentrating on what the car and Leslie were telling her, whilst trying to keep the vehicle straight despite its need to pull to the left. She was reminded again of her horse and realised she needed to just show the car who was boss.

A little later as they hit open road with countryside beckoning, Leslie showed her how to get to third but Evelyn had already begun to shift gear, recognising the sound the engine was making and finding the choreography of the pedal change coming to her quite naturally.

'This is wonderful,' she said gaily to Leslie who merely crossed his arms and looked to his right.

The next time she drove Evelyn decided she'd need to put on some sort of scarf or similar as her throat got incredibly cold as the wind was

THE FASTEST GIRL ON EARTH

chilling her to the bones now she was moving at close to twenty-five miles per hour.

'That's enough,' Leslie said as she changed back to second and skilfully made her way down a narrow street, making the changes as gently as she could. 'I think we've had enough playtime, you can bring the car back now.' Disappointed but understanding and already bitten by the driving bug, Evelyn negotiated the various roads that returned them to the garage and pulled slowly into the large space.

As she reversed everything Leslie had told her at the beginning, she brought the car smoothly to a standstill and looked over at him. 'Not bad for a beginner?'

In answer, he merely got down from the car and huffed, walking off. Evelyn didn't mind. Her head was spinning with the thrill of driving. How the vehicle had bobbed up and down as they'd moved along, how it had sung to her when it needed its gear changing and how at peace with the world she felt from her perch up high.

'You're hooked then?'

Evelyn spun around and saw Sharp smiling at her.

'Why, yes. Yes I am. It was utterly thrilling.' Evelyn grinned and took Victor's extended hand to aid her exit from the car. 'I was just thinking how incredibly clever these contraptions are. Just a few years ago we were only in horse and carts. And now these marvellous, wondrous things are joining them on the road.'

Her boss laughed at her exuberance, the action lighting up his face. 'Indeed. Marvellous. Wondrous. Definitely words I'd use. I was infatuated from the first instance too, they've been my greatest passion ever since,' he spoke with unmasked joy as he held her hand for a moment too long, then dropped it as a slight woman bustled through one of the side doors, brandishing an umbrella at him.

'I told you'd I'd left it here, must have been before the opera.' She stopped as she saw Evelyn standing by the car. 'And who do we have here?'

Evelyn swallowed, guessing who the woman was and held her hand out to her. 'I'm Miss Bloom, pleased to meet you.' Mrs Sharp shook it very quickly, never taking her eyes off her.

'I see, and what do you do, Miss Bloom? Aside from making idle chit-chat with my husband on the Sabbath?'

Evelyn coloured a little.

'Thank you, Mary, that's enough.' Sharp's voice had a slight edge to it which made his wife flinch almost imperceptibly. 'Miss Bloom is my new PA, and, dare I say, likely to be the cover girl for Napier cars – we want to get more women driving, and Miss Bloom is going to help us.' He smiled at Evelyn who was bemused.

'I am?'

Sharp laughed, an unexpected sound that echoed in the garage, then looked in the direction of his wife whose face was contorting with unspoken words. 'Let's go, Mary, the car's waiting for us outside.' Watching his wife as she turned haughtily on her heels and began to make her way out of the garage, Sharp hung back and turned to Evelyn, a hand casually brushing her sleeve. 'I told you I had plans.' He smiled at her in a way which filled her stomach with the kind of butterflies no young man at any of the dances she went to had managed, then followed his wife out of the garage, leaving Evelyn alone in the gloom.

Chapter Three

LONDON

Evelyn walked slowly to Napier's on the Monday morning. The weekend had been a fun one. It had included poets and champagne with her friends and lodgers Hena and Frances on the Saturday, followed by a drive in a beautiful Rolls Royce on the Sunday. Though the car had belonged to Frances' beau, Evelyn had been given permission to drive it and had enjoyed showing off her new-found skills to her friends who were all wild with joy when she'd hammered down Oxford Street.

Already Evelyn's new job had taken her life in an unexpected direction. Of course, she'd been hopeful that in her role as a personal assistant to Sharp she would have a chance to ride in one of the many stunning cars they sold. But she hadn't dreamt she'd be able to learn herself. It was Sharp who'd offered her that opportunity.

She paused to allow a horse and cart to clatter past her as she considered her boss. He was handsome, more so than many of the poets and actors she'd met the weekend before, and in a stark contrast to those young, needy men, Sharp impressed her with his wit, ambition and charm.

Evelyn crossed the road quickly. Since she'd learnt to drive with Lesley she had been out in numerous Napiers with other members of staff and every time she returned it had become a routine that she'd go to the office for tea – made by Sharp of course – and she'd tell him of her journey and what she thought of the car. She treasured those moments when it was just the two of them and she was being treated as an equal as he listened to her feedback. His passion for the cars and what he wanted to achieve with them was contagious, and Evelyn would often leave those meetings feeling as though she was at the very precipice of what modern was. It was exciting, even though being in close proximity to him had begun to feel dangerous when on more than one occasion their eyes would meet, locking her to the spot and she would have to remind herself that he was married.

This state could have continued for months, and would have done until he'd announced the week before that she would need to make plans to move to Paris. For six months. Alone.

As Evelyn pushed the door open to Napier's she found herself stomping her way up the staircase. Why would he send her away to France? For so long? Grumbling, Evelyn leant hard onto the heavy oak door of the office just as it gave way on the other side and she found herself careering straight into the sturdiness of Sharp's chest, one hand resting over his heart.

'Miss Bloom,' he pushed her away hastily, 'what were you doing?' He moved her aside as though she was a speck of dust on his tailored, black suit jacket, his brow furrowed.

She brushed her hands down her immaculate jacket and skirt, as much to distract herself from being embarrassed as to channel the irritation she was feeling at his reaction to touching her.

'What do you think *I* was doing? I was opening a door, the door you assured me was going to be fixed last week. It was stuck,' she replied snippily, forgetting herself for a moment, but Sharp smiled slightly at her.

'You're quite right, Miss Bloom, it's entirely my fault. I will ask again for this to be fixed, wouldn't want to have this happen every day. Would we?' He was beginning to move through the doorway and Evelyn caught a light waft of his scent as he brushed past. He smelt of cigar smoke and coconut hair oil. When she looked up at him, she thought he was going to say something, but instead he made to leave.

'Victor,' she caught herself, 'I mean, Mr Sharp, I wanted to ask you about Paris.' Her words halted him briefly.

THE FASTEST GIRL ON EARTH

'Yes?' In one word he implied asking what her decision was, informing her of his need to dash off and, Evelyn felt, a certain longing for her.

'I wondered why you were so keen to send me away. I haven't been working for you for very long and I suppose I was thinking, whether it might be because I've not done a good job and, you, well, you wanted to get rid of me.' Evelyn stopped talking. She didn't want to embarrass herself any further. Sharp stared intensely at her and she felt her neck beginning to warm, the indicator that she'd soon be consumed by a blush which would spread across her chest and up towards her ears. She tried to stay calm.

'Come here for a moment.' Sharp retraced his steps and walked back into his office, settling himself into one of the red leather armchairs, and indicating for Evelyn to do the same. She sat poised, her hands in her lap.

'Have you heard of Camille du Gast?' The French words, spoken in his soft Australian accent made Evelyn smile but shake her head.

'I don't think so.'

Sharp grinned.

'No, but then, you are an English woman. If you were a French woman you may be aware of her. I know the men are.' He smiled and hurried on as Evelyn looked confused. 'When I raced in the Gordon Bennett Cup a few months ago, she raced too.'

Evelyn gasped. 'A woman raced in a competition from Paris to Austria? How did she do?'

'That's actually beside the point.' Sharp raised an eyebrow. 'It didn't matter that she didn't win because as the only woman racing, it was her car which got the majority of the coverage and drew attention to all the French racing cars that were competing.'

'I see,' Evelyn said, though she didn't.

'I'm not sure that you do,' Sharp replied and leant a little further forward in his chair in earnest. 'I want my own Camille. I want that coverage for Napier and I want recognition in all the press for our racing cars.'

Evelyn was silent, unsure what that meant for her.

'I want you to be our Camille. You're young. You're talented – you're already showing you're a superb driver and, well, let's face it, you're beautiful. You'll look good on the front of newspapers.' Sharp's lips curled up into a small smile and Evelyn sat poker straight in response. She'd never had so many wonderful things said about her, let alone *to* her, by anyone. Least of all a man.

'I see.' She realised she was repeating the last thing she'd said.

'Do you?' Sharp had grasped her hands in his, they were cool to the touch but the shock of his on hers made Evelyn jump a little. 'Do you see? Because if you do, I think that you and I could make a grand team. Think of all the opportunities I could open for you – I have so many ideas. And in return, you'll sell more of my cars. I can't think of a better partnership; can you?'

'I had no idea your plans were so... well thought out,' she admitted and saw Sharp trying not to smile. 'I thought you'd asked me to learn so that I could be a circus attraction for your clients, a little light amusement. I hadn't thought you'd be so,' she looked around the dark oak office for inspiration, 'ambitious on my behalf.'

Sharp breathed out. 'I'm ambitious for both of us. You're not a circus attraction. But you will be good for business. Evelyn, I want you to race in a Napier in the April trial next year, it'll make all the papers.' He grinned.

Evelyn's eyes widened. 'But surely not so soon?'

Sharp nodded. 'Indeed. Which is why you must go to Paris. I want you to be apprenticed. I wish for you to learn all that there is to know about the motor car, all of its little foibles so that when you return, you can race in any competition. All drivers need to be able to fix their own cars on the side of the road and who knows which competitions we'll put you in for, but if you're doing any kind of distance you're going to need to know what to do if something goes wrong.'

He sat back, letting go of Evelyn's hands as if he'd just realised he'd touched her. Evelyn missed the reassuring weight and looked down at her own, where his had been just before.

'You're asking a lot of me, you know.'

'I know. Which is why I chose you, Evelyn.'

His use of her name was what did it, she felt it made them more partners than a boss and his secretary.

'Count me in.'

Chapter Four

Paris

Evelyn had visited Paris once, but it had been with her parents a few years before as part of a larger tour of France and Switzerland, and on arrival to the city she was shocked at how many apartments had been built since her previous visit.

It was a surprise, too, to see so many horses and carts jostling on the roads with cars, bikes and pedestrians, especially around the Rue de Rivoli. There were fewer in London.

The hustle and bustle soothed her nerves. Paris was reminiscent of London in that way, except for its beauty. Everything about the French city exuded charm and romance and Evelyn soaked it all up.

Her father had arranged for her to stay at an apartment overlooking the Rue de Vaugirard. It belonged to a client of his, but as they were touring in the Americas for the next few months it suited everyone for Evelyn to stay there, along with another girl named Isabelle, who had come to the city to study art.

'A *café au lait* for mademoiselle.' Evelyn looked up from the French newspaper she had been attempting to study, as Albert, one of the servants who looked after the apartment appeared on the small balcony.

'*Merci*, Albert.'

'You're welcome, mademoiselle.' Every time they spoke, Evelyn would speak French and Albert would reply in English, but it didn't matter how often she reiterated he could speak in his mother tongue, as it would help her sharpen her rusty French, the servant would have none of it.

It had become a habit of Evelyn's since her arrival in Paris to take her early morning coffee on the balcony overlooking the Jardin du Luxembourg and embrace the calm. She'd usually follow it with a fortifying breakfast of scrambled eggs and another thick black coffee, eschewing the French penchant for pastries and bread in favour of her slight frame. She'd wash it all down with a small glass of orange juice, then, dressed in a white shirt and plain thick woollen skirt, she'd make her way to the Gladiator Cycle Company in Le Pré-Saint-Gervais, along the Seine.

There, apprenticed to Monsieur Abreo, she would work alongside him until midday, learning the many workings of the automobile they were building, stopping only when the men stopped for their lunch, and picking up her work again at 2pm when they returned. She would always look wistfully as they would pack up and make their way to the tabac across the street at the end of their day. However, it had been made clear on her first day that they were only entertaining her due to Sharp's insistence on her needing the expertise. They didn't accept her. And they certainly didn't want the boss's personal assistant tagging along to the tabac with them.

'Evie, I'm glad I caught you.' Isabelle poked her head through the large glass door that led to the wisteria-covered balcony.

'Are you well?'

'Indeed.' Isabelle fanned her pale face, made ever whiter owing to the oversized artist's smock she was wearing to keep her clothes clean. 'I wondered if you might like to join me at Les Deux Magots this evening? There's a wonderful collection of artists and poets who go there. A few of the girls and I are going and I thought you might like a little change to your routine?'

It was, Evelyn felt, a very gentle rebuke of her nearly monastic routine she had picked up since her arrival in France a three months earlier. There had been little change in her weekdays as she worked and returned home, with weekends mainly spent sleeping or visiting the sights around the city on her own. With the various new things she was learning every day, Evelyn was always tired and, though she wouldn't care for others to know, she was a little homesick.

'I'm...' she was going to say too tired, but could see the reaction on Isabelle's face, 'I would love to. Thank you for thinking of me,' she amended.

Isabelle's face lit up. 'That's marvellous.' She brought her hands together in glee. 'That's just brilliant, I was ever so hoping you would say yes, but you are a bit of a closed book so who would know? How about we take a carriage from here, would you be ready for six o'clock? We could have a little light supper before – I know a lovely place just off the Saint-Germain.'

'Sounds perfect.'

'Wonderful. Well, I best be off, can't miss the start of my lesson – again.' She smiled impishly and disappeared from view.

Evelyn finished her breakfast in silence and made her way to work on her light-blue bicycle. She enjoyed the way she could travel across the city unimpeded, swerving around the varied traffic as it afforded her a chance to look at the cars, how they drove, how people in them reacted to different circumstances and how the designs differed from some of their English competitors.

They were, however, all fairly standard under the hood, Evelyn had learnt. Monsieur Abreo had grudgingly admitted that she was a quick learner and she'd gone from merely being permitted to look under bonnets to being consulted on what she thought was causing problems with the cars coming in after breakdowns.

'*Bonjour* Monsieur Abreo,' she called as she jumped off her bicycle and made her way into the garage. Evelyn inhaled the scent of the workshop, a blend of petrol and oil mixed with paint and rubber tyres, and waved at the other men working. They all smiled back, then continued their work.

It was an improvement. Three months of waving at them every day and they'd moved on from ignoring her presence, to at least acknowledging her when she arrived.

'Mademoiselle Bloom, I think I have something you'll like. Yes?' Monsieur Abreo wiped his hands on an oily rag, adjusted his flat cap and blew out the smoke from the cigarette that was permanently wedged in the corner of his mouth. It didn't matter how early Evelyn arrived at the workshop, the men always seemed to be there before her. So rather than in those first few weeks of appearing increasingly earlier to impress them with her dedication, she made a point of turning up at nine o'clock on the dot, just as she did in the London office and getting straight to work.

Pulling on her dark-blue overalls, the thick linen covering her outfit entirely – much like Isabelle's artist's smocks – and fastening the ties behind her back, Evelyn turned up her sleeves to above her elbows and tied a small scarf around her hair to keep it from going in her eyes.

'*Alors, qu'est-cequ'on regarde?*' she asked of Monsieur Abreo.

'Well, we are looking at one of the newest Gladiators on the road,' he replied in his French-soaked English, 'but it has no working. It is,' he spat on the floor, '*capot*.'

Hands on her hips, Evelyn did as he'd taught her and surveyed the car. Walking around it, she checked nothing obvious was stopping the car from moving. There was nothing trapped in the exhaust pipe. She checked there was enough petrol in the fuel tank, it had roughly half a tank so should have been running without a problem.

'Hmm.' She looked at Monsieur Abreo who raised his thick eyebrows at her.

'All correct so far.' He grinned and Evelyn returned the smile. He was, she knew, beginning to accept her too, which gave her a huge amount of relief. The early days had been tough.

'May I?' She looked in the direction of the driver's seat and Monsieur Abreo nodded.

'*Oui, bien sûr.*'

Evelyn took his hand and pushed herself up into the driver's seat, where she pushed and pulled all the levers which should have meant the car would start. Tapping the speedometer she gazed at the mile counter.

'Monsieur Abreo?'

'*Oui?*' He looked at her with a glint in his eye.

'I should like to look under the bonnet, I believe I know the problem,' she said decisively whilst jumping down from the car. 'It's a brand-new car?'

'*Oui*, it was bought yesterday,' Monsieur Abreo concurred.

Evelyn spoke from under the hood of the automobile, her voice slightly muffled. 'And yet,' she pulled a stick out from where the oil was stored and looked at it triumphantly as she saw how clean it was, 'it has no oil in it.'

'Carry on, mademoiselle.' Monsieur Abreo nodded encouragingly.

'Cars only work with oil in and they need to have a fresh pour every twenty miles or so. This car has so little oil in it I suspect either the new owner drove it forty miles from here without topping it up, or...' She allowed the implication of what she'd discovered to settle a little.

'Or?' Monsieur Abreo repeated.

'Oh.' Evelyn looked at the other men in the garage, all working hard and fast to deliver the cars to the clamouring clients all keen to receive their automobiles as quickly as possible.

Monsieur Abreo nodded, his face severe. 'Or someone here forgot to fill it before we sold it, making us look shoddy and unrespectable.'

Evelyn wiped her hands on one of the rags, looking to see if anyone else in the workshop could hear their conversation.

'I'm sure they didn't do it on purpose.' She hoped no one would get into trouble, especially as it was she who'd deduced what was wrong with the car. 'Can I suggest we fill up the oil tank, we fill another can with oil and gift that to the current owner, along with an apology, and we offer a free clean every month for a year?'

All of a sudden, another voice spoke which made her stomach flip.

'That, Monsieur Abreo is a very good way of managing the customer.' Sharp made his way from the small office into the main area of the garage. 'I think you could learn a thing or two about customer service from this lady.' He nodded in Evelyn's direction, causing her to blush and stutter apologies to her mentor, who merely nodded with a smile.

'I think it is a fair trade, no?' he asked of Sharp. 'I teach her how to run a car, she teaches me how to run a business.' The words stung Evelyn until she saw Monsieur Abreo was smiling with genuine warmth in her direction and she realised how concerned she'd been that all the hard work she'd put into their relationship would disappear as soon as Sharp was on the scene.

'How's your apprentice doing, Abreo?' Sharp strode past Evelyn to talk directly to her current boss.

'She's a quick learner,' the Frenchman replied, 'and her little hands are perfect for those hard-to-reach places under the bonnet,' he added. It was a little too overt, and Evelyn blushed, hoping Sharp had missed the innuendo from Monsieur Abreo. Though whether Monsieur Abreo was implying she'd been playing under his "bonnet" or someone else's, she wasn't sure. But the effect was the same on Sharp whose demeanour had hardened a touch.

'I'm sure.' He brushed away the conversation and returned his gaze to Evelyn who shifted a little uncomfortably, aware of her grubby overalls, tied-back hair and general slovenly demeanour.

'It looks as though Paris is treating you well.' He smiled gently at her. She smiled carefully back, aware of Monsieur Abreo's interest in their exchange.

'It's beautiful,' she replied.

'Yes, it is.' Sharp looked at her, the light smile she knew well playing on his lips. His face was alight with something, joy she thought, or lust. She swallowed and reminded herself he'd sent her to Paris to learn a trade so she could fulfil her dreams of a career. What it had also done was give her space from him, because as much as she wanted to fall she knew she couldn't. He was someone else's husband. Just because he was helping with her career, was charismatic and seemed interested in her didn't mean she owed him anything.

'Are you free tonight, for dinner? I'm sure you've found many wonderful bistros you can introduce me to,' he spoke in a way that seemed to imply he knew what her line of thought had been and she blushed, worried she was an open book.

Unwilling to admit she'd spent more time at her apartment, exhausted, friendless and more than a bit homesick, than eating in bistros Evelyn shook her head. 'I'm sorry, no, I'm out with friends.' She saw the effect her words had on him as his features clouded over and he shifted back on his heels a little but it wouldn't do badly for him to realise she wasn't always available. Even if this was the one and only night in the past three months where she'd had plans.

'I see. And tomorrow?' he pressed. 'It's my last day in Paris, I return to London the day after.'

'Let's see shall we?' Evelyn tried not to laugh at the surprise in his eyes at being told no. '*Monsieur* Abreo, I'll sort out the oil on this and carry on with Monsieur William's Renault.' She made her way to the car.

'*Au revoir,* Mr Sharp.'

Chapter Five

Paris

'I can't believe you'll be on your way home so soon.' Isabelle clinked her glass against Evelyn's.

'It's gone quickly hasn't it?' Evelyn replied, leaning back on the dark-brown leather banquette, enjoying the way the furniture held her form for the briefest of moments.

'Stay for longer,' Isabelle cajoled from her seat at the right of Evelyn's at their favourite haunt, Les Deux Magots. 'I have six more months until I'm finished; who else will I get to enjoy champagne with?' She smiled as they clinked glasses again. 'Everyone else is incredibly dull.'

'That's no way to talk about us,' George interjected, causing Evelyn to laugh. At twenty-five, he was five years older than Isabelle, but with his tall stature and her grace they made an attractive couple and Evelyn was convinced they would be announcing their engagement imminently.

'Sorry darling, obviously I wasn't describing you as dull, far from it.' Isabelle rolled her pale-blue eyes in Evelyn's direction. 'All that political talk, *fascinating*, my love.' George held some sort of mid-level position in the British government but was in France for a year working at the British Embassy. Nothing he did sounded interesting as far as Isabelle and Evelyn were concerned, something they'd regularly remind him of.

'And me?' George's friend and colleague, Benjamin was sat next to Evelyn, their legs pressing into each other. They'd met a few months' prior, on the night Isabelle had organised for them to go out when Evelyn had turned down Sharp's dinner invitation. She'd enjoyed a three-month flirtation with Benjamin, which hadn't amounted to much, other than a few chaste kisses. It had been enjoyable enough, and had kept Evelyn's mind from thinking of Sharp too much, but she knew Benjamin wanted more than she was prepared to give. Another reason for looking forward to returning to England.

'Of course I'll miss you; how long have you left here?' she asked, knowing the answer but playing for time.

'Five more months, maybe I'll see you in London? We could go for dinner, just the two of us,' he said meaningfully, throwing a glance at Isabelle and George. 'Without our minders,' he whispered and squeezed her thigh lightly.

'Dinner sounds good,' she replied, though there was something unreadable in his gaze, warm, but a little too measured. He had a way of watching people, not with interest, but with intent, as if cataloguing them.

'What time do you leave tomorrow?' Isabelle said, breaking the tension, and Evelyn, grateful not to continue talking to Benjamin about their unlikely future together, looked in her friend's direction.

'I'm getting the train from the Gare du Nord at midday to Dieppe, then I'll catch the ferry across to Newhaven. Then it's another train to London. I should be there by around midnight I believe.'

Isabelle shook her head, her blonde curls moving as she spoke.

'So quick nowadays? My mother always talks of a time when we couldn't get across countries in less than a week. Now we can do some in a day. Incredible.'

George placed his drink on the glass-topped table that reflected the warm lighting in the bar and reached for a handful of roasted and honeyed nuts that were nestled in a bowl in the middle.

'That's nothing, did you see *The Times* this morning?' he asked the three, looking from one to the next, his eyes absorbing everything in their surroundings – a trait which always made Evelyn feel as though he was waiting for something more interesting to happen than what he was in the middle of.

Evelyn shook her head. 'No, I was too busy saying my goodbyes to the boys and Monsieur Abreo, they gave me a watch as a *bon voyage* gift. So sweet,' she added and Isabelle laughed.

'And to think they didn't even speak to you when you first started.'

Laughing, Evelyn shook her head when George pushed the bowl of nuts to her.

'Well, it was pretty awful,' she recalled, 'they didn't talk to me for the first two months at least, just kept muttering when I went past.'

'She'd be left to eat her sad little lunch in the garage, all by herself,' Isabelle teased.

'Yes, thank you for that. I quickly found a beautiful park and realised how wonderful time by oneself could be,' Evelyn added knowingly to Isabelle who acted shocked at the suggestion.

'Can I finish?' George interjected and Evelyn indicated he carry on as she took a sip of her champagne. 'Good. Listen to this, it's from this morning.' He produced from his side a well-folded piece of newspaper.

Isabelle rolled her eyes. 'You are very bossy.' She stuck a finger over her lips as George stared at her with faux rage and indicated she should be quiet.

'First flight of an airship over London,' he read. 'This afternoon, countless Londoners were thrilled to see a navigable balloon in the sky. The strange device was piloted by well-known aeronaut Stanley Spencer, who has spent the past three months making trial flights from the Crystal Palace. In this, the first flight by a powered aircraft in Britain, Spencer took off from the palace grounds in south-east London at 4.15pm, passing over Tulse Hill and then setting course north-west to Clapham. He finally came to earth at Eastcole, west of Harrow, having covered thirty miles in three hours.'

George looked at the other three, excitement glittering across his eyes.

'Bloody hell, he finally did it. Good for him.' Benjamin spoke reverently and raised a glass to the air. 'Imagine the possibilities.'

George was nodding enthusiastically. 'Exactly, my friend, exactly. Hell of a feat; makes your trip home sound positively archaic.' As he spoke Evelyn imagined what it must have felt like to float over London.

'Gosh, indeed. Still, I've got my speed trial to look forward to in a few months. Who needs a balloon when I'll be racing by myself,' she added proudly.

Isabelle raised her eyebrows whilst looking in her compact mirror as she checked on her lipstick. 'Not entirely by yourself,' she suggested and Evelyn widened her eyes in a bid to stop her friend from continuing.

'What?' Isabelle feigned innocence and Evelyn shook her head again.

'I think I'll freshen these up. Want to help me get a drink for these lovely ladies?' Benjamin asked of George, distracting his friend from the balloon article he'd been studying intently.

'Of course. Ladies, excuse us for a moment.'

As soon as the two men left, Evelyn turned to Isabelle, keeping her voice down in case she was overheard.

'What were you trying to do? Did you want Benjamin and I to fall out before I returned home?' She looked at Isabelle with confusion.

'No, I wasn't trying anything. I was merely suggesting you weren't going to be on your own for this race of yours. Yes, you'll be travelling alone, which, by the by,' she shifted closely to Evelyn's side, 'I think is marvellously brave, but I do insist you bring a gun with you, just to be on the safe side. Benjamin said he'll organise for one to be delivered to you in London. But you'll be driving Sharp's car and it'll be in his name so I'm assuming he'll be somewhere nearby most of the time. You'll only have to turn those big brown eyes on him and he'll be with you for as long as you need.' She began to mimic Evelyn. 'Oh Victor, help me, I'm a damsel in distress.'

'Hardly a damsel. He's had me over here to learn everything I need to know about cars so I'll be fine. The closest thing to distress I'll experience is my hatred for those dreadful driving clothes the women racers are starting to wear – they're appalling.'

THE FASTEST GIRL ON EARTH

Isabelle looked at the dress of palest green Evelyn was wearing, paired with some elegant cream shoes and a few choice pieces of jewellery. She was a well-put-together woman.

'Just wear whatever you want,' Isabelle advised, 'you know better than anyone what you'll be most comfortable in and if you wish to look stylish, you can combine the two. I'm sure of it.'

Evelyn considered her friend's words, Isabelle was right. She'd already been tweaking her wardrobe so she could drive at any given point of the day, but at the same time she'd been getting the balance so that she didn't have to make any change of clothes should she wish to be ready for any socialising which came her way too.

'Shall I come and wave you on your way tomorrow?' Benjamin said quietly to Evelyn as the men returned to the table with a fresh bottle of champagne and new glasses.

Accepting the glass and swirling the bubbling liquid around, she shook her head gently and pressed her hand over his.

'Thank you, but I'd rather say goodbye to you tonight, I don't want a scene at the station.' She smiled lightly to soften the blow. He looked disappointed but nodded, then checked his pocket watch – again. Evelyn noticed, not for the first time, how often he glanced at it. As though he was on someone else's timetable.

'Of course.' He leant in and whispered in her ear. 'But can I just say, you are the most remarkable woman I've ever met. I suspect I'll remember you for much longer than you'll remember me.' He chanced a kiss on her cheek and she smiled.

'Oh no, Ben, I won't forget you. I promise.' She kissed him back and the other two at the table whooped lightly, reminding them they had company. 'Do look me up the next time you're in London.'

'To Evelyn, may her daredevil driving that's been honed on the streets of Paris be put to good use when she's back in Blighty,' caroused George, and the other two cheered his words.

'And to my lovely new friends, who I'm thrilled to have met and for whom I wish only good fortune,' she replied.

'I'll drink to that.' Isabelle tilted her glass to her lips and sipped her drink. 'Cheers.'

1903

Chapter Six

LONDON

A young man, dressed in a leather driving coat, thick black boots encasing his stick-thin legs, with a pair of goggles dangling from one of his hands was looking mock-confused in Evelyn's direction as she got herself comfortably behind the wheel of the Gladiator. It was the car that Sharp wanted to demonstrate in the trials that chilly April morning.

'Are you thinking of taking that to the shops?' He called over with a jeer from where he was standing next to his own car.

'No, she thinks it's time for a picnic. Look she's got a blanket and everything.' His friend, dressed identically, nudged him in the ribs and looked back over to Evelyn. 'Love, you should stop playing now; let the men come and show you how it works.'

Evelyn shook her head and focused on the checks she needed to make before leaving. Her nerves were jangling and she wondered whether she should have made time for breakfast that morning rather than the strong coffee she'd settled on.

'Passengers sit on the other side of the car, love.' The skinny-legged man had come to her side of the Gladiator and was leering. 'Better yet, want to be my passenger? I reckon we could find something interesting to do down a quiet road if you accompany me.' He grinned and licked his lips. Ignoring the lascivious remarks and satisfied with the checks she'd made inside the car, Evelyn decided to double-check under the bonnet to be certain she'd not overlooked anything. She didn't want to let Sharp down.

'Excuse me, please.' She faced the man who was trying to catch her attention and was blocking her route out of the car, his hands either side of the gap. 'I need to get down now.' She kept her chin up. He really did remind her of a rat.

'What if I say no?' the rat replied.

'I would suggest you move yourself Mr Atkins. My colleague has asked you very politely to move out of her way I believe. Am I correct in saying,' Sharp spoke to Evelyn as an equal would, 'that you need to look under the bonnet?' He raised an eyebrow as he spoke and a faint smile was on his lips.

She nodded, then turned to the other man to repeat herself. 'Excuse me please,' she said to Mr Atkins whose face had gone pale ever since Sharp had appeared.

'My apologies, Miss?'

'It's Miss Bloom, and you'd do well to remember her name.' Sharp took a step further into the rat's personal space and he backed down, heading away with his friend and leaving Evelyn and her boss to stare after them for a brief moment.

'I could have handled him,' Evelyn said assertively to Sharp, her jaw jutting fiercely, eyes sparkling with anger. 'I didn't need to be rescued.'

Sharp clasped his hands to his chest. 'You wound me, Miss Bloom, all I was doing was aiding an employee from a,' he leaned into Evelyn slightly so that she could feel the warmth of his body near to hers, 'rather unpleasant, weasel of a man, but don't tell anyone I said that. He is, after all, the son of one of the car manufacturers here.' His laugh rippled through the air and Evelyn caught the tail-end of it. He so rarely showed any emotion, to hear laughter from him was truly wonderful. She wanted to hear it again.

'I promise not to tell – would you like to know what I thought he resembled?' she confided, speaking so quietly Sharp had to lean in close so that she caught his scent, a mix of cigars and hair cream. 'I thought he resembled a rat.' She raised her eyebrows, hoping he'd join her in the joke. For a brief moment Evelyn worried she'd gone too far, the man was still one of Sharp's contemporaries, but then she saw his face crack and his laugh bellowed out.

'That's glorious. A rat,' he remarked, laughing again. 'I knew he reminded me of something but now I see it completely – he's just missing a long pink tail,' Sharp added conspiratorially and Evelyn felt warmed by their shared joke. Ever since returning from Paris she and Sharp had taken every opportunity to give her practice time out in the Napier. This had its downsides, Sharp was quick to point out her errors, regularly asking her to repeat move after move in the car to prove she could handle the vehicle, which would often send her near to despair. But there were many more upsides. He was relaxed and jovial in her company and he always brought a flask of tea for the two of them to enjoy partway through the session.

Over the course of the last few months of practice sessions and dodging bad weather over winter, the two had forged a friendship which Evelyn treasured. And if her heart thumped every time he looked at her with those hazel eyes that gave away little, then it was something she had learnt to ignore.

'Bonnet?' he asked, bringing them back to order. 'We need to get to the start in fifteen minutes. Want to look or do you trust me?' He went around to the front of the car and his face was quickly obscured by the sheet of metal he'd lifted.

'It's not that I don't trust you, but I would be letting myself down if I didn't look too.' Evelyn stood primly next to him, then leant in to check the various parts herself. To be in this close proximity to Sharp felt daring and wonderful at the same time. Keeping herself in check, and telling herself that she needed to focus on driving and demonstrating the car, Evelyn leant forwards to check the oil. Just then, Sharp did the same thing, their hands touching.

'Sorry,' she said quickly, withdrawing her hand, the feel of his seemingly imprinting, searing itself onto hers. He stepped back from the car and wiped his hands on a cloth.

'No, I am. You do it – it's your car, who am I to be getting involved with her anyway? She should be in the hands of someone who deserves her. See you at the start.' He made to leave. Stopped. Then turned to look at her again.

'And Evelyn?' He was still holding the cloth in his hands, moving it from one to the other. Behind him people were rolling tyres, talking in groups of twos and threes and pushing motor cars to the start line.

'Yes?' She could hear her heart beating so loudly in her chest at the sound of her forename on his lips she was sure if she looked down it would be making its way out of her breast, straining at the white shirt she had tucked into her dark-grey woollen skirt.

Sharp looked at her, then away. 'Just... Good luck.' He turned on his heels and walked through the chaos of the start line. Evelyn watched as he made his way through the groups of chattering men and women, hangers on and interested parties, sellers, buyers, and owners, and disappeared into the throng.

Realising she'd been holding her breath for what felt like an extremely long time, Evelyn exhaled and told herself to calm down. Whatever had passed between her and Sharp needed to be forgotten for now.

She had to focus on the trial. It was the reason she was here. She slammed down the bonnet, turned the starter a few times and hopped up into the driver's seat, the engine throbbing in the belly of the car. Evelyn smiled with satisfaction at the ease with which she could do these tasks now.

There were fifty-six cars at the start line for the trial, the first of the year to demonstrate a range of sales points for the varying range of vehicles and give the advertisers plenty of headlines for the makes and models of their cars. Evelyn was well aware she was mainly at the start line to make the headlines for Sharp as the first English woman to compete in a motor race. In her own mind though, what she wanted was to win.

She was desperate to hit the speeds that she'd been scorching on roads in London, including the month before where she'd been pulled over by the police for speeding.

'Hullo.' A man was trying to catch her attention from a Renault, he had an incredibly bright ginger beard and a friendly face. 'I'm Jones, wanted to wish you Godspeed and all that. Best of British.'

THE FASTEST GIRL ON EARTH

'Thanks, and to you. Any advice for a beginner?' she yelled over the sounds of the numerous motors starting with putters and snarls all around.

'Just put your foot down and have a bloody good time.' Jones laughed and waved his cap at her. He was, it transpired, totally bald. His glistening pate was offset by the zesty beard and the whole look was both beguiling and comical.

'Right you are.' Evelyn laughed back, her expression turning to something more serious as she saw the official climbing on his steps next to the outside of the track, holding a white flag.

Suddenly, all the drivers were looking in the official's direction and, were it not for the revving of the fifty or so cars around her, Evelyn was convinced she'd be able to hear a pin drop. Her head was itching under her driving hat and she removed one hand quickly from the steering wheel to rearrange her headgear, only for the official to drop his flag just as she did so. Instinctively Evelyn planted her foot down, smoothly transitioning the gears, listening to her car like she listened to her favourite horse. She was in tune with the Gladiator and quickly picked up speed, roaring past a few vehicles that hadn't been able to start and made her way out onto the track.

The next fifteen minutes went so quickly to Evelyn she couldn't be certain she hadn't dreamt the whole thing, were it not for the quickening pulse in her throat as she and the Gladiator careered over and round the track. The route was on a private field and included a short hilly section which Evelyn found both uncomfortable and annoying. She wanted to go faster but the Gladiator's twelve horsepower kept pulling back, urging her to move down a gear. Once she was through the hills and round a bend, she coaxed her car to go faster but something was holding it back, and, whilst she was making good time, many cars were streaming past her. Including the rat.

Doing what she could, Evelyn pushed the car on to the finish, nodding at the flag-waving official as she crossed it, so he would make a note of her time. As she slowed down Sharp was first to her car.

'Park up over there.' He pointed to a space and she slowly made her way in, aggrieved she'd not achieved anything for Napier cars or

Sharp. But the way her boss was beaming, she'd have been forgiven for thinking she had won.

'What?' she said hastily as she made her way out of the car, holding his hand lightly to exit and finding the ground most solid and reliable after the bouncing of the Gladiator.

Sharp was smiling broadly, his teeth gleaming. 'You, my dear, were absolutely marvellous,' he said, clasping his hands together. 'Wonderful to watch – the way you hammered round the bends, I was thrilled.'

Confused, Evelyn shook her head. 'But I didn't win us anything.'

Sharp shook his head. 'In this case, it doesn't matter. You showed up and you proved despite so many naysayers that a woman *can* drive a car.' He clasped her hands in his, the intimacy shocking her enough to look up into his eyes that for the first time were ablaze with excitement. 'And not just that, she can do it bloody well.'

Chapter Seven
LONDON AND GLASGOW

'I can't believe you're going to do it all by yourself, it's such a long way.' Frances, one of Evelyn's friends and long-term lodger, was lounging on the chaise below the window. As the early morning light streamed silver over her hair she looked as though she was a true-life Renaissance painting – the sensuous curves, cherry-red lips, the curls tumbling down her shoulders – except for the frown that was being aimed at Evelyn.

Pulling back her own shoulders and aware of how diminutive her own curves were, Evelyn wondered if her small breasts were the reason Sharp hadn't made any sign of a move towards her since the trials back in April. Sure, there had been the mildest of flirtation in the office, but his words, always softly spoken, always saying something other than what they really meant, left her more confused than anything else.

'Oh, for goodness sake.' Frances's words broke into Evelyn's thoughts. 'Evie, would you get this thing away, he's at my leg again.' She shook her head as she aimed a swift kick at Dodo, causing him to yip, skittering away, narrowly missing the blow. Trotting over to Evelyn as though nothing had happened, Dodo, a black fluff of a Pomeranian dog, waited for his owner to scoop him up and place him on the chair next to her, feeding him tiny scraps of crispy bacon she'd asked the cook to make just for him.

'I won't be on my own, I'll have Dodo with me. He'll be more than enough company. He's seen the world that dog, he'll be a good companion.' She tickled the animal's chin and smiled into his large eyes.

'Disgusting thing. I honestly have no idea why you don't send him somewhere.' Frances pulled a face and Evelyn ignored her, kissing Dodo on his nose.

'He was a gift from Isabelle and was smuggled into England drugged and hidden in the repair box of an automobile. The least I can do is give him the home he was expecting,' she popped the last of the bacon into the dog's mouth, 'and anyway, I'll need to talk to someone when I'm on my way from Glasgow to London. It's a jolly long way and one may find oneself a touch bored of one's own company,' she declared as she finished her black coffee.

Frances shook her head again. For someone who acted as audacious as she did, forever encouraging the others to spend their nights in low lit bars, Evelyn harboured a suspicion much of it was a front and Frances really craved a life of routine domesticity. Hence why she never fully supported Evelyn's automobile endeavours, unless calling upon her as Frances's personal driver counted. Evelyn had done more trips to Oxford Street and Bond Street for shopping the past three months, than the last three years.

Still, it was more support than her parents gave, the last letter from her mother with its anger and thinly veiled insults resulting in Evelyn throwing it into the sitting-room fire.

Sipping her cup of tea, Frances waggled a finger. 'One should be saving one's kisses for a certain boss.'

Evelyn tried to keep her face from flaming red, she wished she hadn't admitted to Frances her longing for Sharp, which hadn't changed in the past few months, instead it had grown stronger in spite of his lack of overtures to her. She knew he was married, but that didn't stop her from wanting his closeness, or imagining how things could be if he was free to be with her. She didn't want marriage, though she understood most women needed it to cement their status and relationship with a man. But she craved him. Sharp was perfect. Handsome, unattainable and a little arrogant. He wanted to be the best and Evelyn found that attractive. She wanted to be the best too. Though, that wasn't deemed an attractive quality in a woman. She found it desirable in her relationships and discovered the few female friends that stuck around often held that quality.

'Will you be wearing many layers?'

Not Frances though, Evelyn realised. She lacked that element of a personality, but she was fun to be around. Even if she was short of ambition.

Evelyn roused herself to answer. 'Yes, numerous. I thought a few furs would be good,' she replied, gaining a nod from Frances who was getting up, readying herself to dress for the day.

'Agreed. And a blanket if you can manage it, it's a blasted long way from Glasgow,' she reminded Evelyn.

Not that she needed reminding. Every day for the past three weeks she'd studied the route from Glasgow to London, the various minor and major roads she would need to take in this latest endeavour to put Napier cars on the map.

Sharp had been right. Despite her not gaining any prizes in the April competition, she gained a lot of column inches for Napier cars and by proxy, Sharp, just by being in a car at the start. She was pretty convinced had she just ridden as a passenger it would have had the same effect, but secretly she'd enjoyed the coverage, the celebrity.

'When do you go?'

Evelyn was adding to her mental list of items she wished to bring. A gun would be useful, to feel safe. She would bring the one Benjamin had sent her. There had been cases reported in the papers of lone women being attacked and after years of shooting with her father she was a terrific markswoman, so wouldn't hesitate in taking aim should she need to.

She also needed to pack a compact mirror; she found holding one up every now and then meant she could see what was behind her in the road. It had prevented a few incidents where other drivers had come out of nowhere and, on seeing a woman was driving, attempted to overtake her. They *attempted*. They rarely managed it. Evelyn found she had a good knack for speed when she put her mind to it.

'In a couple of days. Victor's picking me up, we'll be travelling most of the way on the train and staying in a hotel overnight, then I'll drive back down the following day.'

Just as Frances opened her mouth to reply, presumably to make some sort of crass comment involving Evelyn and Sharp in the hotel, Hena, Evelyn's other lodger, burst into the room.

'Oh thank goodness, you've not gone yet.' Hena came over to Evelyn and bundled her up in a warm embrace. 'I was worried we'd miss you and not be able to show you this.' She held up a copy of the day's *Telegraph*, then turned to one of the inside pages. She pointed at a small article, just a column, with the headline *Making History* but Evelyn shook her head, unsure what she was being shown.

'It's about you, Evie, they describe you as a "daring scorcher – willing to push Napier's Gladiator to the limit in her pursuit to be the first woman to travel from Glasgow to London non-stop".' Hena laughed. 'You're famous, Evelyn. I've bought ten copies, I think you should sign them.'

This time Evelyn really shook her head, surprised at her friend's joy. 'Oh stop it, it's nothing. They shouldn't have written anything.' She laughed, covering up the joy she experienced at seeing the news.

***

A few days later in a chilly Glasgow Evelyn was more than a little nervous. Photographers were at the start line of the run, jostling to get photos of the twenty-five cars and nine motorcycles signed up to take part.

Evelyn rearranged Dodo in a coat on the passenger seat, ensuring he was tucked in and, despite the mid-May weak sunshine making itself known in the Scottish city, retrieved her hat and veil from beside the dog. She twisted the veil a couple of times and tied it over the hat she'd pinned in place, tying a knot under her chin. Satisfied it wouldn't disappear in a whip of wind, she withdrew her gloves from the drawer under her seat and placed them on. She felt warm just then, the tweed winter coat was buttoned to her waist, her scarf knotted neatly around her neck and her thick skirt giving warmth to her legs, but she knew once she was on the road the cool breeze which whipped past as she got up speed would begin to chill her if she hadn't taken these precautions.

'Hey!' Evelyn heard the voice from the crowd of onlookers as she double-checked her Colt automatic was in reachable distance, should anything untoward take place when she was on the road. Satisfied she

THE FASTEST GIRL ON EARTH

had done enough due diligence on her provisions, including a few chocolates to keep her humour up and a small pouch of chicken pieces for Dodo to nibble on, she looked in the direction of the crowd where the man's voice was still yelling in her direction.

'May I help you?' she asked with a pleasant smile, it was one of many things she'd come to learn. The more pleasing she appeared, the less aggrieved the men on the start line were to her. Most of the time.

'Why aren't you at home? You should leave the driving to your husband,' the stocky, pale-faced Scotsman shouted, drawing titters from the crowd.

Evelyn ignored him.

'Hey, I said, why don't you get back in the kitchen? Pop out a few bairns, that'll put a stop to this nonsense; a woman racing, whatever next?' He shouted again and Evelyn felt a snarl of anger spread across her face, grimacing at keeping her emotions in check.

'I tell you what next, more women racing?' She threw back, enjoying the look of apoplexy that had spread over the Scotsman's face and knowing what he'd hate. 'Better yet, maybe the vote.' She grinned at his hatred and blew him a kiss, drawing a few whistles from the crowd. Pleased she'd irritated him, she stroked Dodo, whose head had popped up in interest as to what was happening around him, and nodded at the young boy who was going between all the cars to start the motors.

'Thank you.' She smiled and tipped him, noticing he blushed as she touched his hand and she shook her head at his innocence. Her thoughts were interrupted as more and more cars were started.

The motorbikes, which were nearest the front had started too and the cacophony of noise filled Evelyn up. Much as she knew many people's souls were balanced from a trip to the seaside or a brisk walk through the countryside, for her, being surrounded by the noise and vigour of these engines – the best in the world – was enriching.

She grinned at her luck, aware what she was experiencing was in most part due to her background. Though it was her personality which had gained her the role as Sharp's personal assistant, it was her father's connection that had got her the original job as a secretary. One which she knew he would rather she was doing than in his words "gallivanting, unmarried, all over the country doing God knows what in God knows where", as he'd politely put it the last time she'd visited them in their Hampshire home, surrounded by his plants and a lack of understanding.

The cars ahead were moving and Evelyn settled her car into gear, pushing forward, away from the Scottish man who had begun yelling obscenities, making her way out onto the open road. She passed the Napier contingency who all started shouting and waving in her direction causing her to smile widely and give a quick wave. The two engineers, along with Sharp and a few other men she didn't recognise all waved back.

They had three cars in the event and, whilst they weren't allowed to offer any technical support on the non-stop race, they were to follow should one of the cars breakdown and need to be withdrawn from the competition. They wouldn't be near enough to help her if she ran into problems such as a blown tyre though – she'd need to fix it. Or if someone took against her and she needed to protect herself.

'That's what the Colt's for though, Dodo, isn't it?' she said to the now very asleep dog and smiled to herself. 'Four hundred miles. Let's go.'

Chapter Eight

Glasgow

Evelyn was thankful for the precautions she'd taken with her clothing. As well as the constant damp that had clung to her since she'd left Glasgow at nine o'clock that morning, the roads were muddy, and small flecks of grit would regularly be thrown up onto her windshield. The loose pieces of gravel would strike her on the face, or the hand, so often that she became used to sharp jolts of pain as she continued to keep up the twenty miles per hour the Gladiator had settled into on the wider stretches of road.

Dodo spent his time sleeping or looking at the passing scenery and Evelyn concentrated on keeping the car under control, which was no mean feat when it was more uncomfortable than riding an actual horse. She could feel the jolts and bumps through her legs, jostling her spine and into her neck.

There were moments in the journey she used as markers that passed a distance or time since leaving Scotland. The first significant one was the halfway point, when she saw the skyline of Leeds after ten hours and she realised London was a very good possibility. The next was when, after driving non-stop for some twenty hours, she began to feel the car pulling to the left.

With fierce determination, Evelyn ignored it for a little longer, until the shuddering began. Looking ahead to where some of her rivals were beginning to pull away, Evelyn banged the steering wheel in frustration, all too aware any stops would cause her to be penalised.

She'd hoped to finish with the maximum one thousand points but pulling over would put paid to that.

'There's no way round this, is there, Dodo?' she asked the black fluff-ball. 'We're going to have to pull over, aren't we?' She guided the car to the left-hand side of the road and pulled on the brake. Stepping down from the car, she was thankful for the small mercy that getting out of the vehicle gave her, stretching her legs for the first time in many hours. Dodo seemed to appreciate the chance to stretch his too and disappeared into the long grass beside the road, whilst Evelyn took a look at the tyre in the rosy light of dawn breaking.

'Ah, easy enough,' she told the dog, relieved the issue was merely the tyre had worked away and needed to be pushed further onto the axel, and a screw tightened. She dove into her repair kit and fixed the wheel quickly, waving at the judge's car that pulled in beside her.

'Are you going to be able to get back on the road? It'll be a shame for you to pull out of the race this near to finishing,' the official was shouting from the passenger seat of his car whilst his driver took a short drink from a small flask.

Standing up to wipe her hands on a small rag before fixing her scarf back around her hat, Evelyn shook her head. 'No, nothing to worry about. I'll be ready to go in a couple of minutes – just need...' she looked around for her dog who appeared as if by magic by her side, 'ah, there we go.' She scooped him up and placed him back on the coat on the passenger side. 'Just a little fix on the tyre.'

'You're doing brilliantly, Miss Bloom, keep it up,' the official yelled, then, after making a note on a piece of paper, nodded at the driver and they pulled back out. 'One more hour should do it and you'll be there,' he added, pointing in the direction of the faint London skyline silhouetted against the sunrise.

Evelyn leapt up into the driver's seat and made her way back out onto the road, thankful she'd been able to fix the tyre. Any slip-ups out on the road the driver couldn't fix meant they had to drop out of the race, not something she was keen to do.

'Look, Dodo.' She began to feel euphoric as her car made its way onto a better-made road, and slowly, hints of civilisation began to make an appearance.

THE FASTEST GIRL ON EARTH

First, there were farmlands, with chickens and cows looking with interest as she passed.

Gradually more houses came into view, but it was the city she was focused towards and as she pushed on, the landscape became familiar. Evelyn laughed as she began to make her way down an incredibly quiet Oxford Street. Just a few days ago she'd had to share the route with horses, carts and double-decker buses, but now she was free to enjoy the space all to herself. There was something eerily beautiful about the closed shops. The decorated mannequins sat primly in the windows of Harrods, ready to stand up and cheer Evelyn on. One dress in particular caught her eye, a draped purple and baby pink affair, and she decided she'd return to order it in a few days' time – it would be perfect for Isabelle's wedding in July.

The car sputtered a little and, widening her eyes in a bid to stay awake, she wrestled with it to stay on the correct side of the road, cursing under her breath as the tyre made a familiar sound.

'Just one more mile. Just one more,' she coaxed the car, 'and I promise we can stop.' She yawned, thinking of the pot of tea she'd be enjoying in her flat in a few hours and hoping her flatmates had left her something to eat.

'Oh, Dodo, look!' As she turned the car into the final few metres, Evelyn beamed at the spectacle in front of her. Bunting adorned buildings at the official finishing line for the drive, and despite the early hour, many people had turned out, clapping in the cars that were beginning to file in.

One motorbike sped past her and, not for the first time, she was thankful she'd done the journey in relative comfort. Even if her lower half was numb from the shaking vehicle. The motorcyclist was sodden and coated in a grey grime, kicked up from the four-hundred-mile route. Evelyn, in contrast, was still relatively dry and, thanks to her windscreen, mainly mud-free, though she was looking forward to a hot, steamy bath, and her back ached something terrible from being in the same position for such a long time.

'Welcome home,' Sharp called as he saw Evelyn, and removed his hat to wave it at her jubilantly as she aimed the car over the finish line.

'Hello all,' she replied as three of the workers from the factory walked alongside the car, hooting and hollering at her arriving in one piece, all of them grinning from ear to ear. One, a youngster of fourteen, offered his hand so she could step down from the car and as she reached out to accept it, she realised she was shaking all over.

'Here.' Sharp placed himself in front of the younger man and offered his own hand and, on grasping it, she felt reassured by his strength. Clutching his warm hands around her very cold ones she stepped down onto the ground, still holding on.

'Got a bit chilly did we?' He grinned and rubbed her small hands in his, then, on sensing his workers looking at them with interest, dropped them quickly, all traces of warmth disappearing.

'Here you go.' One of the men from the factory had brought her a steaming mug of tea. Usually she'd have preferred a bone china cup and saucer, but on this very chilly May morning as the sun filled the sky, it was the best cup of tea she'd ever enjoyed.

'Max, this is wonderful.' She gulped down the drink, enjoying the trickle of warmth which was beginning to fill her body once again. 'I got so cold I think I stopped noticing it. I don't suppose there's a biscuit knocking around is there?' She let out a small gasp of joy as the man opened a small tin which contained sandwiches and a handful of biscuits.

'These are from my missus, she reckoned you'd be starving, cold and thirsty by the time you got in, and she didn't think we'd remember to get you anything,' Max replied, pleased with the foresight of his wife and the fact she'd been completely right. There were no other refreshments on offer to the weary motorists making their way over the finish line. Evelyn coming in a reasonable seventh.

Accepting the tin offered, Evelyn took a sandwich. 'Could you tell your wife she's absolutely top-notch.' She refilled the mug with the flask being offered by Max, another idea of his wife's no doubt, as he leaned in.

'My wife says it's the least she could do; she's blown away by what you're doing. She's hoping to drive one day.'

'Send her my utmost thanks.' As Max went to turn away, she was sprung with an idea. 'And tell her if she ever wants a ride out somewhere, I'd be more than happy to take her, it's the least I can do.' Max nodded, pleased.

'You did it, you bloody did it,' Jones, the ginger-bearded driver she'd met before said as he drove past her slowly. 'I must say, I expected to finish ahead of you. I was told you'd broken down – but look at you, in the flesh. Good work, old girl.' He grinned and tipped his hat, causing Evelyn to laugh, but she was distracted by a hand on her elbow through the crowd.

'I think you could do with going home.' Sharp's voice was by her ear, causing cold shivers to run around her body. 'I should think you need to go to bed.' His voice was heavy with suggestion and, on trying not to allow her knees to buckle, Evelyn merely nodded and allowed herself to be manoeuvred out of the crowd.

'My car?' she asked as they moved away from the noise.

'The lads will take it back, it'll need a bit of love and attention after what it's been through,' he looked around to see if anyone was watching, then caught her hand in hers, 'a bit like its owner?'

Swallowing down the anticipation of what was to come, whilst also fighting the sheer exhaustion the drive had brought on, Evelyn tried to think clearly.

'Victor, I share a flat.' She said the words as though they were just in passing, should she have misread the situation in any way.

Sharp nodded. 'That's fine. I thought... maybe... you could do with a little treat – my way of a well done on the drive.' A smile caught on the corner of his mouth. 'I've booked a room at The Ritz.' They both stopped, measuring each other's response. Sharp was a good degree taller than Evelyn and almost twice as broad, but she knew she was in charge of whatever was to come.

She could say no, feign tiredness. It wouldn't be difficult as she was exhausted, and they would return to the life they'd been leading the past year. One filled with quick glances, light touches and the impossibility of being next to one another without a charge filling the space, begging to be lit.

Or she could say yes and there'd be no turning back for either of them.

Chapter Nine

LONDON

'I call upon these persons here present...' The vicar's voice bounced around the church, filling the building. Evelyn listened whilst watching sunbeams stream through stained-glass windows, throwing pools of multicoloured light onto the stone floor at regular intervals. Then, remembering herself, she looked down at her order of service.

What a hoot for Isabelle and George to get married, and in London of all places. Evelyn had been convinced when they wed, after they'd wired her about their engagement, it would be in Paris. But George had been posted back to London, to continue his governmental work in Great Britain and, as Isabelle had completed her art course, she had returned with him.

Evelyn was looking forward to hearing all about their last six months in Paris later in the week when she was due to call round for afternoon tea at their home in Marylebone and smiled to herself.

'Thinking of when you'll be up there?' Benjamin leaned in next to her, grinning, and she lightly cuffed him around the ear, drawing a squawk of disapproval from one of George's many aunts, sat behind her.

'Not on your life,' she whispered. 'I just like seeing them so happy.' She indicated the couple who were exchanging rings and only had eyes for each other.

Isabelle's dress was a stunning confection of white lace and silk. It had been designed and made in Paris by Paul Poiret, a designer friend of theirs and, distracted by thoughts of whether there would be a time for her to write to Paul for a gown to wear to a ball later in the year, she didn't hear Benjamin whisper in her ear.

'Pardon?' she replied in an undertone.

'I said, you're making waves. I spotted your face in the papers a week or so ago.' He raised his eyebrows knowledgeably and she smiled.

'Trying my best; on land and sea,' she replied demurely, looking briefly in Benjamin's direction. 'I must admit, it was terribly fun.' She was hushed by the aunt again and rolled her eyes at Benjamin who grinned back, then nudged her to look to the front.

'I declare you husband and wife,' the vicar said loudly and Evelyn fought the same unseemly inclination she had at every wedding she'd attended, to applaud the newlyweds as they walked down the aisle past her. She settled on a big smile and nod at Isabelle, her face visible now her veil had been swept behind and her friend smiled back, clutching her orange blossom and rose bouquet, the stained-glass colours altering the pattern on her dress.

Waiting for the rest of the party to leave, Evelyn looked through her tiny black handbag for her lipstick and a mirror to adjust her hat and to check her make-up.

'Come on then, how'd it feel?' Benjamin was watching as she applied her lipstick. The gesture made her feel oddly exposed, as though naked, the way he considered her face.

'What?'

He laughed. 'You are something, Miss Bloom; you do know what I'm talking about. All right, I'll play along. How about entering the Harmsworth Trophy, winning it, and setting the world's first water speed record?' Benjamin looked at her keenly as she closed her mirror and replaced it, along with her lipstick, in her bag.

'It felt exhilarating, darling,' she admitted, grinning, then patted his arm. 'We should leave too and join the rest of the party,' she added, noticing most of the church had emptied out and their voices were echoing around the building.

'I bet it bloody was. And then you won at Cowes last week. You're having a good year.' Benjamin followed her out into the aisle. 'I suspect Sharp has something to do with it?'

Evelyn swallowed. Victor and she had, as far as she was aware, managed to keep their affair secret for the last couple of months. They'd taken every precaution necessary so their friends and colleagues wouldn't know anything was happening between them and had been entirely discreet.

But the nights at The Ritz were Evelyn's highlight of every week. The one time when the two of them could be entirely themselves. However, Benjamin clearly thought he knew something, she realised, looking at his face. 'He's a very good boss,' she replied evenly, studying his response which remained neutral.

He nodded. 'The best, I'd wager,' he continued quickly, 'and it's paying off, you're getting a lot of column inches. Did you see the photos of Cowes?'

Evelyn shook her head. 'No, it's been a busy week. Why? Should I have done?' They entered the churchyard where they waited patiently, watching as the newlyweds had a photograph taken on the stone steps. It was a glorious, hot summer's day and the warmth outside was welcome after the chill of the three-hundred-year-old church.

'There's a good photo of you on the Royal Yacht. Am I right in thinking you were talking to King Edward?' Benjamin took a pipe out of the inside pocket of his morning coat and began packing the tobacco into the end.

'Oh yes, he was very kind. He congratulated me on my pluck and skill,' Evelyn remembered, swelling with pride.

Taking a deep pull on his pipe as he lit the bowl with a match which he then carefully blew out, Benjamin nodded. 'As he jolly should. I can't believe it, you – just chatting with the King. Remarkable. What else did you talk about?'

Evelyn thought back to the discussion aboard the yacht, where she'd enjoyed a glass of champagne with the King and smiled with the memory.

THE FASTEST GIRL ON EARTH

'Well, we discussed, among other things, the performance of the boat. He was very impressed with its speed, and how quiet it was. He mentioned...' She laughed at the memory, interrupting herself.

'Go on.' Benjamin pulled on his pipe again, the embers glowing orange.

'He mentioned its potential for British government despatch work. Well, what would you say to the King of England? I said I agreed it would be perfect, hopefully it'll land Napier with a contract. I only wish I'd mentioned to Sharp I needed more commission.'

Benjamin leant in to speak to Evelyn, but turned suddenly to someone on his right who was attempting to attract his attention.

'Excuse me, but the wedding party are being called for a photograph with the bride and groom,' the photographer's assistant said to them both.

'Best do as we're told.' She looped her arm in Benjamin's, noting the difference between Sharp's solidity and his slighter, more athletic frame. Height wise, he was well matched to her, unlike Sharp's six-foot stature, which made her feel as small as a mouse when they were together.

'Everything all right there, Miss Bloom?' Benjamin was looking sideways at her as they made their way to the group, gathered around Isabelle and George, and took up their positions. Realising she'd been caught staring at him, Evelyn smiled and cleared her throat a little.

'Fine. All fine, thank you.' She patted him on the arm. 'You're a good friend, Benjamin,' she said softly, aware the rest of the group was very quiet. He covered her gloved hand in his and squeezed it gently.

'I know,' he said quietly too. 'I'll always be here for you, you know that.'

'Ladies and gentlemen, if we could all look to the front now please.' The assistant was pointing at the photographer, encased in the hood of his camera. 'Mr Black is ready to take your picture.'

Standing with poise, Evelyn held the same serious face as the rest of the group whilst the assistant kept his hand up to indicate they shouldn't move. As soon as the photographer was satisfied, the assistant dropped his hand and the group began to move again, like statues that had been reanimated.

Making her way over to the newlyweds, Evelyn lightly tapped Isabelle on the shoulder, causing her to turn around.

'Congratulations, darling, you look beautiful.'

'Oh thank you, I was so worried; the dress only arrived yesterday and I was beginning to think I would be wearing my mother's. She'd have been thrilled of course.' Isabelle laughed a little, then pulled a face when she saw her mother looking in her direction. 'Not that it was a bad dress, but... you know...' She trailed off a little.

'You'd have looked sensational in anything; frankly I'm surprised you didn't turn up in your smock,' Evelyn said with good humour, then looked confused at Isabelle's reaction

'I doubt there'll be much time for any of that anymore, what with being Mrs George Savory. My time will be spent on being a good wife, and hopefully a good mother,' her friend replied tersely.

'I'm sure you could find time to paint; even mothers can put paint onto a canvas.' Evelyn replied, but Isabelle shook her head.

'The time for mucking about is over, Evelyn,' she said firmly. 'We can't all spend our time racing cars. Sometimes we have to grow up and realise what's needed of us.' With a determined air she turned away, leaving Evelyn feeling as though she'd been punched in the stomach. She knew most women who married prioritised their husbands but she hadn't expected it of her bourgeois artist friend.

Evelyn had thought she and Isabelle would carry on drinking cocktails and putting the world to rights until they were old and grey. Married or unmarried. Child or child-free.

'Everything alright?' Benjamin had found her again. 'You look awful.'

Shocked and unable to trust herself to speak, Evelyn suddenly felt she couldn't stay a moment longer. She needed to run away from the weight of expectation that weddings brought, and ideally it was going to be into the arms of a certain six-foot bear-like man who would scoop her up and pour cocktails into her.

Chapter Ten

Trouville-sur-Mer

Evelyn stared out to sea from the hotel in Trouville-sur-Mer, her thoughts of racing and boats drifting in and out as she watched the undulating waves. The sunshine was glinting off the water, giving it the look of a beautiful piece of material and she could see why so many painters had been drawn to this pretty area of France.

'Got your racing face on?' Sharp wrapped his arms around her and rested his chin on her shoulder, the weight of it feeling both comforting and burdensome.

She inclined her head to his. 'Ready as I'll ever be.'

Sharp spun her round and held her gently by both shoulders. His look was intense, but he was smiling. 'You're incredible, I have every belief in you. Just go out there and be Miss Evelyn Bloom, the press will eat it up.' He grinned and kissed her on the cheek. 'They've fallen for you, just as I have – wait here a moment.' Evelyn watched as he disappeared to the other side of their hotel suite and searched in his suitcase.

The past couple of days had been like a dream. They'd opted to stay in Trouville, whilst other competitors had settled in Paris, nearer the start line. Although Evelyn had her own room in the same hotel to maintain discretion, she'd stayed with Sharp the whole time, enjoying the luxury of waking up next to him as the light streamed into their room. They'd been careful to meet up in the hotel lobby, not wanting to draw attention to themselves, but other than that it had felt as though they were in a proper relationship. Evelyn had to pinch herself to remember they weren't. This was closer to a daydream than anything real. At any point it could all crumble.

'You look so sad, don't be sad.' Sharp sat her on the edge of their unmade bed where just a few hours before Evelyn had experienced bliss she hadn't been aware could exist in one's own body. Her mind had become so clear with climax it was as though she had floated to the heavens. 'Here, I have something for you.' He produced a brown leather box and held it out to her.

'What is it?'

'You need to open it. I thought it matched the car beautifully.' Sharp said with pride, looking pleased with himself.

Frowning, Evelyn opened the clasp on the box and gasped. Inside was a dark-green emerald pendant. Instead of the ornate and fussy designs popular with so many of her friends, it was a single emerald, the size of her thumbnail, surrounded by diamonds, suspended on a delicate gold chain. For the first time in her life, Evelyn was speechless.

'Well?'

'It's stunning,' she managed.

'Just like its wearer, turn around,' Sharp commanded, and she did as she was bid, lifting up her hair to allow him to fix the clasp, the cool touch of the pendant on her neck causing her to shiver slightly. 'Let's see.' She turned to face him and he looked at her as one would admire a painting. 'I thought so, perfect. The colour is just the same as our cars, but its beauty is comparable only to yours. I thought you may like a good luck charm,' he added, as though he'd shown too much of himself to her.

Evelyn held the pendant in her hand, hugging his words to her. 'I love it. Thank you, Victor. Though it's a boat today, not the car,' she reminded him, then leant in and kissed him gently on the lips. He returned it before pulling back quickly.

'Just make sure you win.' He grinned.

'I'll try, but I think my mind needs clearing a little,' she suggested, sitting across his lap and kissing him deeply.

'I think I can help with that.'

Chapter Eleven
Paris

The Pont de Grenelle was looking celebratory as Evelyn settled into the Napier racing boat with a small crowd gathered on the left of the Seine ready to wave off the eight competitors taking part in the Gaston Menier Cup. As well as racing boats and crews, there were fishing boats in cheerful colours and some sailing boats all bobbing gently up and down on the water.

Trying not to inhale the strong scent of the Seine, for Evelyn was well aware the drainage system was no better than the one in London, she did her last checks of the boat and waved at Sharp who was on the bank.

'Are you absolutely sure you don't want anyone else in with you?' he called over, for what had to be the eighth time that day, Evelyn shook her head.

'Absolutely sure. I'm sure Mr Davis and I will be perfectly fine.' She nodded in the direction of her mechanic sat at the back of the sleek boat, ready for her to begin piloting. Noting Sharp's slight pout, she added, 'The less weight we have, the quicker we'll go – you know that, you're lucky I've said yes to Mr Davis.' She turned to the mechanic, calling past the canvas which separated them. 'No offence, Mr Davis.'

'None taken. We need to get to the start line, Mr Sharp,' he called over to their boss. 'See you at the finish.'

Evelyn waved in her lover's direction. 'See you at the end, get the champagne ready,' she called. 'I'm feeling confident.'

He waved back and applauded them. 'I know my role,' he said, then turned his back on them both as he went to speak to the members of the press clamouring to take photos of Evelyn, Sharp and their boat. Throwing a quick wave over her shoulder to him, Evelyn started the boat and edged her way neatly to the start line, the Union Jack flying proud in the breeze at the back of the Napier.

'All ready for this, Miss Bloom?' her mechanic called from the back of the boat. He was a gnarled man in his late forties, good-natured and he knew his stuff.

'Ready as I'll ever be, Mr Davis.'

'It's Edgar, just be aware of them, and them,' he said, pointing out a couple of other teams competing in Mercedes boats. 'They want this.'

'So do I, Mr Davis, sorry, Edgar. So do I,' Evelyn assured him as she hung onto her steering wheel, ready for the starter pistol to fire, ignoring the looks from some of her fellow competitors. She'd known as she'd stepped into the boat in her form-fitting dress, her black coat adorned with a delightful pattern of toggles which fitted her neatly and a smart black hat securely fastened to her hair, they were expecting her to be a passenger along for the ride to soak up the atmosphere.

So she enjoyed seeing the surprise on their faces when she stood at the front and took up the steering wheel.

She had no reason to hide herself as Camille du Gast did when she raced cars, dressing as if she wanted to hide her gender. Instead Evelyn had made a decision very early on when it came to racing cars and now boats that it wasn't to her benefit to dress in manly clothing. She was a woman and that's what she wished to look like, on whatever form of transport she was favouring that day.

On hearing the pistol Evelyn pulled the throttle and revved the engine, pitching the boat higher in the water and urging it on. She quickly changed gears so she could reach the fastest speed she could with the sights of Paris speeding past her as she hit twenty-two knots. Mr Davis wasn't wrong about her competitors, she noted coolly as two boats roared by, their drivers and passengers making prolonged eye contact with her.

'Come on, girl, come on,' she coaxed the boat. 'You can do better than that.' She pushed down on the accelerator and encouraged the

Napier to get to its top speed, whilst keeping an ear out for the engine straining. She was aware that as it had the same workings as the cars she'd driven lately it could withstand being pushed a little further, but not much more.

'Hold it there, Miss Bloom,' Edgar called from behind her. 'They'll burn themselves out going that fast. We've got five miles to the sea, there's no way they can continue at that speed without a change of oil, and that'll eat into their time.'

Whilst Evelyn enjoyed being responsible for her own wins, to be independent and prove she could do all that Sharp believed she could, she nodded so her mechanic knew she agreed. She had a lot of respect for his experience; he'd built the majority of the boat and knew more about it than she did. So she held the Napier at the speed they'd reached, aware she was sat in fourth place with four others trailing behind her.

Gradually, she was aware that Paris was disappearing behind them as the buildings and the arrondissements, the city streets, tailed off the further they ploughed down the river.

The wind whipped past her face and Evelyn was thankful for the protective canvas canopy set up over the steering wheel, keeping her hands from going numb in the cool air.

'Almost halfway, Miss Bloom,' Edgar yelled.

Evelyn looked to the riverbank and was surprised by what she saw. 'They're cheering.' She waved at the small group stood on the side waving and cheering all the boats.

'Focus on the water, Miss Bloom,' Edgar growled from the back. 'You can't compete if you fall in; keep both hands on the wheel.' Evelyn bit her lip, it was too tempting to reply and irritate him a little. Edgar was quite funny when he was grumpy, but if she wanted him on her side whilst she was competing, she probably needed to listen and do as she was told.

'We have about two miles to go. The rate you're going we should see the finish line in around six minutes,' Edgar predicted.

'I'm afraid that's not good enough for me,' she called behind her. 'That won't put us in first.' She moved the throttle and gunned the engine, knowing the boat had more in it. The extra speed meant more foamy water sloshed on the sides, splashing up and catching her every now and then, but only serving to prove the boat could do better.

'I can only see one boat in front,' she called back to Edgar. 'Who's behind?'

'There's six including the French and the Dutch, but I've lost sight of the Americans, I think they're in front, and I'm sure the German lot were ahead of us, but they're missing too.'

'Right, let's see how things look around that bend. Hopefully we'll be able to see where the rest of them are. If we're in third place, there's a chance I can get around them. Our boat is better than theirs,' Evelyn took the bend a little sharply, hearing a curse from Edgar as she had to reduce the speed to make up for her error, losing precious time.

'Don't panic, Miss Bloom, you've got this. Just keep doing what we've practised,' Edgar yelled from his position. 'I don't want to be tipped into the water.'

Straightening up, Evelyn urged the boat on, the prow of it bumping through the waves, a sign that the sea was getting closer to where it met with the Seine.

Cold. Wet. Her hands beginning to feel both sore and numb at the same time as she gripped onto the steering wheel, its hard leather unyielding, Evelyn did her best to ignore it all.

As the boat engulfed another wave, sending it beneath her, Evelyn felt her feet go and caught the steering wheel just in time to prevent herself from falling to the floor.

'Blast.' She planted her feet firmly down in a wider stance than before and held onto the steering wheel as the boat continued to crest the waves, trying to breathe as calmly as possible.

'Everything all right up there?' Edgar's view of Evelyn was impinged by the beige canvas between them. He would only have been able to see her head.

'Absolutely Edgar, one more mile. Look.' Evelyn said, distracting her mechanic as they rounded another bend, the sea in sight, adrenaline coursing through her veins.

'Miss Bloom, take them on the outside. Just do it,' he said, seeing her look of confusion. 'They won't be expecting it.'

THE FASTEST GIRL ON EARTH

Evelyn hung on to the wheel and still reeling from the shock of almost being knocked off her feet, firmly steered the boat to the right of the competitors in front of her. They had the tighter line, they were tucked in on the left side of the bank and she was certain it would be better to be where they were as they had the shorter distance to the finish line. Uncertainty crossed her mind, but Evelyn shook it away. She had to trust Edgar.

Evelyn changed up into a higher gear, watching as the other two boats pulled ahead. She hugged the right, speeding as best she could until the river opened up once more and Evelyn, to her delight, discovered that owing to a bend on the left of the river, which the other two were now having to slow down to navigate, she was now out in front, easily manoeuvring her way across and ahead of them.

'Oh Edgar, you superstar, how did you know?' She couldn't keep the joy out of her words, but carried on pushing to where she could see the finish line.

'Did a recce of course. But don't get lazy, they're not that far behind and could easily outrun us if they get themselves moving. Go, Evelyn, go.'

She didn't need telling as she was already urging the boat onwards, cutting through the water and breathing into the bumps as they crested each wave. Each jolt was working its way into her shoulders and neck but she clung on, standing proud. As she crossed the finish line she broke into the biggest smile.

'We did it, Edgar,' she screamed, slowing the boat down and pulling into the side, where she could see Victor making his way over to them, shaking men's hands and taking their congratulations.

A journalist made his way over to talk to Sharp, and Evelyn watched on as her win was discussed by them, both looking and smiling in her direction. She accepted a hand from Edgar to get out of the boat and return to dry land, her legs wobbling a touch as she got used to the firmness, keeping an eye on Victor and awaiting his indication to join them.

Any time now the journalist would be talking to her, to ask her how it felt to win. Evelyn retied her hat and rearranged her coat a little to ensure it wasn't creased. It wouldn't do to look scruffy when they took her photo.

Evelyn began to walk to the men, noticing Sharp nodding at the journalist and patting him on the back as the man of the press turned on his heels and walked away. Sharp came over and shook her hand.

'Well done, Miss Bloom, a very good show.' He held her hand a moment longer than was necessary, rubbing his thumb over hers, then releasing it to stand a slightly more respectable distance apart as Edgar appeared from the boat.

'She did well didn't she, Mr Sharp,' he said, wiping his oily hands on a rag.

'Yes indeed, very well.' Victor smiled at his mechanic and Evelyn felt a moment of pride at her ability of being recognised, though she wanted to ask why she'd not been interviewed yet. It was a huge deal to win.

'Just a few more tweaks and I reckon she'll be doing twenty-six knots.' Edgar shook his boss's hand whilst Evelyn realised they were celebrating the boat's success.

Not hers.

Chapter Twelve

London

'Oh darling, come here, you must hear how they've described the competition.' Hena was reading *The Times*, propped up against a mass of velvet cushions that had been arranged behind her on the chaise, a pot of tea to her side. Evelyn had returned from France the night before and was exhausted. She considered returning to her room, closing the curtains and succumbing to the sleep she needed.

'*Miss Bloom won the competition, which was a very competitive race, against the world's cracks, winning the five-mile world championship of the sea, and the £1,750 prize.*' Hena put the paper down and applauded her roommate. 'Bravo, Miss Bloom, bravo. Against the world's cracks, eh?'

Sitting down on the armchair opposite Hena, Evelyn accepted the cup of tea gratefully that was handed to her by her servant, Solomon, and tucked her legs under her whilst she considered her reply.

'So I hear.' She smiled a little thinly and took a sip of the tea. The heated porcelain against her lips made her pause for a moment and recall the blissful few days she'd spent as just her and Victor. Taking breakfast together. Watching the sunset and drinking champagne. His warm mouth on hers.

'Or maybe you didn't notice the competition, maybe you had your heart set on something else?' Hena spoke purposefully, nudging Evelyn to listen a little closer to her friend.

Refocusing on the petite blonde who was looking at her knowingly over the broadsheet, Evelyn shook her head. 'No, I saw the competition. They put up a good fight.'

Hena nodded. 'I see, I had wondered why you'd need to go to France so much earlier than the competition.' Evelyn's heart raced, maybe now she could tell her friend about Victor. 'But it was so you could get extra practice in. Get the edge on them, makes sense now.'

Evelyn sipped her tea in a bid to stop herself from saying anything. What had Victor said to her just the day before?

That they were to keep a low profile, it wouldn't do for people to be aware of their relationship. It would seem improper to some. Not him though. He'd reassured her that they had something special, but it was to be their secret and would affect her future in racing if they were found out. He was sure of it.

Evelyn recalled the hushed conversation they'd had onboard the ferry as they returned to Newhaven, where she tentatively asked why she'd not been allowed to talk to the press after her win at Trouville. He'd hooked his little finger over hers whilst they leant against the metal bars stopping them from falling in the sea, watching the wash as they made their way across the Channel. She recalled the way he'd averted his gaze from hers, instead looking ahead at the water.

'It wouldn't do to have you talk to the press. Remember, whilst we're accepting of you as one of our excellent drivers, there are some people out there who would prefer women stayed at home and brought up babies. They don't like the idea of women competing with men and undermining their efforts.' He paused, breathing in the salty air. 'You're merely the extension of the car or boat. They drive well because of how they're made.'

He'd looked deeply at her then. 'You're *a* story, not *the* story, Evelyn, you'd do well to remember that.' Then, after checking no one would see them, he leant in and kissed her gently, his moustache tickling her upper lip. 'If the press hear about us, your career would be over before it began and the Napier sales would be affected. You don't want that. Do you?'

She shook her head and kept quiet, deciding to swallow down the response. She couldn't see how anyone knowing her personal business would affect her driving opportunities in any way, but Victor was older than her. More knowing. If he said it would, she trusted him.

'I say, old girl, did you hear Solly?' Hena was looking at Evelyn with a strange expression. 'You were miles away – he was asking if you'd like your favourite for breakfast?'

'Gosh, sorry, yes I was. My favourite?'

The servant nodded. 'Yes, ma'am, boiled egg with some toasted bread? Seems to me the sort of thing one would need after a day's travelling?'

She nodded. 'Please, that would be marvellous, Solomon; you're an angel.' She smiled at him.

'It's good to have you home, Miss Bloom, we'll draw you a bath too, I'm sure you're aching all over.' He walked out when she nodded again.

Sitting back on the armchair, the efforts of the last week weighing heavily on her, Evelyn yawned and stretched her arms above her head. She'd just got halfway through a very languorous stretch when a black ball of fur landed squarely on her lap.

'Dodo, my darling, did you miss mummy?' She nosed the animal who fussed around her, licking her neck and jumping to regain as much attention as possible from his owner who'd left him for six days.

'I shouldn't think so, I've treated him very well. He has quite the penchant for macarons.' Frances came into the room and settled herself in an armchair, sighing a little as her heavy frame filled the space. 'Little thing couldn't get enough of them.' As if to demonstrate, she pulled her handbag onto her lap and lifted out what Evelyn assumed was a handkerchief, until Frances began unwrapping it and showing the contents. All of a sudden, Dodo bounced over, tail wagging.

'Sit, darling,' she asked of the diminutive dog who did as he was told. 'Good boy, here you go.' Evelyn watched as her friend hand-fed Dodo little pieces of macaron and shook her head in disbelief.

'You shouldn't feed him that, I'm sure it's bad for him.'

'Nonsense,' Frances shook her brown curls, 'he loves it, look how happy he is.'

Too tired to disagree, Evelyn moved to the breakfast table when she saw Solomon bringing in the tray loaded with toast and a couple of perfectly boiled eggs.

'You know how to treat us.' She began to dig in. 'I hadn't realised how famished I was.'

Hena was eyeing her as she ate. 'Didn't they feed you over there?'

'I should think she worked up an appetite with that boss of hers.' Frances winked as she leant over the table to grab a slice of toast, liberally buttering it. 'Did you see him in the paper? Must be difficult to get any work done.' She raised her eyebrow knowingly and Evelyn reddened.

'I'm sure I don't know what you mean.' She polished off the first egg and began on the second.

Hena smiled. 'No, I'm sure.'

'So, £1,750 prize pot? How much did you get?' Frances munched on the toast, allowing crumbs to drop on to the pristine white tablecloth.

'I...' Evelyn began.

'Oh no. Don't say,' Hena interrupted, interpreting the look Evelyn had made when Frances spoke.

'It wasn't mine to keep,' she began to explain but Frances shook her head.

'You won it.'

Leaning in to grab the last half slice of toast before Frances nabbed it, she shook her head. 'I won it for the Napier company, the boat is theirs. The money is theirs too,' she explained, noticing that Hena and Frances had exchanged reproachful looks.

'Spit it out,' she said quietly, knowing what they were going to say. Hena shook her head, looking as though she'd decided to hold her tongue for a moment.

'Well, at least tell me he's given you a slice of the winnings, or something,' she began and Evelyn nodded, a touch too eagerly.

'Oh yes, he gave me something. Hang on.' She moved out from the table and left the room, crossing the hallway floor to her bedroom where her suitcases remained mostly unpacked, save for a few stockings attempting to escape. She went to her dressing table, catching sight of her tired demeanour in the reflection of the ornate mirror which sat atop, and smiled when she saw what she was going to show the girls.

Grabbing them, she ran back out of the room and into the dining room, interrupting what appeared to be an intense conversation between Frances and Hena. They broke apart as soon as she appeared and turned to her.

'What have we here?' Frances craned her neck as Evelyn unfurled her right hand and showed the two large diamond solitaire earrings Sharp had gifted her the night of her win, to go along with the emerald pendant. Beaming, she placed them in her lobes for her friends to admire.

'My,' Hena placed a hand on her heart watching as they caught the light, 'I've never seen such beautiful examples. They really suit you.'

'They're wonderful.' Frances appeared subdued, which was unusual for her. 'So they're what you won?'

Evelyn shook her head whilst returning to the remains of her breakfast. 'Well, obviously they weren't part of the prize, but Victor, that is, Mr Sharp, felt I should have something for my win and he presented me with these,' she explained, her heart squeezing with warmth as she recalled the last night they'd spent in France. After her win they'd enjoyed a few too many coupes of champagne, and Evelyn, feigning a headache, had explained to the team that she needed to retire to her room.

Sharp had arrived shortly after, to 'check in on her', as he'd put it. There they had embraced in her room until Sharp had scooped Evelyn up and placed her, carefully, on her bed, and had then undressed her as though he were unwrapping a prize possession. Exquisitely, almost painfully slowly.

After they'd made love, they lay sated, drinking yet more champagne, and he presented her with a small black velvet box. For a moment, though she was embarrassed to realise it now, she thought he was going to propose. Despite his own marriage. But then he opened the box and she saw the earrings, and he told her he'd chosen them himself back in London, so sure was he that she'd win.

'And if I hadn't?' she asked, with a hint of mock concern on her face.

'Ah, well then I'd have waited until you did,' he replied, all trace of humour missing from his face.

'Fortunate I won then.' She said, placing them in her ears and allowing him to kiss her, all over her face, down her neck, across her chest and over her ribcage, and everywhere else until dawn had broken.

'So his wife is happy with him buying earrings like this for another woman is she?' Frances's jibe cut through Evelyn's heated memories, and she looked at her friend quietly for a moment.

'It's none of your business.'

'Maybe now's a good time to tell Evelyn of our plans,' Hena interrupted as Frances opened her mouth to reply.

'And they are?'

Chapter Thirteen
Monte Carlo

There was something soothing about the roulette table, Evelyn decided as she slid her black chips on an inside bet, settling them on a street of numbers.

She sipped the martini a waiter had recently refreshed for her and watched the wheel spun by the attractive brunette croupier. Noticing some of her fellow table mates were also looking closely at the croupier, who introduced herself as Marianne, Evelyn flicked her attention to the brooding blond man opposite her. He was staring straight at her and raised an eyebrow when their gaze connected. Discomfited by his attention, Evelyn looked back at the wheel and smiled when one of her numbers came up, accepting her winning chips with grace.

'You have one helluva lucky streak,' the blonde man said. It was the first time he had spoken to her. He had an American accent, she wasn't certain but thought he might be Texan. Evelyn nodded to acknowledge she'd heard him.

'Are you done here? Hena has lost at blackjack again and we think it might be a good idea to leave.' Frances had bent her head down to Evelyn's, a wisp of her hair escaping from its fussy up-do and tickling Evelyn's cheek.

'Your pal can't leave right now, she's winning,' the American said and Frances straightened up, a hint of her rose perfume trailing as she did.

'Honey, there's one thing you need to know about Evelyn. She's always on a winning streak.' Frances smiled at her friend. 'So, what do you think? Supper?'

Part of Evelyn considered staying there at that green-velvet-topped table, where everything made sense. Where she could indulge in a passionate fling with an attractive man who she'd never run into again. Where there were no real repercussions.

But the other part, the one which insisted she said her prayers at night, always said the right thing, the one who realised she loved Sharp and couldn't see a way past it, that part won. So, with a nod to the Texan, she stood up, noticing as she did his eyes trail down her black sequinned dress.

'At least tell me what you'd have placed your bets on?' he asked a little plaintively, and Evelyn shook her head, noticing he was a little older than she'd first thought.

'You're on your own, darling, I must go.' She drained the end of her champagne, and paused. 'But if it were me, I'd be putting it on my age. Though you'll have to guess that one.' She hooked arms with Frances and left the Texan looking at the roulette table.

They made their way through the gambling room of the Casino de Monte-Carlo, the orchid-shaped chandeliers shining glints of light on the gamblers in their tails sat on wooden chairs, puffing on cigars as they placed bets on baccarat, roulette and card tables. Their wives were stood nearby in small groups, dripping in diamonds and gossip, sipping from small bowls of champagne, their enormous rings rivalling the chandeliers.

The thrum of winning was in the air, with occasional roars from a table where someone had won big and Evelyn enjoyed the fantasy the room allowed. It could be night or day, raining or bright sunshine. It didn't matter when you walked into the gambling room, where the drinks flowed and the enormous paintings of beautiful women framed in gold smiled sweetly down on all.

'Hena, come on.' Frances was tapping their friend on the shoulder, attempting to get her attention from the intense game of blackjack she was playing. 'I thought we said to call it a day?' Hena held her hand up gently to acknowledge she was listening, but didn't wish to move.

'Tell you what,' Evelyn leant into Hena and whispered in her ear, 'we'll just be over there. You finish this game and *whatever* the result you come over to us when it's finished. Is that clear?'

Hena looked at Evelyn. 'Of course.' She smiled sweetly, then turned back into the game in front of her.

'Come on, Fran, let's go.' Evelyn pulled on her friend's elbow together to follow. 'We should see if they have any cocktails they recommend here.'

Once they were settled on their dark-green velveteen sofa, Evelyn raised her glass to Frances. 'To friends who have incredible ideas.'

'You're only saying that because you keep winning.' Frances clinked her glass against her friend's. 'You'll have a different attitude when you lose.'

Frowning, Evelyn took a deep sip of her gimlet and looked at her friend.' What do you mean, lose?'

Frances shook her head. 'Oh come on, you must have lost?' She considered Evelyn's quizzical look. 'No, that's ridiculous. There's no way you've never lost a game.'

'I've never lost a game – and I never intend to. I plan to break the bank at Monte Carlo.' Evelyn and Frances were still laughing as Hena made her way over to them with a face of thunder.

'Don't talk to me,' she replied quickly, 'you know what it's like though, I just need one big win and I'll be back in the game again.' She accepted the cocktail the girls had ordered for her and sat down, sinking into the velvet sofa.

'I wouldn't talk to her about it. She reckons she's never lost,' Frances said as she pointed at Evelyn, who was sipping her cocktail.

At the comment, Hena looked darkly at Evelyn. 'Yep, sounds about right. Drives faster than any woman, pilots a boat faster than anyone. Seems like the sort of person who'd never lose at the casino.'

'Only at the roulette table, mind,' Evelyn interjected. 'I know my game. If I played baccarat I'd probably lose every time.' She indicated to the waiter for another round.

'Another? You're sure?' Frances cocked her head in the direction of Hena. 'She's barely begun hers.'

'It's a holiday, and I'm with my beautiful friends,' Evelyn replied, by way of an explanation, 'and I wanted to thank you both for getting me away.'

'Well, we wanted to congratulate you on your win, we're ever so proud of you.' Hena, it seemed, had moved away from her angry slump and was beginning to feel the effects of her cocktail, her gaze slipping into a dreamy, faraway look.

'Thank you, it's very kind of you,' Evelyn began, but Frances interrupted.

'Don't expect this to happen every time you win though. If you do as well as your boss seems to think you will, we'll be well and truly out of pocket if we disappear to Monte Carlo every time. Imagine how broke Hena will be.' The three women laughed hard.

'*If* I compete.' Evelyn's words were out of her mouth before she could catch herself, and her friends' faces showed their shock.

'If? What does that mean?' Frances's face was contorted with anger, but considering how often her friend hadn't been too enthusiastic about her racing, Evelyn wasn't sure why.

'Yes, I'm not sure I want to do it anymore.' Evelyn realised she'd have to explain herself, but at the same time she hadn't thought further ahead than her instinct, which was to stop. She looked over to the roulette tables, itching for the sense of calm she enjoyed there.

The silence from her friends was what pulled her attention back to their table, just in time to notice they were both mouthing silently to each other. Realising they'd been spotted they both stopped.

'Go on then, tell me what you want to say.'

Hena looked at Frances, who shook her head.

'There has never been a time when Frances hasn't had something to say, why are you quiet now? Or Hena, you've always got some advice to give; whether it's wanted or not.' Evelyn's voice was simmering with rage, why weren't they saying something?

'Why would you give up something you're good at?' Frances asked quietly. 'That you enjoy?'

'It's that man isn't it? I told you he'd cause her problems,' Hena hissed. 'I've seen the way he looks at you; it's like he wants to consume you,' she added. Evelyn decided that this wasn't the time to admit to the affair. She pushed the anger down, she needed to tell her friends something which she'd been ignoring.

'My mother wrote to me last week, I received it on my return from Paris,' Evelyn began, forming the words carefully, assessing her friends' responses and noting they were listening intently. 'She said that she and Father have found a match for me. They want me to move to the countryside and make my home with him. He's very wealthy apparently. I could have my own car; apparently he likes motors too,' she added.

There was a silence as she sipped on the new cocktail which had been placed in front of her, suddenly both of her friends spoke at once.

'And?'

'Why?'

'What do you mean, and?' she asked Hena.

'Well, what's the difference now? They're always trying to matchmake you, why is this time any different?' Hena challenged. Evelyn noticed the diamond pendants hanging heavily from her ears and wondered briefly if Hena would always be supported by her parents and then a husband. She had the impression Hena vicariously enjoyed Evelyn's life, safe in the knowledge she would never be troubled by either the need, or drive, to work. Something that didn't sit as well with Evelyn, who though she received an allowance from her father, enjoyed the freedom that came with her own career.

'Because,' Evelyn flailed instead of responding.

'I want to know why you would want to stop when you're just getting going?' Frances added. 'You have an incredible life, you love competing. Mr Sharp has opened more doors for you than anyone else has or could, why would you give it all up? There has to be a reason.'

Because Victor was able to open doors, but then took the glory for his own. Because Victor was happy to roll around in bed with her behind closed doors, but flinched if she got close to him in public. Because she wasn't sure if her need for speed was a need for attention from him. Because she couldn't trust herself not to keep pushing for faster. For more. She was hungry. For winning, for gold, for Sharp.

Because.

'Because it's 1903 and most women I know are settling down with husbands, having babies and living in nice houses,' she replied lamely.

'Pah. You're not like most women I know, why do you want to be?' Frances was angrier than Evelyn had ever known. 'You're gloriously, wonderfully, brilliantly independent. You're clever, beautiful and one of a kind. You're ambitious, one heck of a driver and no one should make you feel like you should change who you are, and conform to what they want. Just because your parents had an arranged marriage doesn't mean that's what you need.' She clasped Evelyn's hand in hers. Hena grasped the other. 'This is a brand-new century, Evelyn. The time for change is coming and I think you're one of the brilliant women who will be pushing for it. A year ago you couldn't drive, now look at you,' she said breathlessly, her eyes shining, 'teaching other women how to do it. Winning competitions. There's so much more for you. I know it,' she finished.

Evelyn looked at both of her friends, could feel their hands gripping hers, willing her to push on for all of them and she gave a tiny nod.

It was a weight she knew she'd gladly carry.

Chapter Fourteen
Southport

Evelyn stroked her jacket, allowing the soft grey fur to calm her thoughts and moved her neck back and forth to ease out the cricks. Closing her eyes to ignore the hubbub around her, she allowed the light to dance a ballet across her eyelids. A cool breeze wrapped itself around her and she smiled to herself, the fur was doing its job to keep her warm, but the cold wouldn't be an issue when she climbed into her car, her focus was on speed today. A simple A to B of showing just how fast her Gladiator could cover a kilometre at Southport as part of the speed trials.

In a moment she'd step out in front of the noisy crowd, jostling to see the cars and cheering the drivers on. She took in a deep breath and opened her eyes, wincing a little as the light hit her retinas, and nodded to herself.

'All right, I'm ready,' she said calmly to Sharp whose face was the epitome of concern. But was it for her, or his investment in her as a driver and "face" of Napier? Evelyn considered his motives for a moment, then pushed them away, filed in her mind under "unhelpful", and concentrated on what she was about to attempt.

'You're going to be brilliant, Miss Bloom,' he said confidently in front of the team, then, when he was sure no one was looking, quickly took her hand in his and stroked his finger on the inside of her palm. Their secret code. He'd told her the night before it was his compromise to her. He couldn't kiss her in public, of course, but it was to be chalked up as owed to her when they could steal a few minutes together. She smiled slightly as he pulled his hand away, just as one of the engineers, Donald, turned round.

'Come on then, Miss Bloom, let's make history shall we?'

Evelyn ignored the nerves in her stomach nodded, trying to look confident. It wasn't that she didn't believe she could drive fast, she'd done it many times in practice, and occasionally on the London streets, but she didn't want to let the team down. Not after the valiant battling Sharp himself had done earlier in the day, achieving close to seventy miles per hour on his forty-five horsepower Napier. And, she realised in a rare moment of complete honesty with herself, she wanted to make the front pages. That was the dream. She was to be the first British woman to take part in a speed trial, and she wanted to do it in style.

'Nothing's changed much since yesterday,' Donald explained to Evelyn as he helped her up into the car, referring to the finals she'd competed in the day before. 'Your class is tough, but you're good. You can do it, miss, I know you can.' He raised his cap a little. 'We're all behind you.'

'Thank you, Donald.' She smiled at him whilst she checked her hat was securely fastened under her chin and focused a little way ahead of them on a chequered flag waving gently in the breeze.

Southport was decked out in its most festive of apparel. The grandstands erected in front of the hotels and houses were packed with fashionably-dressed ladies and gentlemen whilst behind the stout barriers along the roadside thousands of men, women, and children struggled to catch a glimpse of the competitors as they flew past on their machines. Sharp had told her that some fifty thousand spectators had come to watch.

Evelyn couldn't have asked for a more exciting beginning to her speed racing career. The weather had improved considerably on the morning's rain, with occasional gleams of sunshine bursting through the clouds. The only issue was the brisk wind which, she'd noted, was going against her such as it had the day before in the heats. It would affect her speed, but no more or less than her fellow competitors.

THE FASTEST GIRL ON EARTH

The racing cars had had their moment an hour before and, somewhat naively, Evelyn thought the crowds were likely to disperse before her own touring category came up, but instead it seemed they had swelled and a party atmosphere the like of which she'd not seen before had taken over the stands and those behind the barriers.

'Hello.' She waved at one little boy who'd waved at her, and a cheer lifted from the crowd nearby, causing her to grin, which in turn prompted further cheering. Evelyn waved again then shook her head, she needed to focus. They wouldn't be cheering if she failed. At a time when most women were keeping houses and husbands happy, she knew she needed to prove what she was doing was worth saying no to the "normal" route she could have taken.

Lining up her car alongside the others in her race, she nodded at Alex Govan, a friendly enough Scot who had impressed her during the heats the day before. He was some ten years older than her, but was welcoming when they had met at previous competitions in the past few months.

'Miss Bloom.' He tipped his hat, his Glaswegian accent harsh, but his demeanour kind. 'I'm not going to go easy on you, you know.'

Evelyn smiled. 'I should hope not, I don't plan to go easy on you. I want to win this,' she declared.

'Loser buys the champagne?'

She beamed back. 'Best start queuing now, Gov,' she quipped and laughed at his look of surprise.

Turning her attention to the Napier, she made some last-minute checks to ensure she would be ready. Donald turned the starter, waved that he was moving away and her engine kicked into life. Evelyn pumped the various levers so the engine ticked over nicely and carefully made her way to the start line.

Alex lined up next to her, and to the left there was another driver whose name she hadn't caught, but who was in a very smart Newton Pearce motorcar and had driven well the day before. Ignoring the rest of the competitors, Evelyn set her sights on the course in front of her and focused on what she needed to do.

She just had to hammer it across a straight kilometre. And do it quicker than anyone else. That was it.

'Breathe, Evelyn,' she whispered to herself, 'breathe, and focus.' Watching the referee who any second now was about to bring down the flag, Evelyn forced the sounds of the crowd's roars out of her mind. Wiped the thousands of people in their bright colours and their festive atmosphere away. Tuned out the other cars and rid herself of the wind which was wrapping itself insistently around her.

It was silent.

'Go.' The referee fired the starter gun, whilst another brought down a flag and Evelyn's instincts kicked in. Her foot pressed hard down onto the pedals as she allowed her hands and feet to work with seemingly little input from her. Switching up gears. Peddling the accelerator and clutch so she could reach the quickest speed possible in the fastest time.

There was a sound in her ears she couldn't rid herself of. A drumbeat. She thought it was keeping time with her car, that there was something knocking in the engine. Then Evelyn realised. Her heart. It was beating so fast she could hear it in her entire body, feel the blood pulsating from right inside her to the outer tips of every part of her. Even the ends of her fingers, which were clutching the steering wheel, pulsated. It felt good.

Risking a quick look to her right, she saw Alex was keeping up with her, but everyone else had fallen away. Powering, she looked at the speedometer and smiled when it was showing fifty-six miles per hour, but she knew it could do more.

'Come on, girl, you can do it.' She pushed the car, pressing her foot down as hard as she could, urging her car to go faster. She leant into the steering wheel as if by sheer physical force she could push it faster.

The technicolour of the crowd whipped past her. A blur of faces. Sounds hit her again, shouts. The roar of her engine and Alex's. Her heart still beating hard. The end was in sight and she urged the car on, keen to see what it could do even though the wind was pushing into her face, causing her eyes to stream.

And then.

Silence.

All of a sudden, the roar of the crowd was enough to convince Evelyn she'd won, though she couldn't tell until she pulled the car to a final stop a few metres past the finish line.

Alex pulled up alongside her and tipped his hat.

'Looks like I'm buying the champers then. Good job.' Evelyn nodded back at him and beamed at the scenes on either side of her. It seemed as though the entirety of Southport had arrived to watch her race. The cheers were so loud she felt she'd be knocked back by the noise.

'You did it, you bloody well did it, miss!' Donald was alongside her and looked abashed at his glee. 'Sorry, I'm just so ruddy pleased for you.' He said, helping her down from the car to a huge roar from the crowd. 'And I think they are too.'

'They can't believe what they've seen – most of them expect me to be at home darning my husband's socks, Don, that's why,' Evelyn replied, scanning the scenes for Sharp. Her skin tingled with pleasure when she saw him coming through the crowds, but her heart fell when she saw he was with a journalist. She didn't want him stealing the limelight, not like the motor-boat race. Not again.

Decisively, Evelyn shook off other well-wishers and walked quickly over to the two men in conversation, sticking out her hand to the journalist.

'Evelyn Bloom,' she introduced herself, 'good to meet you?' She left the question in the air so as to invite a reciprocal introduction.

'Forgive me,' the journalist took his hat off and shook her hand, 'Ernest Williams, you must think me ever so rude. I was just telling your boss here that I've never seen anything like it. Like you I mean,' he said quickly, as though embarrassed to talk to her.

'Why, thank you. That's very kind.'

'He's not being kind, Miss Bloom, you won in a very respectable one minute and forty-five seconds, he's being mindful of the facts,' Sharp replied, with what Evelyn felt was more than a slight tone to his voice. He was jealous she realised. He hadn't won his event that morning, despite posting the best time across the heats and finals.

But she had.

'Thank you, Mr Sharp.' The journalist nodded. 'I am indeed being mindful of the facts.' He paused, noticeably taking in Evelyn's attire. 'You don't look as I assumed, Miss Bloom.' He indicated her fur coat and she smiled indulgently.

'And how did you expect me to look, sir?' She enjoyed the slight furrow of his brow which seemed to indicate he was a touch embarrassed by his preformed opinions. He removed his hat and smoothed his dark hair down.

'Well, aside from the fact many of the other drivers are in full-length driving coats, you're dressed a little more glamorously than even your European counterparts.'

'Ah, I see.' Evelyn fixed him with a gaze. 'You mean I don't dress either like the men you see driving all the time, or the very few females who race abroad? Well now, wouldn't it be fair to suggest I might be carving my own way through this? Can you even imagine me wearing one of those coats.' She pointed at Sharp's dark-green coat which came to his ankles. 'For one, it would swamp me,' she looked pointedly up at the journalist to emphasise her petite height, 'and for another, can you imagine me in that green? Absolutely ghastly. No, I will wear whatever I deem appropriate for the situation and today it was this beauty. It kept the wind out, that's for sure.'

She stopped to draw breath and noticed the journalist was making rapid notes in his brown leather-backed notepad, the pencil scratching its way across the rough paper.

'It's worth mentioning the wind actually,' Sharp reminded Ernest. 'The wind was hard in her face, she did an incredible job posting the time she did. Many of the others were much slower than their heats, and the wind was no different yesterday.'

Swelling with pride, Evelyn held his compliments to her as though they were a feather that could disappear on the breeze. He was rarely effusive with praise, even when she'd achieved any success, so to hear his comments spoken out loud to a member of the press – who was noting them down – was something she held dear.

The journalist paused in his scribblings.

'Oh, don't worry, we'll mention everything. She—' He broke off and began speaking directly to Evelyn. 'That is, *you*, are very popular with the crowd, they were cheering your name. They wanted to see you win. You did something they've never seen before and frankly if you'd done it in a hessian sack in three hours they'd have been thrilled. That you did it in the style you did, with the passion you showed, the speed, the class. You're a winner in every which way, Miss Bloom, and my article will be a testament to that.'

As though he was used to hearing statements about his staff like this on a daily basis, Sharp accepted the praise with a mere nod, then turned to Evelyn. 'Good, come on, Miss Bloom, you've got more pressing of the flesh to do.' She allowed herself to be led away, basking in the glory of her day, yet deep down down she knew she needed more now she'd had a taste of success.

'Well done, darling,' she heard Sharp mutter through his moustache. 'I really am very proud of you.' He paused, and at first she thought he'd finished but he was looking around and checking the crowds of engineers and drivers wouldn't hear him. 'You're going to cost me a fortune in diamonds.'

1904

Chapter Fifteen

London

'This is wonderful,' Hena yelled whist holding Dodo securely in her lap as the three of them drove at a terrific pace along Piccadilly in London. 'Can you go any faster?' she asked of Evelyn who, with a hat holding her hair securely in place, fastened with a scarf, was thrilled with her friend's enthusiasm.

'Let's see shall we?' She pushed the accelerator down as hard as she dared, enjoying the sound of the engine roaring into life, and scattering a flock of pigeons that had made the error of sitting in the middle of the road high into the air, causing Dodo to bark and Hena to laugh with joy.

It was a gloriously sunny, cold day. The sort of day that had called Evelyn outside with its bright blue skies and white light only for her to realise she needed multiple layers of clothing to ward off the icy chill that spread it sway through the air, and a promise from Hena of a large brandy when they returned to their apartment.

It was the offer of brandy which was urging her on, encouraging her to go faster. She almost didn't see the police officer waving at her on the corner of Hyde Park to pull in, but Hena tapped her on the shoulder and pointed at him.

'Oh for goodness' sake, what does he want?' Evelyn couldn't abide the way the police were against motor cars doing what they were made to do. She was also highly annoyed by the term "scorcher" which she was regularly labelled with for speeding.

'Can we help you, officer?' Hena said graciously, attempting to quell Evelyn's own need to shout at the squat man who was squeezed into his navy uniform, the buttons straining to contain his own sense of self-importance. She did, however, enjoy seeing his surprise that it was a woman behind the wheel, his eyebrows shooting so high into his helmet she wondered if he'd be able to retrieve them.

'You were speeding,' he replied, walking to Evelyn's side. 'Miss...?'

'Bloom, and I wasn't. I was merely putting this car through its paces – I work for Napier,' she said proudly, but pursed her lips when she saw a glimpse of a smile on his puffy face.

'I don't care if you work for the Royal Family,' he replied.

'That's good, because she does,' Hena quipped. 'She taught Queen Alexandra how to drive.'

'I'm sure. And I'm the King's private officer.' He shook his head, quivering with laughter. Evelyn could feel the anger surging inside her. She wanted to throttle him. Her friend could tell she was getting irritated and placed a reassuring hand on her own, willing her to maintain composure. Dodo, however, wasn't to be placated and maintained a constant low-level growl in the officer's direction.

'You were caught speeding, you were doing forty miles per hour and the maximum is twenty,' the police officer said haughtily.

'Oh,' Evelyn was dismayed, 'I was rather hoping I'd clocked forty-five miles per hour. Still, not bad,' she said to Hena who was trying to maintain a straight face.

'This is no laughing matter, you will be summoned to court to pay a fine. You are irresponsible and quite frankly I'd have thought your fiancé would have brought you into line a little more. Women should not be out driving, it's highly irregular. If I had my way you wouldn't be allowed.' The police officer looked at Evelyn with such dislike she snapped.

'Well, I would like to drive over every policeman who gets in my way, but it looks like neither of us will get our wish today.' She watched as he noted her comments in his small notepad.

'Don't,' Hena cautioned, shaking her head as Evelyn went to open her mouth again. 'We don't want any trouble,' she said soothingly to the officer.

THE FASTEST GIRL ON EARTH

'Little late in the day for that, but I have your details. You can expect a summons in the post soon. Good day to you,' he said with clipped tones, then turned on his heel and walked away.

'You don't mean that,' Evelyn hissed, seething.

'Enough, come on.' Hena had jumped down to turn the starter motor. 'Let's get out of here. You need to get ready for that party anyway,' she reminded Evelyn. Isabelle's birthday party was to take place at The Ritz that evening.

'He thought I had a fiancé. Why would he think that?' she asked as she pulled away, irritated at how slow twenty miles per hour felt.

'He made an assumption based on your age I suspect.' Hena shrugged. 'It's not unheard of for women of our age to be married with a child or even two, he wasn't in the wrong for that.'

'I don't know.' Evelyn watched as a woman pushed a perambulator along the pavement, another small child holding onto the frame. 'I'm not sure he was in the right, one can't go around making assumptions about everyone one meets. And anyway, maybe I don't want children. Or to be married.' There was an audible gasp from Hena.

'Never?'

Evelyn turned left into their road and slowly took the car into the side, pulling on the parking brake, then turned to look at her friend who was stroking Dodo. He was calm, as he always was during a drive. He loved the car.

'I just don't see myself as mother material, Hena. Anyway, why do I need to be? There are plenty of other women having babies, I don't need to add to it.' She smiled but Hena wasn't smiling back.

'What? What have I said?'

'I worry about you. You go off to these competitions where it's just men. You hare off at speed in cars and boats with no care for yourself,' Hena leant back and considered her next words carefully before turning to Evelyn. 'I know you're not going to want to hear this, but you're obviously having an affair with that Sharp fellow you talk about. Don't look surprised, it's hard to keep secrets from people you live with – how many bosses give their employees expensive jewellery? He's married Evie, and clearly an utter cad to treat his wife with such a lack of respect. Not to mention your part you've played in it.' She shook her head and reached a hand across to hold Evelyn's. 'I worry that you'll chase after this life for a while until eventually you'll realise you've missed out. Then you'll be alone. I don't want you to be alone, Evie.' Dodo rested his head on top of their clasped hands.

Evelyn was blindsided by Hena's words, her hand weighed down by her friend's as she tried to withdraw it. 'I'm only twenty-three, you're acting as if I'm an aged spinster. I've years until I have any of that to worry about. As for Victor, I haven't said anything because I knew what you and Frances would say. But you don't know anything about us or about how happy he makes me. He plans to leave his wife for me, he's just waiting for the right time. He's a good man, he's just found himself in a loveless marriage,' she explained, trying to conceal her hurt at her friend's outburst. 'Anyway, I won't be alone if it does all fizzle out. I'll have you,' Evelyn added, her eyes staring keenly into Hena's, whose face twisted with concern.

'What now?'

Hena looked away, then turned back to look Evelyn in the eye.

'I'm getting married, Evelyn, and we're –' She broke off, unable to get the words out. 'We're moving to Madeira in a month so Fred can oversee the company there.'

'Oh,' was all Evelyn could muster. 'Good for you.' She avoided Hena's gaze, knowing her friend would see through her. 'I hadn't realised you'd set a date.' Hena and Fred had been engaged for months.

Hena shifted uncomfortably. 'Well, that's because you're not around very much. He's kind. Caring. He's a good match for me. When he told me about Madeira, I knew we needed to get a date agreed.'

Evelyn wondered when the moment had happened that she and her best girlfriend were no longer close, when they'd stopped sharing their deepest wants and desires. Their gossip. She shook her head to drop the thoughts of what the loss of Hena overseas would do to her and instead tried to be there for her friend in a way she hadn't of late.

'I probably shouldn't assume I'll be moving in with you when I'm old and infirm then,' she added, trying to bring some levity to the situation.

THE FASTEST GIRL ON EARTH

Hena smiled tightly. 'Probably wiser to bet on yourself, that way you'll never lose. Come on, let's get out. I'm freezing, and Fred is taking me to dinner shortly.'

'Good idea. We both have plans then.' Evelyn smiled too, though she knew how false hers was.

***

Later that evening, Evelyn thanked the driver for dropping her at The Ritz and rearranged her light-green evening dress after stepping from the car, so that the silk draped itself casually around her, emphasising her hips and bust.

Evelyn took a deep breath as she looked at the entrance of the elegant hotel. Whilst she wouldn't usually have any qualms in sauntering through the gold revolving doors, nodding at a liveried doorman, this evening she felt a little uneasy. Unsettled. It was most likely because of the conversation she'd had with Hena ahead of an evening where she would be in the minority as an unattached woman. So many of her friends were married and having children Evelyn knew she was becoming an oddity.

Not for the first time Evelyn wished Sharp was with her, escorting her inside, holding her carefully. Gently. The way he did when they were alone. But this time it would be in public and she would be able to turn to her friends and acquaintances and say, 'See, I am loveable, I am loved'.

She sighed.

'Penny for them.' Benjamin, who she'd not seen since Isabelle and George's wedding over a year ago, had appeared at her side just before she reached the doors. 'Allow me.' He offered the crook of his arm so she could slip her hand through and they were both swallowed up by the ornate doors, before slowly being revealed to the lobby.

'Are you here for Mrs Isabelle Smith's birthday function?' A tall man in dark-green livery, his over-polished buttons gleaming gold like so many of the furnishings greeted them.

'Indeed we are, good sir.' Benjamin's faux bonhomie grated on Evelyn a little, she hadn't liked it when they were in Paris. This man who always seemed so retiring when in private would switch character and become overly brash and loud in public and she'd often wonder why he felt the need to justify his personality the way he did.

But tonight was not for minor irritations, it was an evening to enjoy oneself. Something, she realised as they were escorted to the ballroom, she'd have no problem with.

Someone had pulled out all the stops for Isabelle's birthday. Evelyn heard Benjamin's low-level whistle at the sight of hundreds of gold stars decorating the walls of the entire room, and hanging from the ceiling. The stars caught the light from the flickering flames of hundreds of cream candles in varying styles, from large church pillar candles clustered on tables, to bunches of skinny tapered ones melting over the fireplace from silver holders. Partygoers in silks of greens, golds and silvers were drinking cocktails from crystal glasses, or dancing with their black tie dressed partners whilst a band played. The effect was mesmerising, disorientating and beautiful all at once, and Evelyn clasped her hands together in glee.

'It's stunning,' she exhaled, turning to smile at Benjamin and catching his briefest glimmer of recognition towards a very pale man, propped up against the bar enjoying a whisky. It was a whisper of a smile but just enough for Evelyn to wonder who the man was that Benjamin had acknowledged.

'Someone from work,' he said quickly as she opened her mouth. 'Shall we dance?' He steered her to the dance floor, twirling her as they reached the busy space where Isabelle was being flung around the dancefloor by an exuberant George.

'Isn't this fabulous?' she said to Evelyn as George pulled his wife in for a fast waltz, causing her to laugh out loud. 'I can't believe Georgy went to so much trouble for me.' Evelyn managed to plant a quick kiss on her cheek.

'It's stunning – almost as beautiful as your wedding,' Evelyn replied as Benjamin grasped her hand and they began to dance. It was a state the four managed to continue for three more songs, before they collapsed at a table, gratefully accepting champagne. Evelyn watched as more couples entered the dance floor, the women's dresses catching the light from the candles and chandeliers, adding their own sheen to the room whilst the men in tails, hair slicked back, held their fiancées and wives with a look of pride.

'I'm going to be all out of pennies if I keep catching you looking wistfully off into the distance,' Benjamin whispered, his lips close to her ear. Evelyn rearranged her features and returned her attention to the table, where Isabelle and George had their heads together and focused on her friend.

'Another party and another win for you, Miss Bloom.' Benjamin's crooked smile showed he wasn't making a jibe, more of an observation. Evelyn kissed him on the cheek.

'Well, if I didn't win we wouldn't have anything to talk about at events like this.' She replied, reaching to wipe her red lipstick from his cheek. Benjamin held her hand as she did, stopping her from wiping his face.

'Leave it, at least this way I'll look taken. Drink?' Evelyn was holding her glass to her lips, she'd barely taken a sip and he was proffering the bottle, an eyebrow raised. Without taking her eyes from his she swallowed down what was left in her coupe and replaced it on the crisp white tablecloth.

'If I didn't know any better I'd think you were trying to get me a little worse for wear.' She nudged Benjamin in the ribs. 'Good that I know you wouldn't hurt a fly.'

Benjamin topped her glass up and returned it to the table. 'To your win. The woman who won a motor-car race one week, then nipped over to France to win a motor-boat one too.' He shook his head. 'The *Championship of the Seas,* so that makes you the champion of the seas then?'

Evelyn nodded as she took another mouthful of champagne. 'I suppose it does, though I didn't think of it like that. It felt more like a sale than a competition.'

'Oh, in what way?' Benjamin's tone was conversational and Evelyn, who had grown used to her girlfriends showing little to no interest in her successes, was pleased to have someone who was.

'Only that it went as well as Sharp and Napier would have hoped it would go. Do you remember I told you King Edward saw the merit of the boat's design so much he bought a few for the British government? Well, after my race this time, when I'd won I was called to a private audience with some trading chap from the French government. They told me they liked it so much they bought the boat, the one I'd just raced in, for one thousand pounds.'

Evelyn enjoyed Benjamin's response, as he spluttered, hastily mopping champagne from his chin and refilling his glass.

'Well, one thousand pounds is quite something. I should hope you're working on commission.' She was basking in his respect of her and her face fell slightly at the mention of commission, a gesture she failed to cover up by sipping her own drink. 'Tell me you're making something from this? The prize pot alone should have gone to you,' he said gently and she shook her head.

'When I first said I'd work for him I signed a contract to say all winnings went to Napier; it's their work after all. It's not like I'd get very far without their car,' she pointed out, 'or their boat. And anyway, I don't want or need any of their money.' She looked off to the dance floor as George led Isabelle out to the middle. Her friend had never looked so enchanting.

Feeling a pang for a sensible relationship, she noticed Benjamin's hand resting lightly on the table as he held a glass with his other. She recalled the many times she'd held it as they'd walked along the Seine. How cool and firm it had always been. How she never felt as though her hand truly fit into his, but that she'd have given anything to feel half of what she felt for him as she did Sharp.

'Sorry, what was that?' She realised Benjamin had said something whilst she was daydreaming of a partner who was out of the shadows.

He raised an eyebrow at her. 'I said, care to dance?' His eyes glinted mischievously.

'That would be lovely.' She realised she meant it as he led her out to the dance floor, his hand resting on her upper back as they began to waltz. Feeling safe with Benjamin she enjoyed the closeness the dance afforded.

'My question, and please don't take this the wrong way as I'm sure you're a fantastic salesperson,' Benjamin said, as they glided across the floor, 'but why would the French government want a British-made boat?'

Looking at him as they rose and fell in time with the music, Evelyn shook her head lightly, it wasn't something she'd thought about. 'I imagine because it's a very good boat?'

'I understand that, but why ours? Why not build their own "very good boat"?' Benjamin's face suddenly looked strained and Evelyn was confused, then remembered he worked in the department of trade and it made sense.

'Silly me, were we meant to do that sort of purchase through you? It seems a little small fry,' she said as the music came to an end. 'It's not like we're supplying their navy, it was just the one boat,' Evelyn mollified and Benjamin's face smoothed.

'Yes, of course. No, I was merely thinking we must consider how to exploit the talent of our British manufacturers, clearly there's a market,' he said a little absent-mindedly, but Evelyn soon forgot the conversation as the band struck up and he pulled her in for a polka, setting the tone for the rest of the evening, where she drank champagne and danced under a thousand golden stars.

Chapter Sixteen

Madeira

'Would you believe this island?' Evelyn stood, looking out across the volcanic landscape which was covered in brightly coloured tropical plants, the like of which she'd only seen at Kew Gardens.

'I told you it was beautiful,' Hena breathed out. 'I pinch myself that I live here.' Evelyn continued to look across Funchal Bay, where fishing boats and cruise ships dotted the seascape, bringing a hive of activity to the island.

Evelyn merely nodded, enjoying the bright white of the buildings that contrasted so starkly against the black volcanic soil. The sky was a much brighter blue than the one she'd left behind in England, it was as though this was what sky was meant to look like. Breathing in a deep lungful of the mountain air, where their guide had walked them to the world's most enviable picnic spot, she inhaled the dampness, the lush dark-green plants she suspected were aloe vera and the dry heat already bouncing off the wall of volcanic stone behind them. It was idyllic.

'Come, let's have some tea.' Hena indicated to where their guide had brought a small table and a couple of chairs and had placed them in the shade of one of the strange trees which stuck out at a right angle from the volcanic wall. Evelyn followed Hena over to the table, settling herself on a chair and rearranging her walking skirt as she did so, hitching it up a little higher than was respectable so as to get some cooler air on her legs.

'Thank you,' she said to the guide, a sombre boy of around fifteen, who nodded with understanding whilst paying particular attention to the tea he was pouring from the pot.

'To you, darling Evelyn, my first proper visitor.' Hena raised her teacup in appreciation and took a small sip, savouring the drink. 'Nothing better than tea and company, is there?' Before waiting to hear Evelyn's response, she'd turned back to their guide. 'Mathieu, I believe we were meant to have a little cake too?' she prompted, then turned to Evelyn, tutting. 'I appreciate having the help, but he's not had any experience as a servant, so he needs quite a bit of teaching.' She took the cake from the guide when he returned and shooed him away, offering a slice to Evelyn.

'Go on, you need it,' she offered again after Evelyn's first response was to shake her head. She rarely gave in to cake and biscuits, it played havoc with fitting into the dresses she enjoyed wearing to balls, but, acknowledging they'd walked a long distance and were soon to walk back down the volcano to the beautiful whitewashed home where Hena lived on Acciouli Street in Funchal, Evelyn took a slice.

'Excellent.' Hena took another sip of tea and continued to look across the bay, the sun highlighting waves as they rolled in, and Evelyn savoured the feeling of peace that came with all her senses being soothed at once.

'I've enjoyed your company these past few days and don't misunderstand me, I'm thrilled to have someone from London to spend time with. But, and I'm only going to ask this once and I won't pry any further,' Hena leant over and lightly placed her hand on Evelyn's own, 'is everything well? I've been inviting you over for months since I got here to no avail, I rather thought you were mad at me after how we left it to be honest. Then one day you arrive on my doorstep with a whole heap of luggage, and you've not explained why you're here. Or what you're running away from.'

Evelyn had been expecting the question since she'd arrived, but had also known Hena wouldn't have pressed her until the time was right. Even so, she exhaled slowly as she tried to decide what to say.

'Victor has gone back to his wife,' she managed, trying, and failing, to show Hena she didn't care. 'I know I have absolutely no rights over him, or what he does. But after the last year we'd grown very close and I suppose...' she stuttered over her words as she tried to stop her tears from falling onto the pale-yellow cake in her napkin, 'I suppose I assumed we would, eventually, be together...' Her words tailed off as the lump in her throat threatened to choke her. Looking at Hena and expecting a thorough telling off, Evelyn was bemused by the sight of her dear friend looking sad.

'I am so very, very sorry to hear that.' She squeezed Evelyn's hand in hers. 'Truly. I was not impressed by him, as you know. But you said he made you happy, that he was going to do the honourable thing and well, that was enough for me. But now – ' She broke off and shook her head slowly. 'Now I'm terribly sad for you. What a waste of a year – of your beauty,' she added, sipping on the fresh cup of tea Mathieu had poured out unasked.

The last statement caught Evelyn unawares and she laughed with surprise. 'My beauty?' she repeated. 'Hena, you of all people should know I don't give two figs about catching a man. I don't want the same as you. I don't care if I'm to become an old and greying spinster. No, what I took most umbrage with was that he didn't tell me. I had to see him at a ball with her,' she almost spat at the memory. 'After he'd told me he was going away for the weekend and had cancelled our plans. He'd cheated on me, with her,' she added, savagely pulling apart the cake and hastily shoving large lumps of the sponge into her mouth.

Hena's mouth was agape. 'He was with his wife, Evelyn, that's not cheating. It's the exact opposite. He was, and I can't believe I'm standing up for him, but he was doing the right thing for once. He was with his wife. You're the person he cheats with,' she admonished and Evelyn was startled by the tone in her friend's voice.

'Cheated. Past tense. We don't do it anymore,' she corrected.

A silence fell between the two women. Where once it would have been a perfectly friendly silence, this felt like a stretch of time which Evelyn would never see the end of.

'Would you do it to me? Or Isabelle?' Hena said softly, her jaw taut with tension and a flash of anger in her eyes.

Evelyn furrowed her brow. 'Do what?'

'You know exactly what I'm talking about. Would you have an affair with any married man?'

A weight plummeted into Evelyn's stomach and she realised why Hena was as angry with her as she was.

'No. Of course not, darling, no. I wouldn't want to hurt any of you, you're my dearest friends.' She reached for Hena's hand and touched it, hoping her face looked as sincere as she felt. 'I didn't begin my relationship with Victor because he was married,' she explained quietly. 'I don't know if it was because we were working together as closely as we were, or the excitement of racing, but it was – still is – love.' Evelyn realised as she said it that she did still love Victor. 'Which is why it hurt so very much to realise that maybe he doesn't love me as much I love him, Hen. That's why I came here.'

Evelyn recalled the week she'd spent in her flat after seeing them dancing together, huge smiles on their faces, the most perfect of couples. And the seething, agonising jealousy which had wound its way around her heart. She'd realised after days on end of being unable to eat and barely leaving her bed that she needed something to change. Then Hena's latest letter with its vivid descriptions of lush plant life, colourful animals, azure seas and a paradise away from home had been placed on her tea tray one morning. She had booked her ticket that day and was on the dock just three days later, bound for Madeira.

'I'm hoping that my time here will help me heal the tear in my heart,' she added mournfully.

Hena smiled sadly. 'If we can't cheer you up here, I don't know where we can. Spend as long as you like, breathe in the air, take more walks, and borrow Mathieu if you need. Discover, tour. Whatever you like. Take the time and we'll rebuild you; then we'll send you home, ready to win whatever competition is coming up next.'

Evelyn looked up, horrified. 'Oh gosh. I hadn't thought. I'm going to have to compete, aren't I? I can't get out of the contract, but I don't want to see his face ever again.'

'Darling, we'll build you up so strong, that not only will you be ready to win again, you won't need to worry about Victor, because the way your career is going you'll be getting offers left, right and centre. You won't even have time to think about him, trust me.'

Looking out to the sparkling sea, Evelyn held Hena's words close to her heart, hoping she was right. Every time she won she wanted more, every time she lost she wanted to prove she was better. Life without racing wasn't something she could contemplate, it met a need in her soul.

Chapter Seventeen
SOUTHPORT

'For she's a jolly good fellow, for she's a jolly good fellow,' the engineers sang loudly, patting Evelyn on the back as though she were one of them, making her laugh with joy as she walked through the large dining room of the Palace Hotel in Southport which had been transformed into a party with servants moving quietly between staff members, offering glasses of champagne to toast her success.

'Let's see them then.' A voice she'd barely heard for the best part of six months was next to her, its owner's unmistakeable scent of pipe smoke, tweed and leather igniting a fluttering in her belly she'd been able to ignore for just as long. Evelyn tried to focus on the team, waving at the ones who were cheering and calling her name, celebrating the fact she'd achieved two medals at the speed trials in Southport.

'See what?' she spoke quietly, determined not to turn around, irritated with her body's response to his voice and nearness, which had sent her every nerve ending into a frenzy.

'I think you know.' The tone was flirtatious, causing Evelyn to blush, then get annoyed with herself for doing so.

'They're over there. With one of the guys, feel free to take a look – maybe even have a wear, and then discard them, I'm sure you know how to do that.' She walked away to accept a glass of champagne from a passing servant, willing herself to breathe.

Evelyn had spent two months in Madeira getting over Sharp and in that time, as well as gaining a strong pair of legs courtesy of the steep walks she and Hena had taken on a daily basis, she'd picked up a keen interest in fishing. There was something incredibly calming about sitting by a stretch of water, rod in hand, waiting to see if something would bite. Evelyn had continued her passion since returning to Britain, and she tried to recall her most recent trip the weekend before to steady her thoughts. She tried to hold on to the calm. The stillness. She willed her mind to remember the sound of the river as it had passed her, the rushing of wind through the grass. Her hope was to calm her heart and mind so that she could at least look at Sharp without wanting to either strike, or kiss him.

'I'm sorry,' he whispered in her ear, lightly touching her waist as he stood behind her. 'I behaved poorly. But I did it for you.' He reached past her to take a glass of champagne, lightly grazing her arm with his. It was enough to send shivers up her spine in a way no one else had done these past few months. Not that she'd been in much male company. Other than agreeing to meet with one match her parents had been thrilled to introduce her to one draughty dinner at theirs, which had gone predictably badly owing to the man in question immediately telling her she was almost a spinster and would 'be lucky to get picked' by him. It had underlined for Evelyn just how little she wanted to become someone's spouse, if it meant giving up everything that made her 'her'. The match her parents had found had said he'd find her a driver – so she could put the whole driving business behind her – as though it were something to be embarrassed of. It had made Evelyn realise just how much freedom she'd had when she'd been in the arms of Sharp. She could have the love of a man, and no expectations she'd need to give up the career she'd forged. It was almost a perfect relationship, if it weren't for the guilt that came with the knowledge he was married.

'How?' she replied to him, interested in his response.

'How what?' He sipped his champagne, a warmth in his voice.

'How did you do anything for me?' She felt him flinch lightly at the sharpness in her own.

'It was the right thing to do. There were...' He broke off, clearly uncomfortable with the conversation. 'Rumours. About us.' Her senses felt as though they were on high alert, she heard him swallow his champagne, felt the slight hitch in his breath as he decided to be honest. 'I didn't want your reputation damaged.'

She spun to look at him, it was enough not to yell at him in such a public setting. 'How very kind of you. So instead you allow me to see you with your wife at a very public event where I couldn't make a scene. Then you keep me away from events, from competing, telling the team I need time off. Keeping me away from the only other thing in the world I love,' she added, realising too late what she'd admitted to.

He smiled as he heard the words, and she felt as though she'd handed herself to him, offering her heart to him to break. 'I brought you back onto the team for the Hereford event didn't I, and the Southport trials?' He raised an eyebrow. 'Seemed like you needed a break after the hard work of last year. And I'd say that I made the right decision. You've driven incredibly well this past few months – don't think I haven't noticed.'

'Maybe that's because you've not been around to distract me,' Evelyn muttered, trying to maintain her irritation with the man who was currently stood so close to her his little finger was grazing hers as her hand hung down by her side. The feel of his touch was enough to turn her stock still, her breathing coming in shallow gasps as she tried to remember everything she'd agreed to Hena and every line she'd prepared to tell him it wasn't going to happen.

'No, Victor.' Her tone was enough to prompt him to withdraw his hand with a look on his face she couldn't decipher.

'No?' His voice was quiet. Surprised. Hurt maybe?

'It's not right. This.' She indicated the two of them. 'You know it isn't, that's why you went back to your wife – completely understandably,' she added, trying to show how magnanimous she was. He moved in front of her, cutting off Evelyn's view to the rest of the room.

'Her mother was ill and sadly died. That's why I tried to be the husband she needed, I was there to help with the paperwork,' he said quietly. 'But after her mother's passing, she has remained in the country where her parents' house is with a very close friend. She and I...' He rubbed his hands together as though the action would move the conversation on further. 'We've agreed to say she's gone to the country to grieve, but the truth of the matter is she will be living there permanently, and I will be living in London for the foreseeable future.'

'And it's taken you all of a few days to realise you don't like being by yourself.' Evelyn crossed her arms in front of her chest. 'I see.'

His eyes flashed. A spark of something she'd seen before, anger. Excitement? 'I've always needed you, Evelyn. But don't you see? Now we can be together,' he said quietly.

Despite everything, and aware her heart was leaping, Evelyn swallowed back her joy. 'Just to be clear, are you telling me your marriage is over?' She realised he was straining to hear her over the hubbub of the team celebrating in the background and matched his volume.

He fiddled with his tie and coughed. 'Well, no. Of course not. You know we can't leave each other, it's not the done thing.' He rolled his eyes at her naïveté. 'She'll still need to come back every now and then to be seen on the circuit. But there can be an...' he searched for the correct word, 'agreement, of sorts, where none of us are hurt by any of the others. Turning of blind eyes and the like.' He patted his pocket handkerchief and withdrew his pipe, fussing with the tobacco, not meeting her eyes.

'I see.' Evelyn realised what he was telling her. She just wasn't certain it was what she wanted to hear. Officially they'd be nothing, but in reality they'd be everything. They'd still need to hide their love, but the guilt she'd felt about the impact on his marriage was less so, as it gave another woman space to live the life she wanted, which was something Evelyn could understand.

Sensing her frostiness melting, Sharp stepped even closer into her space. 'We could be great together, Evelyn. You're my star, I found you. I built you.'

'It's as though I had no part to play.' She couldn't hide her irritation. 'I think I did a little driving somewhere in there.'

He smiled and brushed his finger against her cheek. 'Oh, I think we both know you're invaluable to the team and me.' He whispered into her ear and Evelyn allowed her body to lightly lean into his. She'd missed him.

The rest of the team were taken up with celebrations whilst Evelyn considered what she was agreeing to. She could have everything she wanted, and who got the chance to say yes to that every day? Coming to a decision, she looked up at Sharp, locking his eyes with her own. 'Whatever this is, we need to be honest. From now on, if one of us wants to get out, we tell the other. This isn't a relationship with the same rules as a marriage. And we don't just turn up at a dance with someone else on our arm, only to walk out of the other's life for six months. We talk. And it doesn't affect our work.'

'Deal, Miss Bloom.' Sharp extended a hand to her.

She looked up at him and saw his hazel eyes sparkling with passion that she knew was reflected in hers.

'Deal.'

1905

Chapter Eighteen

London

'So you've taken him back?' Hena looked over her tea at Evelyn and shook her head sadly, her hair swishing over her ears as she did. 'I hope you know what you're doing.' She rubbed her bump and Evelyn wondered, not for the first time, whether it would be a very long while before she saw her best friend again. Hena had travelled back to London with her husband to have her baby, saying she wasn't having her child in Madeira. But once she'd had her child, they would be going back to Madeira, with no plans on returning.

Evelyn took her friend's hand in hers across the table set for tea in her Mayfair flat, righting a cup on its saucer as she did.

'I know what I'm doing, Hena, but I love him. And if loving him means taking on this,' she gestured wildly, 'then that's how it's going to go. He's pretty much moved in here anyway, and has remained true to his word these past three months.' She hoped to convey the enormous bubble of happiness she'd been feeling since Sharp had become a permanent fixture in her life. 'Trust me to know what I'm doing?'

Hena looked out of the window of Evelyn's apartment. Snow had collected on the trees in the park opposite and the streets were quiet as the dull day had morphed seamlessly into a dark evening, and it wasn't even four o'clock.

'I miss the sunshine.' Hena's change of subject didn't surprise Evelyn. She knew it was her friend's way of giving her blessing, even if she didn't agree.

'That's because you live in paradise,' Evelyn replied, helping herself to a petit four. 'I was telling Isabelle about how beautiful the island is, she sends her love by the way. She suggested we all come over, apparently George has some business somewhere nearby.'

Hena looked thoughtful. 'Remind me, what does George do?' She helped herself to a sliver of lemon cake and meticulously cut small pieces with her cake fork before enjoying one of the meagre portions. Even at eight months' pregnant, Evelyn could see her friend was determined to keep her figure, something she was pleased to see. She'd observed too many women balloon with the excuse of a child in their belly.

'Oh gosh, it's something frightfully boring,' Evelyn said, trying to wrack her brain for the answer. 'He's in the trade and commerce section, along with Benjamin,' she recalled.

Hena raised her eyebrows. 'Do you see much of Benjamin?' she asked with a tone Evelyn recognised.

'Yes, I see him, he's often with George and Isabelle when they invite me to dinner, but no, nothing will come of it. He's too...' she searched for the word as she sipped her tea, 'young maybe? Or just a bit eager.' She paused. 'Why?'

Dabbing her mouth with a starched, brilliant-white napkin, Hena shook her head. 'No reason. I just find your group an interesting set-up. Two women, two men. Two of them have paired up, the other two haven't...Has Benjamin met any other women since you?'

Evelyn grinned. 'I know what you're getting at but he's very much a ladies' man, and yes, there have been plenty of women since me – it's been years since we courted. There's always an attractive brunette or blonde on his arm, whatever event we're at. We're good friends and I'm pleased we've remained so. Better that than lovers.' She smiled. 'It's moot now isn't it? I'm taken.'

'For now.'

Ignoring the slight from her friend, Evelyn poured them both another tea. 'Did I tell you about the next competition?' She paused as she sipped her tea and Hena shook her head.

'What's the next big challenge for you then?'

Evelyn smiled and leant in a little closer. 'Sharp has signed me up to drive from London to Liverpool, and back again.' She enjoyed Hena's shock. 'And I'm aiming to do it in two days.'

'But, on your own?' Her friend's eyes were wide. 'That will be terrifying. What if you're robbed, or you're bored or...' She stopped. 'Or you're attacked?'

Unsurprised by the reaction, having had a similar response from Frances a few days before, Evelyn whistled for Dodo and scooped him up onto her lap.

'First, I won't be alone so I won't be bored, Dodo's coming with me.' She fed the little dog a small wedge of cake and he relished the sweet crumbs. 'He'll be my official observer, and I will be completely safe because I'll have my trusty sidekick with me.'

'Dodo?'

'No. My .45 Colt. I've been back down the range to make sure I have perfect aim. And there'll be other people on the road, they won't be looking out for me constantly, but I won't be alone. Many others are taking part,' she consoled her friend, whilst stroking the little dog.

'But none of the others are women,' Hena replied quietly, 'they're all men. You're surrounded by men and none of them know what it is to be a woman in a man's world.' She sighed and pushed away her plate, then scrutinised Evelyn. 'Look at you, you're tiny. You can't protect yourself if a man decides they've had enough of being bested by a woman, or some sort of delinquent takes it upon himself to jump on you whilst you're stopped on the side of the road. The world hasn't been made for us.'

There was silence between the two women. Dodo licked Evelyn's hand and she fed him another morsel of cake.

'Respectfully, I disagree.' She swallowed the pain in her throat which came with keeping her simmering anger at bay. 'The world is opening up to us, we're "new women". Now more than ever we should be taking the opportunities that are out there. That's what I'm doing.' She looked out of the window at the snowy trees. 'There's so much we can do, Hen. I can drive a car and a boat, what next? Maybe I could pilot a plane? But I won't know unless I try. Unless I give everything that comes at me a go. We shouldn't be afraid to do more. To be more. We don't just have to be wives and mothers.' She slapped her hand over her mouth, realising what she'd said.

'I see.' Hena stood up, brushing the crumbs from her bump. 'I understand what you think of me, thank you for making it so clear how much better you are. I'll carry on *just* being a wife and mother if that's all right by you.' She walked to the lobby, indicating with a snap of her finger to Solomon that she wanted her coat, and turned back to Evelyn who was still sat on her seat, mute after her uncensored outburst.

'Be careful, Evelyn. Whatever you believe – it's a man's world, and will continue to be.'

And with that, she walked out of the door.

Chapter Nineteen

BRIGHTON

Madeira Drive looked celebratory in the summer sunshine. Evelyn inhaled the salty breeze making its way from across the sea and enjoyed the sparkles of sunlight that glittered off the waves crashing onto the pebbles of Brighton beach.

Evelyn was enchanted. Intoxicated even.

She adored London life with its glitzy balls and her legendary lunches which would stretch from the respectable midday to the less than respectable midnight. But, she thought as she took huge gulps of the sea air and scanned the horizon, looking at the gaudy Palace Pier and, further away, the more ornate West Pier, there was something rather glorious about being near the sea. She particularly enjoyed the draw of the water as it rattled over the pebbles in varying shades of grey, sand and navy. It was soothing.

Pulling her attention away from the view she focused on the controlled chaos surrounding her on the wide promenade that bordered the shore.

Everywhere she looked, teams of engineers, press, interested parties and hangers on clamoured for a view of the cars set to compete in the day's speed trials. Evelyn placed a hand on her stomach to quell the nerves, which had begun the night before, and breathed out evenly.

'Evelyn?' Her engineer, Donald, beckoned her to the car she was set to compete in. 'Ready?' he asked excitedly, a broad grin on his face.

'As I'll ever be, darling,' Evelyn replied, hoping her bravura would seep into her bones and replace the quaking she felt in her legs.

'Don't worry, love. If you don't want to do it, I'm sure Mr Sharp will understand,' a triallist near her yelled. 'I've heard so much about the infamous Evelyn Bloom, but I have to say,' he paused for effect so more of the crowd would listen, 'the reality is a bit of a let-down. You're no more than a slip of a girl. Albeit a girl who has experienced a bit of luck lately.' He roared with laughter, looking at his circle of engineers and yes-men to fall in and agree with him. They took a brief moment then laughed too.

'Funny, you've heard of me, yet I've never heard of you,' Evelyn replied as she settled herself comfortably into the driver's seat of the Gladiator, tucking her slim legs into the space. 'How about I focus on my speed trial, and you focus on yours?' She looked at his team. 'Word on the grapevine is your car needs all the help it, and you, can get.'

Without waiting for a response, she began steering her car through the throngs of people as Donald brought her to the start line.

This was it.

She, Evelyn Bloom, was about to attempt to set a world speed record for miles per hour driven in a car by a woman. Evelyn had her heart set on the male record, which was one hundred and four miles per hour, though she knew the car that had achieved that had better horsepower than hers. She recognised she'd be the owner of the world record whatever speed she did it in, as she was the first woman to attempt it. But she wanted to set it in style. She wanted to show women could drive just as well, just as fast as men, if given the chance.

Clenching the steering wheel so tightly her knuckles turned white, she acknowledged she wanted the success as a way of proving to her parents, to Hena who she'd not heard from since January, and all the others who'd been against her taking part that it was all worth it. She was making history.

'Evelyn, over here.' A man from the press was holding a camera. 'Smile.' With pride, Evelyn hunched a little over the steering wheel, her fur coat rising up to her neck as she did, and gave the waiting photographer a beaming smile. Satisfied with the photo, he waved his thanks.

THE FASTEST GIRL ON EARTH

'Good luck. My daughter is inspired by you. Wants to drive apparently. I've told her she'll need to marry first. I'm not made of money.'

Evelyn opened her mouth to reply that some cars could be bought quite inexpensively but the photographer had moved away, probably to get himself in a position to take further photos of the attempted speed record. There were some five hundred or so people who had lined the kilometre-long route. It wouldn't just be Evelyn attempting a record that day and she most definitely wasn't the main attraction. More like the sideshow. Most were there to watch the spectacle of the men's speed trials.

But as Evelyn would be attempting hers first they were all going to watch, and that knowledge gave her a warm pulse of excitement.

'Ready?' The official at the start line leant into the driver's side. His breath smelled of cheese-and-onion sandwiches, but Evelyn attempted not to recoil. Instead, she planted a large smile on and hoped he was a supporter of women drivers.

'Very.'

He returned the smile. 'All right then, let's see what you can do,' he said, not in a derogatory fashion, more curious interest.

Standing back, the official grabbed a loudhailer and spoke to the crowd who were clapping their hands and stomping their feet in excitement. 'Ladies and gentlemen, introducing you to our only female entrant in the speed trials. You are, I don't doubt, about to watch a slice of history. Assuming the car starts,' he said with an aside and the crowd tittered.

Evelyn was pleased he'd got the crowd on her side, even if it was at the expense of Napier's reputation. She hoped Victor wouldn't mind. After a quick wave to the crowd she revved her engine.

'Are you ready, Miss Bloom?' The official spoke clearly in her direction and she nodded, her stomach doing a flip.

'Then, three, two, one, go.' The official fired a shot in the air and Evelyn, barely thinking, instinctively shot forward. The car lurched a little at the sudden start, but Evelyn wrestled it, quickly and smoothly moving the levers into the highest gear. She could see the finish line. It was a flying kilometre course, a straight line as fast as she could go. Evelyn could hear the car straining as she kept her foot down. But she knew from past experience on open quiet roads that her car could go faster.

'Come on, girl,' she said with a grimace. Not that she'd admit it to the boys who worked as part of the team, but Evelyn's nickname for her car was Gladys. She and Gladys had an understanding. She pushed Gladys but only as far as she could take it. Evelyn was tuned into every whirr and sound Gladys made and she knew the car had more in her. Evelyn looked at the speedometer. Fifty miles per hour. Good.

But she needed to go faster.

Evelyn pressed harder, urging Gladys on. The faces in the crowd blurred into one colourful mass but Evelyn wouldn't have noticed if they'd disappeared. She was focused on her task.

Sixty-one miles per hour.

Seventy.

Could she go faster? Evelyn had achieved seventy-six on the road before.

'Come on, girl, just a bit more.' As if in answer to her competitive owner, Gladys hit 79.5 miles per hour, then made a whine and Evelyn edged off the accelerator, beaming. Exhilarated. The crowd was cheering and, with a rush of blood to her head and a wash of noise as though her ears had been unplugged, Evelyn tuned back into the environment around her. The applause enveloped her as she came to the finish line and an almighty roar erupted, the sound filling her up. A flashbulb popped, capturing the moment.

The next day the photo would be across all the papers and even her mother would hold on to the clippings with pride. She would take them out, showing them around to visitors to their home.

'Have you read about my daughter?' she'd ask, beaming whilst holding up the headline for all to see. 'She's the fastest girl on Earth.'

Chapter Twenty

LONDON

'This is nice.' Evelyn looked up at the bright blue sky and wiggled her toes, enjoying the warmth of the late-summer's day on her stockinged feet. She clasped her hand in Victor's as they lay on a soft picnic blanket. Life couldn't feel more perfect.

'More wine?' Victor had risen slightly onto his elbow, leaning over Evelyn to the wicker basket that held the remains of the lunch that Solomon had prepared for them. Evelyn propped herself up too and waggled her glass in his direction, watching the golden liquid as it was poured in.

'That's all of it.' He clinked his glass against hers.

For a moment they both stared across Hampstead Hill, watching the other picnickers who had chosen to spend their Sunday as lazily as them. A woman with a tiny dog lumbered past, both breathing heavily as they went by. But it was a girl with a kite that Evelyn couldn't help following with her gaze.

The kite was struggling with the lack of wind, but that didn't deter the girl who Evelyn estimated had to be around ten or eleven. Wearing a white dress to her knees, a white ribbon pulling her hair out of her face, she was the picture of innocence as she repeatedly threw the kite in the air and ran, holding onto the golden string to encourage the toy upwards. When it did catch on the light breeze, Evelyn held her breath in the hope that this would be the time the child would succeed, only to watch it crash to the ground.

But rather than disappointment, the girl would laugh, shout over her shoulder to her family grouped under a tree, and do it again. Just the simple act of doing something she enjoyed was enough, even if it meant constantly trying to improve.

'Penny for them,' Victor murmured into her ear, his moustache tickling her lightly.

'Benjamin says that.' She replied, caught up in the levity of the day, then froze a little as she said his name, remembering how much Victor disliked him. The two men had only met once, at her apartment a few months before and it had not gone well.

Evelyn had been bidding Benjamin farewell after they'd had an afternoon of gossip and catching up. At the time, she'd thought what an oversight it had been on her part to allow the men to overlap. Except now, she considered, it might have been a small test for both of them. Both men were important to her in different ways and she'd have liked it if they'd got on. She'd likened their meeting to two stags in mating season. She could almost hear the hooves scraping against the floor, the antlers swinging slowly.

Benjamin barely spoke, save for a tight hello, which Sharp responded to similarly. Since that meeting, Victor spoke of how rude Benjamin had been and Benjamin alluded to his dislike of Sharp and his "offhand manner". His response had been echoed by her other friend's to meeting Sharp, resulting in Evelyn coming to terms with the knowledge none of them liked him, so they spent the majority of their time as just the two of them.

'I was thinking about how wonderful these past few months have been.' She kissed Victor's cheek in a bid to make up for irritating him. 'You make me very happy.' She picked up her book with the intention of lying in his lap and reading, realising too late that she'd tucked a letter she'd received a couple of days before into it. The white piece of paper fell onto the blanket between them. Evelyn went to retrieve it, but Sharp got there first.

'What is this?' he asked gently, after he'd read the contents. She was bursting with excitement, knowing he'd realise what an opportunity she'd been given.

'Isn't it wonderful?' Evelyn sat up and hugged her knees with glee. 'I've been invited to the first-ever Tourist Trophy race on the Isle of Man; they want me to drive a Mors.' Victor was oddly silent, so she continued to fill the space. 'They're stunning French cars, I saw them when I was in Paris. It's only a fifteen mile course and they've invited me due to the success I've had this past year. It's such an honour.' Victor remained silent and Evelyn noticed he was gripping her letter so tightly his fingers were white. She frowned. 'What's wrong?'

'You know you can't do it, don't you?' Victor didn't look at her whilst he spoke, instead looking out across the hill, at the day trippers packing up their bags and baskets.

Evelyn's stomach plummeted at his reply. 'I can't?' she checked, confused. 'But why can't I?'

Victor turned, anger flashing in his eyes briefly. 'I would have thought a girl as smart as you would know why she can't do this.'

Evelyn shook her head. 'Stop saying can't. Why can't I? You of all people have encouraged me to do things; you've always said it doesn't matter if I'm a woman, I can do anything just as well as the men,' she reminded him.

'You're obviously not as clever as I thought.' He sighed, then held her hands tighter than she'd have liked. 'You can't do it because it's not a Napier. You're linked to my company, you drive my cars, and you don't drive anyone else's.' He released her hands and she rubbed her wrists where he'd held her. 'What if you come last? I need to protect the reputation of the Napier marque, I can't have my driver suddenly bringing shame on my brand.'

'Shame? Why would I bring shame? Why wouldn't I do as well for them as I've done for you?'

Sharp shook his head. 'I hadn't realised. I'm sorry.'

'Sorry?'

'Yes, sorry that you plan to leave Napier. That you're looking to drive for other people, I hadn't realised we were holding you back.' He began packing up the picnic items. 'It's probably time we headed back, I won't stay at yours tonight. I've got an early meeting tomorrow.'

Evelyn was stunned. She allowed him to place her shoes on her feet and gave him her hand so he could help her up. She stood aside from the blanket to allow Sharp to fold it precisely, before he placed it into the basket. He offered the crook of his arm to her so she could slip her hand through it, which she did, and they began to walk slowly down the hill. The girl with the kite was nowhere to be seen and Evelyn closed her eyes briefly, wishing when she opened them that she was back up on the top of the hill, without the stupid letter. It was no use of course.

'I don't want to drive for anyone else,' she said quietly. 'I'm sorry, Victor.'

He turned to look at her. 'If that's what you've decided, then I support you.' He kissed her on the cheek. 'You know I just want the best for you.'

They carried on walking to the bottom of the hill, their silence broken only by the call of gulls overhead, and the distant sounds of horse's hooves.

'Tell you what, let's get dinner from that lovely restaurant you like, and I'll stay this evening,' he offered. They never ate in restaurants in public in London, in case anyone who knew Sharp's wife spotted them, choosing instead to have dinners in her apartment. She tried to force a smile, but it came with difficulty as she turned over the last few minutes in her mind, trying to understand when it had gone wrong.

It had become a little claustrophobic, especially for someone such as herself who enjoyed trying the new up-and-coming bars and restaurants, but lately Evelyn had found it was easier to agree with Sharp than suggest otherwise. She would tell herself she enjoyed being in their bubble. So they stayed in. This evening, though, Evelyn was relieved as they sat in her dining room enjoying the lobster that had been delivered covered with a silver cloche. She'd been so worried he wasn't going to be with her that night, that she'd ruined everything by wanting to take part in a silly race, she was thankful it was just the two of them.

Victor poured them some wine and raised a toast, the glass catching the light of the candles on the table.

'To an *almost* perfect day.' He winked.

1906

Chapter Twenty-One

LONDON

It had been months since Evelyn had visited the Napier offices, choosing to spend her time in the garage, tinkering with her car and chatting to the mechanics, rather than sitting listlessly in the office adjoining Sharp's.

As she walked up the sweeping staircase she had a flashback to the first time she'd made the ascent, bumping into Sharp on her first day as his personal assistant. Never in her wildest dreams would she have thought she'd have the success she'd had. Or the notoriety.

It felt peculiar that other people outside of her social group knew who she was. But following on from countless newspaper articles detailing her success in various competitions, she'd gained a following of passionate women who were keen to emulate her success. She'd also gained a rather overwhelming amount of post from men asking for her hand in marriage, amongst other things. The mail was sent to the Napier offices most of the time, her Mayfair address being, thankfully, less publicly known. And it was this reason she headed into her office.

Victor had assured her he would bring the post home with him that evening, but on a whim, Evelyn had decided to take herself out shopping, and in passing, thought she could collect her post and a few other things from the office.

Her longing to leave the flat had been compounded by the beautiful spring day which had beckoned to her with its wisps of dandelion clouds and multi-coloured blossom seemingly throwing confetti

THE FASTEST GIRL ON EARTH

across her street. When she'd stepped out, her head almost swam at the crisp air, and she realised it had been days since she'd left her home. So few friends called round nowadays and she had a drop-off in social invitations to the extent she could be at home alone for a week if she didn't go to the Napier garage.

Ben called her a hermit when he came to visit, which was always when Sharp had gone to work. But she wasn't, she told herself. She just didn't have much need to leave her home. When Victor was with her, she had everything she needed. And when he wasn't there, she had plenty to keep her occupied. Though the competitions she was keen to enter weren't for a couple of months, she would be back out practising again now the weather had turned for the summer.

As she reached the first floor, though she was certain he'd said he was out looking at a new model of Napier that morning, Evelyn paused outside of Sharp's door, just to be sure she wouldn't walk in on a meeting.

Hearing nothing, she placed her hand against the door only for it to be pulled inwards, taking her with it and throwing her against Victor's shoulder. He looked surprised to see her and held his arm out to stop her from entering his office.

'Why are you here?'

Flustered at his offhand manner, Evelyn felt herself blush as the heat crept from her chest to her neck, whilst she opened and closed her mouth in response, noticing as she did the door to her own office closing.

'Who's in there?' She pushed past Victor, covering her embarrassment with anger, a feeling that was only heightened when he grabbed her wrist.

'Come and sit down.' He brought her to one of his large armchairs, pushing her lightly into one of them and taking a seat in the other. 'I'm sorry I acted like that when you arrived, I was just surprised to see you. I thought you were staying in today.' He looked over at the bottles lined on his bureau. 'Drink?'

'No.'

He leant forward to take her hand. 'Evelyn, darling, I'm sorry for being brusque just now, it's been a very busy morning and, well,' he ran his hand through his hair, tidying it up from its slightly dishevelled state, 'I'd become so used to you not coming into the office, I'd rather forgotten the effect you have on me when you do come in. How about that drink?'

Evelyn frowned. 'I've only stopped coming into the office because you gave me so little paperwork to do.' She looked up and stopped picking the flaking leather from the armchair. 'Although, I'm not really your personal assistant anymore, am I?' She stared as he poured out drinks. 'I've not been for a while. I've been a driver for longer than a personal assistant.'

'Well, exactly, darling, as was our plan.' He offered her a tumbler of whisky she hadn't asked for and she held the glass, unsure what to do with it.

'Speaking of which, there's a race at the end of the month I'm hoping to take part in, with a Napier of course,' she added hastily, remembering his concern at her driving anyone else's car.

'Actually, I have another plan for that one,' Victor replied. 'I don't think you need to bother taking part. Instead, I think you need to aim towards the Shelsley Walsh Speed Hill Climb.' He sipped his drink.

Evelyn was mortified. 'But that's not until June, that's months away. Whatever will I do with myself between now and then?'

'I'm sure you can find some entertainment. Try your hand at the roulette wheel again, you always said you'd make Monte Carlo go bust.' He drained his whisky. 'Look, I'm not saying there won't be any other events for you before June, just that I don't want you doing this one. In fact, I was hoping to send you off for another boat trial if you're keen.'

Evelyn was thrown. On one hand, her true passion was driving and she couldn't help feeling side-lined by Sharp. On the other, the opportunity to race a speedboat again appealed. As did gaining some space from Sharp. She was starting to wonder if something was seriously wrong in their relationship. She'd have liked to talk it through with Hena or Frances. But as Frances had returned to live with her parents and Hena was still not speaking to her, it was difficult to ask anyone. Instead, she decided maybe he was giving her an opportunity for room to breathe even if he didn't realise.

'When were you thinking?'

Victor looked pleased. 'End of the week? We're trialling three different boats, I'd need you to get a handle on them all, then pick the one you prefer.'

'If you think that's best for Napier,' she replied, maintaining eye contact with him. She knew it discomforted him, and on more than one occasion he'd break it, citing she was being too overt, but today they kept their eyes locked. She could feel the tension suffusing the room, smothering the wooden walls, cloaking the dark furniture and sombre paintings.

'I do.'

'And best for us?'

A hesitation. Sharp's eyes skittered fleetingly away, just slightly but enough for Evelyn to catch it.

'Victor?' she prompted. 'I'll be on my own out there, are you sure you're happy with that?'

His eyes snapped back to hers and she saw the emotion that chased itself across his face before he covered it with a smile. Anger.

'We managed six months when you were in Paris.'

'We weren't together then.'

'It was still hard.' Victor relied ruefully. 'I missed you, but knew you'd come back to me. Eventually.' He took her glass of whisky and swallowed the amber liquid down in one loud gulp. 'And this will just be a couple of weeks. I'll come out,' he added, and acted shocked as though he hadn't intended to say as much.

'Actually,' Evelyn realised she'd had an idea, 'I think I'll extend my stay out there. As you say, I haven't got much on until June this year. You've reminded me; I think I'll return to Paris. Just for a little while but I'll go as a tourist.' She watched his face for a reaction. 'Yes, that'll be marvellous. There was so much I didn't do when I was there last. And this time I can make an adventure of it all, with the race midway. I can even go on to Monte Carlo afterwards, spend my winnings.' She laughed, then clapped her hand to her mouth with mock anxiety. 'Oh, but they won't be *my* winnings. Will they? I'll win for you darling, for Napier. Then I'll hand the money over to you, and do as I'm told.'

There was silence in the room and Evelyn knew she'd gone too far.

He was on her in a moment, his hand at her throat.

'Never forget who made you, Miss Bloom.' Spittle landed on her face as he spoke. 'You act as though you're important, and I'm here to tell you that you're not.'

'Victor,' Evelyn gasped, 'I can't... breathe.'

His hold loosened slightly, then he grabbed her chin, pulling her face upwards to look directly at his.

'Everything I do is for us. I want what's best for you. That's why you need to do as you're told.' He sneered at her and Evelyn saw his gums. They were bright pink and vulgar. 'What did I say when I first signed you?' Even if she could have moved to reply, he didn't let her answer. 'I told you to stick with me and I'd take you all the way.' His grip got tighter, she could feel her neck being stretched upwards. 'Haven't I done that? For you? For us? For Napier?' She tried to nod, moving her head a fraction.

He looked satisfied with her response. 'Just remember that. So if I tell you to go out to France to race, that's what you'll do. But don't disappoint me with distractions. You don't need to go to Paris, you need to go out when I tell you to, and you need to race when I tell you to. Then you go to Monte Carlo if I tell you to, and then you come back here. Like a good girl.' His breath was whisky-saturated and it burnt her eyes. She'd seen his anger before, but he'd never hurt her. Evelyn tried to widen her eyes to appeal to him, to ask him for forgiveness.

'If I have to, I'll make sure you remember who's in charge.' He traced a finger down from her neck, past her throat and over her breast. Forcing her to stay still with his other hand against her jaw, he squeezed her breast hard, so that she was convinced his fingers would be imprinted in the soft tissue. 'But right now, I think you'll do as you're told, won't you?' He released the hold on her chin and sat back on his chair. Evelyn rubbed her neck, wincing at the pain in her breast and fought back tears.

'I said you'd do as you're told. I'm expecting an answer, Evelyn,' he growled quietly.

'Yes.' Her voice was hoarse.

He smiled. 'That's what I thought. Now, go back home. I'll have one of the engineers drive you back. We'll have dinner at seven o'clock when I return. See that Solomon prepares it. Don't want you getting involved do we, darling? Can barely trust you with a martini.' He laughed at his own joke and pulled her up quickly by the wrists, brushing his hands over her shoulders as though to tidy her up. Evelyn stood rigid with shock, allowing everything to wash over her. He turned her around and lightly pushed her towards the door. Once at the door, he opened it to push her through, but stopped and turned her around and pulled her into a deep kiss.

It was the type of kiss that before today would have made her weak at the knees. But now she knew who he really was, Evelyn felt as though she were impaled by him. He was leaning her back into an unnatural bend, kissing her so deeply she was sure she'd be suffocated by him. His hand on the back of her head was forcing her face closer towards his than felt natural. She felt smothered. He pulled her up to standing once again and smiled, looking every bit like the Victor she'd fallen in love with.

'If we do that for much longer I'm not sure I'd be able to contain myself.' He kissed his index finger and placed it on her lips. 'Looking forward to our after-dinner entertainment tonight.'

He pushed her out the door, locking it behind her, leaving Evelyn standing bereft on the plush carpet, looking out across the other offices, wondering what the hell had just happened.

Chapter Twenty-Two

Blackpool

The last few months had not gone according to plan.

Evelyn, blindsided by Sharp's behaviour, had privately decided she would only continue racing and remain with him for as long as it took for her to gain an opportunity – off the back of a win – to talk to another car company about moving to them.

She'd also made the decision that she wouldn't talk about how he'd treated her. Evelyn felt too ashamed to admit to it, and had clung to the idea that as long as she performed well in any of the upcoming competitions, she would be able to rid herself of Sharp and Napier at the same time.

However, she'd lost her boat race in France, despite being the favourite, and on her return to Britain she'd practised hard ahead of the hill-climb competition in Worcestershire only to come sixth. She solely blamed Sharp for her failure as her car was the only one competing which was not fitted with non-skid tyres – at his request – and in one hair-raising moment, she and the car nearly went over an embankment owing to the greasy state of the roads. Then in July, hoping to redeem herself, she'd agreed to compete in the Aston Clinton Hill Climb in Buckinghamshire, only to come a disappointing third.

She was, she realised, pinning all her hopes on today's race to redeem herself: the Blackpool Speed Trial, where she hoped to break her own world record, set the year before.

THE FASTEST GIRL ON EARTH

As well as being unable to move to another car manufacturer, she hadn't been able to shake Sharp. It was her own fault. There was an invisible string between them and it didn't matter if they argued, or he became more controlling of her than she would have preferred, something would click inside her before the end of most days and she'd feel a loss if he wasn't in her bed. She'd ache for him to be beside her again.

But when he was with her, she felt revulsion at herself. She'd hear him, how he spoke to her, but it was as though she were floating above her own body, watching him telling her she was ugly, untalented and getting old. She felt separate from herself. Separate enough to know, deep in her heart, that he loved her. However he spoke to her, it was only because he loved her and wanted what was best for her. She was lucky to have found him.

Looking at the crowds gathering for the speed trial, she allowed a small smile to escape. There were more people here for the women's speed trial, than at Brighton the year before.

'It's going to be a busy one, miss.' Donald appeared from the back of the car. 'They say there's near enough ten thousand people come to watch the cars. Best of luck, Evelyn.' He stood a little awkwardly, licking his lips as though he wanted to say something, then shook his head. 'Anyway, me and the boys, well, we're pretty proud of you. You're one of us, don't forget that.' He nodded at her and before she could say anything else, he'd disappeared into the crowd of mechanics and drivers.

'Look, it's her!' a boy's shout came from the crowd and she looked to see where the voice had come from, then waved at the boy and his family. Smoothing down her driving coat, feeling its weight and that of the crowd's expectation of her, she located her gloves in her pocket and pulled them on, beginning her mental checklist of readying the car whilst recalling a conversation between her and Sharp the night before. He'd been warming brandy in a glass, lying beside her in their neatly decorated hotel room, the bedclothes strewn around them. She'd had her eyes closed, visualising the race.

'It's not difficult, you drive from the start to the finish as quickly as you can. You've done it once before.'

'That's why I'm worried, people will be expecting me to do the same as last year, or better.'

'Hardly, there's only you and one other girl. They won't be expecting anything from you, that's why you're the first race. It's the warm-up before the real one,' she heard as he sipped some of his brandy. 'No, you'll know fear of losing when you're up against a field of competitors. Right now, life's easy for you. You're the best at everything because you're the only one doing it.' He sipped again. 'Soon enough, though, that's when things will change for you my darling, when the younger ones start snapping at your heels.'

'Who is the other girl? I feel as though I know her.' Evelyn opened one eye slightly, just enough to spot the reaction on Sharp's face as she spoke, cementing her instinct that there was something going on between him and Julia, the other competitor at the speed trial.

He drained the rest of his brandy. 'No idea, just some girl. They're all jealous I have you, they all want an Evelyn.' He placed his glass on the table beside the bed and leant over her. She was aware of his body's weight pressing on half of her own, pinning her right arm slightly to the bed. She kept her eyes closed. She didn't mean to flinch when his moustache brushed over her lips as he leant in and kissed her deeply.

'Not in the mood, eh?' His tone wasn't one she enjoyed and Evelyn knew the choice was either an argument over why she didn't want to make love that night, which would likely go on longer than the actual act, or she could just smile and get it over with. She shuffled her arm so he could get closer to her and moved her legs a little, to show she wasn't going to put up a fight.

'Not at all, darling. Actually…' She paused, considering if she wanted to anger him. 'I wanted to make sure you were all mine,' she corrected herself, deciding against saying anything else until she had proof. Then leant up to him. He waited a moment, the merest hint of a pause, just to show it was his choice, not hers, and then leant in to kiss her. Their bodies met so easily it was another reason Evelyn felt confusion over their relationship, in this respect it was perfect.

'I'm all yours, and you're all mine.'

'Come on, daydreamer, up you go.' Sharp's arrival beside her in the crowd shocked Evelyn back to reality. A return to the flashes of colour of cars in her peripheral vision, the noise of engines bursting into life or choking and misfiring, and the movement from the crowd.

'Of course.' Evelyn shook her head to clear her thoughts and climbed behind the steering wheel, making a conscious effort to check the levers and the gauge.

'Oh, no, you don't have to do that, I've already checked,' she called over to Sharp who had opened the bonnet and disappeared under it.

'Nonsense, I want to check everything's ship-shape for Miss Evelyn Bloom.' Sharp's face poked around the outside of the bonnet and grinned at her as he wiped his hand on an oil-streaked cloth. 'I'm pleased to report it is.' He slammed the bonnet down hard, causing the car to jolt. 'Only thing left for you is to get to the start line.'

'And win,' Evelyn reminded him.

'And win, of course.'

'And set another record.' She grinned.

'Unless Julia does.' He replied and Evelyn's stomach plummeted. She couldn't consider someone else getting the plaudits.

Chapter Twenty-Three

London

Benjamin rustled the copy of the *Penny Illustrated Paper* which was delivered that morning to Evelyn's flat. 'The sensational adventures of Miss Evelyn Bloom,' Benjamin read over their tea and Evelyn rolled her eyes. '"The sensational adventures of Miss Evelyn Bloom – champion lady motorist of the world." Shall I continue?' Evelyn shook her head and he laughed. 'You eat that marmalade on toast and I'm going to read this to you.' He looked down at the full-page profile, including a photo of Evelyn sat in the Napier after setting her world record of 90.88 miles per hour, blasting her sole competitor out of the water.

'"Miss Bloom, describe the sensations of travelling at the awful pace of world record speeds."' Benjamin cleared his throat and started talking in a higher voice. '"Wonderful. One can hardly describe one's sensations. There is a feeling of flying through space. I never think of the danger. That sort of thing won't do. But I know it is omnipresent. The slightest touch of the hand and the car swerves, and swerves are usually fatal. But I am a good gambler, and always willing to take the chance,"' he wafted his hands around, '"in going that pace, the hardest thing is to keep in the car. Half the time the wheels don't touch the ground at all, and when they do touch, you must be prepared to take the shock and lurch, else out you will go. It is far harder work to sit in the car than to ride a galloping horse over the jumps in a steeplechase."'

'That's enough of that.' Evelyn took the paper and flattened it on the table to read herself. 'No mention of the bonnet of course,' she muttered as she chewed thoughtfully on the toast.

'Yes, I rather think your Victor has done some smoothing over there.' Benjamin raised his eyebrows. 'You break a record, create a new world record for women by driving at an incredible ninety-one miles per hour, and then you have a near-death escape because part of the bonnet works loose. Which, had you not pulled up in time, might have blown back and beheaded you.'

'Well, I don't know...' Evelyn dabbed at her mouth with the starched white napkin.

'A bonnet which you swear was fine when you checked it, but it was Sharp who'd touched it last.' Benjamin eyed her over the newspaper, then, on receiving no response, folded the paper and placed it next to him on the table. 'Evelyn, when are we going to talk about what happened?'

Evelyn poured some more tea out for them. She didn't really want any more, but she hoped to stall a little. They both watched as she stirred her tea before carefully placing the spoon on the saucer, the action breaking the silence in the flat. She sighed a little, rearranging the silk scarf around her neck and looking to the window. It was a cheerfully sunny morning which only further served to irritate her mood. Why couldn't the weather be dreary and grey? Why was it unseasonably warm and beckoning to be enjoyed?

'Evelyn.'

She looked at Benjamin, who rolled his eyes.

'Fine. I was driving wonderfully, my foot was wedged tight onto the accelerator and for a pure, blissful moment, it felt as though I was flying.' Evelyn recalled the race the week before fondly. 'I knew I'd broken my record and this, well, this was my victory lap. Well, not lap, but return journey; I don't think the organisers would have appreciated me doing another loop, would they?' Benjamin shook his head. 'Anyway, as I was driving, I heard... something.' She furrowed her brow. 'It rattled, and I thought, well, I'm not surprised, old girl, I'd be rattling too if I'd been pushed to that limit. I just thought she was groaning a little at what I'd put her through but no sooner had that thought crossed my mind then whoosh, the bonnet started to rattle and come loose and I realised I either pull up, or die.'

'And?' Benjamin prompted gently, sipping his tea.

'And, nothing,' Evelyn replied irritably. 'I pulled up, everyone cheered because they just thought I'd finished my lap and they wanted to celebrate my record. It was only Donald and Victor who'd seen what had happened. They both came to the car, Don inspected the bonnet and kept repeating his apologies.' She dropped her head in her hands. 'But I know he didn't do anything. We both checked that bonnet before the race. It was secure, all the nuts and bolts were fine, no issues. No wear. There was no reason for it to have flown up.'

'But you said –'

'I know,' Evelyn answered, cutting him off. 'I know what I said. I said Victor checked it last but I can't honestly...' She looked at Benjamin. 'You can't honestly think his plan was to kill me. Was it? I'd much rather believe what he suggested, which was that the car had gone the fastest it had ever gone and the wind under the bonnet was enough to push it up.'

'I know that's what you'd prefer to think—'

Evelyn stood up, throwing her napkin on the table, cutting him off mid-sentence. 'It is what I'd prefer to think, Benjamin, and I plan to put that whole business behind me so I can focus on a move to a different company, which has been my plan these last few months.' She moved to a small table and retrieved a cigarette, lighting it and taking a deep pull before she continued. 'I'm going to use all my experience and then I'm going to get away from Napier. And Sharp.' She blew the smoke out with fierce determination, eyeing her friend keenly.

'What about...?'

'Enough, Benjamin, that's enough. I've told Victor I need some time away from him. I've told you I'm going to leave Napier. In a few months' time I'll be free and able to drive for someone else. Now would you please just change the conversation? Or leave.'

She stood, hand on hip, a cigarette dangling from her other hand whilst Benjamin considered his response.

THE FASTEST GIRL ON EARTH

'You and I are going shopping,' he replied, causing Evelyn's eyebrows to shoot up and her mouth to pucker a little.

'We are? And where, might I ask, are we going?'

'Nowhere if you don't change out of that and put something on,' he remarked, looking at her turquoise silk kimono, the cord tied neatly around Evelyn's tiny waist. It was a gift from Isabelle, sent from one of her and George's travels. She blushed, as he knew she would.

'I'm only dressed like this because you arrived at some ungodly hour,' she reminded him.

'I don't believe nine o'clock on a Saturday morning is classed as ungodly for anyone, but it is after ten now and I think we should make the most of the day, not wallowing in this flat anymore.' He nodded at Solomon to clear the breakfast dishes away. 'When we were in Paris, you'd love a shop,' he reminded her, 'said it took your mind off almost anything.'

Evelyn narrowed her eyes at him. 'That's not true, that was Isabelle. I'm far happier fishing. Or riding.'

'Was it? I'm sure it was you.' Benjamin looked confused for a moment, then picked himself up. 'Still, I can't abide fishing and we're not going out riding today. Let's just get out and do something fun,' he stroked her cheek tenderly, 'like we used to.'

On the one hand, Evelyn knew she shouldn't encourage Benjamin as she had no romantic notions towards him, but on the other, as her friends had abandoned her over the last few months, it wasn't as though she had plenty of other invitations.

'Where?'

'Where else, darling? Harrods. I think we should get you a new dress and then we'll go out tonight to somewhere wonderful.' Benjamin grinned. 'Even if you don't want something, I need a new pair of gloves. Look at these.' He held up the threadbare leather pair he'd worn to the flat. Evelyn couldn't think how he'd managed to get them in such a terrible condition, they looked torn, but she agreed they needed replacing.

'I need a few minutes to get myself ready.'

Chapter Twenty-Four

LONDON

'Don't you just love this place?' Evelyn breathed in the air of the department store as she walked through the doors, enjoying the sight of the enormous dark-green ferns draping down from the upper balconies and the many glittering chandeliers lighting the way. 'I really think I could live here.' Evelyn paused for a moment as she inhaled the heady mixture of perfume, leather goods and polish.

'But where would you park the car?' Benjamin walked a little ahead of her. 'Take a look here. New driving hat maybe?' She followed him to a milliner stand, where he pointed at a deep burgundy hat with pheasant feathers tucked into its side.

Evelyn touched the brim lightly, stroking the soft material. 'It's beautiful, may I?' she asked the assistant.

'Of course,' the assistant replied softly, carefully removing the hat from the display and waiting for Evelyn to remove her own, before helping her fit it gently on her head.

'It really suits her, doesn't it?' Benjamin asked of the sales assistant.

'You look quite enchanting,' the assistant replied and Evelyn wondered if she worked on commission.

'I like it. Though I wonder if it'll stay on whilst I'm in the car.'

'Oh, don't worry about that, my sister wore one of these over the weekend and went out for a drive, it didn't budge,' the assistant said confidently, assured in the quality of what she was selling. Giving Evelyn cause to grin.

THE FASTEST GIRL ON EARTH

'That's as maybe, but would it stay on if the car were to drive faster than say, thirty miles per hour?'

The girl smiled. 'Why, yes of course, though why you'd want to go faster than—'

'Or, say, forty miles per hour?' The girl frowned as Evelyn continued. 'Maybe sixty miles per hour? What if I were driving near-on one hundred miles per hour, would it stay on then?'

'Well, I suppose, but no one drives that fast and anyway, I'd tell your husband to slow down,' she replied, looking at Benjamin for help.

'Evelyn, stop teasing the poor girl,' he replied, then turned to the assistant. 'We'll take the hat. And the matching gloves, she does like to drive in style,' he added.

'She?' Evelyn watched as realisation dawned on the assistant and watched with interest in how it played out. 'You're, oh my, are you?'

A smile played on Evelyn's lips. 'Am I?'

All of a sudden, the assistant's face lit up with joy. 'Well, of course it's you.' She leaned over the counter to whisper her admiration. 'You're the fastest girl on Earth, that's what they call you. Don't they? Evelyn Bloom, you were in the papers last week. My father showed me and he's not going to believe me when I say I sold you a driving hat.'

'And gloves,' Benjamin added kindly, and she nodded, locating two pairs so that Evelyn could choose the ones that fitted best and watched as she slipped them on her hands.

'I wish I could drive.'

'To my mind, everyone should,' Evelyn replied, handing her the pair she wanted. 'Driving needn't be an expensive pastime. Ask your father to allow you to drive his. Has he got a car?'

'He does,' the assistant spoke keenly.

'Then ask him to teach you.'

'I'm not sure he'll want to spend the time.' The girl looked sad. 'He doesn't mind me working here, it's Harrods, but he's keen for me to be married and once that happens I'm not sure I'll be driving anywhere.'

'Nonsense. Don't be silly, women can drive whether they're married or unmarried. I'm unmarried.' Evelyn said, making her point and the girl, looking confused at Benjamin, caught on. 'I've been able to make a career out of it. Not that you'd need to do that, but there are other woman drivers. I've met quite a few fabulous ones – I've even taught a few. Tell you what, how about if your father won't teach you, I will? I'll be back here again soon no doubt and if you haven't had any luck, I'll get you behind a wheel.'

'Oh, that would be marvellous. Thank you,' the girl handed Benjamin the hatbox and Evelyn a dainty bag containing her box of gloves.

Evelyn and Benjamin bid the girl farewell as they made their way to the gentlemen's outfitters.

'That's a very kind thing to suggest,' he said as he offered Evelyn his arm, which she took. 'Are you sure you want to do it?' He tipped his hat to a man he recognised who walked past them mirroring his gesture.

'Actually yes, and I've decided I'm going to write a little handbook for women, a way of introducing them to driving so they can teach themselves if need be; and take away the worry of learning. It's certainly something I could have benefited from.' She looked longingly towards the women's area, where the latest fashions were on show. 'I wouldn't mind looking in there for a moment, may I meet you?'

Benjamin nodded. 'Of course. I don't think I'd be welcome there and I'm sure it'll be boring for you buying some gloves with me. I'll see you in the oyster bar in half an hour?'

Evelyn made her way to the dresses she'd spotted, whilst at the back of her mind considering what her book would contain when she heard a familiar voice call over.

'Well I never, Miss Evelyn Bloom, it's been a while.'

Turning on the spot, hardly daring to believe it, Evelyn looked over. 'Isabelle?'

Her friend smiled and walked away from a dress she was discussing with an assistant to embrace her. '*Ma chérie*, it's been too long.' She kissed both cheeks in the Parisian fashion, the scent of roses meeting Evelyn's nostrils, bringing her back to the apartment the two had shared all those years ago.

'It has. I didn't know you were in town.' Evelyn was hurt, and tried not to let it show. She'd accepted so many of her other friends had turned their backs on her since she'd been serious with Victor and she knew now he'd encouraged it, though she hadn't seen it at the time.

But she was surprised not to hear from Isabelle, who was distanced from the London life living in Paris with George. But if Evelyn were not mistaken, Isabelle looked a little shamefaced.

'I'm sorry. We weren't meant to be here this weekend. Well, at all actually. We've been all over the place lately, I'm losing track of where I'm meant to be. Still, we've bumped into each other, so why don't we see if we can find someone who'll furnish us with a glass of champagne, and we can catch each other up?'

'That sounds wonderful, I need to let Benjamin know,' she added as they walked out of the department and it was Isabelle's turn to look hurt.

'Are you?'

Evelyn shook her head quickly. 'No, no. Though I think he'd like to,' she confided. 'I've finally broken up with Victor and before you say anything, I know, but I've done it, and that's that. I've finally seen the truth. Oh, that's darling.' She pointed at a stunning three-foot tall vase filled with fresh flowers, momentarily distracted by its beauty. 'But Benjamin has been looking after me,' she said, by way of explanation of the only person who'd stayed with her.

'I see,' Isabelle replied, but Evelyn could tell she couldn't. It was an unusual relationship that she and Benjamin had. But she counted him as a close friend and confidant, and they'd been thin on the ground lately.

'He wanted some gloves, so he'll be here.' They rounded the corner to the men's outfitting section and Evelyn saw Benjamin, but he wasn't alone, he was in deep conversation with another man she didn't recognise.

'Hello, Benjamin,' Isabelle called and Evelyn shrank a little. She wasn't sure Benjamin had wanted them to see who he was talking to, a thought compounded as he looked up, made hasty conversation with the other man then walked quickly to the two ladies. Evelyn was sure she could see a trace of worry on his face, but by the time he'd kissed Isabelle hello and exclaimed at not knowing she was in town, it had disappeared.

The thought crossed Evelyn's mind that whilst he was her confidant, she wasn't his.

***

'Oh, that's jolly good.' George guffawed, and pinched his nose in a bid to stop the wine spurting from it whilst he clutched his side.

'No, it's entirely true. Whilst I'm teaching one of the princesses how to drive a policeman has to run alongside us in case I kidnap them. Though he struggled last week when I encouraged HRH to drive at more than fifteen miles per hour.' She caught Isabelle's eye.

'Oh, you're too much. I can't believe you've been tasked with that – how did it happen?'

Evelyn thanked Benjamin for topping up her glass. 'I taught the Queen a couple of years ago and she wanted her daughters to learn. I was introduced to them all after I sold the King a boat the last time I was in France.'

'You sold the King a boat?'

'Three actually,' Benjamin interjected, swallowing a mouthful of the beef stew Solomon had put together for the four's impromptu supper, which had followed a day of catching up. 'She talked the King into buying three Napier speedboats, and she didn't get the commission,' he added, shaking his head pityingly.

'What would she do with it anyway?' Isabelle looked longingly at Evelyn's deeply furnished flat. 'What I would give to have a permanent place to live and for it to look half as beautiful as this,' she added, stroking the back of the chair George was sitting on. 'This velvet is divine. So soft.'

Briefly recognising the support her father had given her over the years, Evelyn had a moment when she felt as though she was floating above the dark oak table, the remains of a meal scattered across it, cutlery strewn on plates as they awaited collection by Solomon and she blinked, to steady herself. She remained above the table, as though looking down on her own life and that of the others. Evelyn took a deep breath, blinked hard again and returned to the table, looking directly at Benjamin, who was staring intently at her.

'All well, old girl?'

'Hmm? Yes, yes, quite,' she added quickly, sipping the wine, noting the flavours of damsons and chocolate in the earthy red.

'Thank you, Solomon, another delicious dish. Can't tempt you to come travelling with us?' George pressed the servant who shook his head, then cleared the plates and detritus away, quietly and unassuming.

'You're not staying in London?' Evelyn returned to Earth with a bump. 'Where are you off to next?' For a moment she felt bereft, Isabelle and George had only just returned to her, and they were leaving again.

'No, I have some work to sort,' George replied. 'Actually, Benny, shall we have a cigar out on the balcony? Let the ladies catch up?' He nodded at the two women, and the men left the room. A moment or two later Evelyn caught the scent of the cigars and for a moment wished she were there too.

'Shall we?' She indicated the living room to Isabelle and they both made their way to the chaise, where, as though they were back in the Parisian apartment, they curled up together, Isabelle lighting a cigarette, and after taking a pull, passing it to Evelyn who inhaled deeply.

'What's next for Evelyn Bloom then?' Isabelle accepted the cigarette back and blew a long plume of smoke into the air. The two women watched as the spirals of smoke curled sinuously towards the ceiling.

Evelyn stared up at the smoke. 'I don't know.' She realised it was the first time she'd honestly answered the question since the bonnet incident. Her mother had pressed her to come home, insisting she'd had her fun and now needed to settle down. Whereas Benjamin was sure she should continue driving in any way she saw fit, Victor was no longer guiding her and suddenly, Evelyn felt lost.

'I told Benjamin I was going to keep driving for Napier until someone else saw how good I was and offered me a contract, but I don't know if I could do that. Not really,' she admitted. 'I owe a lot to Napier, and…' She trailed off, blowing some more smoke.

'Victor,' Isabelle finished for her. 'But you don't. Of course, they've made you a household name, but only through your own tenacity and success – they provided the vehicles, you did the hard work. You're in an incredible position right now, I promise. All you need to do is decide what you'd like to do next.'

Evelyn turned on her side to get a proper look at her friend, who raised an eyebrow inquisitively.

'What?'

'I'm trying to decide if you'll laugh when I tell you what I want to do,' she admitted, and Isabelle frowned.

'When have I ever laughed at your ambition? And anyway, I know about the book, Benjamin mentioned it – I think it's a jolly good idea,' she remarked. 'Where are you going?'

Evelyn jumped off the chaise and made her way over to a small dark oak bureau inlaid with mother-of-pearl. Isabelle watched as she finished her cigarette, grounding it in a heavy marble ashtray and waited for Evelyn to return with whatever she was looking for in the desk.

'I want to fly.' She presented Isabelle with the clipping she'd seen in the paper a few days before. 'I want to learn to be a pilot.' Isabelle leant over to take the article Evelyn had cut out, and read it before saying anything.

Evelyn sipped on the tea Solomon had brought into the room and lit another cigarette.

'Well, this confirms it.' Isabelle eyed her friend over the cutting. 'You are quite mad, but I love it – how terrific.'

Accepting the clipping back, Evelyn re-read the article she'd seen in *The Telegraph* a few days ago, even though she knew it off by heart. A woman in France called Martinique Margritte had successfully piloted a plane across a distance of a few hundred metres, before bringing the plane in to land safely. The thrill of being in the air had captured Evelyn's imagination.

'Mad? Do you really think so? I think it would be beyond exciting – think how fast I go in the Napier, and then imagine the pace upped furiously and in the air. What a ride.' She beamed, her eyes shining with excitement whilst Isabelle looked on and shook her head.

'That doesn't sound thrilling to me, it sounds terrifying,' she began, as George and Benjamin entered the room.

'What's terrifying? What are you up to now, old girl?' George took a seat across from the women and settled his slight frame into it. Evelyn often compared him to a sparrow, he looked so fragile, as though a small gust would take him away. Yet his intense stare was enough to imagine he could see into her deepest thoughts.

'Evie wants to fly,' Isabelle explained, and George looked to Benjamin enquiringly.

'Does she?'

Evelyn furrowed her brow. 'Yes, she does. And she can speak for herself, as well as make her own decisions,' she interjected before anyone got the idea Benjamin had any sort of control over her. She'd learnt that in an all too painful way from Victor. But Benjamin merely walked over to her and squeezed her shoulder gently.

'I obviously have no say over what you do, darling,' he said over her head, as though George and Isabelle were his audience. 'I think the reason old George over there was looking at me is because we were just talking about our plans for the next few months.' He shared a glance with George, who gave the tiniest of nods. 'George and Isabelle are going to France for a while and I had been wondering if you fancied doing the same. Bit of a change and all that. And it just so happens your Martinique – yes, I've read the clipping you've been clutching these past few days,' he said as an aside to her, 'she is training at an aviation school in northern France. If you like, I thought we'd sign you up. I'll come along to keep you company.'

'We're going to France?' Isabelle seemed surprised. 'But I thought we were going to Germany,' she said quietly and her husband shook his head. 'Well, if that's the plan, how marvellous.' She clapped her hands together. Evelyn wasn't completely taken in by the performance, but decided against calling attention to whatever was going on in their marriage. She knew Isabelle would divulge it at some point.

'What will you do though?' she asked of Benjamin. 'When I'm learning to fly? Surely you can't take lots of time away from your job?'

'I can be with you, but on occasion I may need to return to London, though we'll see how it all goes.' Evelyn sensed there was more to what Benjamin was saying and wondered just how many secrets her friends were holding from her. But the opportunity to learn to fly in France was too much to pass up. Her thoughts whirled at the practicalities of leaving her life behind and how possible it all really was.

'When do we leave?'

1909

Chapter Twenty-Five

Mourmelon-le-Grand

'It's beautiful.' Evelyn took a look around the airbase, a strip of parched land flanked by fields of what would be lavender in the summer.

'I'm not sure it's beautiful.' A woman dressed simply in a white shirt and beige trousers came to Evelyn's side, shrugging on a leather flying jacket. She extended her hand. 'Martinique, but everyone calls me Mart.' She spoke excellent English with a light French accent and the surprise on Evelyn's face was apparent.

'Finishing school, England,' she offered, by way of explanation, as Evelyn took her hand and shook it.

'A pleasure to meet you, Mart, I've read a lot about you.'

It had taken much longer for Evelyn to get to France than she'd hoped. Three years longer. Firstly Victor had insisted on holding her to the Napier contract for over a year, forcing her to take part in ever more unappealing events. Until finally, in one particularly heated evening she confronted him and threatened to tell the papers about their relationship and that of the replacement woman who was driving for him. Despite his bluster that he couldn't care less whether the world heard of his affairs, Victor finally released her from her contract and wished her luck with her "latest distraction".

During the following three years she was offered some journalism work, writing about motoring for *The Telegraph*, which itself had turned into an offer of a book. Not wanting to turn down the op-

THE FASTEST GIRL ON EARTH

portunities presenting themselves, and in need of a distraction from her break-up with Victor, Evelyn had thrown herself into everything available. The years whirled by in a haze of society events, celebrity and success, until one day, Benjamin, a regular presence in her life, told Evelyn he'd secured her a flying opportunity, if she was still interested. She was of course. Despite her enjoyment of celebrity the past few years, she still craved excitement.

Benjamin had arrived with her a few days before her tutoring began, settling them into a little cottage with two bedrooms – he still hadn't become anything more than a good friend, but had been a regular houseguest at her Mayfair flat. He said he would have to return to London in a week for an indeterminate length of time whilst he recruited for his office. It amused Evelyn to think of Benjamin in any position of power but she knew he was high up in the trade section of government and as the UK's connections to the rest of the world were strengthened, the trade opportunities became more varied.

'You have?'

Evelyn was brought back to the present, where she stood in an aircraft hangar that was little more than a weathered barn, housing two small planes.

'I have what?'

Martinique laughed. 'You said you'd read a lot about me, is that true?' She lit a cigarette, and offered one to Evelyn who accepted.

'Oh yes, any time I've seen something about your latest achievements I've taken great joy in reading how you've done it.' She inhaled the cigarette and, surprised at how strong it was, began coughing.

'Oh la la, what are you doing? You're so English, with your cigarettes that don't taste of anything.' Martinique patted her a little on the back and watched Evelyn whose eyes were streaming. 'You need to take it slow, inhale gently, then you exhale, like this.' She blew out the smoke languidly.

'Effortless.' She shook her head.

'Mart, time to give this one a go, I've been tinkering with it,' said a man in his late fifties, introduced the day before to Evelyn as Renoir, the owner of the airfield. He was wiping his hands on his overalls whilst striding towards them. '*Bonjour*, Miss Bloom.' He nodded.

Martinique's head whipped around. 'Miss Bloom?'

Evelyn nodded. 'The very same.'

'Oh, I've heard so very much about you too, you're the fastest woman in the world, *n'est pas*?'

Evelyn smiled, then frowned a little. 'I am – was. I set the record, someone broke it this year though.' Her eyes were unfocused for a moment, lost in the memory, it hurt she was no longer the best in the world.

'But you've set so many records, I'm in awe.' Martinique clapped her hands and turned to Renoir. 'You've got your hands full here,' she nodded in Evelyn's direction, 'once she gets a handle on it, I think she'll be zipping through the clouds in no time. *À bientôt.*'

Evelyn, who wasn't due to begin lessons for a week, watched as Martinique performed a series of checks on the plane, similar to the ones she did on her cars before she drove. Satisfied, the Frenchwoman climbed into the cockpit and pulled the glass cover over herself. Aiming a thumbs up in Evelyn's direction, the barn was suddenly awash with noise as the plane's rotor blades began to whirr.

Watching as Martinique skilfully manoeuvred the plane out of the shed and onto the runway, Evelyn was struck by how fragile it looked. The tail appeared to be bumping up and down as Martinique moved into position on the runway and the wings juddered on each side. Unsure how something as unwieldy as that could possibly get into the air, much less stay there, Evelyn watched as the plane lurched forward and began to pick up speed.

She realised how quickly the plane moved down the runway and her heart thudded with excitement and fear that she'd be doing the same too. Eventually. All of a sudden the little aircraft lifted into the air, pulling up so that it was high above the barn. Evelyn ran out to try and catch a glimpse of Martinique and was astounded at the speed and dexterity of the plane as it weaved amongst the clouds.

'Your turn soon enough.' Renoir was stood next to her, looking into the sky.

She watched as the plane disappeared into a little dark spot against the clouds, and turned to Renoir with a huge smile on her face. 'Can't wait.'

THE FASTEST GIRL ON EARTH

***

The days went past quickly and soon Evelyn found herself on the airfield once again, but this time taking her first steps towards flight.

She was a natural, Renoir and Martinique had said. She understood the mechanics of the plane quickly, modifying her knowledge of a car's engine with that of a plane's, and understood how it remained in the air.

'You did great today.' Martinique leant against the side of the barn and offered Evelyn a cigarette. She took it and inhaled gently so it didn't burn her throat. '*Bien*, much better. Looks like you're adapting to everything we're throwing at you.'

Allowing a small moment to accept the compliment, Evelyn looked across the dry runway. 'It was good to sit in the cockpit – though even that is much higher than it looks from the ground,' she admitted, exhaling a long plume of smoke. Both women watched as the tendrils of their cigarettes intertwined.

'Just you wait until you're in the air, then you'll feel higher than a bird.' Martinique elbowed Evelyn lightly in the ribs. 'Then you'll say to me, "I can't believe how small everything looks". Anyway, you're a little way off being up there, you'll need to do a lot of taxiing to get a feel for the plane before you do anything else.'

Evelyn turned to face Martinique, studying the dark eyes which looked back at her, the sharp black bob. 'What does it feel like? When you're up there?' She didn't want to admit it, even to herself, but she was starting to worry she wouldn't like the feeling of losing contact with the ground.

Martinique dropped her cigarette and ground it out under the heel of her sturdy boots. She looked towards the sky, watching a gull dipping through the cloud.

'It's like, it's meant to be.' She frowned. 'We have a saying, "*a coeur vaillant rien d'impossible*". For a valiant heart, nothing is impossible. It's like that. When I'm up there, it's just me. There's noise from the engines and there's a lot to concentrate on, but the feeling, the euphoria each time when you leave the runway and you're just, there, in the air, you could go anywhere. It's freeing.' She turned to face Evelyn. 'The saddest I feel is when I return to the ground, I prefer being amongst the clouds.'

Evelyn recognised what the other woman was saying. 'That's the sensation I used to get when racing. When everything was perfect, when the car was working just right and I could hear she was happy, I was happy. Even when the car would kick and pull, I'd pull her right back in, like an unruly horse and I'd get her under control, then we'd speed along in harmony and it would feel incredible. Joyous really. I think I've been chasing that feeling for a couple of years now. I hope flying will give it to me,' she said as she exhaled the last of her cigarette.

Wrapping an arm around Evelyn's shoulders, Martinique grinned. 'Darling, once you've mastered the art of flying, nothing will be out of reach – you can go on daring adventures and forever have that feeling. It's marvellous, just marvellous.'

'Have you had many daring adventures?'

Martinique tapped her finger lightly to her nose. 'One day at a time.'

Chapter Twenty-Six

Reims

Evelyn tucked a stray piece of blonde hair in place and secured it with a grip. Standing back to assess herself in the mirror she nodded at her reflection. She had chosen a stylish suit in navy linen, aware it was a little more relaxed than what she'd wear for an evening in London but for supper at Martinique's, it was more than sufficient.

The sharp tailoring nipped in her already slight waist and the trousers fell in gentle gathers to her ankles, giving her movement grace. She stepped into a pair of low heels, also in navy, and winced as her back spasmed in disagreement. The past few weeks learning to fly had pushed her in so many ways, both physically and mentally and whilst she'd been exhausted from the many different tasks she had to learn, her body grumbled at the taut position she took up in the plane.

On gathering up her handbag, she stopped and surveyed the small cottage.

Benjamin had returned to London the week before, having spent a week with her, taking her out for meals and generally providing a light countenance to the training. Pausing to tidy one of his newspapers away, Evelyn noted the pang of absence she felt when Benjamin wasn't with her. She enjoyed his conversation and the ease with which they fell in with each other but it wasn't until he went away that she realised how accustomed she was to having him by her side. Gradually, over the last year or so, she realised she'd fallen in love with Benjamin, but it was a gentle sort of love. Not the visceral, had-to-have-him lust she had felt for Victor. Instead, it was a kindness between them, a gentleness. Evelyn shook her head a little, she needed to ignore the feelings because she wasn't certain he felt the same after the years of her pushing him away.

Indeed, he seemed to spend more time acting friendly towards her now than lovingly and she realised she'd probably missed the opportunity for them to be anything more.

There was a knock at the door and Dodo barked to announce a new arrival. Evelyn dusted her trousers down to ensure she was pristine, then strode to the door expecting to see Martinique's driver, the clacking sound of her heels breaking the silence of the cottage.

'*Bonsoir, ma chérie*, I thought I'd pick you up.' Martinique beamed at her, thrilled with the look of surprise on her friend's face. 'My wheels.' She stepped back to allow Evelyn to see the car she'd been talking about all week.

'I didn't expect you to collect me – but when you have a car like that, I can see why you have. She's stunning.' Evelyn returned to the inner sanctum of her cottage, picked up her light summer coat of white cotton, then returned to her friend.

'Is it going to be my turn to take lessons?' Martinique asked as the two women pulled themselves up into the car.

'Oh no, I expect I'll be learning from you again.' Evelyn pulled her coat around her and held onto the passenger bar. 'Besides, I haven't risked driving over here just yet, I've stuck to my trusty bike.' She watched as Martinique pulled slowly out of the driveway and onto the country road.

'I love the smell here.' Evelyn shouted a little over the sound of the engine as Martinique increased the speed and they pelted past the hedgerows and fields. The countryside in northern France was very similar to Sussex, where she had spent a lot of time driving with Victor in the early years of their relationship. Though the light was incredibly different, lending the vista a golden glow as they rattled along that summer evening, the scent of lavender and hay from the fields wafting pleasantly around Evelyn, removing all thoughts of Sharp.

There was little chance to chat as the sound of the car's engine drowned them out, until Martinique slowed down to take a right along a thin unmade road. The car bumped from side to side and Evelyn winced as her back grumbled.

'Not much further, I promise,' Martinique shouted over the rumble and soon they were in a clearing. The track opened to a large sweeping drive edged by fruit trees, that Evelyn guessed to be apple and pear, which took them down to a grand, if slightly dilapidated, mansion. 'Been in the family for years,' Martinique added, by way of explanation. 'Always needs money spent on it, so as it's just me and Jeffrey the butler, it doesn't bother me. I tend to stick to the same few rooms.' She pulled into a garage, alongside two other cars. One seemingly in the process of being repaired, the other in slightly better condition. 'A hobby.' Martinique said by way of explanation, before making her way down from the car.

Evelyn did the same and looked at the view around her. 'You live in such a beautiful place,' she enthused, looking out across the large pond to the left of the house, the golden light reflecting across the surface.

'*Mai oui*, but you do too, *non*? You live in Mayfair. I've been to London, I know how fancy that area is. Now, you must be hungry? Yes? I know I'm starving, let's see if Jeffrey has made anything worth his salary.' She strode off to the house quickly, and Evelyn rushed to catch up.

'Don't you get lonely?' The house was entirely on its own and Evelyn hadn't seen any other properties for many miles. She followed Martinique through a set of heavy double oak doors and stopped to look at the decorations carved across the top of the doorway, trying to work out what it said.

'Family motto, "live well, live long",' Martinique threw over her shoulder as they walked across a wide hallway and into a cosy dining room. 'We'll eat in here, maybe cognacs on the terrace. Even though it's summer, it might get cold here later, so we can always light a fire and drink them there.' She pointed to two well-worn armchairs that were sat together. For a moment Evelyn recalled the chairs in Victor's office but in stark contrast to his taut, cold leather seats, Martinique's looked cosy and welcoming.

'Kir royale?' A man, who Evelyn presumed to be the famous Jeffrey, appeared in the doorway holding a silver tray, two glasses perched carefully atop.

'Kir royale?'

'It's crème de cassis and champagne. It's delicious, you will love it,' Martinique said confidently as she took both glasses from Jeffrey and turned to Evelyn. '*Salut.*'

'*Salut*,' Evelyn chimed in and took a sip. The drink was every bit as good as Martinique had promised. 'Oh, this is heaven, I could have a few more of these.'

'I like to have one as a little pre-dinner treat, then we can enjoy a glass or two of the white burgundy I've found in the cellar. Knowing my family it's either going to taste of dust, or be wonderful, there's no happy medium when it comes from down there.' They sat down in the armchairs and Evelyn breathed out a sigh of deep relaxation whilst she sipped her drink.

Martinique lit a cigarette and leant forwards a little, eager to hear from Evelyn. 'So, how are you finding it all? Have you got the flying bug?'

'Oh, definitely, I love it. It was frightening to begin with, but once I got past the first flight it's been wonderful. Though I'm not sure I enjoy it more than driving a car or speeding across the water.'

'Such an action woman, just like me.'

'I don't know. You've done a lot more,' Evelyn replied, then sipped more of the sweet blackcurrant aperitif.

'Yes, but I've not had a handsome man helping me succeed. Or is that not how it was?'

Evelyn felt herself flush. 'Oh, Benjamin? No, he's not helping like that, other than being a good friend of course.'

Martinique shook her head and waved her glass quickly, almost sloshing the dusky pink drink over the side of the coupe. '*Non*, I meant the other one. The one you work for? Victor was his name? Yes? He helped you?'

Staring into the unlit fire, Evelyn tried to ignore the stab of pain that she felt anytime Victor's name was mentioned. She had hoped the feelings would disappear, but after more than a year, the way he had treated her as their relationship had intensified and then deteriorated was still painful to consider.

'Sorry, you don't have to talk about him, he was your... sponsor... *non*?' Martinique felt around the gaps in the conversation and Evelyn forced herself to look at her friend. She wasn't going to allow Victor to ruin what she'd achieved.

She drained her drink. 'Yes, he was an advocate for me to be a driver. He'd spotted a lady over here doing it, and she'd achieved a lot of attention in the press for her company. He wanted to replicate that success with me.' Evelyn stood to go to the table as Jeffrey, who had appeared in the room silently, placed plates of food on the table covered by silver cloches. 'I like to think I achieved that for him.'

Martinique joined her and allowed Jeffrey to fuss around them, removing cloches to reveal a dish comprising fish in a creamy sauce with tiny cubes of carrots, peas and some potatoes. The butler poured a small glass of white wine for both women and exited the room.

'You managed that and more,' Martinique tucked into her meal, 'though, and I wish you no offence, it did seem he got everything from you only to drop you last year, just when you were on the cusp of being a magnificent driver.' She dabbed her mouth with a starched linen napkin that had pink flowers embroidered across it. 'I don't understand why you weren't racing, I hear Brooklands is a wonderful circuit, *n'est pas*?'

Evelyn swallowed her mouthful before replying. 'It's meant to be an incredible course, but they don't allow women drivers.' She laughed at Martinique's incredulity. 'I know. But that's the case, even though they're new and could do whatever they please, they choose for women not to be allowed. England likes to add limits to women's enjoyment, they don't want to see us spread our wings too wide.'

'Which is why you're learning how to spread them here. To Evelyn and her wings,' Martinique raised a glass to Evelyn and the two clinked glasses.

For a while they ate their food in companionable silence, allowing Evelyn's thoughts to wander a little to her other girlfriends. Not in all the time when she shared her flat with Frances and Hena did either of them treat her ambition as a positive thing. It was merely indulged, with their assumptions being she would grow tired of it and get married.

Isabelle was different, but she'd met Evelyn when they were both in Paris and known her only as the girl who was learning about engines. Nothing Evelyn did surprised her, though Isabelle had quickly settled into the prescribed role of wife, which didn't include Evelyn very often. It was with a great wave of sadness that Evelyn recognised how alone she was.

'*Ça va?*' Martinique looked concerned on hearing the sigh that had escaped her new friend's lips. Evelyn smiled, to cover her mood, and gripped Martinique's hand in hers.

'*Bien, merci*, I was just having a moment. I was being self-indulgent, but I'm fine. Really, *très bien.*'

'Ah, we French have a saying for that too.' Martinique said as Jeffrey came in with the second course. '*Qui n'avance pas, recule* – there can be no standstill in life, only evolution or devolution.'

'I like that.' Evelyn inhaled the mixture of herbs that coated a small chicken sat on the plate, surrounded by creamy mashed potatoes and some delicate vegetables. 'This is heavenly. Please tell me you eat like this every night.' She began to slice a little morsel of poussin and speared a bright-green asparagus tip.

'Oh, I wish. No, this is all for you, Evelyn. All these flying hours, you need the energy to enjoy them,' she said tenderly and Evelyn's heart warmed along with her stomach.

'Thank you, it's a real treat. I'm maybe not as good at looking after myself as I should be. When Benjamin is here we go out for dinner and he enjoys visiting the boulangerie for our lunches, but when he's not, I sometimes forget to look after myself.'

'Ah yes, Benjamin, can we talk about him?' Martinique said with a little twinkle in her eye. 'He is your lover, yes?'

Evelyn flushed. 'No – he was... well, not a lover as such, more a friend who I kissed a few times many years ago, but then our lives went in different directions,' she said hastily. Hers in Victor's, she thought sadly. 'Now we're friends. *Just* friends,' she reiterated, much to Martinique's obvious disappointment.

'Really? But the way he looks at you. In fact, the way you look at each other, it's as though there's some great understanding between the two of you, I thought... well, I assumed...' She shrugged, lighting a cigarette and offering Evelyn one. 'Well, you know what I assumed.'

'Yes, I can guess, but no, nothing like that. Not yet.' The words were out of her mouth before she realised. She clapped her hand to her lips as though it would stop any more truths escaping. Martinique had heard her, though, and raised her eyebrows.

'Ha, *je comprends*. I see what's going on here, you do like him but you're waiting for him to show he likes you, or you'll get hurt.' She put her head on one side, exhaling smoke and surveying Evelyn. 'No, that's not right, you've already turned him down before and so now he's concerned you'd say no, but you don't want to make any moves in case you lose him. And his friendship.'

'How did you...?' Evelyn was speechless.

'It's a gift. I know people.'

'Well, you're correct.'

'Of course I am. But he has other secrets too. I've seen the way he looks at you, of course, but I see more there too. More than I think you know.'

'Ah, it was good guesswork,' Evelyn breathed out, relieved, 'because Benjamin isn't hiding anything. He would tell me. We don't keep secrets from each other, so you're not right there.'

Martinique cocked one eyebrow and nodded slowly. 'If you insist.' Just then the door to the room opened again. 'Ah, Jeffrey. Dessert, *encroyable*.' She clapped her hands together as the butler delivered a mountain of meringue, cream and strawberries to the table. Martinique turned the conversation to the various problems the propellers were giving Renoir and her. Evelyn nodded and contributed to the conversation that continued long into the night, but the whole time she was considering what Martinique had said.

Was Benjamin hiding something? And if so, what was it?

Chapter Twenty-Seven

Mourmelon-le-Grand

'Bravo, Evelyn, bravo!' Benjamin clapped his hands together heartily as Evelyn made her way over to where he stood in the plane's hangar. He unclipped her helmet and removed her flying goggles. 'You looked incredible up there.' He pulled her in for a hug and they kissed each other's cheeks.

Evelyn was breathless. Her adrenaline would always surge when she was behind the controls but as soon as she reached the ground once more, it was as though she'd been running for many miles. She took some gulps of water Benjamin offered and sat on a wooden chair to get her breath back, whilst she watched him pour tea into cups from a flask.

'Thought you might be parched. Fancy one?'

She nodded and accepted the cup gratefully. 'So you saw me then?'

Benjamin sat next to her, holding a cup in his hands. 'Oh yes, I came over about half an hour ago, I've watched you swoop and turn as though you've been doing this for years.'

'That's what I told her,' Martinique said, appearing in her flying gear, 'she is an absolute natural when it comes to this. I think she'll be teaching me soon.'

'Oh, you are both too kind, but I do love it almost as much as driving.'

THE FASTEST GIRL ON EARTH

'And shooting,' Martinique added, reminding her of the weekend they'd just spent at the run-down château, taking part in the local pheasant shoot.

'Yes, she's good at that too.' Benjamin looked at Evelyn fondly. 'Tell me, Mart, has she taken you fishing yet?'

'*Non* – don't tell me, are you good at that too?'

Evelyn shook her head. 'That's enough. I'm terrible at fishing, but I do enjoy the calm of being beside the river. Though I did catch a rather large trout the last time we went, didn't I?' she said to Benjamin. She noticed an odd look on his face which he covered quickly.

Martinique looked at the two of them.

'Well, you've not seen each other for a fortnight, I suspect you have a lot of catching up to do.' She raised her eyebrows meaningfully and Evelyn blushed. 'My turn to go up in the clouds – I'm practising dropping items in fields,' she added by way of explanation as she shouldered a large canvas bag.

The two watched her walk away.

'Whatever would she need to do that for?' Evelyn asked.

'I think we need to talk.'

Both looked at each other as they spoke at the same time.

'You go first,' Evelyn suggested, concerned at the seriousness in Benjamin's tone. He looked around and shook his head.

'Not here. Back at the cottage, it's safer there.'

Frowning at the cloak-and-dagger nonsense coming from Benjamin, Evelyn rolled her eyes. 'We're in the middle of nowhere, Ben, look where we are – who will hear us?'

'Just trust me – you do trust me, don't you?'

Evelyn thought for a moment, then nodded. 'Of course.'

They made their way back in a car Benjamin had borrowed. He drove whilst Evelyn looked up into the bright blue sky, enjoying the breeze as it rushed past her face. Barely a single cloud could be seen and the sun warmed her to the bones. She'd been in France for six months and would be sorry to return to London in a few weeks' time. She wasn't sure what she was returning to London for though, it certainly wasn't for friends. And her parents had said the next time she returned to theirs she would be set up in a marriage with someone they considered "suitable". Evelyn sighed and Benjamin looked at her with concern.

'Malaise?'

'No, just, wondering what I'm going to do with the rest of my life.'

'Ah, as simple as that then.' Benjamin steered the car carefully down the track to their cottage. Evelyn always thought of it as theirs, even though she'd been staying there the most.

After they parked, Evelyn stepped down from the car and stretched, rolling her neck from side to side and briefly imagining what it would be like if Benjamin were to rub it gently.

'Are you coming?' Dodo had escaped out of the front door and was propelled by his wagging tail across the garden so he could reach his favourite person. She scooped him up and buried her face in his fur, inhaling the mustiness and herbs which meant he'd been playing in the back garden whilst she'd been out.

'Come on, Dodo, let's find out what this is all about.' She popped the little dog back on the ground and they made their way into the cottage. She notice Benjamin had already tidied, and thrown open all the shutters to let in the warmth and daylight of the late summer. He'd placed a jug of cut flowers on the table and was in the process of cutting up a baguette, which he was laying alongside some cheese and cold meats. Evelyn's stomach rumbled in response.

'Sit down, I'll serve you,' he said. 'We can't talk about serious things on an empty stomach.'

Evelyn's stomach was suddenly filled with butterflies, she wasn't sure she had room for food. As she looked around the cottage, considering all the little tweaks Benjamin had made, she suddenly wondered if all the efforts he was going to was because he wanted to propose to her and her heart skipped a beat. They'd never discussed a relationship, but in the time he'd been away Evelyn had spoken frankly with Martinique, analysing her feelings for Benjamin and she realised how much he meant to her. Certainly she couldn't imagine a life without Benjamin. Suddenly she realised he was looking at her, a plate held out.

'Sorry, did you say something?' She tried to recover her thoughts.

Benjamin smiled. 'Only that I wondered how much food to give you. But I decided you could have more if you needed it.' She accepted the plate and set it in front of her, whilst he looked at her in a way which made Evelyn's heart skip a beat. He filled their glasses with a crisp white wine, his movements considered and slow. Evelyn wondered if he was stalling for time.

'Aren't you going to eat? Dig in.'

Evelyn began to tear small hunks off the bread and slathering them in butter, but was having trouble concentrating, all too aware of Benjamin's presence across the table. She looked at him properly, really taking stock. He had sprouted a few grey hairs in his black hair, but it was making him look ever more distinguished. His demeanour was one of a strong, resolute man, but she knew that not too far under the surface was a gentle, sensitive soul who didn't take well to any criticism or rejection. He dressed well and his broad shoulders called out for her head to rest upon them. There was no way round this. She'd fallen head over heels for Benjamin. She knew if he proposed, she'd certainly say yes.

'Evelyn, there's something I want to talk to you about.'

His words broke her concentration and she looked up slowly from her food.

'Do we have to, right now?'

It was Benjamin's turn to roll his eyes. 'I'm returning to London in three days, so yes, I think now would be a good time.' He leant forward. 'I have a proposal for you.'

***

'A spy?' Evelyn spluttered as she choked on her bread, flapping her hands to wave away Benjamin's help.

'At least have some water,' he said, offering to top up her already drained wine glass. He watched her closely as she slowly sipped the water to dislodge the bread and to gain a brief moment to gather her thoughts.

'It's a very cheap description, you know.' Benjamin was sat back, relaxed, his arms behind his head. 'We prefer "undercover operative".'

Evelyn tried to make sense of what he was saying. 'When did you become an "undercover operative"? And why didn't you tell me?' Benjamin shook his head and leant over the table to grab the bottle of wine sat between them. Without asking he poured himself, and then her a generous glass.

'For the shock,' he said, indicating the glass. 'Have a sip, it might help.' Evelyn did as she was told and sat the glass back down on the table a little firmer than she'd planned.

'So you've been lying to me for how long?' she said, challenging him to respond, but not giving him a moment to reply. 'You do know how much I hate liars, Benjamin, don't you?' He opened his mouth but she continued. 'I told you when I broke it off with Victor, one of the worst things anyone could ever do, was lie to me.' She got up from the table abruptly, unsure what to do with herself and pressed her hands to her head to rub her temples.

Benjamin stood up too and edged round the table before standing in front of Evelyn and taking her hands in his.

'I didn't lie to you.' She went to pull away, but he held her hands tight and she relented. 'You need to hear this. I had just been scouted when we were introduced in Paris all those years ago and I didn't know if we were to become anything. I didn't want to put you in any harm. But we've remained in each other's lives and as the time has gone by, it's been harder and harder to explain to you what I do.'

'So why now?'

Benjamin exhaled audibly, and Evelyn realised he was nervous.

'Because...' He leant in and kissed her lightly on the lips, then pulled away. 'Because I think we could make an incredible team,' he said, smiling at her disbelief.

'What do you mean? Are you proposing marriage?' Evelyn was irritated at asking him to spell it out, but to her surprise he laughed.

'Well, yes and no,' he said quickly.

Evelyn walked over and sat on the floral chaise placed nearby under the window, trying to make sense of what was happening. In every version of him proposing that she'd imagined, none of them involved spying. 'Which is it, Benjamin?'

He took two paces to reach her and sank to his knee beside the chaise.

'I need a wife when I arrive in Paris. The border patrol won't look at a recently married couple on honeymoon, but they will pay close attention to a single man. Things are... getting interesting at the moment.' He raised his eyebrows. 'I've seen everything you can do and I think you could make a rather incredible agent, and if I'm by your side, you'll have someone to protect you.'

There was a silence as she wondered what to say. 'It's not quite the proposal I was expecting,' she admitted.

'You were expecting a proposal? From me?' he asked quietly, his confidence slipping for once, showing something Evelyn hadn't seen before. She softened a little towards him, her heart hammering. It was time to tell him the truth.

'Benjamin, you do know that I'm in love with you, don't you?'

For a moment there was only the sounds of birds outside the cottage, then Benjamin cleared his throat. 'It would seem I've gone about all this in the wrong way. I do think you'll be an exceptional operative and it does make sense for you and I to be married as a cover, but...'

'Yes?' Evelyn urged, hoping he wasn't about to break her heart.

'It's not quite the proposal I had in mind either. I had wanted to do it in a grand way in a few month's time, when I knew for certain what your feelings were for me. But events have changed and we need to speed up plans.'

'So I'm just part of a plan for you?' she challenged, her irritation growing at laying her feelings bare and getting only confusion in return. He shook his head fervently, his kind eyes looking keenly up to her.

'Let me do this right,' he held her hand in his, his grasp warm. 'Evelyn Bloom, I have loved you from the moment I met you in Paris all those years ago. I have followed every aspect of your career, fighting the pride I had in your numerous successes, with the dislike I had for Sharp and his manipulation of you. You have no idea the amount of times I've wanted to take you into my arms and kiss away the pain on that beautiful face, but I've settled with friendship. I've listened to the terrible matches your parents have suggested for you, all the while wanting to tell you that you should be with me. That I would love you forever. So now, Evelyn Bloom, I'm asking you to be my wife.' He pulled out a navy velvet ring box and opened it to reveal a single sapphire. 'Say yes, and make me the happiest man in France – even if the proposal is under slightly unusual conditions.'

She looked into his eyes and saw love for the first time. Torn, Evelyn bit her lip. She wanted to say yes, but realised this yes came with an enormous caveat. It wasn't a normal proposal, she was agreeing to be a spy as well. It wasn't the normal happily ever after she'd imagined either. But, she acknowledged, when had she ever decided to follow the normal process in anything? Being a spy – an operative – did excite her in a way that only racing and flying had.

'I assume there's no way I can say yes to one thing and not the other?'

Benjamin had the decency to look a little awkward. 'Let's put it this way, it's a lot easier if you say yes to both. I need a wife to arrive in Paris with, and I'd much rather a woman on my arm that I'm madly in love with.'

'Madly?' she repeated.

He looked up at her and inclined his head to one side. 'Madly. So, is that a yes?'

She felt the corners of her mouth curve up, and noted the joy in his face. 'I'd need to understand how life will work as a spy. But yes darling, it's a yes. I want to be by your side, however that might look.'

Benjamin shot up from the floor and in a few long strides had reached the small icebox in the back of the kitchen.

'Thank goodness, otherwise I don't know what I'd have done with this,' he called through, picking up a couple of coupe glasses and brandishing a bottle of Laurent Perrier.

'Hah, so I must have been a dead cert even before I told you I loved you.' She accepted the glass of champagne he offered and knocked back the drink in almost one gulp. 'Another please, it's been a very strange hour.'

Benjamin sat next to her and refilled the glass she held out. 'You weren't a dead cert and I had to pick my moment. Although I was fairly confident you'd say yes.'

Evelyn was astonished. 'How? I didn't know for certain I would until about ten seconds ago.'

'I know you. You crave excitement, you need your blood pulsing or it's not worth being alive. You need adrenaline. Speed. Fast cars and faster planes. You need to feel as though you're doing something brand new, that no one else has ever done and you need to carve your own way through this world. But you can't do it with a husband acting as a deadweight around your neck. You need freedom,' he finished, sipping his drink. 'I can offer you all of that, and so much more. Just you wait and see.'

Evelyn sipped her second glass of champagne thoughtfully. 'You're right. Well, most of what you said was right. I do want freedom.' She thought of Victor's jealousy towards her success. 'But I also need real love,' she said, looking at Benjamin. He finished his glass, and placed it on the table beside them. He took Evelyn's glass from her and placed it next to his.

'I thought I told you.' He leant in closer. She could smell his hair balm, a sweet lemony tang which she always associated with Paris. 'I'm madly in love with you, I want to give you everything.' He leant in so his lips lightly pressed against hers, before pulling back a little.

'Ben,' Evelyn whispered, reading the hunger in his eyes, knowing it was reflected in hers as he leant in and kissed her again, deeper this time. They'd kissed before, when they'd briefly courted in Paris, but this was different for Evelyn. She sensed that Benjamin was in tune with her. As their lips met again she felt as though she were his instrument being tuned, warming her, readying her. She was compliant.

Ready.

He took his time. Feathering kisses across her collarbone and lightly unbuttoning her silk blouse, allowing the material to slip between his fingers onto the floor. He made relatively short work of her corset, chemise and slip, discarding them too. The cool air from the nearby open window blew across Evelyn's skin, raising goose bumps of pleasure and she shivered. Benjamin threw his shirt on the floor, quickly followed by his trousers and undergarments and resumed kissing her mouth and neck, the warmth of his chest burning her skin at its touch.

As he worked his way lower he removed her skirt and she wriggled free from her bloomers, leaving her naked on the chaise.

Evelyn looked up at him, at the patch of hair on his chest she hadn't known existed until now, and traced her finger across it, drawing a shudder from him.

'I need you,' she said hoarsely, unable to contain herself for much longer. Benjamin's face broke into the crooked smile she knew and loved.

'I better do as I'm told,' he said as he lay her gently back on the sofa. He held both her hands down above her head in one of his, whilst his other raised her up to meet him. The exquisite torture of both being unable to move, whilst being held in a position which caused her most pleasure brought Evelyn to a shuddering climax and Benjamin released himself immediately, as though he'd been waiting for her.

As they lay together, their sweat mingling and cooling, Evelyn traced her finger over his chest and felt compelled to confess, 'I've never felt that, I mean, I didn't,' she stuttered, a sudden shyness overcoming her and Benjamin kissed her on the lips.

'Well, I said you liked brand new. Maybe you want faster next time too?'

Evelyn laughed. 'I'm not a car.' She kissed him back, her longing for the feeling again spurring her on. 'But faster sounds good.' She manoeuvred herself so she was sat on top of him. Victor had liked her taking control, so the position wasn't new to her, but by the look on Benjamin's face and the growing hardness between his legs, she was teaching him something too.

'We're never going to get anything done now we've crossed this line,' he groaned as she moved onto him. 'But for tonight, I really don't care.' He bucked into her and Evelyn moaned lightly in response.

'We can get to work tomorrow,' she agreed, allowing bliss to fill her mind and body.

Chapter Twenty-Eight

Reims

'*Salut*, my friends,' Martinique said, raising her glass towards Benjamin and Evelyn. 'I told you so, *n'est pas*, Evelyn?' She drained her glass. '*Encore, si'l vous plaît, encore.*'

'You did.' Evelyn looked at Benjamin and when he held her gaze for a moment she felt her heart squeeze, she'd never known such all consuming love for someone. Their small wedding had taken place swiftly after the proposal, under the watchful eye of the mayor, who had given his blessing. But Martinique did not want their nuptials to go past without a celebration, so she opened her home to Evelyn and the few friends she'd made on the airfield at Mourmelon-le-Grand.

Evelyn looked around at the abundance of cream roses Martinique had organised along the dark oak table in a collection of ceramic and glass vases, all, no doubt, heirlooms of family members who were once residents of the mansion. Large pillar candles with wax dripping down their sides were grouped in clusters on the stone window alcoves and dotted around the room, giving a festive feel. Evelyn inhaled the scent and leant into Benjamin.

'Heavenly, isn't it?' she said, then placed a light kiss on his cheek. He turned, lay his arm around her neck and pulled her in to kiss her on the lips, garnering a smattering of applause from the ten or so guests enjoying a pile of profiteroles courtesy of Martinique's talented butler, Jeffrey.

'Speech,' Marie, one of her fellow pilot friends called down the table. She felt Benjamin moving next to her and watched as he stood up.

'*Bien*,' Benjamin started, but was quickly interrupted.

'In English is fine,' Marie heckled, making the rest of the women laugh. 'We know your French is worse than our English,' she chided and Evelyn grinned at Benjamin's amusement.

'Well, all I have to say will translate across both languages,' Benjamin said, turning to face Evelyn, his look causing her face to burn, remembering their nights of passion over the past week.

'As you all know by now, Evelyn is something special. As well as being incredibly talented at seemingly everything she turns her hand to, adding officially qualified pilot to her achievements now, she is also a wonderful woman. She's been a dear friend for the last seven years, and I'm relieved she's finally seen sense and settled for me.' He raised his glass. 'To Evelyn, may she always do the impossible.'

'To Evelyn,' the rest of the women chorused. As the loud chatter began once more around the table Benjamin turned to his new wife.

'I didn't settle, you know. I wanted to marry you.'

'That's as maybe, but it's not exactly the start to married life you'd have imagined, is it? Disappearing off to Paris for your first spy operation.'

Evelyn considered it. The way they'd decided to marry was a touch unconventional but she'd never been married before, much less imagined how life would be once she'd said "I do". They were due to travel to Paris the next day so that Benjamin could do whatever his assignment called for and she was excited at the prospect.

'Personally I think it's a wonderful way to begin married life, far more interesting than any of the dull honeymoons our friends have gone on. Or worse, marrying due to being with child. No, I think this i s *exactly* how I would like my marriage to begin,' she leant in and whispered in his year, 'and it's "undercover operative".'

Benjamin laughed and raised a glass. '*Salut* to that.'

THE FASTEST GIRL ON EARTH

***

The next morning, Benjamin packed up the car with the few belongings they needed for travel to Paris. Evelyn was sad to leave the little cottage she'd called home for the last six months, but knew whatever the future held she'd return – Martinique had made her promise the night before.

They were to drive for the next couple of days, leaving the car on the outskirts of Paris before entering the city on a train, as they would do if they had travelled from London. Benjamin already had their papers which had been created to show their fake journey.

'It's a long way, I hope you'll be all right,' Benjamin said as Evelyn settled herself into the passenger seat and pulled her thick fur coat around her to protect from the slight autumn chill which was creeping in, coating the farmlands around them in a light grey mist.

'I think you forget who you're talking to. I drove non-stop on my own from Glasgow to London. That was hours of driving and I was perfectly fine when I arrived. This time I have you and Dodo to keep me company, I'm sure I'll be fine – I'm more concerned about you. Are you sure I can't do some of the driving at least? I miss it,' she admitted.

Benjamin looked as though he would refuse, then changed his mind. 'Actually, yes, go on then. If I can't be driven by the world's best driver, I really don't know who could be better,' he said, as they crossed over in front of the car, kissing each other briefly as they did. 'The fastest girl on Earth, wasn't it? Try not to break any records in this I'm not sure she'd take it.' He patted the side as he got up into the car.

Evelyn settled herself behind the wheel on the left-hand side and became familiarised with the levers on the right of her.

'This should be jolly fun,' she pulled forwards, 'Paris here we come.'

After a few hours of driving, Evelyn pulled over in a small village and the couple made their way into a tabac for cigarettes and to stretch their legs.

'Oh look, Ben, lunch.' Evelyn realised she was famished, and at a nod from Benjamin took a seat at the bar. The lights were dim but she could make out a few shadowy figures sat in groups, eating the special of the day. A low murmur of French male voices restarted after their entrance and for the first time since the garage in Paris with the mechanics, all those years ago, Evelyn felt self-conscious, all too aware her fur was worth the equivalent of half a year's salary for these men, let alone the rest of her belongings. She surreptitiously moved her rings around that her jeweller father had gifted her for various birthdays, so the diamonds wouldn't catch the light, and casually unhooked her small diamond pendant from her neck, placing it in her bag.

'Two glasses of red wine, a packet of these,' Benjamin slid some cigarettes in Evelyn's direction, 'and we have a plate of *coq au vin* coming our way soon. Ah, *merci*,' he said in the direction of a man with a face so full of wrinkles Evelyn couldn't imagine what he'd looked like as a youngster. He made his way over and placed a small basket of bread on their table.

'I'm not sure we should be in here,' Evelyn whispered to Benjamin who lit a cigarette. He puffed, his eyes narrowing against the smoke, and frowned.

'Why? It's a rough place, most of these places are but I've found they can be guaranteed to give you a good plate of grub. You should eat up, I don't know where we'll stay tonight,' he advised, taking some bread and buttering it carelessly, allowing crumbs to drop on the table. His expression changed to concern when he saw she wasn't doing anything. 'Evelyn, everything is all right. This is a decent place. We won't be doing anything dangerous this trip, I promise.' He paused and looked at her as she reached for a piece of bread. 'But maybe the next tabac we go into, lay off the diamonds and furs?'

She laughed a little, relieved at his candour and chastised herself for allowing her anxieties of Paris to leach into their lunch in a remote spot of north-west France. Soon they were both tucking into the most delicious *coq au vin*.

'Do you think I could ask the cook for his recipe?' Evelyn half suggested, as she saw Benjamin's look of concern. 'Not for me to cook, for Solomon,' she clarified.

'Good, because I've never eaten your cooking and I'm pretty certain we can't assume you'll be good at it, just because you're good at everything else.'

A movement out of the corner of Evelyn's eye caused her to glance in the direction of the bar.

'Benjamin,' she whispered, nodding towards the bar. 'I think they're talking about us.' Sure enough, the man who'd been talking to the barman was walking towards them. His gait slow, but powerful, as he stood under one of the few lights. He looked, Evelyn felt, as though he spent his days working the fields. He was muscular and appeared exceptionally strong. Her heart began beating rapidly.

'English?' he said, in a strong French accent. Evelyn was about to speak when Benjamin began in a quick, loud German. Her heart in her throat, she saw the reaction on the man's face as he took a step towards Benjamin.

'Diamonds.' The farmhand pointed at Evelyn, who had begun to quake a little but Benjamin was faster. Standing up quickly, he caught the man unawares by grabbing his arm and twisting it behind his back, he then spoke rapid-fire French whilst eyeballing the man, not giving him any room to move.

Whilst she had a good grasp of the language, Evelyn didn't need to be able to understand what Benjamin was saying, the tone and the intention was clear. When he released the farmer the man slunk away, back into the shadows.

'Finish up,' Benjamin said, as he sat back down in his chair. She looked around the tabac, aware there were a lot more of the farmers' friends in there.

'I said finish up,' he said calmly. 'Or bullies like that will think they've won.'

She looked at her new husband who was chewing deliberately slowly as she tried to calm her breathing, and began to really understand for the first time about the seriousness of the world Benjamin had invited her into.

Chapter Twenty-Nine

Paris

The following evening they arrived in Paris, having abandoned the car on the outskirts, as planned, and travelled into the city together via the recently built Métro. As they emerged into the weak Parisian sunshine Evelyn enjoyed the familiarity, still impressed by the French version of the underground, though she felt a pang for London.

'The hotel is just around the corner.' Benjamin was holding the small light-brown suitcase that contained their belongings for the evening. Evelyn had hoped to bring a few more dresses, but Benjamin had been insistent she wouldn't need them and when they reached the hotel, she realised why.

'It's a bit unpleasant, don't you think?' she said quietly as she looped her arm through the crook of his.

He looked at her. 'Well, we can't draw attention to ourselves, can we? We're a loved-up young couple, but we're not rich or poor. We're very much in the middle. The best thing for anyone right now is to ignore us completely, you see? All we need is to turn up, attend the dinner this evening and then return tomorrow,' he said carefully, as he pretended to consult his map.

Evelyn frowned. 'Benjamin, I think there's a problem here. I'm travelling under my name?' She checked for confirmation and he nodded. 'So, I'm me?' He nodded again, this time looking more than a little irate. 'Well, I wouldn't stay there,' she pointed at the slightly downtrodden hotel, 'I'm me, Evelyn Bloom, and I'd stay at The Ritz, wouldn't I, darling? I always do.' This time it was his turn to frown and she continued. 'Wouldn't it look a lot more convincing if we stayed where I always do? We live the way we always do, and we just so happen to have this dinner tonight, whilst on our honeymoon?'

She watched the traffic as it trundled past her. There were more cars on the road than when she'd last lived in the city. She marvelled at the sight of them whizzing past and wondered whether Paris would ever have too many cars, then smiled to herself about the preposterous suggestion.

'Oh, Evelyn you're right. Of course. We're married – for real, and you're you, of course you are.' Benjamin suddenly looked concerned, his face pallid. 'I should have said as much to Fergie. Our handler,' he explained as Evelyn looked confused. 'I'll introduce him to you soon, but for now we're in a bind. I listened to him and didn't consider the reality of being married to Evelyn Bloom, the one who's photograph may well have made it into the Parisian papers. Of course you'd stay at The Ritz, we both would if we were honeymooning. I got so caught up in the last week or so of being your husband, I hadn't considered the details of a plan made in London many weeks before.'

Evelyn leant in to kiss him on the cheek. 'I'm caught up in you too, and because of that my darling, I'll be able to get a place at The Ritz, no questions asked. I assure you. Though in future I'd like to be consulted on any plans that involve me, I may want to make a suggestion or two. And I will need more clothes than what you're carrying,' she said, laughing at the expression on his face.

A little while later they settled into a suite after the desk clerk of the prestigious hotel recognised her from her previous stay, when Evelyn had competed in a hair-raising race around the city. Back then she'd been accompanied by Victor, but if the doorman or the hotel manager had any thoughts on her new husband, nothing was said. Of course not, it was The Ritz.

Evelyn checked her reflection in the gilt-edged mirror set apart in the dressing room of the suite and was satisfied with her appearance, her small waist enhanced by the smart navy dress she'd had sent from Poiret, her designer friend.

She called through to Benjamin. 'Honestly, darling, I'd have wanted it anyway. Frankly you've done me a favour.' Her voice dropped a little as he walked into the dressing room. 'I should try packing light more often,' she said, as his hands encircled her waist.

'I'm not sure you've quite caught the concept of packing light,' Benjamin whispered into her ear, causing goose bumps to appear across her neck and down her arms. 'But I agree the dress suits you.'

There was a knock at the door of the hotel room and Benjamin went to answer. He popped his head round a moment later. 'It's the wine we ordered. Shall I pour us a drink?'

'Yes do,' she said, watching as Benjamin plucked a bottle from the silver wine bucket filled with ice and began to open it. Evelyn enjoyed watching his concentration and careful opening of the bottle, before he poured some of the drink into the gleaming polished crystal cut glasses. Everything about Benjamin was considered, one of the many traits she loved about him. Somehow she would need to speak to whoever Fergie was, to ensure he didn't make mistakes with operation planning in future. There was no way she'd let anything happen to Benjamin now he was hers. Evelyn had learnt from her driving days that the more straight talking she was with gentlemen, the more likely they'd see her point of view. She hoped this would be so of Benjamin's handler. He was her handler too, she corrected. There was a lot she needed to learn.

Evelyn accepted the glass from her husband and took it out onto the balcony which overlooked a stunning view of Paris. Evelyn took a sip, enjoying the bubbles on her tongue and looked across to the Sacré-Coeur. She was going to take Benjamin there tomorrow. A proper day's holiday. He joined her at the bistro table placed neatly on the balcony and set his drink on the table near to hers.

'We need to talk about tonight. The chap we're meeting is called Antoine and as far as this evening is concerned, everything has to appear as real as possible.'

Leaning closer to her husband, Evelyn looked across to the blush pink sunset stretching its fingers towards them. 'Well, we're definitely real, but I am a little nervous about meeting Antoine. You haven't told me much about how I fit into this evening. Or what I'm meant to be doing.'

'Basically, Antoine wants what I have,' Benjamin replied.

'Which is?'

'It's better if I don't say too much, I don't want to drag you any further into this than necessary,' Benjamin said evenly.

'No.' Evelyn stood up, catching the table with her dress, almost toppling the glasses over. 'No, you can't do that. I've married you, I've said I'll help with this. I've said yes to being a part of this Benjamin. Whatever is going on, however it needs to be done, I'm here with you. And that means you need to tell me exactly what's going on.'

Benjamin breathed in slowly, assessing his response. 'Fine, but I want you to know I suggested someone else for this job, I didn't want to bring you into this. HQ insisted.'

'Who would they have had you marry?'

'It doesn't matter. When it got to it I realised if I was going to marry anyone it had to be you. If I were to marry someone else and you got wind of it... I wouldn't, couldn't,' he corrected, 'couldn't have lived with myself knowing I'd have hurt you in that way.'

'So you thought a spy mission would be better?' Evelyn laughed at the situation. 'I can see, you were in a bit of a predicament.'

'He's selling secrets about our government to the French,' Benjamin explained. 'He's paying our men to tell him everything they know about the weapons we have, the agents on our books, the vehicles we own. Then he's telling the heart of French government, and getting paid by them.'

Evelyn sat down. 'But why? Who is he?'

'Well, that's what we don't know. We know he's doing this. We've traced him. We know the agents who are selling him secrets but we don't know who he is. He's French, but seems to be able to get the English on board easily, and seems to have connections with Germany too. Tonight will be the first time anyone from our end will have met him face to face.' Benjamin smiled tightly, showing how nervous he was.

'If he knows everything, and knows where you are, and knows who I am, why would he show himself to you? Surely he's going to know he's being played?'

Benjamin looked down at his hands, then back up at her.

'Because I've said I want to join him.'

Chapter Thirty

Paris

Evelyn tried to focus on what Benjamin and Antoine were discussing but she could only hear her own thoughts screaming at her. She was a fool to have said yes to Benjamin and his plan. A stupid fool who did something completely out of character all because of love. Yet again she was in a relationship where her heart was going to be crushed, though this time it would be because Benjamin had pulled her into a world where they were likely to be kidnapped or killed. Why hadn't she decided her feelings for Benjamin were just a whim and ignored the butterflies in her heart whenever he was near? Then she could have been a lot safer than whatever this turned out to be.

'Is your wife quite all right?' Antoine, who was red-headed and pale faced was staring at her, raising his extraordinary red eyebrows in her direction and, Evelyn realised, Benjamin was staring too. She could almost hear him telling her to pull herself together. But it was all right for him, he'd had training for this. What was she to do? She'd already spotted the other man had a gun tucked into the waistband of his trousers, he'd not tried to conceal it all that much as they'd sat down to dinner.

'I say, are you all right? Need some air?' the man said to her and she swallowed.

'Gosh, I'm ever so sorry – I think I was daydreaming a little. I think it's all this man talk, I can't get my head around it. Would you both excuse me for a moment?' She stood and grabbed her beaded black clutch bag, giving Benjamin a tight smile and hoping he'd understand she was fine, she wasn't going to let anything go wrong and she was, in fact, pulling herself together.

'Ah yes, well, we don't expect the fairer sex to get themselves involved in all this – must be very boring for you,' the red-headed man replied, and she wondered if he was mocking her. Ignoring him, she walked as calmly as she could to the powder room of the restaurant and closed the door behind her.

'Cigarette, *mademoiselle*?' the attendant asked her, and Evelyn nodded, throwing a few francs the way of the lady and not thinking to correct her that she was in fact a *madame* now she was married.

'*Merci*,' she replied, lighting it and inhaling it deeply. The rush of the nicotine was a balm almost immediately and she took a seat on the shell-pink chaise to gather her thoughts. A minute or two later another woman came in. Evelyn smiled, and she received a smile back. The woman went into one of the cubicles and a little later came back out to powder her face, she looked over at Evelyn who was stubbing out her cigarette in one of the white marble ashtrays on the gilt-edged table.

'Who are you hiding from?' the woman asked and Evelyn raised her eyebrows in surprise at the English accent. 'Daphne Earl, I know who you are of course, I've seen your face all over the papers in England. Evelyn Bloom, you're the reason I drive. I have your book, *The Woman and the Car*.' She smiled.

'Oh, you're my reader,' Evelyn said with a grin rising to shake the other woman's hand. I must just...' She indicated the cubicle and the other woman nodded.

'What are you doing in Paris, Miss Bloom? Are you racing again? I thought you'd given all that up.' The voice came floating through the door to Evelyn who finished up and came back out.

'I've just got married,' she admitted, showing her ring to Daphne. 'Please, call me Evie,' she said, drying her hands on a soft pink towel, which was immediately whisked away by the attendant.

'Congratulations, Evie.' Daphne paused and looked at her face in the mirror. 'So is that why you're hiding in here? You're avoiding your husband?' She removed a hair grip and replaced it, smiling satisfactorily at her reflection.

Evelyn reapplied her lipstick and shook her head. 'No, I'm not avoiding anyone,' she lied. 'I just needed a few minutes to myself. My husband and I met with an old friend this evening and you know how it is. These men, they get into their stories and that's enough to send any of us to the powder room,' she elaborated, hoping her story sounded plausible enough. Daphne nodded, seemingly satisfied with the explanation.

'How much longer do you need? We could share another?' She pulled a cigarette case out of her handbag and offered one to Evelyn, who shook her head.

'No, fair enough. One does want to be able to taste one's food,' Daphne lit her cigarette, 'I must say, I rather expected you to keep racing, you know. You just seemed to stop overnight, why was that?'

Evelyn thought on her response carefully. 'I decided I'd fulfilled all my racing ambitions. I still drive of course, and I write, as you know. And I've been learning to fly.'

Daphne's mouth fell open wide. 'In a plane? What, by yourself? Surely not.'

Turning to face the other woman, Evelyn composed herself. 'Of course, why is that so shocking? You already know I race cars.'

Daphne ruminated on her reply. 'I suppose flying just seems a whole lot more dangerous,' she decided. 'At least in a car if it's all going too fast you can just pull over.'

Maybe that was why she'd suddenly become afraid when confronted with the realities of spying. There was no way she could just pull over if things got too much.

'I think I just enjoy that sense of almost peril,' she replied to Daphne. 'I'm in control and it's up to me to bring the plane up in the air and reliant on me to get it back down safely. I like that responsibility.'

'But aren't you...'

'Frightened? I suppose,' Evelyn admitted as she considered what she and Benjamin would be getting themselves into over the next few months. 'But it's worth it.' She gathered up her lipstick and compact and placed them in her bag, clicking the clasp shut. 'Thank you for buying my book, and keep your fingers crossed I'll always stay in the air.' She didn't wait for a response from the other woman before heading out of the door, deciding she needed to get herself back out to the restaurant before she lost her nerve.

As she returned to the table she saw Benjamin and Antoine shake hands.

'Ah, there you are, we were starting to think you'd got lost.' Benjamin stood as she sat down.

'No, I've found my way back. I'm here, what are we shaking on?'

'A new partnership. Your husband will be an incredibly useful asset,' the man said, his accent a mixture of English public school and German. 'I look forward to getting to know the both of you very soon. I hear you've gained your pilot's licence.' He looked at Evelyn, as though he could read her thoughts.

'Yes, recently.'

'Interesting,' the man said, nodding. Then turned to face Benjamin. 'I think you're right, you've found quite the star here. I certainly think we've got something interesting to work on in the future.' He stood and gestured for the couple to stay seated, then placed a slightly too small bowler hat on his head.

'I need to go, but I've sent for another bottle of *Dom Pérignon* for you lovebirds to enjoy.' He picked up Evelyn's hand and kissed it lightly. 'Keep up the flying, you'll never know when it'll be needed.' He tipped his hat at Benjamin and walked away.

'Don't say anything,' Benjamin cautioned quietly, placing a hand over hers. 'Who knows who could be listening.'

As a waiter filled their glasses, they sat in silence, Evelyn watched the other diners, evaluating who might look as though they were listening in on a loved up couple. But to her, everyone looked like they should be there and she wondered what the giveaway signs were.

'To us, my sweet Evelyn.' Benjamin raised his glass, bringing her attention back to him. 'And our exciting future.'

As Evelyn toasted Benjamin's success she prayed fervently that they'd have any kind of future, exciting or other.

1910

Chapter Thirty-One

LONDON

'How long will you be gone this time?' Evelyn hated herself for scolding Benjamin from her bathtub. 'You've barely been home more than a week.'

He walked into the bathroom, undoing his tie and rubbing his face as he sat down in a chair next to the bath. 'You knew this was how things would be,' he replied quietly. 'I told you I'd be away a lot.'

Evelyn turned to face him, allowing water to slosh over the sides of the bath. 'But you'd said I'd be with you – I'd be doing things too. Not just waiting around in London for you to come back.'

'Oh, my darling, I know it's hard but we're getting there. I promise.'

'Hard? No, I go shopping, I go for lunch, I drive, I attend parties, I give parties, I gamble, I fish, I shoot,' Evelyn listed. 'No, it's not hard. It's bloody boring. I'm not a housewife, I can't waste my days with fashion and gossip.'

Benjamin picked up a sponge and started gently brushing her shoulders with the suds. 'But you're always so terribly well dressed, I thought you liked fashion,' he said, with a tone in his voice Evelyn recognised. If she had looked around she knew he'd have been grinning. She wasn't going to allow him to get away with it that easily.

'Not wanting to dress as a man whilst driving, that's different to being obsessed with the fashions of the day. Honestly, who cares? I can't see why they waste their brain cells on which stripe detailing to choose on their summer dresses.'

THE FASTEST GIRL ON EARTH

'Mmm...' Benjamin had begun to soap her neck, and was wiping the sponge across the top of her chest.

'You're not listening to me, Ben.' Evelyn held onto his hand, stopping him from going further. 'I'm lonely and I'm bored. If I'd wanted to be either of those I'd have stayed with Victor. I need to do something.'

He exhaled, his warm breath tickling her neck. 'You're right, I'm sorry. I've been so caught up ensuring our man doesn't cotton on that I'm working both sides, I suppose you've been my port in a storm. A way of just being myself. But you're right. We can't have you on the side-lines any longer.'

'Really?' Evelyn turned and planted a kiss on Benjamin's hand. 'What do you have planned?'

'One of our assistants was meant to deliver a letter to a contact in Hyde Park tomorrow, but she's fallen ill. I think you should do it.'

'Assistants?'

Benjamin smiled. 'Yes. We don't call them operatives, it's not as easy as all that I'm afraid. But believe me when I say they're vital – and you will be too.'

Evelyn was disappointed, she'd barely had a chance to call herself a spy and now she was downgraded to an assistant. But she'd worked hard to get where she did for Napier, and she'd do the same at the British Government. Deciding that something was better than nothing, she smiled at Benjamin. 'I'm your port in the storm am I?' she said, leaning up to kiss him deeply.

'Oh yes, somewhere to place my anchor.' He leaned forward on his chair to kiss her again.

'I see.' Evelyn looked thoughtful for a moment, and then grabbed him by the tie, taking him by surprise and pulling him into the bath fully clothed. 'Better come aboard then, sailor.'

***

The next day, a Saturday, Evelyn made her way along Rotten Row, towards the intersection which took her towards The Serpentine where she enjoyed the sight of children running with sticks and big imaginations. Their shrieks of joy added to the other noises around her, from chirruping birds excited for spring, to those of gossiping women, strolling arm in arm.

It was an ideal morning for a stroll, and even if she hadn't had an assignment from Benjamin, Evelyn would have chosen to walk somewhere akin to Hyde Park, to enjoy the first few whispers of spring and to revel in the beauty of the cherry blossom which seemed to flood London at this time of year.

As was the case though, she chastised herself, she shouldn't be looking for birds or blossom, instead she ought to be searching out the bench she'd been told to sit at by Benjamin that morning over breakfast.

'Remember,' he'd added as he'd piled a dangerous amount of marmalade on an inadequately-sized piece of toast, 'you must be just Miss Bloom. Be yourself. You are out for a walk, you'll decide you need to rest a moment on this bench.' He'd marked an X on a map for her. 'There you'll enjoy watching life go past you, until a gentleman will sit down on the same bench and ask you for a light.' He bit into the toast and winced at the sharpness of the oranges. 'You'll nod, then you'll pass him this, as you lend him a lighter.'

Evelyn could see in her mind's eye the piece of cream paper, folded so small she was concerned she'd lose it, pressed up against her lighter in the inner pocket of her handbag. As naturally as possible, she settled on the bench she'd agreed with Benjamin and looked ahead to see if the children with the sticks were still running around. As though it would offer some comfort, she stroked her handbag, the calfskin soft and supple under her fingers, and considered the contents of the silver-grey bag. She hoped whatever information she was passing on wasn't something which would cause anyone harm.

Benjamin had told her not to consult her watch, in case anyone was watching and assumed she had a prearranged meeting. But the urge to find out as time passed, if she was early or her contact was late, started to fill Evelyn with a pressing need to sneak a look at the dainty gold watch her father had given her the previous Christmas. Her parents had been so relieved she was married, and in their minds, "finally" respectable, they'd welcomed Benjamin with open arms into the family, which had meant matching watches as Christmas gifts.

She was just about to give in and consult it, when a man of average height, average build and gently greying hair sat down at the other end of her bench. He was so nondescript, Evelyn wondered for a moment whether he could truly be her connection.

'Have you a light?' the man asked, holding a cigarette.

Evelyn's heart thudded. It was happening. 'A...?' she stuttered, trying to work out how she would pass the note and the lighter to the man without it looking odd.

'A light? Do you have a light?' He looked irritated and Evelyn was reminded of the man who taught her how to drive. How irritable men get when women don't behave as they should, she thought, rummaging in her handbag, though knowing full well where the lighter and note were.

'Here.' She moved up the bench to reach the man a little easier, and passed him both. 'You should probably light it yourself. Wouldn't want people thinking I make a habit of lighting men's cigarettes.'

He took the items from her hand, quickly, and lit his cigarette. He paused, staring at her for a moment and Evelyn wondered briefly if she'd got the wrong person. Then he stood up and shoved one of his hands into his coat pocket as he smoked with the other.

'Don't,' he said, then stopped.

'Don't what?' she said, quietly, unsure if this was all part of the set-up. Benjamin hadn't said there would be any more exchanges.

'Don't make a habit of it. Maybe just stick to one or two,' the man said, his face lighting up, giving him a flash of something a little more handsome. 'Men – whose cigarettes you light,' he explained, then winked. 'Best be off.'

Evelyn watched him walk away, then stood up, dusting herself down a little as she'd been sat for so long, then continued her walk to The Serpentine.

As though it were just a normal Saturday.

1912

Chapter Thirty-Two
MONTE CARLO

Over the last two years, Evelyn's role in gathering intelligence for the British government had grown to such an extent she had become used to long periods away from home. There was no need for a cover, with her personality reason enough to travel to Monte Carlo, Berlin or Paris. It was widely accepted she was something of a socialite who enjoyed fast cars, late nights and good champagne.

The fact that whilst she was at any of those places she would hand over a small note, or receive something similar, would go unnoticed. So, too, would her sit-downs with men in politically sensitive roles. No one questioned a woman who gambled so often with men in high society enjoying a drink and chat with them afterwards.

'Darling, you were incredible today,' Nathaniel, an Austrian diplomat who Britain had concerns was selling secrets to the Russians, whispered into her ear. He was, she knew, a little drunk, but that only helped. She had questions about a rumour that was persisting in England, and she hoped to gain some knowledge for HQ back home. Her handler, Fergie, had been insistent.

'As were you, what a shame you lost it all though,' she said, as she indicated to one of the staff to take her chips and bank them. 'You never win against me, do you?'

'It's because you're too enchanting, Evelyn. How can a man focus on cards when he has this beauty in front of him?' He raised a glass. 'To the wonderful Evelyn Bloom.'

'Now, now, that's enough of that,' she admonished. There was a stark difference to being there and being *seen* to be there. She didn't need to have too much attention.

'How's the old man?' Nathaniel asked. They'd run into him the year before in Berlin, and Benjamin had taken an instant dislike to him.

'He's well, I think,' Evelyn admitted. Nathaniel looked up from his glass hopefully.

'You think? Are things not going well?'

She shook her head. 'Darling, no, it's all wonderful. It's just we don't see much of each other, that's all.' Privately though, she was beginning to get more than a little concerned. It was four weeks since Benjamin had last made contact. He was usually very regular whilst he was away, and to not hear anything was odd. When she'd asked Fergie, a brusque man with a fantastically blond moustache of her husband's whereabouts he'd said he'd know more by the time she returned from Monte Carlo. Evelyn had decided when she returned to London at the end of the week she'd be visiting Fergie at the Foreign Office and she wouldn't leave until she knew her husband's whereabouts.

'What was that?' She caught a half-missed sentence from Nathaniel.

'Nothing.'

'No, you said something.'

'Only that he clearly doesn't know what he has if he doesn't see much of you. I know I'd like to.'

Attempting to overcome the revulsion that Nathaniel brought out in her, Evelyn smiled and laid a hand on his.

'That's very kind, but we're fine. I'm very happy,' she added.

'Take each minute when you can,' Nathaniel said, cryptically. 'Who knows how much longer this peace will last.'

'Oh?' Evelyn held her breath. This was what she was good at, gaining confidences from men. She squeezed his hand a little and smiled in what she hoped was her most beguiling way. 'You'll be telling me there's going to be a war.'

'Not yet, but there will be the way these countries are dealing with each other,' Nathaniel predicted gloomily. 'We have Austria and

Serbia and it's a hissing pot of snakes. They're just waiting for one to bite and then it's going to be a fight to the bitter end. I'm sure of it.'

Evelyn twisted a piece of her loose hair and sipped her champagne. 'Well, that all sounds frightfully negative,' she said. 'How could you possibly know all that? Tell you what, let's get a drink. Something stronger than this?' She held up her glass and beckoned a member of staff over.

An hour or so later, after Nathaniel had gone to bed considerably drunker than when they'd first met, a sober Evelyn sat very still at the table he'd just left, digesting everything she'd heard. She'd become good at that, filing away every piece of information, shuffling it, and producing it at a moment's notice.

'Everything to *madame's* satisfaction?' A waiter in white tails stood patiently next to her table, a tray balanced in his right hand. 'Would you care for anything else?' he said, sweeping his free hand in the direction of the bottles and glasses on the table.

'No, thank you. It's all been perfect, *merci*.' Evelyn nodded, but just as the waiter was due to depart, she remembered something. 'Actually, is there somewhere one can make a phone call – without interruptions? I want to call my husband.'

The waiter, if he had made any assumptions about her drinking companion, nodded deliberately slowly. '*Oui, bien sûr*. I'll show you the way.'

She followed him, noting that very few people had remained in the casino, though when she checked her watch she realised it was after one in the morning, it was no wonder things were winding down.

'Here you go, *madame*.' The waiter showed her to a small glass booth down a quiet corridor where sounds were muffled by a thick burgundy carpet underfoot, and, after seeing she was settled in comfortably, closed the doors on her and walked away.

Evelyn brought out a compact mirror from the small satin handbag entwined around her wrist, and patted a little powder on her nose, all the while looking to see if anyone had followed her, or if the waiter was hovering and listening. Satisfied there was no one around, she picked up the handset and spoke quietly into it.

'London 2591, *s'il vous plaît*,' she said to the operator and for a while the line went very quiet. Evelyn touched her hair, it was stiff from too much hairspray, and she thought impatiently of a bath and her bed. It had been a long day.

'London 2591, who may I say is calling?' the man Evelyn knew to be both butler and security to the person she was ringing, answered.

'It's Flora, I'm sorry to call so late, but I must talk to my father.' She used the code name she'd been known as for the last two years to check in with Fergie.

'Certainly.'

The line went silent again and Evelyn tried to push any thoughts of Benjamin to the back of her mind. He would be safe, he had to be. But for it to have been four weeks without a word, she was beginning to worry.

'Flora, what time do you call this? I was expecting a call two hours ago,' Fergie said as soon as he got onto the phone, raising a half smile from Evelyn. He certainly embodied a father figure and if anyone was listening they'd be fooled into thinking she was merely calling her father to check in as she was in a foreign country.

'Sorry, Father, I got chatting to a friend and things got a bit late.' She left the sentence to hang in the air, to give Fergie a chance to reply.

'I see,' there was a pause, 'and was this friend one I'd approve of?'

'I'm not sure, Father, he was certainly very outspoken. Maybe even a little too chatty, though I don't much understand politics, as you know.'

'Well, of course not. Is this friend likely to be anything more, or was this a one-off meeting?'

Evelyn hesitated, weighing up what she wanted to say against how she could say it.

'I think he could become something more, though he doesn't spend much time in England. I'll probably only be able to bump into him here. He told me he visits once every couple of months, though.' She looked briefly at her compact mirror resting on the shelf to be certain no one was listening. 'From what he was saying, he probably won't be coming back here in the near future. He seemed to suggest his gambling days would be over in about six months and he'd have to remain in Austria-Hungary after that.'

'Hmm, gambling, eh? I don't think I like him,' Fergie played along.

'No, probably not. He's not a big fan of the English anyway,' she added, hoping that she'd be able to speak to Fergie directly soon because what she'd found out that evening had chilled her.

The arms race between Austro-Germany and the Franco-Russian alliances appeared to be accelerating. From what Nathaniel had said, each were looking to demonstrate their power to the other.

And Britain was currently sat on the outside, looking in.

Chapter Thirty-Three

LONDON

A few days later and Evelyn was waiting impatiently outside a stark, black glossy door. The office hours were nine to five, and the employees within kept to them very punctually.

And Evelyn was five minutes early.

She consulted her watch again, noting that time really didn't move nearly as fast when you were waiting for it. What she would have given to have had this level of inexpedience when she'd been racing. To slow time in such a way, she could have covered routes in seconds.

'Morning, Miss Bloom, punctual as ever.' Fergie swept past her and pushed open the door. Evelyn rolled her eyes, she hadn't considered checking to see if the door was open or not. Casting aside her irritation, she made her way through the entrance, whilst Fergie held open the door for her.

She followed Fergie to his office, listening to the other members of staff chatting as they arrived. Evelyn allowed the ache of jealousy to wave across her for a moment, she missed having people she could nonchalantly natter with. Gone were the days of sharing her apartment with Hena and Frances. She hadn't heard from Frances in over five years, though the gossip was she'd moved abroad to live with a married man. Of Hena, she'd burnt her bridges.

Martinique corresponded occasionally, but Evelyn knew she was mixed up in work not dissimilar to hers. Their paths had crossed a year or so before at a bar in Paris, where, over one too many martinis,

Martinique had admitted she was attempting to recruit and teach women to fly so that the French would have the advantage, should any air attacks be necessary.

Other than Benjamin, the only person Evelyn saw more than once a year was Isabelle, and usually that was with George in tow. And soon she'd have a baby. Evelyn shook her head. Really, wasn't it enough to be married? Why did her friends have to keep getting wed and pregnant? It turned them into terrible bores.

'Tea?' Fergie was showing Evelyn to a comfortable, if a little shabby, midnight-blue chair. It would have looked more at home in an old woman's sitting room than in the office of a man as important as Fergie. Mind, the government wasn't awash with money, she knew that. That was part of the reason they kept her in their employment, she often funded her own trips abroad, as much to cover the reason for her jaunts as to save the British Secret Service the embarrassment of trying to cover the cost. She wondered what her father would think if he knew his money was being used in that way.

'Please,' she replied, closing the door and sitting, somewhat uncomfortably on the worn velvet seat. She accepted the plain cream teacup and saucer and sipped at her tea.

'So,' Fergie rubbed his hands together, 'if what you say is correct, it would seem we need to be more on our toes than the current thinking.' He sipped his drink, leaving droplets of tea on the edges of his moustache, which he dabbed away with a handkerchief that had seen better days.

'Nathaniel said a lot at the casino, some of it was nonsense as he'd been drinking heavily, but I think most of it was in the right area.' Evelyn paused to consider how she'd frame her next sentence. 'It feels... worrisome, does it not?'

If she'd been hoping for soothing words, Fergie's face did nothing to calm the nerves she'd had since her Monte Carlo meeting.

'It's not the only intelligence we've had that something's rumbling,' Fergie replied carefully. 'We don't think something will happen imminently, but alliances are being made across Europe which are troubling. There's a whisper of war.'

Evelyn knew she wouldn't get more out of Fergie, so nodded, dutifully. 'Is there anything I can do?'

'I think you've done more than enough, you've been an absolute trooper.' Fergie finished his tea and wiped his moustache. 'You should head home and enjoy a little downtime.'

The thought of being alone again caused Evelyn to drop her head sadly. 'I can't enjoy it when I don't know where Benjamin is, or if he's all right,' she admitted, hoping against hope that Fergie would give her an idea of where her husband had been the past five weeks. And whether he would be back any time soon.

'Ah,' Fergie fixed her with a piercing stare, his dark eyes boring into hers. 'Yes, well, with our new information we think it's high time we got him out of... wherever he is, and bring him home. At least for the next few months.' He smiled at Evelyn's clear relief. 'I take it you're agreeable?'

She nodded. 'Very, but I hope that won't affect anything?' She wasn't sure what Benjamin had been doing or to what end, but if events were escalating, she was torn between wanting him beside her, or allowing him to work for his country.

Fergie shook his head. 'Not at all, we'd planned to get him out sooner, truth be told, but he'd turned up some interesting things for us. We'll leave it there though... all right?' He was back to talking in whispers and half-sentences, something Evelyn found very hard to get used to. She needed plain speaking.

'Well, of course. I'll be off then – and nothing for me then either, I take it?'

Already looking at some papers that sat on his desk, Fergie didn't even look up to answer. 'Not for now. Go home, ready your house for your husband and we'll be in touch, soon.'

Never one to do as she was told, in this instance she quietly complied. As Evelyn let herself out of the office that was still humming with chatter and business, she thought on how important Benjamin had become to her life and happiness.

She had never enjoyed being alone and her life, to this point, had ensured she hadn't been. From living with her parents, to moving into her own apartment where she'd live with the two girls, to Victor spending most of his time at hers, Evelyn had managed to manufacture a life of constant companionship.

The only times she'd been truly alone were living in France whilst she trained as a pilot, and these past few weeks without Benjamin. Evelyn had found a rhythm to her solitary life, but it was one of managing. Not enjoying.

So she took great pleasure in knowing Benjamin's return would be imminent, and began to run through all the necessities she knew he'd enjoy.

The next few days Evelyn spent devising menus with her staff to ensure he was built up on his return. She'd found on his trips abroad he'd come back with tales of the awful food he'd had to digest, often leading to him either gaining a little around the midriff or losing weight that didn't need to be lost. By organising their food she knew they'd have delicious light lunches and suppers which would get him healthy and lean once again.

She spent time in Harrods, choosing flowers for all the rooms, though she knew Benjamin didn't care for those sorts of things. It was a way for her to show just how well she'd coped by herself. "See", she could say, "I've been alone but I've not let standards drop".

Evelyn sourced a new driving bonnet and gloves and on a whim bought Benjamin some too, with a plan to take off on a little sojourn together once he was ready. A little trip to somewhere in the countryside. She'd enjoy driving a longer distance than the short hops she'd been making around London.

'You seem miles away.' Evelyn spun round to spot the owner of the voice.

'Victor.'

***

He had aged.

That was the first thing Evelyn realised when it came to her past flame. And he was with his wife, both still acting the charade of a married couple, if the way the woman hung on Sharp's arm was proof to go on.

'Miss Bloom, how wonderful to see you.' Sharp smiled, though his apparent joy didn't reach his eyes.

'King,' Evelyn corrected and Victor frowned. 'It's Mrs King now, I married Benjamin,' she added, by way of explanation.

Victor's wife tapped him on the shoulder. 'I told you, I read it in the society pages,' she said quietly. Her eyes were set just a little too far apart and gave her a look not dissimilar to that of an owl. But the loftiness which she'd shown all those years ago had gone, instead she appeared smaller than Evelyn remembered. Sharp flapped his hand at his wife to stop her talking and Evelyn bit back the relief she wasn't in his wife's shoes.

'Why don't you go ahead, I'll be right behind you.' He said to his wife who did as she was told. Of course she did. Everyone did what Sharp told them too. Everyone but Evelyn.

They both watched as the owl disappeared into the revolving doors of the department store.

'So, how is married life – where is...Mr King?' Sharp asked, pointedly looking behind Evelyn.

She smiled, sizing him up and considering what she'd seen in him. Maybe it had been an attraction to power, because even in the soft summer light his features had a harshness to them and his eyes held malice in their dark pools.

'He's away, working, but I expect him home in a couple of days,' she said. 'Speaking of which, it was lovely to catch up but I really must head off.' Evelyn went to walk away but something in Victor's face made her stop. He looked sad. Something she hadn't expected of him.

He stepped a little closer, the light dimming a little as he did so. 'It's not the same you know,' he said quietly, his words barely making a dent on the thrumming in Evelyn's temples. She could feel a headache coming on. Something that only happened when she was very anxious.

'What isn't?' she said, replying in what she hoped was a haughty, offhand manner.

THE FASTEST GIRL ON EARTH

'Everything. The racing; no one can come close to what you achieved,' he said, surprising Evelyn with what appeared to be honesty. 'And... you know.' As he spoke he reached out to remove something from her shoulder, his thumb lightly grazing the fabric of her coat. It was a gesture so intimate she flushed.

'Yes, well,' Evelyn stepped back, forcing him to move his hand away abruptly, 'I'm afraid you'll have to forgive me for not feeling quite the same. It was you who decided to drop me from the team, was it not?' she carried on, not allowing him to reply. 'And it was you who got bored with me and ended us, too?'

Sharp's mouth opened and closed, shocked at her robustness. It had been over five years since she'd seen him and a lot had happened in those intervening years which had changed Evelyn. Defined her. And she knew he didn't have a place in this life she was building.

'Goodbye Victor, enjoy shopping – with your wife.'

At that, and not even waiting to see his reaction, Evelyn made her way over to her car, where a man in Harrods livery of the finest dark moss green, was stood to its side, keeping an eye on the contents.

He tipped his hat at her. 'All your purchases are here, ma'am.'

Evelyn nodded. 'Thank you.' She pressed a small coin into his white-gloved hand and briefly watched Victor walking away. Satisfied she no longer had an audience, Evelyn pulled herself up into the car and only then could she allow herself to breathe deeply, ruminating on whether she should have spoken to Sharp in that way and allowing her heart rate to slow back to its norm.

The familiarity of the car soothed her and soon Evelyn was able to start the motor, the irritations of the exchange with her past suitor tempering down into a smaller, more manageable puddle of annoyance.

By the time she arrived at her apartment in Mayfair she had quashed all thoughts of Sharp and his owl of a wife and was excited to return home to ready it for Benjamin's arrival.

But she was greeted on the kerbside by Solomon, hurrying out to her with a telegram. 'Mrs King, it's your father. He's been taken ill.'

Chapter Thirty-Four

HAMPSHIRE

If the death of your father wasn't enough to age you, seeing your own mother sob violently on the side of his grave was.

The illness had taken him quickly, Evelyn had been reassured by a doctor, who seemed to think that would calm her.

All she could be thankful for was the ever calm, ever solid presence of Benjamin by her side. He had returned to their home the morning after she'd learned of her father's death, as Evelyn oversaw her luggage being packed by Solomon. A difficult task as she was unsure how long she would be expected to remain at the family home when she returned.

Benjamin, without a beat, had taken a quick bath to wash his journey from him, asked Solomon to pack up his luggage, dashed down a swift breakfast followed by a pot of tea – the drink of victory, as he always described it – and was ready to sit alongside her, in her car, just an hour after returning home.

If he'd been disappointed at the lack of romantic reunion, or Evelyn's distractedness, he hadn't shown it. Instead, he'd kept up a stream of anecdotes about his adventures over the past few weeks as she negotiated the roads out of London, towards the countryside to Hampshire, and Solent House, where her parents l ived.

Parent.

Evelyn caught herself. It was just her mother. A woman who, in the years since Evelyn had moved out, had withered, giving in to age as much as her daughter had embraced living.

'I think you're needed,' Benjamin said quietly, looking in the direction of the small group of mourners who had gathered in the drawing room, accepting cups of tea from the servants. Evelyn felt like shrinking and hiding. She'd relegated everyone in that room to the past. Not one person had reached out to her when she'd left for London, nor had they celebrated any of her wins. But she caught sight of her mother, hunched over and smaller than she'd ever looked before, gripping a cup and saucer so fiercely Evelyn was worried it would shatter.

'Shall I take that?' she said, moving in her mother's direction and taking the cup and saucer without a fight. Handing it to one of the staff, Evelyn touched her mother carefully on the elbow and guided her to a hard-backed upright seat as delicately as though she were guiding a new-born.

'Good God, it *is* you,' Evelyn's Uncle Tom boomed from his seat from across the room. 'I thought it was, but Petunia wasn't sure, were you?' he said loudly to his prim-looking wife who continued to just hold her head high, as though she hadn't heard a word her husband had said.

'Yes,' Evelyn said quietly. 'Well, it's been a few years since we last saw each other, I suspect I've changed a little since you last saw me, Uncle Tom,' she said, aware the majority of the twenty or so mourners were listening in on their conversation.

'Why was that? Why haven't we seen you? Too busy with your London life?' he replied, leaning in earnestly. 'Weren't you, ah, let me think,' he scratched his woolly beard in thought, 'weren't you working as a secretary?'

Evelyn swallowed down her irritation. 'Is that what Papa said?'

Uncle Tom began to smile, caught himself and shook his head. 'No, the old man didn't tell me much about your life, truth be told, just that you'd said no to his latest match and continued to cost him a pretty penny in that Mayfair apartment of yours.' He barked a laugh, caught himself and rubbed a handkerchief under his eyes as though mopping up a tear.

Trying not to show her surprise, Evelyn ignored her uncle, then turned to her mother.

'Do you need anything? I think I could do with a some fresh air.' She hoped her mother would understand the insinuation to her father's brother and his continual annoyance.

'Actually,' her mother's voice was dry and brittle, 'I could do with some too, can you take me outside?'

Evelyn nodded and the two stood, their black crinoline dresses rustling as they made their way slowly down a light filled wood-panelled corridor that had no place being bathed in soft, dappled early afternoon sunshine on such a wretched day.

They were silent, but it was welcome after the many hours of small talk Evelyn had been forced to make since the morning. Ever since they'd begun preparations for the funeral, making their way to the church for the service, then to the cemetery where her father was interred in the family's plot, before returning to the house with their interminable entourage. Evelyn so wished it had just been her, her mother and Benjamin, but knew, were it her own funeral, she would prefer to have more than three people sad she'd left the world.

The thought was maudlin and Evelyn tried to ignore it, but it lodged there like an undigested bit of food, reminding her of her own mortality. Not in all the times she'd raced cars, boats, planes or, indeed, spied for Britain, had she contemplated her death. She'd assumed it, made peace that it was inevitable, but she'd thought of it as one would think of dreams. At a distance. She was only thirty, she didn't need to concern herself over death and dying, not yet. But still the thought persisted. What had she given to the world that it would mean one jot whether she lived or died? And who would come to her funeral? Right now she could only guarantee Benjamin, and if they were able to, Isabelle and George, but even they were a stretch.

'He's a liar.' Her mother broke her thoughts.

'Who is?'

'Your Uncle Tom. Your father was immensely proud of you – we both are, were,' she corrected herself. 'No, we were both proud of you and I... continue to be.' She stuttered her way through her sentence as though words had no place to be in her mouth. 'We love you dearly, and wouldn't want you changing your life in any way than how you want to live it.'

Evelyn clasped her mother's hand. 'But what about the latest match Father sent?' She hadn't mentioned the potential landowner her father had spoken to her of, just a month before she'd married Benjamin.

Her mother smiled, a little sadly. 'It was his way, I think, of trying to bring you home – we were selfish and wanted to see you, but he knew you wouldn't be happy until you'd found your own husband. You are happy, aren't you?' Her mother looked into Evelyn's eyes, her own light-grey ones reflecting back. 'That's all we've wanted for you.'

'Very happy, Mother, I assure you,' Evelyn replied, realising, all too late that she'd built a life away from her parents, arrogantly believing herself to be better than them, or unheeding of their lives, whereas now she would give all her independence up for one more hour with her father.

'It's yours, you know,' her mother said, looking out towards their gardens, the sunshine throwing rays across the neatly manicured lawns.

'What is?'

'Well, everything eventually. But for now, the Mayfair apartment, it's yours – in deeds and all, your father made sure it was legally under your ownership once you turned thirty. Now you'll always know you have somewhere to call home – wherever you are in the world, even when—' Her mother broke off, but Evelyn knew.

Even when they'd both left her, that's what she'd wanted to say.

1916

Chapter Thirty-Five

London

Evelyn looked up and down the busy station. Waterloo was a hive of activity, with families bidding tearful farewells to soldiers in uniform on their way to fight in the war which had been going for two years, and others waiting for their loved ones to return from the front. But she didn't care about any of them just then. She had eyes for one man. A man she hadn't seen in close to three months.

Scanning the platform, she absentmindedly played with the delicate gold penny medallion hanging on a long chain around her neck. It was a gift from Benjamin which she hadn't removed since he'd given it to her, his way of being in her thoughts. Any time she felt the ache of his distance she would rub it, with the hope he would know on some level that she was with him.

'Penny for them.' The familiar voice was at her left side and she spun round with relief, allowing herself to be swept up in a deep embrace. Benjamin's face was rough with stubble but his touch was the same. As soon as they kissed she felt the electricity of his closeness.

He held her at arm's length to assess her. 'Let me guess what you were thinking about. Was it how much you couldn't wait to see your handsome husband?'

Evelyn laughed, a little at the comment but mainly with relief that he was here. Benjamin had been returned to her. He cocked his head a little to the side in an unasked question.

'I'm so happy you're back,' was all she could manage, her voice cracking with the emotion. 'I've got so much to tell you.' They began walking in-step, and Evelyn, who had never before considered she was in need of another human being, felt instantly whole again having him by her side. His presence was reassuring, but whenever she looked at him, there was something about the way he made her feel. With Victor she'd never felt more than an object, to be held up and admired, placed on a pedestal. But with Benjamin she found she liked who she was in his eyes. He treated her as a partner. An equal.

'Walking home I'm afraid, cabs are few and far between and I'm not sure you'll want to go on the tube?' The question was loaded, she didn't know where Benjamin had been, and she wasn't certain he'd tell her. But she could see behind his pleasure at returning to her a haunted look as though he were being chased by an unseen nightmare. Her instinct told her he would enjoy the open air and walking through the streets of London, rather than trundling under it. His quick nod confirmed her thoughts, so she took it upon herself to fill their walk with chatter to catch him up on the last three months. All of it light. None of it asking the questions she really wanted to know the answers to. Especially the main one – when would he be leaving her again?

'I'm afraid we're a bit limited on what we could get hold of, and as we only knew you were returning two days ago things have been a little fraught. But Solomon and I have managed to scrounge enough goodies together to make you feel like you're at The Ritz,' she said. 'And I thought after a lunch, you might like a hot bath. I won't tell anyone,' she grinned conspiratorially, 'but we both know you love a good bath, and I'm even going to share some of my precious salts with you.' At the last remark, Benjamin, who had been looking ahead, to all intents and purposes as though he couldn't hear, looked to her and smiled, a touch of crinkling around his eyes and the greying at his temples the only difference to when they first met those years ago in Paris.

'You think of everything.' He caught his hand in hers and her heart swelled at the squeeze he gave. They carried on with the last of their journey in silence, Evelyn watching the world and his wife as they scurried across the London streets. A light drizzle had begun, but even that didn't darken her mood – she had Benjamin back. The thought that crossed her mind of "for now" was pushed away into the recesses. She wouldn't think of him leaving again. He was here now.

'It's funny,' Benjamin said, breaking their silence as they turned into their road, 'I've only been gone three months but it feels like a year. The city feels different – is that possible? It feels more broken than before.'

It was Evelyn's turn to give him a look before replying. 'I don't think I've noticed. Of course, people tend to hurry around more now, there's always the possibility of a bombing raid.' A zeppelin had dropped bombs over Bromley and Chelmsford just a month before. It was shot down by the British, but Evelyn hadn't been in London. She'd been flying over northern France, dropping radios to the British troops, new ones to ensure the Hush WAACS, who continued to break the German codes could contact the Brits at HQ in London.

Since Benjamin had brought her into the Secret Service it had mostly meant flying missions for the most part. The Service quickly relied on her flying skills when the realisation had dawned not long after Great Britain declared war on Germany in 1914, that most of the other pilots were unavailable as they were fighting for their country. And so, after a couple of months of training on the south coast near to Folkestone, it had become a regular occurrence. Evelyn would receive to be given a piece of paper with coordinates, the merest of briefings and very little warning, before she flew to somewhere, usually in France, where she'd collect or drop items, and return to England.

When she'd return to the city – her city – she'd met the devastation of the latest attack with a lack of surprise. She had her suspicions that the Germans would soon come up with a more effective air-based bomber, one that wouldn't be so easy to spot or shoot down as the zeppelins. It was just like the cars and the boats she'd driven. The people in power were always looking at ways to improve them. But she couldn't share any of that with Benjamin, just as he couldn't share anything he'd done. The yawning chasm of things left unsaid filled their conversation, like the darkness around the stars in the sky. She knew something had to be there, but neither could say what it was.

She brought herself back to the present, holding her husband's hand because they were both alive, and that was a lot to be thankful for. 'But I think Londoners are pretty stoic. A lot of the young men are at war as you know, so maybe that's what you're noticing – a missing generation on the streets. It's happened in such a way I hadn't noticed it as starkly as you. But when I've caught buses and trams I've noticed much older men driving now, even a woman every now and then,' Benjamin looked at her with surprise. 'I know, it's quite shocking isn't it? I rode all the way to Balham and back the other day just because a woman was driving and I enjoyed the wonderful novelty.'

They began walking up the two flights of stairs to the apartment, their breathing quickening due to the steepness.

Once they reached the top floor she paused, they were at her door. Their door. 'Not that I've been wasting my days whilst you've been away of course,' she said, as much to reassure him as to ensure he knew how decadent her last statement had sounded compared to whatever he'd been doing. 'I was on the bus for a reason,' she dropped her voice to a low whisper, 'I was practising tailing people, Fergie says I need to be better at it. So I've taken to picking out strangers at random and following them.' She pushed the door open and was surprised as Benjamin caught her at the waist and kissed her.

'Evelyn Bloom, you constantly astonish me. Do you know that?' He pressed his body into hers and she kissed him back, then pulled away.

'Come inside, what will the neighbours think?'

'When have you ever worried about that?' He embraced her again and she laughed, letting him kiss her neck, and over her face, the action bringing waves of pleasure to her. Kicking the door shut he pressed her against the wall and held her face in his hands, then pressed his lips lightly to hers, the action so gentle Evelyn emitted a small moan at the tenderness of this man.

'Lunch is going to have to wait,' he said, picking her up and carrying her along the hallway, his shoes clacking across the black and white tiles and into the haven of their bedroom, shutting the door and the world out behind them.

A little later, true to her word, Evelyn ran Benjamin a bath filled with hot water and bubbles, along with a generous sprinkling of salts. The bathroom smelled divine and as he climbed into the claw footed bath, hot water sloshed dangerously close to the top of the steep side.

'Do you want company or shall I give you some space?' Evelyn was in a white silk robe, her hair tied up, trailing her hand in the water as she sat on a stool next to the bath. Benjamin caught her hand and held it.

'Stay. Always stay. I never need space from you,' he said, kissing her palm and the inside softness of her wrist.

'In that case, I better sponge you down,' she said, knowing it was one of his favourite things for her to do. She picked up a sponge and squeezed the hot water along his shoulders, watching him visibly relax. He closed his eyes as she continued her ministrations, carefully wiping around his ears and removing the many weeks of travel and distance between them.

Cautiously she sponged down his back, mapping the trail of old and new bruises under his skin lightly with her fingertips. A smattering of green and purple down his right side that looked like a footprint, along with numerous smaller cuts that marched across the base of his back. She knew he wouldn't talk about them. She knew she couldn't. But their presence caught on her heart and brought tears to her eyes. Evelyn continued to sponge him, wiping his arms, his chest, the black curls of hair. Further down his legs, along to his feet, which were again cut and sore. Looking over to see if she'd hurt him by wiping a particularly deep cut on his left foot, Evelyn smiled at the sight that greeted her, Benjamin's chest was rising and falling slowly, his mouth open slightly. It wasn't the first time he'd fallen asleep in the bath. Every time he came back from his missions she found it was the way to bring him most peace. It was as though the warmth, the water, brought an infantile response out of him.

Evelyn couldn't pull him out of the bath, and he would have to be woken when the water cooled, so she did what she always did when he slept like this. She stayed, watching his chest rising and falling, praying for the day when he would come home to her for good.

1917

Chapter Thirty-Six
GHENT, BRUSSELS

'*Non, madame, non merci.*' Evelyn kept her head bowed to deflect the attention of beggars proffering meaningless trinkets and charms for a price as she wound her way through the cobbled streets.

She pushed the flat cap further down over her head, keeping her fingers crossed that any hints of blonde hair were hidden out of sight, and no one gave her a second thought.

Cursing herself for the bad luck in coming down later than she should have, Evelyn pushed on, walking quickly in the subdued dawn light, wishing again that she'd been earlier so that she could have done the majority of this walk in the dark.

She walked past buildings with German flags fluttering outside, her steps, though light, making a soft thudding sound as she moved quickly past shuttered shopfronts and houses with curtains pulled tightly across windows as though to keep the rest of the world away.

She didn't need to consult any instructions – she'd destroyed them anyway – but she knew where she needed to get to. A small hotel, just a little way from the centre, nicknamed "Buck Palace" by the British, where she was to pick up a parcel and deliver it back to London as quickly as possible, and not attract the attention of the Germans.

A noise to the right of Evelyn made her halt briefly, all too aware she could be being followed, but she breathed in relief when the blackest of cats ran out of an alleyway and up the street.

Looking around to be certain there hadn't been a reason other than her presence to frighten the animal, she listened out for other footsteps. A quick breath. A cough. But nothing. She was alone.

Aware her heart was racing but satisfied no one was following her, Evelyn strode quickly around the corner, and knocked on the plain grey door, noticing as she did that a German sign had been hung over the original French name. Whilst she could understand a good deal of the language, she was still learning and hoped her French would be acceptable whilst in the Belgian town.

There was no answer at the door, and Evelyn shifted a little, the cold seeping into her feet. It had already been a very long night, having left an airfield in Sussex in the early hours, with very little notice from HQ that she was heading to Ghent. She'd not stopped for any breakfast and was beginning to feel nauseated at the effort and mental agility she'd performed in landing in the pitch black, albeit in a farmer's field.

The door opened, just a touch, and a man's face looked out. ' *Bonjour*,' he whispered.

'*Bonjour, monsieur, je cherche un petit-déjeuner, est-il possible de s'arrêter ici un moment?*' Evelyn asked quietly, hoping he'd say yes to the breakfast, then she asked the coded question, '*et, si possible, récupérer votre courrier?*'

He nodded quickly, letting her in and swiftly closing the door behind them both.

'George?' he asked, her code name, but before she nodded, Evelyn looked around to check who else was in the darkened room. She hoped she hadn't walked into a trap.

'But you are...' The Frenchman left the implication hanging in the air, like the scent of rotting cabbage the hotel was permeated with, and she ignored it. It was better, she had come to the conclusion, to have as little as possible to do with whomever she picked up from when she ran these missions. That way there was less chance of them being implicated in anything should she get caught, and vice versa.

Evelyn smiled tightly. By not speaking too much it could be assumed she was a young man, but if she were to talk, it would be a giveaway if, indeed, it was a trap.

'However, you are not 'ere for conversation,' the man continued, speaking in hushed tones and nodded at her with recognition in his eyes. 'I understand, I shall get the... package.' His English faltered and she smiled again, to show she appreciated him helping.

Shrugging off her thick khaki canvas backpack, Evelyn crouched down and opened it, knowing it was as empty as it could be, but reminding herself of what she could leave, if, indeed, the package was bigger than she'd assumed. In the last three missions she'd collected barely more than a scrap of paper, and, in one case, something contained within a metal lunchbox.

Her water canister was inside, as was an apple – which she picked out and began to eat, the sound of the skin breaking as she bit into it tearing into the silence of the desolate hotel.

"Buck Palace". Evelyn smiled to herself. She appreciated the British sense of humour, there was certainly nothing she could correlate between this house and the beautiful palace she'd visited on numerous occasions when teaching Queen Alexandra how to drive.

A different life.

That part of her life was in the distant past, confined to a page in history when women could be record-breakers. She shook her head, ridding herself of memories sparkling with cocktails and celebrity and bringing herself to the present. For the most part her recent missions had been reconnaissance, a simple "checking out" of where the enemy were so that she could let British HQ beware, so they could work with troops on the ground. She didn't relish those ones as, more often than not, they put her in incredible danger.

Twice she'd been shot at these past few months, so it had been with some relief she'd been given the package run to Ghent.

'ere we go.' The hotelier had returned, but rather than a package, wrapped in brown paper and secured with a string, Evelyn was presented with a scrawny man, no older than eighteen, his flat cap held tightly. The whites of his knuckles were showing as he moved the cap between his hands, the tension visible in his whole demeanour.

'*Non, monsieur,*' Evelyn said, cautiously. '*J'étais censé récupérer un paquet.*' She indicated her bag. '*Un paquet,*' she repeated, miming a parcel. '*Pas une personne.*' She wagged her finger in the young man's direction.

The hotelier's response was merely a shrug of his shoulders, followed by a rapid and very quiet discussion with the young man, which Evelyn couldn't follow. The next thing she knew he was forcing a baguette wrapped in brown paper into her hand and trying to put it into her bag, whilst hustling herself and the young man out of the door.

Evelyn tried to think during the commotion and decided the best thing was to get this boy to England, deliver him to the drop-off point and then hopefully someone else could be responsible.

But for now she had to get them both out of Ghent.

Chapter Thirty-Seven

GHENT

Day was breaking, with tentative rays of sunshine leaking round the gloomy corners of the street where they'd emerged, the door to the hotel shut firmly behind them. Evelyn pulled her cap further down over her head and cast a quick look up and down the street.

Seeing it was clear, she glanced behind her at the young man who was blinking in the sunshine, his hand raised to cover his eyes, exposing holes in his jumper in the seams that ran under the arms of his coat.

He looked younger than she'd first thought.

'We must leave,' she said in quiet French to him. 'Now.' She made to walk away but he didn't follow. Evelyn stopped and turned back. 'I say, are you deaf? I said we need to go.' She tugged on his sleeve and inclined her head in the direction of the right of the street. 'This way.' This time the boy did as he was bid and moved, silently, behind her. He was so quiet she had to keep looking back to ensure he was following.

They walked quickly and turned down into another, thinner street. Evelyn beckoned the boy to walk alongside her and as their strides fell into step, she continued scouting for anyone who might see them.

'We need to keep an eye out for any police, but look confident. We mustn't attract attention,' she cautioned, walking with her head down a little, to avoid confrontation. As they reached the end of the street, they could hear scraping along the cobbled paving and Evelyn held her hand up to stop the boy.

Cautiously, she looked into the street and saw a café owner and his boy apprentice setting up chairs and tables outside a café festooned with German regalia.

'This way,' Evelyn whispered, and the two strode purposefully into the main thoroughfare, walking quickly back along the route she'd taken earlier that morning. There was a loud crash behind them, causing the boy to jump and Evelyn's heart to hammer, but she'd been in tighter spots and maintained her poise, looking forward and working out what other routes she could take back to the field where her plane waited.

Allowing herself the quickest look behind, she noted with relief it had only been a chair that had crashed to the ground. She could see the man lecturing his boy apprentice and she turned back to carry on. As she did, she noticed a German soldier walking towards them. Attempting not to attract any attention, Evelyn cast her eyes around to see if there were any detours they could take to avoid the officer, but very quickly she concluded there were no options. Even if there had been, they would have attracted more attention by darting out of sight. She cursed the time it had taken her to get to Ghent, land, and find the boy. She should have been in and out hours ago. They were better off walking as quickly past the German as they could she reasoned. She just had to hope he didn't spot she was a woman, or the fear in the boy's face.

She could feel the boy slow as the German turned to them as they passed in the street. Evelyn smiled politely at him, remembering a millisecond too late that she wasn't dressed as a lady and therefore had no need to act like one.

'*Guten Morgen*,' the officer said, crisply.

'*Guten Morgen*,' the boy replied. '*Sieht so aus, als würde es trocken sein*,' he continued, looking up to the sky. With Evelyn's smattering of German she surmised this was vaguely about the weather.

The officer looked at them both and considered them for a moment, then dismissed them.

'*Einen schönen Tag noch.*'

This time it was Evelyn who felt her sleeve tugged lightly, as the boy quickly communicated that the conversation had come to a close and they needed to leave. She nodded at the German and began walking on, with the boy close by.

'You speak German?' she asked, but he fell silent again. Evelyn furrowed her brow in irritation, but aware they needed to press on and reach the field before their cover was blown, decided not to push the matter any further. As she made a left, the boy tugged on her elbow and looked to the right.

'No, I came this way,' she answered quietly.

'Boat,' came the reply.

'Boat? Show me,' Evelyn realised if they were on a boat they could make the journey quicker.

They went to the right, winding their way down smaller backstreets until the boy stopped at a corner, the sinews in his shoulders stiffening a little, the breeze carrying with it the scent of the canal. Evelyn stopped too. Then followed close to him as he walked round the corner of a pink building and onto the side of the canal, the side edged with smooth bricks.

Looking up and down, ensuring there were no onlookers, Evelyn ran over to the side to join him, just as he began clambering onto a small speedboat. Not dissimilar to the ones she used to race.

He beckoned to her, offering to help her in, but she shook her head and swiftly leapt into the boat. The boy immediately strode towards the controls, flicking switches in a way which suggested he wasn't too sure what he would do if the boat did flicker into life.

'No – stop. *Arrêt*,' Evelyn said as loudly as she dared. The boy stopped and looked at her, confused. 'We can't start the motor up yet, people might hear.' Just as she spoke another boat whirred past, a chunky dark-blue one that was heftier than theirs, but, importantly, it was making a noise. She encouraged the boy to start the engine as she freed the tether from the side, but he shrugged.

'I don't know,' he mustered and his confidence disappeared immediately, leaving a young boy in its wake again.

'I do. You navigate us out of here,' she replied, taking up her familiar position at the stern, firing up the engine and easily negotiating it from the side. The boat was fairly quiet as it puttered down the canal, and Evelyn relaxed into the familiar controls.

She watched as the scenery moved past. The houses were a riot of different colours and as the wash lapped against the sides they gleamed in the dewy morning light. Ghent was beautiful and she made a note that when this was all over, she would revisit with Benjamin.

She became aware of movement to her left and saw the boy. Looking in his direction to see what he was doing, she noticed he had opened a small hatch and was removing a little bag.

'This is your boat?'

He nodded. Evelyn felt better knowing they'd not stolen someone else's property.

'Father,' he said quietly and again Evelyn detected an accent, but couldn't be sure with so few words to go on, quite which it was. Belgian? She didn't think he was German, she couldn't imagine a rescue mission from the UK for a young German boy. Though he did speak it well.

'Oh, it's your father's? Well, I'll be kind to her, I promise.' She smiled in what she hoped was a reassuring way, though her heart was hammering a little as she considered what a sitting duck they were on the water. Maybe he'd only directed them to the boat so he could get his bag with no thought as to whether it was the safest option or not.

Panicking rarely overcame Evelyn. She took a deep breath and assessed their situation. She had a boat, which she could navigate. She was heading in the right direction to the plane, the only issue was getting there now in the very bright sunshine. And that was assuming no one else had noticed it. Evelyn had landed at night using the coordinates British HQ had given her, allowing the plane to roll to a stop behind a thick cluster of trees that camouflaged it from any passers-by. But originally she had been due to leave before dawn broke, giving her plenty of cover.

'How far?' she asked, noticing the houses on either side were beginning to thin out and the canal had become a little less loved in places.

The boy trailed his hand in the water and Evelyn watched him with a modicum of pity – he'd probably done this with his father many times. Maybe he was worried he'd never return. He looked over at her and held up his hand to indicate "five".

THE FASTEST GIRL ON EARTH

Whether it was five minutes or five knots away, Evelyn couldn't be certain, but it meant it was nearby. Scanning the horizon to get her bearings, she tried to locate any sort of landmarks she'd seen on her walk into town during the night. Try as she might there was nothing familiar. Though, she admitted privately, she hadn't been able to see much in the dark so she had to rely on guesswork.

A church spire appeared and disappeared in the distance, and she realised the canal was coming lightly to the right. The boy cleared his throat.

'Here?' she asked, realising how trusting she'd been to get herself in this situation. Because, whilst she'd thought "boy", he was, of course, on the cusp of being a man. She could easily be overpowered by him, if it were to come to that.

She touched the gun in the waistband of her trousers. It was tucked out of sight, under her shirt and grubby waistcoat. Invisible yet within reach. And she had some rounds of bullets stashed in her rucksack. Both brought her peace of mind.

She hadn't killed anyone. Yet. But she had shot a man on a mission a few months before, and she was willing to do it again if she had to.

Evelyn expertly brought the boat into the side and the boy leapt out, tying off the rope around a stub of wood jutting out.

The boy extended a hand to pull her onto the side and Evelyn took it. She had to trust him.

He pulled his bag onto his shoulder and waited as she rearranged hers on her back. Then he looked in the direction of a street, snaking out of view away from the canal and Evelyn nodded a quiet confirmation.

They traipsed in silence. This was out of the centre of town, where German names had disappeared and a quiet Belgian resistance seemed to exist. There were only houses, no cafés or bars, but every so often Evelyn spotted a French place name, a reminder of Ghent's previous life.

At another corner Evelyn recognised where she was, just a few were minutes away from the field where she'd left the plane – left as inconspicuously as a Bristol F.2 two-seater could be. As she stepped forwards the boy grabbed her arm.

Something had spooked him and he pulled her into a doorway. She frowned, but didn't speak.

In the near distance they could hear men's voices talking in quick German.

They were coming closer.

***

She could smell the boy's sweat. Hear his shallow breaths. Straining her ears to listen for the German soldiers Evelyn willed herself to disappear.

Suddenly the door behind them opened and a tiny old woman, bent over with age, pulled them into her home, firmly but quietly closing the door. Inside was dark and the scent of fried bacon filled the air.

The old lady turned to them both and beamed, beckoning them with a crooked finger to follow her.

Evelyn looked at the boy who shrugged and turned to follow the woman. But they froze as the voices of the German soldiers stopped outside the sitting-room window, where the trio stood just out of sight.

The old woman pressed her finger to her lips and they all stayed stock still. Evelyn counted the seconds on the clock on the mantelpiece, unable to follow the quick German phrases. It was the longest minute and a half she'd ever experienced. No driving attempt could compare.

Finally the men walked off, their boots scraping along the street, disappearing to a faint trace. The old woman was the first to stir, crooking her finger at them once more to follow her to the kitchen. Evelyn's stomach grumbled as she watched the woman placing fat rashers of bacon in a pan.

It had been a long time since she'd enjoyed bacon. Even though she had deals with her local butchers, things were highly rationed in Britain. She had assumed it was the case abroad, and, seeing the boy licking his lips she got the impression this was a rarity for him too.

They both sat at a tiny wooden table by a window that looked out onto a beautiful and neatly kept garden. Evelyn was enchanted by the roses still blooming in the autumnal light, and watched as insects flew from flower to flower. The old lady placed a doorstep of a sandwich in front of each of them and gestured to eat, something they didn't need repeating.

'You stay here today,' the lady croaked in thick French. Her rural accent was strong and Evelyn tried hard to follow. 'Tonight you...' She mimicked flying and Evelyn nodded, then frowned.

'How did you...?'

'When you get to my age you don't need much sleep anymore – it's as though you need to soak up what's left of life. I spend my nights looking out at the stars. I can here.' The woman pointed at her spot in the kitchen where a shabbily worn armchair had pride of place. 'Last night, I saw something moving in the night sky. Then you arrived – I've never known a plane land so quietly,' she added.

'I cut the engine and glided in,' she explained.

The old woman's face broke into a mix of surprise and delight. 'I thought maybe the person who arrived under the cover of darkness didn't want to be found. So when I saw two strangers walk past my window this morning I decided to take a risk and meet this incredible pilot. But, I must admit, I thought it would be you.' She looked at the boy, who had continued to stay mute. 'A woman pilot. You're very brave.'

Evelyn shook her head. 'I think maybe I'm stupid. I'm trying to work out how I got myself into this.' She drained the coffee the old woman had given her. The drink was thick and black and bitter as hell. 'You've been very kind to give us sanctuary.'

'Tsk, I would give anyone sanctuary who was sticking a finger up at those,' she searched for the right word, 'bastards,' she settled on.

'We're trying.'

They spent the rest of the day alternating between resting, eating, and making conversation with the woman. The boy seemed exhausted and slept for the majority of the day. Evelyn had a short rest, but her adrenaline was running and she knew she wouldn't be able to sleep deeply until she returned from her mission.

She did, however, accept the lunch the woman gave her and enjoyed the conversation. She got the impression the old lady didn't have much company, and if the bargain for safety and food for a day was companionship, Evelyn was happy to acquiesce.

Once light fell, a tension entered the room as the boy and Evelyn readied themselves to leave. They'd kept an ear out all day for German soldiers and had heard nothing since they were rescued earlier in the day.

Whilst she wanted to leave under the cloak of darkness Evelyn needed to arrive in Britain in the dead of night too. She couldn't give away to any spy planes the location of the airbase and though it took just a few hours to fly from Belgium to England, she had to use a circuitous route to ensure she kept anyone off her tail.

They agreed to leave at midnight. The old lady, despite her claims she could stay awake, had nodded off at around ten, so it was with a heavy heart that Evelyn had to lightly shake her to let her know they were leaving. She squeezed Evelyn's hand and pointed towards the back door. They'd agreed the quieter they were the better, so both the boy and Evelyn left through the kitchen door, having said their many thanks to their saviour earlier in the day.

As she brushed past the roses their scent caught in the clear night air and Evelyn inhaled. When she returned home she would fill her apartment with roses. When the war was over, she corrected herself. She never wanted to forget the beauty of this evening.

The boy opened the wooden gate that opened straight out onto the field and stopped. Evelyn held back, straining to hear if there was anything untoward. The boy seemed happy and moved forwards.

Evelyn followed, the two walking quickly towards the thick cluster of trees that hid her plane. The wind rustled the long grasses and Evelyn felt a crawl of fear over her back. She looked behind and saw nothing in the deep black of the night.

Keeping the boy at her side, they both instinctively ran towards the trees. Relieved to find the plane seemingly intact, Evelyn climbed up into the pilot's side. She watched as the boy ran round the other side and, knowing there was no time to waste, pressed the starter motor.

THE FASTEST GIRL ON EARTH

The sound rattled out across the quiet of the field and Evelyn pressed the control buttons to start the propellers.

Suddenly, there was a sound of gunfire from the right. Evelyn saw a flash of light and looked to see the boy climbing up.

'Hurry,' she yelled. She had no idea who this boy was, but she wasn't going to let him be captured. She pulled him in behind her and he slammed the door shut.

Another gunshot rang out and Evelyn manoeuvred the plane, steering it out of sight of the barn so she could use the field as a short, but just about manageable runway. A gun fired again, nearer this time.

Evelyn yelled at the boy to hold the steering column and he did as he was told, leaning over from his place behind. Grabbing her gun, Evelyn cocked it and hung out of the side of the plane so that she could feel the door pushing deeply into her ribs. She looked in the direction of the gunfire and steadied her aim. It was so dark it was almost hopeless, but she had to do something.

'Straight,' she yelled at the boy who was trying to steer the plane.

A bullet whizzed past, the sound of damaged metal shocking Evelyn into action. She aimed in the direction of the shooter and fired twice.

Aside from the noise from the blades of the propeller there was nothing else. With no more shots coming and the pitch black surrounding her, she could only hope she'd caught the shooter.

Ignoring the feel of nausea in her throat, Evelyn gunned the plane and pushed it hard. She knew the houses at the end of the field were going to make this ascent particularly difficult.

Casting a quick look at the boy who was holding very tightly onto his seat, she pushed the throttle.

Her heart was thumping, but her mind was as clear as the first time she flew. She took in a deep, calming breath.

'Now or never.'

Chapter Thirty-Eight

LONDON

'They knew I was coming,' she said angrily to Fergie as soon as he sat down on a bench in Hyde Park a little distance from her. 'They seemed to know far more about my mission than I did,' she added, finally being able to speak her mind, the thoughts that had kept her awake the previous night, many hours after touching down safely on the airstrip in Surrey.

'Had you told anyone where you were going?' he asked, his face obscured by a paper, the words reaching her around a copy of *The Telegraph*.

Evelyn almost spat. 'Had I told anyone? I'd barely had time to digest the pickup coordinates and get to the airfield myself, let alone call all and sundry to let them know.'

'What about Benjamin?'

This time, when she spoke, spittle flew from her mouth in rage. 'Firstly, Benjamin is not a double agent; he wouldn't put my life in jeopardy. Secondly, he's out of the country; and I suspect you've got a much better idea where he is than I do, and thirdly...' She counted the third point on her finger but slumped as though the wind had been knocked out of her.

'Thirdly?'

'Thirdly, even if he was in the country it's unlikely I'd tell him, bearing in mind we've not seen each for the past six months – as you well know,' she said through gritted teeth, whilst trying to focus on the book held uselessly in her gloved hands. They had to keep up a pretence she wasn't involved with the government, for fear of blowing her and Benjamin's cover, but she wasn't sure who this level of deception was for. Certainly the Germans wouldn't have given a fig who she was.

'Not Benjamin then,' came the helpful voice.

Evelyn shook her head irritably. 'Enough of this now, Fergie. Aside from the fact if I hadn't been armed we may not have made it out of there yesterday, I found myself picking up a person, a young man, not a package as I'd been led to believe.' She blew out the breath she was holding. 'The whole thing left me in the bloody dark, and I wouldn't have minded any of it – not a bit – if I'd been briefed properly, not treated like some sort of puppet that can be tossed around whenever you feel like it.'

The trees shivered, loosening their leaves as chilly afternoon air blew in, yet a few children played with hoops and sticks nearby. It warmed Evelyn to see some aspects of life was still going on, in spite of the war.

'We don't think you're a puppet, Evelyn.' Fergie put his newspaper down and looked directly at her. She noticed how tired he looked. His dark navy suit was still impeccable, without a speck of dirt. 'We think you're an incredibly accomplished woman we are proud to have on our side.'

'But—' She stopped as he held a hand up.

'No, my turn. An accomplished woman, who is, as yet, unrecognised by the government. A woman who got herself into trouble yesterday, and not just that, almost lost a civilian in the process. A woman,' Fergie looked at her, his eyes boring into hers, 'who takes too many risks, when she should wait for help. It wasn't your place to bring that boy home. There had been a mistake, clearly, and you should have said no when he was presented to you, insisting on the package instead. Not some boy who is of no interest to us.'

'Of no interest?' She was incredulous. She'd risked her life for nothing.

'None. The owner of the hotel has admitted he wanted to get his son to safety, and he took a chance on the next runner. He wanted his son to gain refuge here in Britain. Apparently he has a sister who lives in Birmingham, the boy is going to live with her.'

Evelyn digested this information slowly. 'And the package...?'

'Was meant to be a list of codes, a way to break into some of the German's plans. But you left them there.' He looked at her keenly, all trace of the pretence to know know each other disappearing as the anger – or frustration – he had at her, was vented.

'No, I asked and was told there was nothing.'

'Did you? Did you ask?' Fergie had gone back behind his paper.

'I...' Evelyn stuttered.

'Because I think you just did what most women do when they're spoken to by a man in charge.' He stood up, rustling his paper back into a tidily folded rectangle and tucking it under his arm. 'As they're told.'

He tipped his hat in her direction. 'Goodbye Evelyn. I'll be in touch if I need you.'

He walked away, leaving her with a mouth wide open in shock. She'd done all of it – risked her life, shot the soldier, flew at night. All of it, for no one.

For nothing.

1918

Chapter Thirty-Nine

LONDON

As the months changed to a year, with no sign of Benjamin, and no call up from the British Government, Evelyn remained in London as the war raged on and threw herself into helping anyone and everyone.

She drove ambulances through blown out streets, discovered a knack for locating items on the black market for people in need and generally made herself useful.

At the base of it though she was lonely. Her heart felt tight from waking to when she fell asleep numb with tiredness after every day. She knew she couldn't continue living in this state.

With so little for him to do, she'd had to let Solomon go, encouraging him to return to his family. Gradually Evelyn had taken to using just the bedroom in her now cavernous flat. Retreating there. She didn't enjoy the echoing silence that met her every time she returned, missing Benjamin, her friends, and her long since passed dog Dodo.

In the beginning, Benjamin's disappearance hadn't been that unusual. He'd been sent on various missions after their marriage. But since the onset of the war his stretches away from home had increasingly grown, so that he was away more than he was with her. She'd become used to her own company, but gradually, when it had been a year since she'd last seen him, she suspected he'd returned to the country, though not to her.

THE FASTEST GIRL ON EARTH

Certain items of his have, I'm sure, been removed from the apartment, she wrote to Isabelle at her friend's address in France, concerned she was losing her mind.

Not altogether. And not all at once, which is why I didn't notice it to begin with. But now I realise that his favourite jacket is no longer in the cupboard. The silver-framed photograph of his mother is gone. The question is, did he take all these items the day he bade goodbye to me all those months ago? I can't remember. Did he know he was going for a long time? Did he plan it? Or did he go away and whilst – wherever – he decided he'd had enough of me? And has he taken his items by stealth when I was out? But if the latter, why not just speak to me? I'm an understanding woman. Neither option gives me much comfort. I thought all was well between us. How foolish of me.

With nothing to keep her in London, and the bombing raids increasing, Evelyn decided after multiple requests, to move to her mother's home in the new year.

She was fed up of waiting. Waiting for Benjamin to appear from wherever he'd been. Waiting for Fergie to give her an opportunity to work on behalf of the Secret Service, because in spite of her years of unparalleled success for the department he had chosen to punish her with silence. She should have been commended. Not chastised.

Once she'd decided to leave London it hadn't taken much organising to pack up what she needed to bring to her mother's, aware she may be leaving her flat for the last time.

In mid-January, on a cold and blowy winter's day that made London look even greyer than usual, Evelyn made her way to Waterloo Station, noting the welcome buffet for soldiers who were returning home. Whilst she wished to drive to her mother's, the cost and scarcity of petrol meant she couldn't. Instead, she'd had to park the Napier in a garage some distance from her flat, locked away until such a time when she'd be able to return to it. To her life. Or whatever was left of it.

On the train she sat opposite a soldier who slept the entire three-hour journey. Evelyn went from ignoring him, assuming he'd need space, to studying the boy as he sat, arms crossed, a hat pulled down over his eyes. He could have been mid-twenties, but he looked a hundred. His hands, she noticed, had bright-blue veins which swam through to his bony wrists. He appeared to need at least a month of fulsome hot dinners. With heavy desserts, topped with custard. Though the chance would be a fine thing, with the sugar rationing in full force. Any desserts would need to be made frugally.

'Hardly worth it,' she mumbled to herself, accidentally waking the poor soldier for a moment. He opened his eyes wide, the stark blue frightening her with the terror they held, before he rearranged his hat and leaned a little closer to the window for comfort. Evelyn was impressed with the speed he fell back asleep, but realised he was likely making up for months of deprivation.

When they arrived at Winchester station, no sooner had the conductor blown his whistle on the platform than the boy, blinking himself awake, slapped his own face – a move which took Evelyn by surprise – before rearranging his uniform, pulling his hat to the correct angle and standing stiffly. He looked every bit the captain despite his years and she saw how the war had made men out of these boys.

She followed him as they both disembarked and she watched as he strode with impeccable precision along the platform, before he was leapt upon by a young girl – no older than ten – who threw herself into his arms and kissed him on either side of his face. The way he responded, by dangling her by the legs and swooping her back up again, before rubbing her head in an affectionate manner gave Evelyn cause to assume it was his little sister. An assumption made certain when a woman in her late forties and a little life-worn embraced him in a tight hug.

'Evelyn.' Her mother had appeared by her side, and held her closely.

'Mother, I wasn't expecting you to meet me.' Evelyn was shocked, expecting to see the driver. Her mother had never done it herself for as long as she could recall.

'Just act pleased to see me,' Evelyn's mother whispered into her ear. Taking the lack of reply as a response in itself, her mother continued. 'I have been asked to put you back on the train and send you back to London,' she said rapidly, holding her hands.

'Why?'

'You're needed. Abroad.' Her mother's lips trembled as she spoke. 'I didn't know you worked abroad.' She looked deeply into Evelyn's eyes. 'I thought you drove for the Royal Flying Corps?'

She hadn't enjoyed lying to her mother, but had felt it was better she knew little of her escapades.

'I do, I did,' she replied. In fact, she'd flown for them – once – but for the most part, there was nothing on Evelyn Bloom in any records. As far as anyone was concerned she'd never flown for her country. Let alone killed for it.

The platform had gone quiet, and Evelyn's mother leant in again, the hint of her Chanel perfume mingling with leftover steam from the train that had departed. 'Someone sent a telegram to my house, I don't know how they knew where you'd be, but the haste is clear.' She withdrew the telegram from her overcoat pocket and showed it to Evelyn.

Briefly looking around before she read it, Evelyn cast a quick glance over the short message.

`Sticky situation. STOP. Holiday needed in Paris. STOP. Musée opens at 10am Friday. STOP. Bring clothes. STOP. F.`

F stood for Fergie. Evelyn wracked her brains as to why he'd need her in Paris. Sticky referred to Benjamin, it had been his idea as his name contained the word jam. So Benjamin needed her, in Paris. And she was to meet him at the museum. But clothes. She knew the whole message was coded. Clothes wouldn't mean clothing. She'd need to consider it.

'Your train is in forty minutes, we could have a cup of tea?' Her mother nudged her elbow a little. 'It'll be good to catch up and stay warm.'

Evelyn nodded. Whilst they sat in the steamed-up café, sipping on weak tea and sharing the only slice of rock cake left in the building, she listened to her mother who was so happy to see her.

'I've opened the house to the medics of course,' her mother continued, topping up her cup, 'doing my bit as they say. You wouldn't recognise the gardens. They're all dug up – vegetables everywhere. But you know my opinion on fresh vegetables, a carrot solves everything, so that's what we're doing. Feeding the boys.'

Evelyn gulped a little more of the tea and checked the time on the clock behind the counter. Ten minutes and she'd be back on the train. Evelyn interrupted her before she continued with her tales of housekeeping injured men. 'Mother. You know I love you very much, don't you?'

'Of course, my darling, and I love you very much too – such a pity we can't spend time together, but I'm ever so busy too. So I suppose we wouldn't have seen each other all that much. After the war, when it all goes back to normal, you and I will be able to enjoy teas in the drawing room and delicious, sugary cakes.' She smiled.

Evelyn held her mother's hand and smiled back as she listened, trying to drink in every memory she had of this moment. Aware she may not return from France.

Whilst her mother talked, Evelyn realised what "bring clothes" meant. "Come armed".

Chapter Forty

Paris

Turning up her collar against the frigid air, Evelyn pulled the thick woollen coat tighter and thanked her foresight for putting the sheep-fleece-lined gloves in her backpack. They were two sizes too big, but she'd poked small pieces of newspaper into the ends which only added to the warmth, though if she wanted to work the Colt which was currently tucked into the waistband of her trousers, she was going to have to take her gloves off. She just hoped, fervently, that it wouldn't be the case. She wasn't certain she could shoot at point-blank range, even if her own life depended on it.

Or Benjamin's.

Casting a look to the left and right, Evelyn felt conspicuous even though no one was paying her any attention. She pulled the cap down a little further over her head, to serve the dual purpose of keeping her warm and preventing her from being identified. One of the things she did know, since Mata Hari was executed for being a spy last year, no one took pity on a female intelligence officer. Worse still, having the wool pulled over their eyes by a woman seemed to result in a harsher sentence than that of their male peers.

Her focus was on Benjamin though. She had to believe he was would be here. She'd followed the meagre instructions from Fergie and was standing by the Eiffel Tower. Checking her wristwatch she saw it had turned one minute past ten. He was late.

She'd rushed back to her Mayfair flat from the station and as quickly and efficiently as possible had packed her rucksack with the basic essentials and changed into more appropriate flight gear. She was unsurprised when she walked out, just an hour or so later and found a car with a driver who nodded at her and opened the door. He had took her straight to the airfield in Surrey and she boarded the two-seater that was fuelled and waiting for her, with just two disinterested staff in grubby green overalls waiting to kick the bricks away. By this point the winter night had closed in tightly and she took off in the pitch black.

Evelyn landed in a field outside of Paris a few hours later, leaving it in plain sight. She knew she wouldn't return to it, she just hoped it wouldn't be destroyed.

In a bittersweet replay of their honeymoon, she had travelled into Paris on the train, changing to the Métro as she closed in on the outer arrondissements, the streets that curved themselves like a snail into the centre of the city. She spent a few weary hours trudging across the city until early morning when she had found an open lodging house for very few francs in the Montmartre area, where she collapsed, exhausted and slept for a couple of hours.

And here she was. Fuelled by half a dry croissant and a weak espresso made by the landlady of the lodgings, she was propped up against a metal support that eventually grew into a leg of the Eiffel Tower.

Looking for her husband.

The musée. It had made her smile to read that. Benjamin and she had always referred to the tower as the Amusements, in a nod to Blackpool's tower, so she had guessed "musée" referred to the "amusement". But now, looking at her watch again, and noting it was five past the hour, she wavered in her assuredness of how she cracked the code.

She decided to give it five more minutes and considered the view from the base of the tower. The last time she'd been here Benjamin had made her swoon, dipping her in a deep embrace as they stared out at the layout of the city below them, looking in every way like a real-life map.

Unaware she was doing it, Evelyn brushed her hand across her cheek, as Benjamin would.

'That's my move,' came a brusque voice beside her.

THE FASTEST GIRL ON EARTH

Evelyn turned to her left and appraised the handsome man stood a foot away from her. Forgetting everything, forgetting protocol, forgetting the distance they'd had for months, forgetting the journey, the terrible coffee and the lack of sleep, Evelyn threw her bag to the ground and ran into his arms.

Benjamin held her and kissed her deeply. His moustache, a new addition since she'd last seen him, tickled her face, though not in an unpleasant way. She pulled back.

'What is it? Am I a terrible kisser now? It has been a while.'

'No. I just wanted to check it was really you,' she held him at arm's length, 'you've lost weight and you've gained a moustache.' She let him pull her back in.

'I've lost weight? You look like a rake, you didn't have much meat on you before.'

She laughed, it had been a long time since the heaviness in her heart that had settled around the rest of her body had lifted. 'Before we do anything like that, I need to know where you've been.'

He looked across to the view of the Seine making its way through the city, a dark-grey snake pushing its way past the cream buildings. 'You know I can't tell you that.'

'But why the telegram? Why haven't you been home? Have you been sending for clothes?'

Benjamin turned to her and grabbed both her hands, looking over her shoulder in a way that made her nervous. 'Soon, I promise, but I can't. Not today. I didn't want you over here... but the Service, they insisted.'

Evelyn looked at him. 'What's going on? What aren't you telling me?'

'Nothing.'

'You're not telling me something, I know that look, Ben. Something's going on, and it's not a lover's reunion, is it? Otherwise there'd have been no reason why I needed to come so quickly. Or armed.' She had whispered the last few words as two women cycled past.

Benjamin's shoulders sank. He looked quickly around him, then guided her to a bench a few feet away. As Evelyn sat down she felt a moment of relief, the exhaustion was seeping into her bones, and sitting down lifted it a little. She recognised the same response on Benjamin's face and she smiled in recognition of the man she'd pledged to be with for the rest of her life. Then scowled.

'Why haven't you come home? I've heard nothing for months – Fergie wouldn't tell me a jot.' She paused and looked up at the dark metal of the tower looming above them. 'You could have at least sent a letter, to let me know you were well. Alive. I've been desperately worried, I thought I might be a widow.'

Benjamin took her hands in his and stared keenly in her eyes. She noticed the lines around his were far more pronounced than before, the last time they'd been together.

'All I can say is, I'm sorry, Evelyn. I truly am. But it was all for the best – I assure you.'

'Best for whom?' She broke eye contact and resumed looking at the intricacies of the tower. She preferred Blackpool's, she decided. The circus underneath was a lot more fun. Paris took itself too seriously.

'Best for us. Best for Britain,' Benjamin exhaled.

'Ah, that old thing.'

'Evelyn, you need to do something. And I'm sorry to have to ask, but I'm going to need you to go out to dinner tonight.'

He stopped. Cleared his throat. Looked at the sky as though that would get him out of the predicament he was in, then back at her again. 'You need to go out, and accidentally bump into one of our own, a chap called John, we need you to...' He pressed his hands together, willing himself to continue. 'To become a companion to him. We believe he's a double agent and is sending information on our plans to the Germans. We need you to find out if that is true. It might take some time of course, but hopefully you can build up a... rapport... with him.'

Evelyn turned to face him during his stuttering speech. 'Pardon?'

Benjamin shook his head. 'Don't make me say it again, it's terrible enough just knowing what I'm asking of you.'

'But... me... why?'

'Because, you're you, Evelyn, you can be anything. You're brilliant. And beautiful and witty and, really rather extraordinary.'

'And if I am as brilliant as you suggest, why is it then that my husband,' she punctuated the word by slapping her own thigh in anger, 'is sending me to another man? To what? To become his whore?'

Benjamin was stricken. 'No, that's not it at all.'

Evelyn was tingling with anger; the frustration of not knowing where Benjamin had been this whole time was hurting her more than she cared to admit, and now they were reunited he was pushing her further away.

'Really? Because I can't think of any other way of describing it.' She looked at the stunning view of Paris and hated every aspect of it, choosing to hang her head and cover her face with her hands. 'I don't know why I'm here. I shouldn't have come.'

There was a silence. There was still the background hum of vehicles moving and somewhere nearby a baby cried. Reminders that other people's lives were continuing – but no words were spoken.

'I'll do it,' Evelyn said eventually.

Benjamin exhaled briefly for moment, as though he'd wanted her to say something else, before speaking. 'Thank you.'

'Wait, let me finish.' She locked eyes with Benjamin and for the first moment in a very long time, truly felt she was herself again. 'I will do whatever is being asked of me, for Britain. But, let me be very clear here, this,' she indicated the two of them with a brief wave of her hand, 'whatever we are. Whatever we've been. This is over.'

'Evie.'

She held her hand up, she'd had enough of his voice. 'No, Benjamin. You have absolutely no idea what the last year has been like for me. I only rushed over here because I thought you were in danger; that you needed me. But I realise now it was just a ruse. A way of using me. Just tell me one thing.' She paused and he looked up, a broken man.

'Anything.'

'Did you ever love me? Or was this all a way of recruiting me. Using me?'

She allowed him to grab her hand and kiss it, noting the sadness in his eyes as he spoke to her. 'I have loved you for a very long time, Evelyn. I loved you when you were here, in this city, as a green young thing with not a clue about the world. I loved you even when you went off with that rat, Victor, and I've loved you every day since we married.'

She shook her head and removed her hand from his. Then stood, dusting down her coat.

'Words, Benjamin. Just words. You use them to weave stories. You've spent so long living multiple lives you don't know what's true anymore.' Her breath misted in front of her. 'I think I do now.'

Evelyn took a couple of steps towards the grandeur and romance of the Eiffel Tower. She wanted to burn it to the ground.

'I'm at the Hotel Davenport. I'll await further instructions and an excellent evening dress. Goodbye Benjamin.'

Chapter Forty-One

Paris

If she had known what was to come would she have done anything differently?

Evelyn tried to imagine any other outcome than her leaving him that way, but the sound of bombs overhead blocked any thoughts. She told Benjamin it was the last time she'd talk to him, but that was when she could still change her mind.

Tonight, though, she feared that option had been taken away.

Some time, not long after nine o'clock, when she began her appetisers with John, a bland man who clearly only had eyes for his own sex, they'd only got as far as one drink and a bite of fish, when Evelyn recognised a foreboding sound.

Gotha bombers.

The Germans were bombing the city seemed they were aiming to obliterate it completely.

It had taken Evelyn's date no time at all to clear out of the restaurant, leaving her with the bill to pay, refuge to seek and nothing to report back to London. Unless she counted his sexual proclivities, which could have explained some of his subterfuge to the British government.

Instead of the night of wooing and sharing secrets, Evelyn found herself stranded in the middle of a city facing a terrifying bombardment. The restaurant manager ushered those who hadn't fled into the streets into his cellar, and it was there that Evelyn was sat on an upturned crate that once used to contain potatoes, listening to what sounded like the end of the world.

It felt as though every minute they were sat there they would hear another bomb, the aftermath of which would be felt through the walls of the cellar. Evelyn knew being underground was a wise idea, but she still couldn't shake the feeling she was a sitting duck.

She coughed as dust that had accumulated over many years left undisturbed in rafters was shook over the twenty or so diners who had sought refuge in the cellar every time there was a quake overhead.

Evelyn watched as a crack in the red-stone wall traced a journey further along, behind shelves which contained all manner of canned goods. She had to give this restaurant credit, they'd been able to maintain standards even with the rationing. The manager caught her looking and came to sit next to her. He was a short man, with a terrific moustache quite at odds with the size of his face.

'You're wondering how we have so much? When others have so little?'

'I suppose, yes.'

'I have friends, let's say, in very high places.' Evelyn enjoyed the way the man spoke, his French unhurried and easier to understand. 'They make sure we're stocked, so they can be well looked after when they come to me.'

'I see.'

Evelyn shivered a little. Her evening gown that had been dropped off for her was no more than a slip of silk the colour of moonlight, and she'd left her fur wrap back in the restaurant. The air was damp in the basement and she was beginning to curse her lack of foresight.

'Have this.' The manager shrugged off his topcoat.

'No, I couldn't.'

'No, I insist. We cannot have a lady freezing down here. If we survive the bombs, I'm not letting the cold kill you.' She took the coat gratefully.

'Thank you, you're very kind,' she said, looking in the direction of the others huddled in groups in the basement. 'You're kind to accept us all in here.'

THE FASTEST GIRL ON EARTH

'Well of course,' the manager, who introduced himself as Pierre, said. 'It's my restaurant, it's my duty to look after you all.' He leapt up and frantically searched the shelves. Just as Evelyn wondered what he was doing, there was a sickening sound as a bomb exploded very close by.

Many of the inhabitants in the basement shouted exclamations, and the women screamed in fear. But whilst more dust fell on them and the very skeleton of the basement seemed to have been disturbed, no bricks fell. No walls collapsed. They were safe. For now.

Evelyn clutched the coat around her, the shock which had been present started to dissipate a little, but she was shaking all over. A mixture of cold and fear, perhaps, but she couldn't control it.

'Here, take a sip.' Pierre, who had made his way along all of his guests, bending over each small huddle and offering them items from his shelves, handed her a bottle of brandy.

'For the nerves. And the cold. It'll warm you up from the inside.'

'*Merci*.' Evelyn accepted the bottle and took a small sip. He was right, the spirit instantly warmed her body, bringing it back to life.

He shook his head as she tried to give the bottle back. 'A little more I think.'

Evelyn took a deep swig and allowed the heat to roar in her belly. It felt like a fire had been lit down the back of her throat.

'Much better.' Pierre took the bottle from her and then produced a hessian sack. 'It's not quite the same as your beautiful gown, but it might keep you a little warmer, no?'

Gratefully accepting the sack, Evelyn placed it over her legs, aware of the goose bumps covering her.

'Thank you again, you've been wonderful.'

'Well, *madame*, I couldn't help but notice you were on your own and I wanted to make sure you were looked after.' He paused for a moment as they heard another bomb explode, further away this time. 'I hope your young man is safe, I noticed he disappeared quickly.'

Evelyn was grateful for the gloom that hid the face she pulled. 'He wasn't my young man.'

Pierre held his hands up. 'I am so sorry, *madame*, I had thought you were out with your husband.' He directed a look at her hand where her gold band was still on her wedding finger. She covered it with her other hand.

'He wasn't my young man,' she repeated, hoping to close down any further conversation.

'I'm relieved,' the manager said, leaning in as though to impart a confidence. 'He has come to the restaurant a great many times and I never liked him. Never leaves a tip,' he explained, making Evelyn laugh.

'You shouldn't laugh. I judge all men by the size of their tip,' he said very seriously.

'As do I.' Evelyn grinned at the double entendre, the brandy giving her a little of her old self back. Pierre laughed too.

'You're a funny one. So, can I ask, where is...?' He looked at her ring to ask the question. 'Or do we not want to discuss?'

Evelyn sighed, and reached for the brandy. After another emboldening sip, she spoke. 'I am married, but we have been separate for a long time. I don't know if we'll ever divorce because, well...' She shrugged at the impossible nature of the task. 'But I don't think we'll see each other again. He asked too much of me, Pierre.'

The manager nodded, understanding. 'Sometimes life has a way of surprising us, *madame*. I think this war, if it hasn't taught us anything else, should teach us that. Maybe he asked just the right amount from you, but you weren't ready to listen?'

Before she could reply, Pierre's attention was taken by someone calling for him from the other end of the basement.

'Duty calls, *madame*,' he squeezed her hand, 'we will persevere, *oui*?'

'*Oui, merci*, Pierre.'

For the next few hours Evelyn sat in the semi-darkness, her ears picking up every explosion and her mind filling in the gaps of what was outside. She imagined buildings blowing out and people dying. She'd seen enough aftermath in London to know what a bombardment such as this could look like.

But at the centre of it, all she could think about was Benjamin. Was he safe? Did he know she still loved him? Her heart ached that the last thing they had done was argue.

He may have gone to his death not knowing how loved he really was.

Evelyn vowed that the next morning, when the bombing had stopped, she would make enquiries and find her husband.

They would start again.

***

The next day as Evelyn emerged onto the street, nothing of what she'd imagined had come close to what faced her.

It was as though the whole city was enveloped in a cloudy fog. Everywhere she looked Evelyn could only see a few feet in front of her. The fog was a mass of particles in the air that came from obliterated buildings, dust, mixed with debris and other lightweight detritus, swirling together to form a blanket which blocked out the weak January sunshine.

Pierre's restaurant had escaped the worst of it, but when the diners emerged, blinking into what light there was, the full impact of the damage revealed itself as they picked their way through streets of rubble.

News trickled through that overnight four squadrons of seven German Gotha bombers had appeared over the city and suburbs to drop two hundred bombs.

It felt to Evelyn as though no street had escaped the Germans' attentions and she found it hard to hold back the tears that threatened to overcome her as she walked slowly through the city she had once known and loved, hoping that her hotel was still standing. She had little else with her, and cursed herself for neglecting to bring her trusty backpack.

Though the backpack would have looked a touch incongruous if she had taken it, hence the tiny silver pouch that dangled uselessly from her hand. She caught sight of her reflection in a shop window that was unscathed. Her once beautiful silvery dress was filthy from a night sitting in a basement, and her feet, out of their stylish heels, bled as she stumbled barefoot over rubble. With no choice other than to keep moving forwards in the hope she'd get to her hotel, she continued to place one foot in front of another, refusing to acknowledge her pain.

She knew people had died. Families had lost loved ones and many other Parisians were injured. She did not have the right to feel discomfort over some sore feet. Evelyn shook her head and carried on. She would not allow herself a moment to dwell on any sort of emotion, least of all grief or sorrow, until she'd established where Benjamin was. And if he was safe.

That morning, whilst the walk would have usually taken forty minutes or so to cross various arrondissements, the combination of the freezing January temperatures, her bare feet and the constant disruption of blown-out buildings and the clean-up operation, meant it took Evelyn closer to three hours before she arrived at the street where her hotel was. She felt gloomy and exhausted, thirsty, hungry and tired and didn't hold out much hope for the hotel to still be standing, as she rounded streets to find block after block had sustained damage.

As she turned the corner, Evelyn realised she was holding her breath, willing the hotel to be there.

Miraculously it was. Evelyn sent a prayer up to a god she rarely acknowledged, and moved quicker towards the entrance, all thoughts of cold leaving her.

'*Madame*, you're here,' the woman behind the desk – Evelyn thought her name was Imelda – rushed around the side and embraced her. 'I didn't like to think. I kept your room. I've kept everyone's rooms, for now, but only half of you are back,' she whispered into Evelyn's hair. 'I can't bear to think of where my others are.'

The exhaustion and relief collided and suddenly Evelyn found herself on the floor, with the ceiling spinning above her.

'*Madame*, you need food I think. And some water?' Imelda disappeared for a moment, before reappearing by Evelyn's side. 'Here, lean on me.' The woman, who seemed a similar age to her mother, pulled Evelyn up a little from where she had slumped and had her rest against her shoulder. She handed Evelyn a teacup with water and guided it to her mouth. She watched as Evelyn sipped, then gulped the water down.

'Good, now this.' She offered her a wedge of dark rye bread, with a scrape of butter. 'I'm sorry there's nothing else, there haven't been any deliveries today, as you can imagine.'

'It's good, *merci*.' Evelyn fell gratefully on the bread, demolishing the day-old, tough rye as though it was a soft buttery croissant. After she finished, she closed her eyes briefly.

'I think you need to sleep, *madame*. Let's get you upstairs.' Imelda slipped herself under Evelyn's shoulder and helped her up. 'Oh, you're freezing; I'll try and find another blanket,' she offered, whilst guiding Evelyn towards the dark staircase.

'No, I must go. I need to find my husband.' Evelyn's exhaustion was making her thoughts fuzzy, but she knew she had to find Benjamin. Imelda looked at her and shook her head.

'But why wasn't he staying here? I haven't checked him in.' She looked confused.

'I came a day earlier, he was due to meet me,' she lied to the receptionist. There was no way of explaining her situation, especially with the truth.

'I see. But still. Your man knows where your hotel is – do you know where his is?'

Evelyn shook her head.

'I see.' Imelda didn't press any further. 'In that case I think you're in the right place. You should sleep, get yourself a bath, though I think we only have cold water. He knows where you're staying, so why not wait for him to come to you?'

Tiredness was seeping into Evelyn's bones and she nodded more to halt the conversation than to agree with Imelda's plan. She allowed the older woman to open her hotel-room door and guide her onto the bed.

Seconds later she was fast asleep.

Chapter Forty-Two

PARIS

Rough hands grabbed at her shoulders, waking her up.

Evelyn flung her arms out to protect herself, throwing punches blindly and yelling, only for something cotton-like to be shoved into her mouth, preventing her from making a sound further than a whimper.

'Where is he?' A man's voice spoke in quick French, pinning her to the bed with his weight, but it was all Evelyn could do to shake her head in terror, *I don't know*, she communicated wildly with her eyes. *He hasn't returned to me.*

She was wrenched upwards into a sitting position, her arms fastened in front of her at her wrists, vaguely aware she was still only in her light evening gown. A soiled, bloodied, ripped, evening gown. And that was all she had to protect herself from the man who was working quickly to tie her ankles together with rope, looping the excess through the bindings at her wrists so she wouldn't be able to walk, or work her hands free to remove the gag.

He pulled her close to him. His face was covered by a balaclava and he was wearing army fatigues. She wondered briefly if she could knock the gun he was holding from his hands and use it on him.

But could she use it? It wasn't something which came naturally to her. Killing. But if her life was on the line...

If.

THE FASTEST GIRL ON EARTH

It felt certain she was going to die. The man pulled her from the bedroom, the only place she'd found peace in the last twenty-four hours, and dragged her along the landing, her bare back flayed as she was pulled along the wooden floor. There was no respite as he dragged her down the stairs by the ankles, her head thumping with a crack on each step. Twice her head hit a step so hard she felt as though her skull was being split. She focused on the ceiling above, praying she wouldn't pass out from the pain and hoping Imelda, the receptionist, would see her and come to her aid. But as they reached the bottom step and the man used her wrist bindings to pull her upwards so she was stood, stooped over, she spotted the receptionist at her desk. If she'd thought Imelda was on her side, one look at the self-satisfied smirk on the receptionist's face immediately brought her to her senses. She'd been played.

'*Merci, mademoiselle.*' Her kidnapper nodded in Imelda's before brusquely picking Evelyn up and tossing her over his shoulder, then hastily shoved his way out of the hotel's door.

Immediately, gusts of cold January air wrapped around her, causing her to shiver, but she mustered every ounce of herself to not show any weakness. Biting down on the cotton wad still in her mouth, Evelyn ignored the sharp jolts of pain radiating from her head from where she'd been dragged down the stairs and tried to focus on an escape plan.

Any hope of seeing someone on the street who would rescue her disappeared quickly as Evelyn realised there was no one around. But even had there been, she knew they would have looked the other way. The city was still coming to terms with the level of bombing it had seen the night before and she knew she was one insignificant fragment in the whole.

The man opened the passenger door of a light-blue car parked on the street, its cream roof pulled over to cover the seats, and threw her inside, her arm catching one of the levers, causing her to wince with pain. She tried to focus on something else to push the thoughts away of the injuries she'd sustained, noting the car was an Ariès, a newer version of the car Evelyn's friend Martinique had driven before, in those halcyon years, when she was learning to fly.

She watched as the man started the car, noting as he did that there was a knack to getting this one going.

'*Merde*,' the man said under his breath, throwing his gun onto the dashboard nearest to him and trying once more to get the motor to start, then sitting back in relief when the rumble of the engine caused vibrations in their seats. 'It would be much easier for you if you just said where your husband was,' the man said calmly as he steered the car out into the road, rolling his balaclava up to his forehead so that it became more of a hat than a face covering.

Showing his face, a distinctive one that was covered in freckles, could only be a bad sign for Evelyn. It meant he was confident she'd never need to identify him to someone.

Looking out the window, Evelyn watched as the cityscape of Paris disappeared, replaced by the fields and farms which encircled the outer arrondissements whilst trying to keep the prickle of terror away. Gradually, before long, all she could see were fields, and a partially unmade road, pockmarked with loose gravel and stones. She hadn't seen a soul for over twenty minutes. Wherever they were going, help wouldn't appear anytime soon.

She shuffled, the ties around her wrists and ankles were biting into her skin and the bound position was making itself known in her back as shooting pains spread from her hips upwards and the car was only slighter warmer than outside. Her teeth would have been chattering had she not had a wad of cotton stuffed in her mouth, which was – due to it being in there for some time – making her retch. She wished there was more slack in the rope so she could reach the gag to pull it out.

Something had to happen. Boring her eyes into the man's side she willed him to look over at her, which he eventually did.

'*Quoi*? What do you want? Changed your mind? Remembered where your husband is?'

Evelyn nodded.

'*Bien*. I tell you what; we'll pull over up here, and then I can pull your stockings out of your mouth, and you can tell me where that spying husband of yours is. Don't look shocked, we both know he's a spy. That's why I want to... have a little chat,' the man said.

Evelyn nodded again.

'Of course, it's probably wise for you not to make any long-term plans, but maybe, just maybe, if you're nice to me, I'll be nice to you.' He raised his eyebrows and looked at her lasciviously. Evelyn held back a shudder of revulsion.

The man pulled onto the side of the road. He kept the car going whilst he turned to look at her, the leather seats squeaking in protest as he did so.

'Are you going to be a good girl? Bear in mind, there's no one around to hear you scream and if you make one stupid move, I'll shoot you. *Vous comprends?*'

She nodded again, slowly.

'I think you and I are going to get on very well,' he said, stroking a finger over her cheek, down past her clavicle, stopping at the neckline of her flimsy dress. Evelyn willed herself to stay very still, any minute now he'd ungag her. He took her lack of movement as acquiescence and allowed his finger to drop lower, skimming the outline of her breast, then suddenly pulled his hand back as though he'd been electrocuted. 'Look at this, you're distracting me... I tell you what, I'm going for a piss. After that, I take off your gag. Then... you tell me where your husband is, and then I think you can thank me for sparing your life.' As he spoke he continued to grope her.

Evelyn saw a flash of fire in his eyes as he wrenched down hard on her dress, ripping the light material and exposing her breasts to the cold air. She bit on the gag and tried not to cry.

'Something for me to remember when I'm old and grey,' he said, laughing, as he undid the car door, leaving her bound and gagged on the passenger seat.

But Evelyn wasn't thinking about how exposed she was, or what would happen when he returned to the car.

Because she'd spotted two things.

One, he had left the car running. And two, he was so caught up in committing her breasts to memory, that he'd left his gun on the dashboard.

Watching as he walked over to a tree and faced away from her, Evelyn took the only opportunity she had. She painfully shuffled over the gearstick and into the driver's seat, silently sending up a prayer of thanks that she was small enough to manoeuvre into position. Checking he was still at the tree, Evelyn, her hands still bound in front of her, clumsily groped towards the dashboard in a bid to pick up the gun. She tried twice and struggled to get purchase. Frantically, she looked up and saw her kidnapper was coming back from the tree.

He was whistling and she tried once more. Her breath caught in her throat when her hands brushed successfully over the gun, enabling her to clasp it in both hands.

'What are you doing?' The man had opened the driver's door to be greeted by the sight of a semi-naked Evelyn, pointing the gun directly at his face. He lunged for her hands and she leaned back, throwing her legs up in the direction of his crotch and sending up the second prayer of the last ten minutes at how high the car was, because she caught him exactly where she needed to, causing the man to yell out in surprise and pain.

'You bitch,' he began, and Evelyn shook her head, holding the gun steady. She knew how to use it. And not just that, she knew she would use it on him. Something the man seemed to realise too.

'Don't shoot. Please.' He held his hands up in surrender. 'I have a wife and a child.' Evelyn shook her head. She didn't care. He hadn't cared about them a moment before.

'I can take the gag off?' he asked, his hands coming down. Immediately Evelyn pointed the gun at his head and shook it a little, causing his hands to fly back up again. 'You don't want me to take it off you. Fine. Your wrists maybe? I could undo those?' Evelyn knew she needed to be untied to drive the car. But for him to untie it he'd be very close to the gun, and it would be too easy for him to knock it out of her hands and kill her.

He saw her hesitation and moved.

Instinctively, Evelyn pulled the trigger.

At the close range and with her shooting experience it was of no surprise to her when the man's body slumped to the ground.

The look in his glazed eyes, though, told her it had been a shock to him.

Chapter Forty-Three

Paris outskirts

Evelyn took stock of where she was and what she needed to do.

The car was still running, she was still bound and the dead man was slumped on the ground a couple of feet away. Panic seized her as she considered her predicament. The stockings he'd stuffed in her mouth were blocking her throat, tickling the back of it and causing her to gag every minute or so. She desperately needed to get them out of her mouth so she could breathe properly again.

She needed to gnaw her binds to rid herself of them, but she couldn't do that with a stuffed mouth. And she couldn't take the stuffing out without the use of her hands.

For what may have been only the second time in her life, Evelyn felt truly and utterly helpless as she allowed the tears to drip from her eyes. She sat, shivering, whilst big, fat tears rolled off her cheeks and onto her legs and cursed herself for ever saying yes to Benjamin.

At the thought of her husband, Evelyn's tears shuddered to a stop. Whatever had taken place between them, someone was after him and she loved him too much for that to happen. The man, though he had been speaking French to her, may have been German. And if they were after Benjamin she knew there would never be a second chance for them, and their marriage.

She needed to inspect the man's body to find out any more clues about who he was and had to get moving soon, as others may be on the lookout for them.

Turning carefully in her seat, aware she didn't want to knock a lever or nudge the handbrake, Evelyn slipped down from the car, her feet meeting the damp mud of the road keeping watch on the man. But he didn't move. And she could see from where she was that his chest was still.

Slowly, but with more assuredness, she shuffled her way across the grassy verge, the rope tying her wrists to her ankles making movement awkward but eventually she stood over the body. If she hadn't known she'd shot him, she'd have guessed he was asleep. The shot had travelled cleanly through his heart, perforating his clothes. But as they were so dark, the blood wasn't apparent until she got closer.

By now, Evelyn was shivering uncontrollably. Whether it was the cold, the shock or the relief her ordeal with the man was over, or all three, she wasn't sure, but her whole body was beginning to shake. She knew she needed to get herself fixed up and back in the car before she froze to death.

Scanning the man, and satisfied he was indeed dead, Evelyn kneeled beside him and patted his body, feeling around for anything which might help her identify him and save her. In an outside pocket of his coat, her hand alighted on a cool, metal object. Heart racing, she withdrew her hand and gasped, the gesture making her retch at finding it was a multi-use knife; one she'd seen some of the soldiers use. They would use them for all sorts of things, she was sure one part of it was a corkscrew even. But most importantly, there was a knife to it.

Holding it clumsily in both hands, she carefully eased out what she hoped was the knife part from the side of the tool with her thumb, relief coursing through her as it revealed itself as a sharp blade. Carefully she pushed the knife further away from her thumbs, and managed to turn it round so that the blade was pushed into the rope which was binding her wrists.

With extreme concentration, Evelyn worked the blade up and down across the binding, thankful that the man had looked after it well, as it was sharp and quickly severed the strands of rope. The better it worked, the quicker Evelyn moved the knife. A biting wind was beginning to chill her hands, and a pain like no other was sitting in her bones but she concentrated on working the blade back and forth

THE FASTEST GIRL ON EARTH

until suddenly the resistance of the rope gave way and she was able to slip her hands free.

Rubbing her wrists and moving her hands around to get feeling back into them, Evelyn quickly pulled out the gag from her mouth, gasping as she could breathe fully again before hacking through the ropes around her ankles, wincing at the deep red welts the ties had left.

Making for the car, Evelyn remembered the minimal training she'd been given by Fergie when she'd been recruited into the service and spun back to look over the dead man, to see if there was anything else she could use.

The first thing that sprang to mind was his coat. It had blood on it, but it was made of a thick, rough, wool. Working as hard as she could, Evelyn heaved the man to sitting, his limp body heavy as she sat behind him and wiggled the coat from his unforgiving arms. She lay his body back down and pulled the coat on. It was enormous and fell to below her knees, something she was thankful for.

With his coat off, his cream cotton worker's shirt had a large scarlet patch that stretched across his chest and Evelyn stood briefly for a moment to take in the horror of what she'd done.

'He'd have killed you,' she reminded herself, her voice rasping as she spoke in the cold air.

Evelyn patted his trousers and pulled out a handful of centimes, but could find nothing else on him. Eyeing up his black, heavily-laced boots, she considered if she should wear them as driving in bare feet was going to be close to impossible.

She pulled a boot off grimacing at the size difference. There was no way she could wear them. But his thick socks would provide some comfort.

A little later, sat in the car with warm feet and the feeling of blood back in her hands, Evelyn drove away, leaving the body on the side of the road. She couldn't return to Paris, so she decided to try and track down Isabelle and George. They were in a village not too far from Paris, she just needed to find the way – though with the short January days, the light was already dimming.

As Evelyn drove the car down the road, she spotted another car in the far-off distance. It was still unusual for women to be seen behind the wheel, and she'd heard unsavoury tales of what happened to ladies who were found driving on their own by solo men. Especially at night.

She wasn't taking her chances again and looked around the car to see if she could find anything to disguise herself with, then spotted the man's balaclava. Evelyn grabbed it from the seat and pulled it onto her head as best she could, as she tried to keep the car straight. She pulled it down to her ears, tucking away her hair and sat up as much as possible to prevent her diminutive size being noticeable.

Behind the wheel of the other car a man in a flat cap raised a hand and waved. She did the same and a few seconds later they had passed each other. Evelyn exhaled with relief.

Further down the road she came upon a dilapidated road sign, but she could just make out the words *Château-Thierry*, which she knew was not too far from Isabelle's village. Turning right, Evelyn hoped she had enough petrol to get her to her destination.

After an hour or so, and following signs she half recognised, Evelyn arrived in a small village, a replica of all the others she'd driven through and her heart sank. She didn't know how much farther Isabelle's village was, and this one appeared to have no signs. All of its shops were closed, save for a tabac where the glow of a light came from within, illuminating a withered old man sat on a bench with his Alsatian beside him. Both watched as she drove past them slowly, their faces turning to follow the car in unison.

Evelyn felt a pang in her stomach. It had been a very long twenty-four hours, and she'd not eaten properly since dinner in the restaurant the night before. It was hard to believe she'd experienced a bombing and a kidnapping in those subsequent hours, but her body was reminding her.

She was tired, her whole body was aching with cold and the pain of the beating she'd sustained from the man when he'd awoken her hours ago.

The light had gone and, though she had headlights and was skilled at driving in the dark, she realised that her exhaustion would kill her if she didn't find a safe place to stay.

Up ahead, a cottage was positioned on its own, a little way from the village. She could smell the welcome scent of a fire and drew alongside the home. Candles flickered in the windows, as though warding off any evil spirits, and Evelyn decided she could take the risk.

Cautiously, she walked up the path, her socks soaking through as she stood on the damp ground, and she knocked at the door.

As she heard footsteps, Evelyn suddenly remembered to remove her balaclava, and wondered at the fright she would look.

The door opened, bringing a flood of welcome light to the path.

'Evie?'

Chapter Forty-Four

Crécy-la-Chapelle

'Who is it?' a voice called from inside where the warmth and light was; where she wanted to be. Evelyn had never craved that sense of safety so much as that very moment.

But she didn't move, because in front of her stood Isabelle silhouetted in the doorway, and she was shaking her head.

'No one,' Isabelle called over her shoulder and Evelyn opened her mouth to speak, but closed it quickly when her friend held her finger up to her lips and indicated silence.

'Must have been the wind,' she called again, and closed the door. The light, and with it, Evelyn's hope, disappearing with it.

The night had fully drawn in and Evelyn shivered, despite the thick coat, wondering what her options were. Unsure as to why Isabelle wouldn't help her, Evelyn was stuck with indecision. She considered knocking on the door again and demanding to be let in, or walking away to the car.

She was tired. Her limbs felt as though they were tingling with overuse and she'd had enough. Just as she began to march back down towards the cottage, her arms swinging at her sides, the door opened again and instinctively, Evelyn jumped behind one of the many bushes which lined the path.

Isabelle, this time wearing a thick coat and boots, adjusted her buttons whilst calling over her shoulder, 'I'll be fine, just a touch of something. Nothing to worry about. *Bonsoir*,' she said, then swiftly walked down the path.

'Evelyn. Come on, I know you're around here, I saw you jump into the bush,' she whispered. 'Come on, or don't you want somewhere to warm up?'

Shakily, Evelyn stood out on the path and her friend rushed to embrace her.

'I'm sorry, I'll explain everything, but for now, we need to get you out of sight – jeepers, you're freezing.' Isabelle's words came tumbling out in a mixture of elation and concern.

'Where are we?' Evelyn was cut off by Isabelle steering her down the road, a little further away from the cottage, hushing her at the same time. A few minutes later, the two women – one cold, tired and angry at being kept quiet, the other throwing furtive glances over her shoulders before opening the door to another stone cottage and pushing her friend through – finally had a chance to talk.

'You look a fright, what in God's name...?' Isabelle's words faded away as she took stock of Evelyn, standing in a thick German coat, a ripped, muddied and bloodied evening gown and thick, mud-coated socks.

'Oh darling, come on.' She pulled Evelyn into the kitchen, and stoked the fire, coaxing the embers into a stronger flame. Evelyn sat on a hard wooden chair, numb to everything and just watched Isabelle as she busied herself in the kitchen.

Ten minutes later Isabelle had warmed up enough water to half-fill the tin bath that she'd placed in front of the fire and pulled Evelyn to standing.

'Off with this stuff.' She took the coat off, the weight of its departure shocking Evelyn from her stupor.

'Why couldn't you speak to me?'

'Now this,' Isabelle said, ignoring the question, pulling the gown over her head and tutting at the bruising and blood coating Evelyn. She helped Evelyn into the bath, where the water soothed her legs, and seeped into the numerous cuts she had across her body from fighting off her attacker. Wincing at the heat of the water on her wrists and ankles where the ropes had cut dark-red marks into them, she allowed Isabelle to sponge her shoulders and neck.

'You've so much dust on you, you look as though you've been travelling for months,' Isabelle said sadly. 'Though I don't think it's been as fun as all that.'

Evelyn allowed Isabelle to wash her hair. And with every drop that hit her skin, an ounce of the fear which had resided in the pit of her stomach began to evaporate.

Once she was satisfied Evelyn was clean and soothed, Isabelle brought a large, albeit scratchy towelling cloth and held it to her as she stepped out of the tub. She handed her some clothes to change into, which had been warming on a rail by the fire.

'I don't have much food in; we're due to leave in a couple of days. But there's some bread and a hunk of cheese.'

'Anything.' Evelyn accepted them both greedily and tucked in quickly, nodding at the pot of tea Isabelle offered and taking a large gulp of it.

'So—'

'How did you find us—?'

The two women spoke at the same time.

'You first,' Isabelle said, and Evelyn recounted the last twenty-four hours. She left out the argument with Benjamin, she didn't want to remember, but everything else – the bombing, the kidnapping, the man she shot and killed. She told Isabelle it all.

'I knew you were around this way but then the light faded and I couldn't be certain where I was, so I hoped to get help from someone, hence me knocking on what turned out to be your neighbour's door.' She shrugged. 'Someone was looking out for me I guess.'

Isabelle shook her head.

'I think that's typically you. The way you used to race, the audacity of flying a plane, it's you. Someone might have been looking out for you, but I'm guessing deep down somewhere you remembered our address from the cards we've sent over the last couple of years,' she said, smiling fondly at her friend. 'But you're lucky – we're leaving shortly. If you'd arrived on Thursday we'd have gone for good.'

'Why? Where are you going? And why are you keeping me secret?'

Isabelle sighed. 'Come upstairs.'

Evelyn followed her friend along the narrow landing where a couple of candles glimmered and lit the way. Her friend pushed a door open carefully and inside, snuggled in a cot, blankets wrapped tightly around them, was a child of two or three, the flames of the fire in the nursery throwing golden shapes across the room onto their face.

'This is Phillipe, he's my son,' Isabelle whispered, then indicated they return downstairs.

Once settled at the table, Isabelle sipped some of her tea. 'Men came for George a fortnight ago. They didn't find him because a neighbour alerted us. He was out walking his dog and spotted an odd car in the village. He knew a little about George so he tipped us off.' She drank some more tea, her eyes darkening as she spoke. 'We had minutes to make a plan, we don't know how they found us. He disappeared into the woods and has, I hope, made it out of the country to England. We agreed I'd follow on in a couple of weeks with Phillipe, but I had to act like I wasn't going anywhere. I can't be certain I'm not being watched.'

'By...?'

'Probably the very same neighbours I was eating dinner with this evening,' Isabelle said. 'They have some links with the Germans but it's not clear how. I dined with them in the hope they'd be convinced all was well with me. Then you showed up.'

Evelyn whistled through her teeth.

'Cigarette?' Isabelle lit one off a candle and passed it to Evelyn. 'I need something stronger than tea. And we need a plan,' she added, locating a bottle of brandy and two glasses, pouring out healthy measures for the two of them.

'If they're looking for Benjamin and George, then someone has given up their contacts.'

Isabelle took a deep gulp of brandy and looked at her friend. 'They know where I live and once they find the body of that man you've left on the roadside, you can bet they'll turn up here looking for blood.'

Chapter Forty-Five

CRECY-LA-CHAPELLE

The plan, much like anything concocted after too many large measures of brandy, was nowhere near as straightforward as it had seemed the night before.

In the cold light of day, the idea was almost ridiculous.

Almost. But not quite.

Evelyn believed in the plan. She had to. It was the only one they had, but it was not without its problems.

They were to leave that night. Taking only Phillipe and the basics they could carry, they had decided to risk using the dead man's car for a portion of the trip, but discard it somewhere near to Reims before they got too close to their destination, for fear it would give them away.

After that, they'd be on foot. Isabelle estimated it would be a day's walk until they reached Martinique's château in Mourmel-on-le-Grand. Assuming she was there, they planned to borrow a fixed-wing or a helicopter. Then it was over to Evelyn to fly them out of France and back to England, where they had to hope they would be safe.

Evelyn tried to ignore the problems she could foresee. Bringing a small child. Being seen. Getting to Martinique's home only to find she was no longer there. Evelyn was aware her friend worked for the French government, so might be on her own missions.

There were many more problems. Nonetheless, they needed to move on.

That day, the two women spent as much time as they could trying to sleep, or at least rest, aware they'd need as much energy as possible to see them through the next few days.

Phillipe didn't make it easy though. He was only two, but he was big for his age and, it appeared to Evelyn, he never needed to sleep. He certainly wasn't swaying her opinion on children.

'Where do you think they are?' Isabelle said into the fire, her face in her hands.

The two covered this conversation in many different ways over the past few hours, each wondering aloud where their husbands had got to. For Evelyn, she was undecided whether she preferred Benjamin to have been blown up by the bombs in Paris, or captured by the Germans. At least the first outcome could mean a quick death. The third, that he simply chose to leave her after she pushed him away on that fateful day at the Eiffel Tower, was more painful to consider, so she ignored it, closing her heart to him walking away.

For Isabelle, the two women prayed that George had managed to get himself out of the country safely. They didn't want to voice any other possibilities, though they were the ones that hovered between them, cluttering up their thoughts.

'I said, where do you think they are?' Isabelle repeated and Evelyn shook her head grumpily.

'No, we've gone over this. We don't know, we can't guess, we're better off not knowing – for now.' She tied the backpack Isabelle had given her and ran through the provisions, mentally ticking them off.

'Did you check if the car was still there?' she asked.

Isabelle looked up from her own backpack, whilst attempting to stuff yet another cloth nappy into the bag. She had maintained a normal routine that day to reduce any suspicion and had gone to the boulangerie to get what she could.

'Yes. I didn't want to draw anyone's attention, especially as Monsieur Barr is already suspicious after I left their dinner so early last night. But as I returned from the village I knocked on one of the villager's doors under the pretext of asking them about coal. They live down the same lane as the one you parked in, and it was still there. They weren't in, and I realised that the other two cottages are empty.

So, we shouldn't have anyone either interested in the car or witness leaving this evening, though I'll need to pop back and top up the petrol. George has a can in the garden.'

Evelyn exhaled. For now they had luck on their side. They also had the time of year, it was barely four o'clock and the day had darkened already. Within an hour it would be pitch black outside and they could make their escape.

Phillipe screamed, breaking the silence and making Evelyn's skin crawl with his primal energy.

'He can't make that noise when we're out. You know that, don't you,' she hissed at Isabelle who was soothing the child on the floor.

'He's two years old, Evie, he has no idea what's going on. Just that his father disappeared a couple of days ago and a strange, angry lady has appeared in his place. Be kind to him,' Isabelle said, smoothing Phillipe's hair and crooning soft words of sympathy as she cradled him on her lap, whilst sat on the cold stone floor.

There was a moment, a brief, glorious but frightening moment, when Evelyn considered leaving the two of them behind. The journey would have been easier, of that she was certain, but as soon as the thought had crossed her mind she chased it away. Isabelle was her friend. Phillipe was her son. She no more wanted the two of them to die, as she did Benjamin. It was her own fear that was at fault. Her fear of being caught could cause her to make rash or wrong decisions.

She inhaled and exhaled, forcing some control over her breathing and reminded herself of all the other times she'd been in trouble and survived. This was just another land speed record she had to complete. As long as she kept in mind the end goal, getting to England, she could be in control. And calm.

'It's time,' she decided, the firmness in her voice alerting Isabelle to movement, who reacted by setting Phillipe on his feet and dressing him in a warm coat.

Evelyn pulled on George's wax jacket, turning up the sleeves to fit her arms. The coat dropped to well below her knees, and could have fastened twice around her, but it had deep pockets, perfect to fit the gun she'd taken from her kidnapper in and more besides, should she be separated from her backpack.

'I must look quite a fright,' she said to Isabelle, in a bid to make up for her earlier outburst. 'What would they say in Harrods if they saw me now?'

Isabelle looked away from doing up her son's buttons and smiled at her friend. 'I don't know, I think French farmer fashion could be the nouveau style, darling, *très chic*. You look good in a boiler suit. I should know, I saw you working as a mechanic, remember.'

The two women held hands, their shared history intertwined. It barely felt any time since those untroubled days in their apartment in Paris, where they'd drunk champagne and gone out for evenings filled with poetry in bars, meeting strangers who came and went throughout the night. That was before the racing. Before celebrity. Before the war. A lifetime ago.

'*Bonne chance*, my friend.' Evelyn kissed Isabelle on the cheek, and she did the same. 'I think we will all need it.'

***

The reality of leaving in the middle of the night became apparent almost as soon as they crossed the threshold of Isabelle's home and the hinges on the old farm door complained noisily. Against the silence of a sleeping village, every step they made sounded to Evelyn as though they were wearing metal-soled boots.

Loose stones skittered across the road as they walked carefully in the pitch black. Evelyn followed Isabelle closely, so as not to lose her way, her eyes struggling to make out more than a hazy shape in front of her, and on occasions larger, sturdier shapes either side of them, which she assumed to be cottages.

It should have only taken them ten or so minutes to arrive at the car, but between Isabelle having to stop and rearrange the sleeping Phillipe on her shoulder and the inky darkness that prevented them from seeing further than their hands, it was closer to half an hour when Evelyn touched the reassuring solidity of the car.

Isabelle hoisted herself and Phillipe into it and Evelyn carefully closed the door, alert to any sounds from the cottages nearby, sure there was no one there.

Satisfied they wouldn't disturb anyone, Evelyn pulled herself into the driver's seat. Then stopped.

'What is it?' The two women had barely swapped a word during the walk to the car, and Isabelle's voice, despite it being barely above a whisper, sounded as loud as a gunshot.

Evelyn turned and saw the tiniest glint of light in her friend's eyes. Now that her own had become more accustomed to the darkness she was able to make out more than outlines.

'I can't start the car. Even though there's no one around here, we will need to get past a few other rows of cottages to get out of the village. There's no way to avoid them hearing us.'

There was a silence as they processed the situation.

'We could push it?' Isabelle suggested.

'Only one of us could, the other would need to steer,' Evelyn reminded her.

'I could push it, you could steer; you're the driver after all.' Before waiting on a reply, Isabelle had placed Phillipe carefully on the seat, wrapped in a thick blanket, and slipped out of the door again.

Evelyn heard a light bang on the back of the car which she took to mean Isabelle was going to give pushing it a go, so she released the handbrake. To begin with nothing happened and Evelyn started to wonder if they'd have to start the engine and hope no one noticed. But then, slowly, the car began to move, its wheels crunching on the stones as Evelyn navigated the vehicle, turning out right onto the main road that led out of the village.

A small camber seemed a slight obstacle for Isabelle who appeared to slow briefly, but again, the car moved forward and Evelyn concentrated on keeping the car on the road, no mean feat without the headlamps, holding her breath as they moved past the row of cottages, one of which held the neighbour inside that Isabelle was certain was talking to the Germans.

THE FASTEST GIRL ON EARTH

As the car crunched slowly along, Evelyn allowed herself to believe they were going to be all right and considered at which point they could safely put the headlamps on.

In the quiet of the night a dog suddenly barked somewhere to the left of them. The car crunched to a stop and Evelyn looked around, her ears straining to hear any other sounds. She willed Isabelle to keep pushing. Why had she stopped? The worst thing now would be if they got caught leaving under the cover of darkness. That would take a lot of explaining.

Something wooden banged. Evelyn wasn't sure if it was a shutter or a door but it sounded nearby. She shivered. Despite George's coat the icy chill of the wintery night was bitter and seeped into her skin. She briefly blew on her hands to prevent them stiffening whilst she waited for Isabelle to move the car, her pulse hammering in her ears as she listened for someone, anyone, coming out and finding them.

Next to her Phillipe made a light sound, and kicked in his sleep. Evelyn re-tucked his blanket around him when, after what had felt like an interminable time, the car began to move again.

And then, suddenly, they were leaving the village behind, an open road in front of them and Evelyn could start the engine, just as Isabelle appeared in the passenger door and pulled herself up.

'Go,' she pointed at the road ahead, 'we need to go now.'

The two women, one driving, the other holding her son close to her to keep him as warm as she could, didn't speak as the car, struggling in the cold, puttered down the road. Deciding if they would be heard, they may as well be seen too, Evelyn flicked the headlamps on and breathed a sigh of relief at being able to see where she was driving.

It was well-timed as the road was unmade, with loose stones skittering under the wheels, occasionally causing the tyres to skid. But Evelyn kept the car on a straight route and, after a few minutes of reacquainting herself with the vehicle, began to push the speedometer up.

'Careful,' Isabelle said after a particularly loud grinding sound had come from the gearbox. 'We don't have many choices when it comes to escape vehicles, it'll be nice if this one stays intact.'

Evelyn grinned for the first time in hours. 'I'm keen to make up for some of the time we lost back in the village, it all took much longer than we'd planned,' she reminded her friend.

'Hey, you could have jumped out of the car and given it a push – it wasn't easy you know.'

'One of us had to steer.'

'Yes, I think I may have managed that, but it turns out my years of working in the garden here, hauling bricks out of the earth to make space for my flowers, might have helped. Oh...' Isabelle stopped talking and Evelyn took her eyes off the road to look at her friend, but she could see little in the darkened cabin and resumed looking ahead.

'What is it?'

'It's nothing. It's silly...' Isabelle started, then went quiet. Knowing better than to push her, Evelyn waited.

'It's just that I'll probably never see my beautiful cottage and its garden ever again,' she admitted. 'I know that sounds ridiculous considering the position we found ourselves in, but I loved that cottage. It was our first proper home in... years...' The last few words were uttered amongst sobs.

'It's not ridiculous,' Evelyn said into the quiet that was punctuated with the smothered sniffs of her friend. 'You'd managed to find somewhere that was away from the madness and carve out somewhere full of peace and joy – who wouldn't miss a home that provided that?'

There was silence again and Evelyn wondered if she had said the wrong thing.

'You're right, Evie. And anyway, my home is wherever this little man is.' The affectionate tone in Isabelle's voice had a slight catch in it. 'And George of course.'

'Of course.'

'Sorry, here's me going on and you must be missing Benjamin too.'

Evelyn wasn't sure how to explain to Isabelle how she and Benjamin had left things. How regretful she was that he could be dead and the last thing she'd said to him was to get out of her life. She hoped that if they managed to get to Britain, he'd be there too and they'd be able to work out a way to be husband and wife once again.

'Watch out,' Isabelle shouted and brought Evelyn's wandering attention back to the road. She swerved and narrowly missed a large hole. 'You have to pay attention,' Isabelle said, soothing Phillipe who woke with a start when the car lurched on the road. 'We can't assume we're home and dry just yet.'

'May I remind you this was my idea, this is my car and I'm taking you to my friend's home where hopefully we can leave this country in a plane that I will be piloting,' Evelyn replied. 'I have zero expectations of being home and dry. I don't even know if we'll make it yet.'

The air crackled a little with the tension but neither woman spoke to break it.

'We should stop for breakfast in a little while,' Isabelle said, a mile or so later. 'The sky is lightening, which means we'll need to take cover somewhere soon if we're going to complete as much of this journey in the dark.'

Evelyn gripped the steering wheel tightly. 'I'd like to drive for as long as possible, until it's as bright as we can cope with. These winter mornings can stay dark for some time and it's foggy, I don't want us leaving the road until we absolutely have to. Better to make up as much time as possible when we can – heaven knows when we'll be able to get back on the road this evening. We don't know if it's a busy route or not.'

'You might be used to gambling, I'm not,' Isabelle replied. 'I don't want to risk our lives just because you have some sort of point to prove.'

'I don't have a point to prove, I just want to get home. I want to be there now,' Evelyn shouted, 'and I think I can get us to Reims before the day gets too light. But you need to trust me.'

After a brief moment Isabelle cleared her throat. 'I always trust you, even with my life.'

Chapter Forty-Six

En route to Reims

It was the petrol that gave out before Evelyn's will to stop. Though she had driven as conservatively as she could, the car only had a small petrol chamber so it was no surprise when the vehicle began to shudder, shake and then grind to a halt.

Isabelle woke up, confused, and Evelyn envied her moment of unknowing before reality set in. 'Where are we? Why have we stopped?'

Once the decision had been made to drive until they couldn't risk it any further, the two women had chatted amicably about this and that, mainly to keep Evelyn awake and focused.

Isabelle told her of the last couple of years, how George had been given a role to "oversee operations in France" which meant little to her other than he'd occasionally disappear to Paris for a few days and then return. Whilst there were reports of German soldiers nearby, nothing ever happened. And so, she, George and Phillipe had lived a quiet, fairly undisturbed life.

There were a few questions about a couple from England living in France, when they could barely speak the language. But, Isabelle told Evelyn, they were brushed quickly aside when they explained George had moved to Paris to work for a French motor company, only to make the decision to move himself and his family out of the firing range of the city to somewhere safer in the countryside.

According to Isabelle, no one had questioned their story, just allowed them to live within the community until the last six months, when the neighbour a few doors down began to pay more attention to them than usual.

'He would ask why George wasn't working that day, or what he did for money. Or where he'd gone, as he'd go away for a couple of days to liaise with government officials and leave myself and Phillipe. I would just say he needed to travel to Paris every now and then, and leave it at that. I knew he wasn't convinced though. And in the meantime George became increasingly worried his cover was blown.'

According to Isabelle, she and George were preparing to leave, but they were sold out quicker than they'd assumed, hence why he could escape, but it was too unsafe for them all to leave.

'The petrol has run out,' Evelyn told a sleepy Isabelle. 'So it's on foot from now on.' She began looking through the glove compartment to see if the dead man had left anything of use to them. 'I don't know how close we are to Reims, but I don't think it's very far. We should find somewhere to hide now though, an abandoned car is likely to attract attention.'

Phillipe began to whimper a little, and Isabelle looked in her bag for a corner of bread to give him. Soon he was sucking on the crust, perfectly happy in his little world.

The two of them lifted the bags out the car, and Evelyn pulled on her backpack when she heard a sound.

'Isabelle.' She looked in the direction of clattering noise and quickly turned to see if there was anywhere they could hide. But everywhere she looked she could only see farmers' fields stretching out to the horizon, a few dotted with sullen cows. 'Of all the places to run out of petrol.' She cursed herself for not thinking it through. Too intent on making up the miles, she'd not considered the capacity of the engine. What would Benjamin have thought of her, being so unprepared?

Shouldering Phillipe, and looking at the empty road which stretched up and down with no end in sight, Isabelle shrugged a little.

'We can't hide, Evie, they'll see the car and there's nowhere we can go. Let's face whoever it is, and we say, quite honestly, our car has run out of petrol, and, slightly less honestly, that we're on our way to our aunt in Mourmelon-le-Grand. Though we'd hoped to get to Reims first.' She shrugged again. 'What's the worst that could happen to two women on the road with a child?'

Evelyn bit her tongue. There were many horrible, awful things which could happen to them. She'd seen some of those things, and she'd escaped others.

She patted the pocket of her jacket and reassured herself that the gun was in there. Evelyn knew there would be enough bullets to either kill whoever was coming in the cart towards them, or, if need be, herself, Isabelle and Phillipe if they ran out of options. Best a quick death than anything the opposition could do to them, she reasoned. Though the prospect was so awful she hoped she wouldn't have to consider it.

As a cart, drawn by one slowly plodding horse, came into view, it became apparent to Evelyn she didn't have to worry. The driver was a man with a bright white beard and wrinkled face, he wouldn't be doing any of them any harm, not before she could do to something to him anyway.

'*Ça va?*'

'We're well, monsieur, but our car has broken down,' Isabelle said, taking the lead and speaking quickly in French.

'I'm going to Reims – would that help? I'm afraid I don't have any gasoline, I don't need any for old Tomas here,' the man said, his eyes twinkling with affection as he leant and patted his horse.

Evelyn and Isabelle exchanged a look. If they could get a lift, it would hopefully keep them mainly out of sight should anyone be looking for them on the road, and would save their legs for the last part of the journey.

'*Si'l vous plaît*, if you're sure? We're heading for our aunt's in Reims,' Isabelle explained, using the story the women had agreed on.

'*Bien sûr.* We can't have two lovely ladies and such a handsome boy left on the side of the road, now can we? Who knows who's out here?' The man indicated the back of his cart with a nod of his head. 'There's room up there, I'm afraid it's not as chic as your current transport, but there's space.'

'*Merci*, we appreciate it,' Evelyn said, smiling at the man. 'Can we give you anything for your troubles?' She hefted her bag off her shoulder to look for her purse, but the man shook his head fiercely.

'*Non*, I'm going that way anyway. Now I have a little company, you will be a little chattier than Tomas.'

Isabelle climbed into the cart first and Evelyn passed Phillipe up to her. The boy, sensing adventure, enjoyed the view from the cart and Evelyn couldn't help get caught up in his excitement as she climbed up beside them.

It was still cold. The wind was bitter, but the three settled next to each other towards the back of the cart and Evelyn pulled a threadbare blanket over to keep them warm. A musty scent of hay and years of hard work wafted up as they settled into place. The man clicked his tongue and Tomas began his steady plod.

Relieved they had secured an unobtrusive means of travel, one which wouldn't draw attention and was, happily, designed in such a way they couldn't be viewed from the road. Evelyn rested her head against the cart and allowed herself to relax. The only sounds were those of the horse's shoes and the cart's wheels clicking against the loose stones of the road, and Isabelle's quiet words to a sleepy Phillipe.

The movement of the cart was soporific, slowly rocking Evelyn's weary body.

She knew she'd need her wits about her soon, but her body was craving sleep, pulling her deeply down, and she found it impossible to resist.

***

'*Allez, mademoiselles.*' The old man stood at the side of the cart, looking outwards, away from them. 'You must leave, there are *gendarmes* on the outskirts of the town and,' he coughed, clearing his throat, 'today's not a day I'd like to have a run-in with them.'

Evelyn looked around blearily, quickly getting her bearings. 'Where are we?'

'You're one kilometre from Reims, but I cannot take you further, a friend passed me and said a blockade has been set up by the town,' the man continued, leaning against his cart, not speaking directly to them. 'I don't know who you are, or your aunt, and I don't need to know. But I suspect you don't want to have a conversation with them? *Oui*?'

Isabelle secured all her items in her backpack and handed Phillipe down to the man. 'How did you know?'

The man touched his finger to his nose. 'Ask me no questions and I'll tell you no lies. But I meant it, I didn't want to leave two lovely ladies by themselves, even ones wearing oversized British army-issued coats,' he nodded at Evelyn and raised an eyebrow, 'and carrying a gun.' He looked meaningfully at her pocket.

'*Merci*, monsieur, you're very kind.' She leant forward and kissed the old man on the cheek.

'*Merci*.' Isabelle did the same.

The man blushed a little. 'Enough, now go. And *bonne chance*, my little friend,' he said to Phillipe, who was hiding behind Isabelle's legs. 'You be brave, just like your *maman* and friend.' He winked at them both then walked up to the front of the cart, clicked his tongue and he and Tomas disappeared slowly into the distance.

The two women watched for a moment, both deep in thought.

'And now we walk,' Evelyn broke the silence.

'No, now we hide. Look.' Isabelle pointed out a disused shepherd's hut that had fallen into disrepair on the side of the road. 'And we have something to eat.' Isabelle was right. They'd been fortunate with the lift, the last thing they needed was to be caught out on the road in daylight.

They crossed over to the tumbledown shed and Isabelle forced the door. Inside was dusty and looked as though it hadn't been used since the turn of the century, but there were a couple of stools lying upended on the floor. Evelyn turned them back round and sat on one. A small window, covered heavily in grime, let in the only light. What spirits she had begun to plummet.

'Hey, Phillipe, tell Auntie Evelyn how high you can count,' Isabelle prompted the boy, who was squatting on the floor, drawing pictures in the dust with a finger.

Evelyn turned her attention to the boy, indulging the two-year-old who had kept far quieter than she'd ever imagine. 'Oh yes, tell me, Phillipe.'

The little boy stood and looked solemnly at his mother and then Evelyn. '*Un, deux, trois*, four, five, six, *sept, huit*, nine, ten.' He smiled, thrilled with his success, and Evelyn felt herself grinning at the mixture of French and English.

Isabelle smiled too. 'We've been teaching him French words for things but obviously he hears us speak English at home, and then when he's in the village none of the residents speak much of it, so he only hears French out and about. To him it makes perfect sense.'

'I love it,' Evelyn said, cheered. 'Frankly I think we should all speak like that – why not.'

'*Je m'appelle* Evelyn, a pleasure to meet you Phillipe, *ça va*?' she mixed, and the boy laughed.

'*Non*, Auntie Evie, you're saying all the wrong words,' he said, giggling. 'You are speaking funny.'

'Oh, he doesn't realise he's mixing it up,' Isabelle leant in and whispered to Evelyn. 'We haven't thought to correct him as such. I suppose I thought he'd always need French as we'd be here forever. I've been particularly naïve this time, Evelyn. I think I thought we'd finished running. That we'd settled.'

Evelyn was glad of the gloom, otherwise Isabelle would have seen her raise her eyebrows. Isabelle wasn't stupid, she knew George was working for the government, was a spy. She'd known for far longer than Evelyn had that Benjamin was involved. In fact, it was Evelyn who'd been last to know about a lot of it, which hurt.

'I think we should try and get some rest. Mourmelon is around twenty miles from here, and even when we find the village, I think Martinique is a little way out the other side. So it could be another mile or so on top of that.'

'Twenty miles is a long way,' Isabelle said after a while. 'How long will it take us?'

LISA BRACE

Evelyn blew on her hands, they felt stiff with the cold despite the shed which offered some shelter, but was still merely a wooden hut and the temperatures had dropped to almost freezing outside. The night would be even colder. She wasn't certain Phillipe would manage, but she didn't mention any of her fears to Isabelle.

'I think on a good day it would be about seven hours walking. But I don't think we're going to manage it as quickly as that. We have our bags and Phillipe, it'll be dark and very difficult to navigate, plus the cold will make walking harder.' She thought for a moment. 'It might be more likely to say ten hours from here, give or take.'

'And that's assuming it doesn't snow,' Isabelle added. This time it was her turn to sound demoralised.

'Let's cross that bridge when we get to it – I'd like to suggest we could wait out any weather here, and decide to leave tomorrow in the day, but I think time is of the essence. We need to press on,' Evelyn said, trying to inject a note of confidence in her voice. 'We've got food and warm clothes, good solid walking boots and currently, we're well ahead of anyone who might come looking for us. Let's face it, how likely will it be that anyone actually is on the lookout for us? It's George and Benjamin they're really after.'

There was a silence, punctuated only by the lone cry of a bird outside.

'As rousing speeches go, I'm going to say you'll need to work a little harder on them,' Isabelle said.

Evelyn found herself grinning, then giggling. Isabelle joined in, and soon the two were laughing until tears streamed down their faces. Phillipe watched the two adults and merely shook his head, resuming his drawing in the dust as he spoke.

'*Mon Dieu.*'

Which only served to make the two laugh even harder.

Chapter Forty-Seven
OUTSKIRTS OF REIMS

The day passed as much as any day in a cold, wooden, draughty hut in winter would. Isabelle held Phillipe to her, and the two women sat as close as possible to keep warm.

On occasions they'd hear a horse and cart and once, a car drove past them, causing the two women to stiffen in anticipation.

But nobody came. No one looked for them, or even stopped near to the hut and they passed the day in relative silence, surrounded by dusty gloom, the cold chilling their bones.

As the weak light that had been straining through the clouds all day began to disappear and was swallowed into a pitch-black night, all three tucked into a day-old baguette and some hard cheese, chased down with sips of water.

'I think we should start.'

'It's only early,' Isabelle began. 'It's barely five o'clock?'

Evelyn shrugged. 'It's dark, no one will be on the road, we may as well start now and get as much walking in before it gets really cold.' She put her backpack on and could hear Isabelle doing the same.

'No, I'll take that, you take Phillipe.' Evelyn took the bag from her friend. 'Tie him on with this,' she unwound a shirt she had tied around her waist, 'and we'll take it in turns.'

Grateful to her friend, Isabelle shifted Phillipe onto her back, with the two women fumbling in the dark as they proceeded to tie the wiggling two-year-old in place.

'You need to hold on to me, Phillipe,' Isabelle said firmly to the boy, who settled down.

Evelyn finished tying the shirt and stepped back to assess her work, pleased with the result. 'He won't be going anywhere for a while. Let's get going.'

They pushed open the door, which creaked in protest, and stepped out. It turned out the shelter had protected them far more than they'd been aware. As soon as they began to walk, a bitter wind wrapped itself around them, chilling them almost instantly.

'I can't see us doing ten miles tonight, let alone twenty,' Isabelle puffed, and Evelyn heard her stumbling behind. 'We're on a fool's errand.'

Evelyn secretly agreed with her friend but she didn't want to give her any reason to give up. They just needed to get on with things, and eventually dawn or warmth or shelter would appear. That's all she could hope for.

'Let's go.'

Over the next few hours the small group walked along what passed for a road, Evelyn in front navigating her way along the verge, Isabelle keeping pace, every now and then placing her hand on her friend's shoulder to reassure herself she was heading the right way. Occasionally loose stones would slip under their feet, crunching into the heels of their boots, causing them to lose their footing, and when the moon went behind a cloud they would have to wait until it reappeared, giving them a slight glimmer of light to navigate.

Every hour or so, the two would stop and swap their loads, with each woman taking a turn to carry Phillipe or the backpacks and Evelyn would set the pace.

'Come on Isabelle, we need to go faster,' she called as she hefted Phillippe a little higher up her back, the boy's weight unbalancing her a little. 'Did you pull him tightly enough on? I feel like he's shifting a lot.'

'I can't walk any quicker, and if you're going to complain about my son's weight, kindly wait until he's not in earshot,' Isabelle replied with a huff.

Evelyn rolled her eyes and bit the inside of her cheek so as not to reply with an angry retort. She'd noticed Isabelle was struggling to match her speed, but she knew the only answer was to keep going.

'Evelyn, stop walking so quickly. I don't know where you get this energy from but I can't keep going like you. Some of us have been struggling to find food you know.'

'Oh, and you think I've had it easy?' Evelyn began to walk quicker, her anger rising.

'I didn't mean it like that.' Isabelle moved quickly to catch her up.

'Didn't you? Because it sounded like you think I've been living a life in luxury in spite of there being a war on.' Evelyn's back was aching, Phillipe was awake and kept wiggling, causing her to shift her weight as she walked.

'No, just...' Isabelle tried to keep up, stumbling a little as she did so. 'You didn't seem to have the same problems as us. Any time we were in touch, you'd be disappearing off somewhere. Learning to fly. Gambling in Monaco. What were you even doing in Paris?'

Sweat was dripping down Evelyn's back where the heat of Phillipe added to her own exertions, and in spite of the cold night, she could feel a warmth rising from her collar and rushing to her face. She hated getting overheated. It stopped her from thinking practically.

She marched on, looking ahead only at darkness. It was time Isabelle knew the truth. 'I was spying. I thought you knew that – George did,' she said honestly, briefly turning her head to see her friend. 'For the last six years I've been working undercover for the government.'

'You?' The tone in Isabelle's voice was incredulous.

'Me.'

'But it was Benjamin who was working for them, that's what George eventually told me.' Isabelle walked quicker, almost catching up with Evelyn. 'What could you do for our country?'

'Drive. Fly. Shoot. Speak three different languages. What can you do, Isabelle?' Evelyn stepped forwards and felt the ground under her disappear, and suddenly found herself off the side of the road, in a steep ditch. In the millisecond that she had to make a decision she knew she didn't want to land on Phillipe and twisted herself awkwardly to prevent it.

The pain was instant. She had landed so her foot was twisted and knew instantly it was broken. But was concerned for the child, because despite rolling away, Evelyn wasn't certain she'd avoided Phillipe being injured and he was eerily quiet.

'Isabelle,' she called, hoping her voice wouldn't betray the worry she had.

'I'm here, just finding my way down, hang on,' her friend replied and in a short time was by Evelyn's side. 'Oh, Phillipe.' Evelyn felt Isabelle wrestle the child out from her back. She felt as though there wasn't a sound around them, save for her own quick breaths catching with pain, and Isabelle's words of comfort to a boy who wasn't responding.

'Is he alright?' Evelyn asked quietly, smiling with relief when Phillipe wailed loudly.

'He'll be right as rain, just a bit of a surprise. I think he had the wind knocked out of him, but you took the force of the fall,' Isabelle said, whilst soothing the boy to a light whimper as she hugged him closely. 'What about you? Can you stand?'

Evelyn shook her head, gritting her teeth to bear the pain. 'It's my ankle. I think it's broken. I felt a bone snap.'

'We need you out of this ditch. I'm going to put Phillipe up on the road with some bread to suck on, then I'll come back and help you out of here,' Isabelle replied. Evelyn heard movement alongside her and could sense, more than see, Isabelle carrying Phillipe away. A minute later and she had returned.

'Let's see if you can bear any weight.' The anxiety in Isabelle's voice gave Evelyn something to grab onto. If she didn't get up, she was as good as dead. There was no way Isabelle would be able to come back for her, and what if other people working were out looking for them? They had to keep moving.

Isabelle crouched behind her and put her arms through hers, under Evelyn's armpits. 'On three, I'll pull, you need to stand on your good ankle.'

'On three,' Evelyn confirmed.

Isabelle counted and pulled her friend up, not an easy endeavour in the dark, on uneven ground, but they managed it. Evelyn leant against her friend to catch her breath and could feel her heart beating quickly from the exertion.

'Now we need to get onto the road so I can bandage you up until we get to your friend's,' Isabelle said, placing an arm behind Evelyn's back, 'you need to lean on me and I'll try to lift you up as much as I can.'

'I'll try,' Evelyn replied.

Slowly, the two women began to move across the ditch, one shuffling, the other grunting with the effort to keep them both upright. As they reached the side of the road Evelyn instinctively put both feet down, only to cry out as her broken ankle shot daggers of pain from her foot to her knee.

'Hush, you can do this.' Isabelle squeezed Evelyn's hand. 'I don't want you worrying Phillipe. Let's get you bandaged up.'

'And then what?' A miserable Evelyn could barely see straight for the pain causing white circles in her brain, let alone imagine how she'd walk the many miles needed to get to Martinique's home.

'One step at a time,' Isabelle huffed, pulling Evelyn up onto the gravelly road. Small sharp stones stuck into Evelyn's hands as she leant back to swing her legs onto the road, but she brushed them off, focusing on her friend's plan. The pain was intense, and she began to wonder if she was still awake.

'Stay with me, I can't have you fainting.' Isabelle sat behind her, propping her up whilst reaching for the bag she'd left by Phillipe who was sat quietly on the side of the road. 'I'm going to bandage you up with this.' She brought out a cloth nappy of Phillipe's, 'I just need to find a stick.' After a brief search, Isabelle returned to Evelyn's side with a sturdy stick to bind onto her ankle to act as a splint.

'This is going to hurt isn't it?' Evelyn asked. She'd felt pain before, and she knew she'd survived other ordeals but this felt like one more thing Evelyn would have to manage and she felt exhausted by it.

'It might hurt a bit, and I'm sorry. But it'll be worth it,' Isabelle replied. She gave Evelyn a quick glance then removed her shoe and sock, ripping her trouser leg some way so she could get access to the ankle. Even in the moonlight both women could see it was ballooning, with purplish blooms spreading across her bone. Unfazed, Isabelle began binding Evelyn's ankle with the first of the cloth nappies she'd pulled out of her bag. The pressure was intense and it was all Evelyn could do not to cry out, but she didn't want to scare Phillipe who had made his way over to the two women, intrigued by what they were doing on the side of the road.

Soon though, Isabelle had added the splint, continued to bind Evelyn's ankle and was quickly tying off the cloth. She looked over at Evelyn, concerned.

'Sore?' Evelyn was focusing on anything but the pain and couldn't reply. 'I can give you something for that too,' Isabelle looked in her bag and produced a small bottle. 'Just a couple of drops should take the edge off – not too many though,' she advised. Evelyn stuck her tongue out and let Isabelle place a couple of sour-tasting drops of liquid on. The effect was almost instantaneous. A tingly wash of relaxation poured over her, numbing her ankle but also bringing a sense of bliss she hadn't experienced since the headiest days of making love with Benjamin.

'Goodness,' she exhaled, and Isabelle nodded with understanding.

'I was given it after having Phillipe, I kept hold of it just in case. I'm so, so, sorry, Evelyn. I keep snapping at you when in reality I'm just angry with George for leaving us in this situation and honestly, your words were much too close to home.'

Evelyn smiled dreamily and leant on her friend. 'No, I'm sorry. I shouldn't have said you had nothing to offer.' She giggled, then covered her mouth. 'Sorry, I didn't mean...' She tailed off, unsure what she was saying and Isabelle shook her head indulgently.

'It's an opioid, it can make you a bit... giddy,' she explained. 'Don't worry about what was said – we were both in the wrong. Let's leave it there. We need to push on, and find somewhere to rest that's out of sight.' She took one look at Evelyn on the ground. 'Probably sooner than we'd planned.'

Chapter Forty-Eight

REIMS

The night drew on. Isabelle had Phillipe tied to her front, and the two bags on her back. Alongside her Evelyn shuffled, using a long stick they'd found as a crutch, occasionally leaning on Isabelle for further support when the painkiller began to wear off. Every now and then they'd pause so Isabelle could rearrange the bags and her son, and placate Evelyn with more opioids.

After what felt like hours, but was probably closer to just three, Isabelle spotted a farm shrouded in darkness. She could make out a few outbuildings, one of which could serve as a place for the three to gain some rest and warm up.

'Evie, look, we should aim for there.' She pointed in the direction of the buildings, a field away.

Evelyn's mind was scrambled. She couldn't remember where she was heading, but she knew she was in pain. She followed Isabelle across the field, leaning heavily on the stick. Her ankle protested at step she took now that the medication was wearing off, but she needed to reclaim clarity or she'd never remember where she was leading them.

Eventually they reached the farm. A dog barked some way off and the two paused, hoping it wouldn't continue. Isabelle pointed to a barn on the outskirts of the farmstead, away from the main house, and they made their way as quietly as possible to the building.

Inside, they could smell the scent of musty hay, and something a little like iron and a lot like animal, though no sounds came from within the barn. But it was warmer than outside, and the hay provided a comfortable place to lie down. Isabelle settled Phillipe down, wrapped in the shirt they'd carried him, and he immediately fell asleep.

She made her way to Evelyn who was sat down against a hay bale, breathing deeply, the exertion of the last few hours taking every ounce of strength from her.

'Let me see.' Isabelle began to roll up Evelyn's trouser leg and even in the half-light she couldn't cover the wince she made when she saw her friend's ankle. 'You're not going much further on this, are you?'

'I think we need to, I don't think there's another answer.'

Isabelle shook her head. 'What a mess we've found ourselves in. Damn this war.' She sat back on her heels and rubbed her eyes with her hands roughly. When she took them away her eyes were glistening. 'We should have stayed in the village.'

'And risk being captured by the Germans? Don't forget I've already had one close call these last few days,' Evelyn reminded her. 'I don't think they'd have been any kinder to us when they caught up with me. I shot one of their men remember.'

'How did you manage it? Were you scared?' Isabelle asked, her arms wrapped around herself as thought to get some comfort.

Evelyn nodded. 'It was me or him, Isabelle, I chose me. I still choose me. And you. And Phillipe. We've done what we've needed to do and we'll continue to do whatever it takes to stay alive. And if that means me walking on this crooked ankle, then so be it.'

'And flying a plane?'

'Martinique!' Evelyn shouted with glee, punching the air and shocking Isabelle.

'Shush,' she said, glancing nervously towards the barn's opening, where the wind blew through carrying their words towards the house.

'Sorry,' Evelyn whispered. 'But I'd forgotten some key points. We're going to Martinique's, aren't we? Borrowing a plane? Escaping to Britain?'

Despite herself and their situation, Isabelle laughed. 'You say it like it's that simple. But yes, that's the plan.'

Evelyn rubbed her hands together and nodded. 'Excellent. I think we need to rest, and if possible stay out of sight until the evening again, though we'll have to see what the day brings.' Her stomach rumbled, and she ignored it. Isabelle had heard though and dug into her bag, removing an apple. She offered it to Evelyn who shook her head.

'Keep it for Phillipe. He'll need it – anyway, I've got a few things still. I cleared out your cupboard,' she giggled, 'sorry, I think the drug's leaving my system.'

'Do you need any more? That's got to hurt.' Isabelle said, looking in the direction of Evelyn's ankle.

'No, I need clarity. I forgot where I was for a bit back there. The pain is...' she broke off for a moment to consider how to explain the background thrum of heat, 'consistent... but I need it to hold onto something. Odd as that might sound. I can't trust myself to fly if I'm confused. I might forget how to do everything.'

Isabelle looked concerned, but said nothing to the contrary. 'Let's rest.'

The two settled themselves around Phillipe, forming a protective barrier around the boy and, despite assuming she'd be awake due to the pain, Evelyn fell to sleep almost as quickly as Isabelle.

***

'*Bonjour.*'

Evelyn awoke with a start, sunlight was streaming into the barn and she rubbed her eyes hard to remind herself where she was. Then the pain in her ankle shot through her leg, shocking her awake and she looked up to where a boy of no more than ten was standing, frowning at what he'd found.

Patting Isabelle gently, Evelyn roused her friend so that the two women were staring, blinking into the light, the boy's face out of focus as he stood blocking the door.

'*Ça va?* Do you want some bread?' He was holding out what seemed to be a freshly baked baguette and Evelyn's stomach growled in reply.

The boy dropped to his knees alongside them, allowing the light to float over them all, and broke his baguette into three evenly-sized pieces. He solemnly gave a piece to the women, and a bleary-eyed Phillipe who began gnawing on the crust.

Evelyn tore into hers, and Isabelle did the same.

'Your foot is sore?' The boy pointed at Evelyn and she nodded warily, He nodded in response and disappeared out of the door.

'We're sitting ducks. We should have woken earlier and hidden,' Isabelle said, worried. 'I can't believe how long we slept.'

Evelyn finished her bread in a couple of mouthfuls. 'What's done is done. I'm not sure we'd have got very far.' Her foot was obviously swollen, with deep, dark-purple and greenish bruising spreading all over, in spite of Isabelle's nursing. The two women sat in the weak winter sunlight, caught up in their own thoughts.

'*Maman, ici*,' they heard the boy say outside and a moment later, a woman in her forties arrived, a blue-and-white striped apron tied to a sensible dark-brown dress. She was lean and her hair was tied back from her face which had a smattering of flour in patches. When she saw the trio in her barn, she stopped short and placed her hands on her hips, then said something quickly to the boy who ran off.

'And you are?'

Evelyn spoke first. 'Lost.'

'I'd say, no one comes this way unless they're buying from me.' The woman indicated the other end of the barn, where the metallic smell was explained – rows of carcasses were hanging, some dripping blood on the hay-covered floor.

'We're looking for a friend,' Isabelle began.

'Is that so?' She thanked the boy for bringing a bag, and moved further into the barn. 'My son says you need some help. That looks sore.' She came over and looked at Evelyn's ankle then searched in the bag with a cross marked on the side. Isabelle cast a glance at Evelyn.

'Are you a nurse?'

The woman frowned as she carefully undid the makeshift bandages. 'These were done well, though I think we're going to need to reset your ankle before it heals in the wrong place. It's going to hurt though.' She began to feel around Evelyn's ankle, carefully touching the swollen areas. Evelyn bit back her tears. 'I'm not a nurse, though

I was training before the war.' She took the stick which had been on her ankle and handed it to Evelyn.

'Bite down.'

Evelyn did as she was told and thought for a moment as the pain seared white hot across her brain, causing a cold sweat to wash over her that she'd pass out. But as quickly as the woman had moved her bones back to where they needed to be, the pain began to subside. Efficiently and quickly the woman tied a long bandage around her ankle.

'Of course, it would be better if we could set it in plaster, but this will have to do. I'd suggest no weight on it if you can.' She stood up and dusted herself down. 'Would you like some breakfast?' She noted the look of concern between the two women. 'My husband is fighting in the war. It's just me and him.' She pointed at her son. 'And the animals. Maybe once we're inside you can tell me where your friend is and I can help.'

The women looked at each other, they had to trust her, and breakfast did sound good. Isabelle and the farmer's wife each took an arm of Evelyn's and helped her across the farmyard, where chickens scratched at dusty stones and the sweet scent of horse manure reminded her of journeys into the English countryside. With a longing for home, Evelyn reminded herself that, as weary as she was, they could be there soon.

Once they were sat at a large oak table, in a kitchen warmed by a fire that crackled in a grate, the woman poured each a large cup of coffee and offered them more slices of baguette, along with buttery scrambled eggs.

The two women gorged on the food as though it were a feast for royalty. Barely a word was said as they ate and drank their fill, though Isabelle watched closely as Phillipe dipped his bread into a bowl of the darkest hot chocolate, concerned he'd make a mess in the woman's kitchen.

'He won't be worse than my boy, let him enjoy it.' She smiled indulgently. 'We have plenty, and we're fortunate because of it.'

After a while, both women sated, the woman poured another cup of coffee for them and sat, quietly, waiting for the explanation that Evelyn knew had been coming.

She decided to be honest.

'We're trying to get to Martinique Margritte in Mourmel-on-le-Grand, she's a friend. And we really need a friend at the moment, we need to get home to England,' she began, tears unwelcomingly pricking at her eyes.

'I'm a friend, I'm Sara,' the woman said, smiling kindly at them both. 'I knew you weren't French, though I did wonder why two English women and a child were hiding in my barn. But,' she held a hand up of warning when Evelyn opened her mouth to explain, 'I don't want to know. What I can do, though, is help you get to your friend, because she's mine too.'

Chapter Forty-Nine
Mourmelon-le Grand

'What a sight for sore eyes you are, *chérie*.' Martinique ran into the driveway and swept Evelyn into an embrace that continued for some time, causing her to wince as she tried to avoid putting weight on her bloated ankle. 'I've missed you.' She turned to see Isabelle, properly registering her for the first time.

'My dear friend, Isabelle, and her son, Phillipe.' Evelyn made the introductions as Phillipe held out his hand to shake Martinique's.

'*Mai oui*, what a polite chap, *non*?'

'I'm leaving these with you, I need to go and make my rounds,' Sara said and smiled at the group. '*Bonne chance, et au revoir*. Martinique, I'll see you on Friday for bridge. Your time is coming,' she said, as she climbed onto her cart, clicked at the horse and left.

Martinique's face turned serious as she looked at Evelyn. 'You must be in trouble if you've wound up here, looking like that.' She pointed at Evelyn, who took stock of what her friend saw. She realised her face would be bruised from the fight with the German, her hair was full of dust, mud and debris from their journey, and her ankle of course, there was no hiding how damaged that was.

'What's the English phrase? Someone did a number on you?' Martinique said, as she helped Evelyn into her home, guiding her towards the kitchen. Evelyn looked around, it had been a long time since she'd been in this house, but the fond memories came back straight away.

'Something like that, but that's all in the past,' she said painfully as Isabelle and Phillipe joined them. 'What we need now is help in getting to Britain.'

'I see.'

'I think you know what I do, because you do it too, Martinique – I know you do. We have... mutual friends... and I know you've been flying missions on behalf of the French government.' She looked knowingly at her friend. 'I believe you were responsible for the aerial bombing of a German military base in Metz? You don't need to say anything. All I need is to borrow your plane, I'm hoping you have one still?'

Martinique settled Evelyn on a wooden stool next to a table that had a white cotton cloth laid over it. She busied herself boiling water to make tea, her back to the others, disguising any giveaway or reaction to Evelyn.

'How will you return my plane?' She turned to face them, pouring hot water into delicate porcelain cups to warm them, a reminder of a bygone time when she and Evelyn would set the world to rights between flying lessons.

'I'll figure out a way,' Evelyn replied, her mind racing to come up with a solution, whilst gratefully accepting the tea.

'And how will you fly – your ankle, it's going to become miraculously better? I'm intrigued as to how you'll work the foot pedals.' Martinique looked pointedly at Evelyn, who had propped her leg up on another stool. It was obvious how much pain she was in.

'I'll manage. I've flown in worse conditions.'

'You haven't.'

'All right, but I've flown in poor conditions, a busted ankle won't be too different. And anyway, Isabelle could do it, if I taught her.'

Isabelle paused from sipping her tea where she'd remained quiet, listening to the exchange. 'No I won't. I don't know anything about flying.'

Martinique sat at the table, alongside Isabelle, facing Evelyn. 'I'll fly you.'

'I can't ask you to do that,' Evelyn protested.

'You're not. I'm telling you – I'm not giving you my plane, or risking not getting it back because you've crashed into the Channel on some ridiculous mission and have too much pride to get help. You have two options, you fly with me, or you go elsewhere.'

Isabelle looked with hope at Martinique. 'Thank you – you're a wonderful person.'

Martinique blushed. 'I haven't done it yet.'

'And I'm still not convinced you should – I don't want your involvement on my conscience, along with...' Evelyn broke off.

'With?' Martinique prompted.

'Nothing. I just don't want you coming back to haunt me because you didn't listen. This could be dangerous. The Germans were after both of our husbands, and...' she faltered for a moment, 'we suspect they're after me too. We don't know whether they're interested in Isabelle, but it's not safe for her here – they could capture her and Phillipe and use them as bait to flush George out. If he hasn't made it back to Britain already.' She stopped and took a deep shaky breath in.

'Finished?' Martinique shook her head. 'Honestly, you'd think you were the only one involved in dangerous missions these past few years. You know some of what I've done, but not all – not that I'm going to share it with you – and if I can lessen some of my guilt by getting a son reunited with his father, then I insist on helping you.' She leant over the table and took Evelyn's hands in hers. 'And I won't take no for an answer.'

Evelyn looked at Isabelle for her friend's permission. The two exchanged a glance of knowing and it was settled.

'I recommend you stay here for a night or two, it's the weekend and if we do anything that looks out of place these next two days I think we'll draw unwanted attention,' Martinique advised. 'And it'll give you all a chance to sleep a little.'

As soon as she mentioned rest, Evelyn began to feel tired.

'Let's get you into bed.' Addressing Isabelle, Martinique pointed to a bag with a cross marked on it, similar to Sara's. 'Bring that up, I think she could do with some painkillers to ensure she sleeps well tonight.'

Isabelle did as she was told and between them they managed to get Evelyn into a bedroom. Martinique lit a fire and the room quickly warmed up.

'Have some of this.' Martinique dropped some liquid onto Evelyn's tongue, which, though she tried to move away, the two women held her and insisted.

'It's good for you, Evie, it'll take the pain away,' Isabelle said, stroking Evelyn's hair. The relief was welcomingly immediate as Evelyn chased the tingly bliss across her body, sighing deeply that she was finally somewhere safe and would be home soon. She had to pray that's where she'd find Benjamin. She fell asleep quickly, dreaming of their reunion.

***

As agreed, two days later Evelyn bade farewell to Isabelle and Phillipe. The plane was only a two-seater and they'd decided Martinique would bring Evelyn home first, so she could have her ankle looked at. Martinique would refuel, return to France and the following evening – assuming they hadn't attracted any attention – would bring Isabelle and Phillipe home. It would be a squeeze, but it was doable. Evelyn had been concerned about leaving the two at Martinique's house, but Isabelle had been certain it was the right thing to do, telling her it would be like a holiday for her.

'A cold château in February, sounds like a riot.' Evelyn laughed, but she could see the attraction after the last two peaceful nights' sleep. The rooms that Martinique used, such as the kitchen and two of the bedrooms, had fires that were well stocked with plenty of fuel. There were cosy blankets across the sofas, and Isabelle's bedroom, once a fire had been lit to chase the chill away, held a bed of such comfortable furnishings, that Evelyn found herself jealous of the night's sleep Isabelle and Phillipe would be enjoying whilst she flew across the Channel.

But she had her home to look forward to. And she had to hope Benjamin would be the warmth she'd find in her bed. She had decided the only way she could let Martinique risk her life for hers was to be optimistic about Benjamin and push aside any niggling doubts.

'We should go,' she said, a littler sharper than planned, but now she had Britain in her sights, she wanted to get home. It had been almost a week since she'd last seen Benjamin. She needed reassurance he was safe.

'I was going to say the same,' Martinique agreed, 'I think you've almost outstayed your welcome.'

With a quick embrace of Isabelle and a promise she'd track down George so they could be reunited when they made it to Britain, she followed Martinique slowly to her car, hobbling with the use of a cane they'd found in the house. They would drive to the airfield, then Martinique would fly her two-seater across the Channel, landing somewhere near to Southampton, where Evelyn would be able to send a telegram to Fergie and get picked up.

Looking up at the clear February night sky, Evelyn spotted a bright star poking its way out of the velvety blackness and focused on it intently. If ever there was a time to make a wish, this had to be it.

'Keep us safe and bring me home to Benjamin.'

Chapter Fifty

LONDON

'We don't know where he is.'

'But, Fergie. I've...' It was hopeless, Evelyn tried to find the words to explain the harrowing last week. A week where she'd only had the courage and drive to push home with the promise, the urgency, of finding out where Benjamin was and if he was safe.

'I know this is hard to hear,' Fergie pushed himself out clumsily from behind his heavy oak desk and moved closer to her, 'but I think you need to accept he might not be coming back. You're lucky you managed to.' Evelyn knew he was trying to make her feel better, to giver her a way of moving on, but it only made things worse.

'It doesn't feel lucky.' She sniffed, and accepted the large handkerchief from Fergie's outstretched hand. 'How can you be sure he's not safe?'

'Truth be told, I can't be, but my guess – based on whispers from Paris and the fact he hasn't called in, which as you know is one of our rules, leads me to assume he's either dead or been captured and I'm afraid right now we don't know which.'

'Oh,' Evelyn felt tears welling and she willed herself not to cry.

'I can keep you updated of course, but I think for now you'd be better off going home and looking after yourself – that looks painful,' he said, indicating the cast on her leg.

She looked down. Her foot to her knee had been enveloped in plaster of Paris in a bid to aid recovery, but according to the doctors, though Isabelle and Martinique had done their best for her, her ankle was never going to be fully functioning again.

They weren't sure how well she'd walk on that side once she came out of the cast, something Evelyn couldn't quite believe. It was, as she was at pains to point out, just a broken ankle. But the surgeons insisted she had surgery to try and manipulate the bones back into place. According to them she'd suffered fractures in three different places – and walking on it had exacerbated the breaks.

'It's fine,' she waved away Fergie's fake sympathy, 'I could cope better it if I knew more about Benjamin.'

'I need to ask...' Fergie poured a whisky for himself and Evelyn. 'Back in Paris. How did it go?'

Evelyn looked at him, confused. 'How did what go?'

'Your mission. You were meant to do something – we hadn't known about the Gotha bombings of course, terrible business.' He sipped his drink, then perched on the desk near to her. 'But you were meant to do something for us. Meet someone?'

Draining her whisky, Evelyn leaned heavily on her walking stick and pulled herself up. 'Fergie. It was a week ago. There was a mass bombing during my mission – a mission which, in case you hadn't noticed, nearly cost me my life, and may have cost Benjamin's, so no, I didn't get anything from that chap, except for a hatred of cellars.'

With that, as she walked as carefully as she could to the door, Evelyn realised it had been Fergie's doing, asking her to go to Paris. That Benjamin would have found it the worst thing to ask of her, but had been between a rock and the British Secret Service. She turned to Fergie one last time. 'It'll come as no surprise, but I'm done with all of this. You know where I am and if you hear anything about Benjamin – anything at all – I want to be the first to know.' Satisfied she'd said all she needed to, she turned and called for Solomon, who had been all too happy to resume his position when she'd arrived back in England, grateful to return to the life he knew. He appeared quickly in the doorway with a wheelchair that she sank gratefully into, holding her head high as she left the office for the last time.

***

Later that day she sat propped up by a collection of overly stuffed cushions on one of the armchairs in her flat, her leg resting on a stool in front of her. Evelyn smiled widely at the familiar face escorted in by Solomon. 'You made it.'

Isabelle sat opposite her and waited as the servant left the room. 'How is it?' She pointed in the direction of Evelyn's leg, who grimaced.

'Fine. Though I won't be driving for a while.' She shifted a little uncomfortably. 'How was your journey over?' She heard how Martinique had flown during a particularly rainy night to bring Isabelle and Phillipe to Britain. Fergie told her that all three had arrived at the Southampton airstrip shaken, but intact. It could have been a very different story if someone less competent than Martinique had been in charge of the plane. Gloomily, Evelyn presumed he'd meant they had been in better hands than if she'd flown.

'Fine,' Isabelle echoed, 'put it this way, we won't be choosing that form of transport any time soon.'

The two women broke off as Solomon re-entered with a tea tray that contained a pot of tea and, Evelyn was thrilled to see, his very own boiled fruitcake. A treat now they were still facing sugar rationing. They waited until he'd left the room, before resuming their conversation.

'And Phillipe?' Evelyn realised she'd grown to have deep affection for the little boy, despite her initial reservations.

Isabelle's face changed to one of sheer joy as she began to pour tea out for them. 'Oh, he's so happy, we're at my parents' house in Surrey where he's excited to see the chickens and a horse.'

'And you?'

Isabelle exhaled, unsure whether to reply honestly to her friend. 'Relieved to be home.'

'And to have George back too?' Evelyn asked without any malice. George's successful return to London, via a journey far more treacherous than theirs, was one which gave her optimism.

'That's a relief too. I'm sorry, Evie.' Isabelle placed the cup and saucer next to Evelyn on a small table, then put her arm around her friend. 'I'm so sorry about Benjamin.'

Evelyn looked confused. 'Why are you sorry? He'll come home. I'm sure he will.' She watched as Isabelle patted her eyes with a handkerchief then sat back down, lifting her cup up to toast. Evelyn did the same.

'To Benjamin, who will definitely come home.'

'And to George, who did,' Evelyn added.

'Cheers.'

Both the women drank in a peaceful silence, lost in their own last few days.

'I think that's my lot,' Isabelle said, after a while. 'I need to get the train back. George isn't in great shape and needs a lot of looking after, it's not fair on my mother to do it all.'

She stood and Evelyn looked up at her. She was pale and forlorn, a shadow of the Isabelle she'd known before the war, a sight Evelyn assumed she reflected. But, Evelyn supposed, that's what war did. None of them would ever be the same as they were before. All of them had seen too much.

'You take care of yourself – let me know if you need anything,' Isabelle said, squeezing Evelyn's arm. 'As soon as you hear anything about Benjamin, you let us know.' She arranged her hat so that it sat artfully on her hair, and placed her handbag in the crook of her arm.

'Goodbye Evelyn.'

'Goodbye Isabelle, give that lovely boy a hug from me.'

Isabelle took one step away from the table, then turned and swept Evelyn up in a tight embrace.

'I'm not sure how I'll ever be able to repay you for everything you did for Phillipe and me. We'll be forever in your debt, I assure you.' She kissed both of Evelyn's cheeks, then walked away quickly.

Evelyn stayed seated in her chair and waited for her friend to leave before calling for Solomon to replace her tea with a gin and tonic. One went down quickly, so she called for a second, then a third, the alcohol numbing the pain in her foot, and the ache in her heart.

The silence in the apartment felt as though she was underwater and she craved the time sixteen years ago when it had been her, Hena and Frances living together. She smiled as she remembered the nights spent drinking cocktails and champagne, swapping love stories and fashion tips. She thought too of Victor and their time together. So many memories.

But she knew she'd give them all up if she could have Benjamin back.

Chapter Fifty-One

LONDON

Evelyn raised a toast in her apartment to the photo of Benjamin on her mantelpiece from her chaise after hearing the announcement on the radio.

'The war is over, my love. Time to come home now.'

She drank deeply from the glass of cognac as though it were water, then quickly refilled it. The brandy glasses never held enough, barely a thimble's worth as far as she was concerned. Evelyn drank a third and a fourth. Gingerly she stood up, wincing at the now familiar pain in her ankle and walked to the kitchen, looking for something bigger to pour her drink into.

In the last ten months since she'd escaped France, Evelyn had stuck to her word. She hadn't attempted to contact the Secret Service, nor they her. There had been times when she'd picked her way carefully over the paving slabs and cobbles, around bombed out buildings and dirt covered windows of a London that was at once all too much, and completely unfamiliar to her, when she was sure she'd seen Benjamin. A face in a crowd, or the back of his head in a shop. At those times she'd rush over to the man and tap him on the shoulder, only for a stranger's face to turn around, with a look of surprise and incomprehension on their face. She would apologise and bid a hasty retreat, always devastated she was wrong.

There were times too, when she was convinced she was being followed. By whom, she wasn't sure. To what purpose, she wasn't certain either. But she was aware she had done her fair amount in the name of her country. That could mean she would be considered better off dead. On those days, when she was certain the shadows were holding dangers, she would hurry back to her apartment, cursing the flights of stairs that took her to the top floor, flopping with exhaustion on her chaise with an exhalation of relief. It was on those days too when she'd turn to a couple of drops of opioids to ease the pain in her ankle, washed down with whatever bottle of wine she could find.

Looking out her window, on the day that peace had been called Evelyn watched the merriment of strangers as they hugged each other in the street. There was so much joy on their faces. So much hope. Maybe she could have hope too. The war was over, and if Benjamin wasn't able to make his way back to her, she would make her way to him.

Evelyn wiped a tear that had crept its way down her face. She was Evelyn Bloom, the fastest girl on Earth and she had to do something. She wasn't going to wait for him. She would find him.

1922

Chapter Fifty-Two

London

D ying was nowhere near as exciting as living.

In fact, Evelyn pondered, as her soul began to exit her body, had she known how boring it was, she would have preferred to have disappeared off the face of the earth in a fiery ball of flames, or submerged fifty feet underwater.

Instead, she had this.

A morphine-infused calm that had coated the pain of her ankle injury in a sheen of otherworldliness but which, she admitted to herself, had become an addiction. Over the years she had replaced the love of a good man with the love of a beautiful drug, which always reassured her and kept her in its loving embrace.

But lately its embrace had become harder and harder to find. She'd upped the dosage for her injury years ago, surreptitiously adding a few more drops here and there when the pain from her ankle, that had never set properly, would flare up.

Or, and again she felt she could admit it to herself now, when the pain of living got worse.

Despite years of searching for Benjamin, being told by the government there was nothing to say he'd died, but nothing to prove he'd survived in Paris all those years ago, she'd spent the last few years using whatever means necessary to track him down. She had chased ghosts across countries, had been told of sightings of Benjamin in places across Europe and even America.

It hadn't been enough. She burnt contacts and bridges and spent all of her money. She became angry, aggressive, hardened. She was beginning to cause problems internally within the Service and Fergie had stopped talking to her.

Her friends had disappeared too. Not that she cared. Didn't she bring it on herself? Even Isabelle. Her promise of never leaving her quickly disappeared when her friend fell pregnant again and her world was taken up with nappies and feedings. She couldn't even go to her mother, who had passed in the spring.

Nothing mattered anymore, she just wanted absolution. Needed Benjamin to tell her he didn't hate her, that he pardoned her. Forgave her for sending him away that fateful night, instead of standing by him where, even if he'd been caught up in the explosions – she'd have gone with him.

Coughs wracked her body, Evelyn pushed herself up to sitting to try and ease the pain in her chest. Pneumonia, that's what the doctor had said when he'd called in a couple of days before. She'd seen his look of confusion as he'd taken in the faded glamour of her Mayfair flat. There was little else left other than the apartment itself, save for her threadbare chaise, trophies and photo frames, one of which held an image of Benjamin. She'd sold almost everything to fund her chase across the world for him, and had nothing but poverty to show for it.

Pain seized her chest and Evelyn took a drop of morphine on her tongue to ease it. The doctor had prescribed it, but as she enjoyed the numbing sensation the drug gave her, Evelyn wondered when she'd last had some. It had been a few hours, hadn't it? Touching her hand to her forehead she noted how hot she was, and how cold she felt. Her head hurt and her lungs rattled with every breath she took. A drop of morphine would help. She paused after allowing two drops to land on her tongue, had she done that recently? Her thoughts were confused. She wasn't certain if it was today the doctor had been, or yesterday, or the day before. The morphine was almost gone, a week's prescription, it must have been seven days since he came to see her. She was so tired.

As the morphine took hold, Evelyn lay back on her chaise longue and rested her head on the feather-filled cushion. It was a lot easier just lying there, not asking too much of her lungs. Evelyn's mouth felt woolly and she tried to put her finger on why she felt so free, wondering if the morphine hit was different this time. Her eyelids felt ever so heavy and she allowed them to flutter shut for a moment.

She was well aware that she'd seen and done more in her forty years on this planet than most people would fit into three lifetimes.

But right then, as she forced her eyes open, wondering if she was taking a final glimpse around her Mayfair apartment, furnished with just her trophies of past sporting glories and silver-framed photos of a life when she was loved, she wondered why, when the whole world had been at her feet, she had been left to die alone.

Closing her eyes, Evelyn allowed herself to be lulled into a foggy half sleep. The sound of a bell tinkled close by. It was as though angels were singing to her. Was it time, she wondered. Was it time to go? She grasped the penny medallion around her neck, Benjamin's gift that she could never be parted from. Her only link to him, and she held it firmly.

A noise came from somewhere nearby, maybe she was entering heaven. The sounds, they were louder than she'd expected.

'Penny for them.' The voice so familiar by her side, Evelyn felt rough hands shaking her. Waking her.

Blinking to clear the fuzziness in her brain she opened her eyes slowly, unsure of what she'd see.

The image came in slowly, like a photograph that had been poorly developed. An outline of someone she knew began to take shape, colours and light filled the space. A voice. His voice? Was it? Was it really? After all this time?

'Evelyn.'

'Benjamin?' she coughed, the pain nothing compared to the wonder that he was back with her. She felt his rough hands stroking her face, felt his moustache tickling her cheek. He was both familiar and unfamiliar. It had been four years. He was solid. He was transparent. She wasn't sure where she was.

'I'm here, darling, I'm here. I was captured in Paris. Almost killed. Held as part of negotiations with the British government – Fergie knew. My love, I'm here. I'm right here. I'm with you.'

A torrent of words. Rushed out. Was it in case she didn't hear?

Weeping. Was it him? Or her? Her cheeks were wet.

'I looked...for you...I looked everywhere...'

Her eyes closed again, listening to his words. 'You found me. You did it Evelyn. I'm here.'

He was kissing her. Holding her.

They were together at last.

Afterword

The more I learn of this era, the more my interest in the early 1900s to 1920s continues to grow.

When I'd finished writing *Swim*, I knew I needed to write another historical fiction novel celebrating the successes of women who had been forgotten about. It seemed so sad that in just over one hundred years we had no knowledge of their successes.

With that in mind, I actively sought out the 'next big idea', and instead I found two incredible women. Dorothy Levitt, a woman who set many records whilst driving a car for Napier motors, and the woman who was described by one paper as *The Fastest Girl on Earth*. She was a well-dressed daredevil and many aspects of Evelyn's life and character are based on Dorothy's glittering fame.

The problem with Dorothy's story, if I were to tell it fully, was after around 1912 all records or mentions of her vanish. I couldn't find anything that referenced her again until 1922, and that was her death certificate. Aged just forty the inquest records state, "the cause of death was morphine poisoning while suffering from heart disease and an attack of measles. The inquest recorded a verdict of misadventure."

From my point of view, I had a woman who could drive fast, owned a gun (and knew how to use it), had achieved record breaking speeds on a motorboat AND flown a plane. All of this is recorded. So why was there nothing about her for such a long time? My writerly mind couldn't shift the idea that maybe, just maybe, she was picked up as one of the new network of female spies who were recruited in the First World War (and who very little is documented about).

Enter my second incredible woman. Marie Marvingt. In France Marie's name is known everywhere. She died in her late eighties after an inspiring career which involved her identifying a need for an air ambulance service. She also attempted to fight for France, imitating a man, and in 1915 Marvingt became the first woman in the world to fly combat missions when she became a volunteer pilot flying bombing missions over German-held territory and she received the *Croix de guerre* (Military Cross) for her aerial bombing of a German military base in Met.

It is possible that her and Dorothy's paths crossed, as Dorothy went to France to learn to be a pilot at the same time Marie was learning in a similar area of France. The character of Martinique is a nod to Marie.

This *is* a work of fiction. Evelyn's racing triumphs however, are all Dorothy's. She did all the incredible motoring endeavours Evelyn did, including learning to be a mechanic in Paris, driving from Scotland to London with just her dog Dodo, and a gun in the glovebox. She set the land speed records, and the various other motoring achievements are all hers.

I don't know if she was a spy, but I hope she lived her final years audaciously.

I also hope she doesn't mind me giving Evelyn a little more of an optimistic ending than she had.

Just as I did with my first novel, I have meticulously researched every aspect of this book. It's been edited, proofed and fact checked more times than I want to think about, but there will be something that's slipped through, and for that I take all the responsibility. Just don't let me know or I might cry.

Lisa Brace, April 2025.

Acknowledgements

Thank you to the reader. I was incredibly surprised by how successful *Swim* was last year, and I've been really touched by the many of you who have been in touch to tell me how much you enjoyed it. I hope you like this one too.

Writing can be a very solitary game. You create worlds from your own random thoughts and try to explain it to others, who often look a little confused by what you're telling them. That's why it's so valuable to me to have so many writer friends I can call upon should I need a bit of help and support (or someone to tell me to get myself in gear).

Top of the list has to be best writing buddy, Daisy White. An absolute powerhouse who is always available to put my fears to rest. She read this in a weekend when I was at the point of deleting the entire manuscript. I'm very glad she told me to keep going, and that it was good. Thank you. Hope your mum likes it too.

Thanks to my editor, Ian Skewis. It's because of you that my characters shed enough clothes in their 'intimate' scenes – still my favourite editing point.

Thanks also to my Horsham writing group, a lovely team of bright young things who are always available for writing sprints, cheering on and being in each other's corners. I recommend everyone finds a group like this in life!

There are many other groups who I've been able to glean advice from, including the Savvy author's group on Facebook, where I'm now friends in real life with a wonderful bunch of West Sussex based writers, all of whom support each other.

Books like this need a lot of research. I have folders of references regarding every aspect in the period I've written about, but nothing beats seeing it in the flesh. Thank you to Worthing Museum for allowing me access to the clothing of the time, and to Beaulieu Motor Museum for answering my many, many, questions on how the cars in the 1910s worked. Not quite the same as my beaten up Citroen...

Finally, thank you to my family. My children for realising my daydreaming is usually my way of fixing a tricky plot point, and my husband for his meticulous read throughs – and excellent choice in wine as an incentive to get things done.

Editor – Ian Skewis (ianskewis.com)
Cover designer – Agnes (thatagnes.co.uk)
Publisher – Blue Pier Books (bluepiercreative.co.uk)

About the author

Lisa Brace is an award-winning writer, who combines penning novels with running her own business in the beautiful surroundings of West Sussex.

She has worked as a journalist and copywriter for over twenty years, giving her the chance to be nosy without getting into trouble.

When she had two very young children she decided she didn't have enough on, so gained a BA Hons degree in English Literature and Language via the Open University, where her love for creative writing was sparked.

Her debut novel, *The Fame Trap* – a psychological thriller, was published in March 2024, swiftly followed by her first historical fiction novel, *Swim*, in June 2024, and *The Fastest Girl on Earth* in June 2025.

When not writing, and running writing retreats in the south of England, Lisa enjoys walking her dog, reading everything she can lay her hands on, and baking elaborate cakes.

Website – Lisabrace.co.uk

Instagram – lbrace_author

Facebook – Facebook.com/LisaBraceAuthor

If you have any questions or would like to get in touch with Lisa email hello@bluepierbooks.co.uk

Printed in Great Britain
by Amazon